COME HELL OR HIGH WATER

PART THREE:

DELUGE

By
Stephen Morris

Come Hell or High Water, Part 3: Deluge is a work of fiction. Names, characters, places and incidents are the products of the author's imagination or are used fictitiously. Any resemblance to actual persons, living or dead, or events is entirely coincidental.

ISBN 978-0-9847731-6-9
eBook ISBN 978-0-9847731-5-2

Cover design by Elliot Kreloff

To
Elliot and Rob,
without whom this trilogy would have
never seen the light of day

By Stephen Morris

Come Hell or High Water, Part One: Wellspring

Come Hell or High Water, Part Two: Rising

Come Hell or High Water, Part Three: Deluge

Acknowledgments

There are many more people to whom I owe a debt of thanks than I could ever adequately thank here. First among the many without whom the trilogy would never have been born is Rob Fisher, who first suggested one evening as we stood on the incredible Charles Bridge in magnificent Prague, "You know the legends of Prague and the practices of medieval magic and theology—you should do something with it all!" But it was the sale of my first short story—written in response to a challenge Cal Trovato and I issued to each other—that gave me the self-confidence to begin the book that became this trilogy.

I am grateful to Billy Dotter, Jaana Hinkkanen, Richard Myer, Marta Rojo, Conan Power, Jan Sedláček, and Roman Sedlar, who each encouraged me and whose interest in Magdalena, Fen'ka, and the others helped sustain me when my own energy flagged. Ivana Husakova and Blanka von Kannon also helped with Czech–English translations. Any errors that remain are my own.

Furthermore, Marta Tanrikulu was the best editor I could have asked for and working with her was a dream!

I must also thank Lester K. Little for his marvelous 1993 book, *Benedictine Maledictions*, in which he describes the rites French monks would use to call down God's wrath on the nobility who sought to steal from the monasteries. Professor Little's descriptions of these curses first conjured the image in my mind of an old witch dying in the flames and using some of those same imprecations to curse those who were killing her.

Finally, I would like to thank my partner Elliot Kreloff for all his help, support, and comments, as he not only read each chapter but also listened to my musings aloud as the story developed and provided invaluable assistance in the final stages of the book's production.

Part Three Chapters

Chapter 1:
The Chariot (*Sunday night, August 11, 2002*)

Chapter 2:
"Curse their wives and children!" (*fall–winter 1356*)

Chapter 3:
Wheel of Fortune
(*Sunday night, August 11, 2002–Monday, August 12, 2002*)

Chapter 4:
"Let the shadow of death stalk them in the night!"
(*January–February 1357*)

Chapter 5:
Eight of Cups (*Tuesday, August 13, 2002*)

Chapter 6:
"Let the river swallow them up!" (*early to mid-February 1357*)

Chapter 7:
Nine of Swords, reversed (*Tuesday, August 13, 2002*)

Chapter 8:
"As this fire dies…" (*mid-February 1357*)

Chapter 9:
The Tower (Wednesday, *August 14, 2002*)

Chapter 10:
Death (*Wednesday, August 14, 2002*)

Synopsis

In mid-September 1356, the old woman Fen'ka is burned at the stake as a witch by a mob in the Old Town Square of Prague. Dying in the flames, she calls out a series of curses on the city, including: "Curse their wives and children! Let the shadow of death stalk them in the night! Let the river swallow them up!" She concludes the curse, gasping her last breath in the smoke of the flames: "As this fire dies, let all their nightmares come to life!"

In the spring of 2002, Magdalena—a young secretary at Charles University in Prague—is drawn to the ghost of Fen'ka beneath the Charles Bridge. Fen'ka implores Magdalena to clear the old woman's name and put an end to the injustice she had suffered; Fen'ka promises that ending the injustice done to her will, by extension, set right a host of injustices and expose centuries of lies that have justified the oppression of the weak. Magdalena, also at Fen'ka's behest, conjures two spirits that will bring two people to Prague to assist Magdalena in this project.

Magdalena serves as assistant to a professor who is co-organizer of interdisciplinary conferences (one about evil, the other about monsters) that will meet in Prague that summer (August, 2002). At the conferences, she meets George (a handsome Jesuit from New York) and Elizabeth (a beautiful Dublin professor) and discovers they have been brought to Prague to help clear Fen'ka's name and set right the wrongs of centuries.

George reveals to Magdalena that in addition to his academic and parish duties, he is the Grand Master of a network of covens in New York and offers to teach her the secrets of his occult power. He and Magdalena cast an elaborate spell together to summon Svetovit, the ancient four-faced god worshipped in Prague before the advent of Christianity, after George explains that Svetovit's assistance is critical to their project of achieving justice for Fen'ka. But Magdalena's friend Victoria suspects that George and Elizabeth had other, less lofty and more sinister motives. So she casts her own simple spell to expose the two professors she felt were stealing her friend. As Victoria casts her spell on the night of August 8, 2002, she does not realize that George and Magdalena are casting their elaborate spell at the same time.

Victoria's spell gathers a small group of seven academics also attending the conference, including Fr. Dmitri, an Eastern Orthodox chaplain at a small college in the United States. These academics see a vision of the destruction of Prague that will lead to the unraveling of modern society if Svetovit is set free in the modern world. These academics, each of whom is well-versed in the study of magic and folklore, have never practiced magic or any occult discipline and find it both difficult to believe that they have encountered authentic magic here and that what they have spent their lives studying is real. Eventually they each come to accept the necessity of practicing the magic they have previously only studied. They set out to collect the four magical tools of Prague (including a medieval rabbi's staff from a medieval synagogue attic and a knight's sword buried in the foundations of the Charles Bridge) to use in defense of the city, but Magdalena, George, and Elizabeth are collecting the four tools as well and always seem to be one step ahead of Victoria and her new comrades. Realizing that at least one academic, Peter, is also attempting to collect the four tools, George instructs Elizabeth to destroy him. She lures him to an empty park alongside the Vltava River and follows George's instructions but does not realize

Fr. Dmitri's wife Sophia is nearby and witnesses this.

Thwarted, Fr. Dmitri and the academics realize that not only is George an adept practitioner of black magic but also that Elizabeth is a unique variety of Irish vampire known as the Dearg-due, who cannot be destroyed but only driven back into her grave in Ireland—and then, only if a small cairn of stones is assembled atop the correct grave in Waterford in southeast Ireland. Sean, a professor from Dublin enlisted by Victoria's spell, sends one e-mail to his nephews and another to one of his graduate students and asks them to build a cairn atop each of the three purported graves of the Dearg-due.

Meanwhile, on Sunday night, August 11, the academics—desperate to stop George, Magdalena, and Elizabeth—hope that burning tarot cards with salt along the Royal Road, the medieval route of royal processions through Prague, will reawaken the ancient magical defenses submerged there. Elizabeth, to stymie these efforts, kills Alessandro, one of the academics, and attempts to kill Sophia, who escapes thanks to her use of a medal of the Infant of Prague. The remaining academics nevertheless set out to burn the tarot cards along the Royal Road, only to discover Elizabeth and Magdalena in the Old Town Square attempting to break the Astronomical Clock, one of the four magical tools of Prague. Elizabeth sends Magdalena away and attacks the academics, killing yet another, Wilcox. Preparing to strike again, she is stopped as the cairn of stones is constructed atop her grave in Ireland.

The Chariot

(Sunday night, August 11, 2002)

THE CHARIOT: THE SEVENTH OF THE MAJOR TRUMPS, THE CHARIOTEER STRUGGLES TO STEER THE STEEDS THAT THREATEN TO PULL HIM TO PIECES

George had two errands to run now that Magdalena was gone. He needed to meet Fen'ka and Jarnvithja, who were to deliver the great sword of Bruncvik to him. And he had another task to attend to on his way to get the sword.

Before sending Magdalena with the magical staff of Rabbi Loew to meet Elizabeth in the Old Town Square, where they were to sabotage the Astronomical Clock, he had spoken to the hotel desk clerk about arranging an appointment with a local prostitute.

"I would like to meet at her apartment, not here at the hotel," George had confided to the clerk, winking as he adjusted his clerical collar. "It might not look good, you understand, if she were seen coming to my room."

"Of course, Father." The clerk answered the Jesuit from New York in a bored voice, as if accustomed to requests like this. "What time should I make the appointment for?"

"I would also appreciate meeting someone who is—how to say?—not adverse to light bondage," George explained. "She should have her own rope and be ready for a session that involves…" George fumbled for the right word. "I understand that this can cost extra. The cost is of no concern."

"I understand. Of course." The clerk also seemed to have

11

heard this request many times before. "I will need to make some phone calls. What time did you say you wanted to make the appointment?"

George gave the clerk the approximate time he'd like to meet the woman later that evening, and a short while later, a bellhop had delivered an envelope to his room. Inside was a note that simply indicated a woman's name, her address, and the price in Czech currency.

Now, George waited to be sure Magdalena was well on her way from the hotel and slipped a few supplies into his pocket. Then he stepped out of the hotel, found a taxi, and gave the address to the driver. The driver nodded and quickly deposited George at the door of the apartment house a few blocks away. George walked through the lobby and up a flight of stairs to a door on the next floor. He knocked. The door swung open.

"Good evening." The woman at the door was young and lovely, a beautiful sheer robe revealing her provocative curves as a silk sash hugged her hips.

"Good evening," George answered. He stepped inside and closed the door. "It is a pleasure to meet you…"

"Agafia." She smiled and leaned over to kiss him on the cheek. He slipped a hand inside her robe and pressed his palm against her breast. She winked and placed his other hand against her hip.

"You received my instructions?" George whispered into her ear, feeling himself respond to her attractions.

"I did," she purred. "Come right this way." She turned and kept one hand entwined with his as she led him down a short hallway to a door on the left. They entered a room filled with sumptuous Victorian-era style furniture, a Tiffany lamp casting a warm glow across the scene. A few candles twinkled around the edges of the room. A dining room chair stood alone on a plush Turkish carpet in the midst of the richly detailed parquet floor. Coils of silken white rope sat on a nearby table, its surface polished to a glossy sheen.

You will excuse me, my dear," he explained as he stepped away from her, "but I am a man of strict habits and there are certain—shall we say, small fetishes?—which are necessary."

"Such as?" Agafia asked.

"I must make a slight rearrangement of the furniture," he told her. "May I?"

Agafia nodded, seemingly intrigued by his request.

George turned the chair slightly so that a person sitting in it would face north. He also brought a candlestick from a shelf and set it on the edge of the rug. Then he pulled a small object from his pocket and bent over, his back to Agafia, and traced a circle on the floor around the chair and rug. He slipped the object back into his pocket and turned to face Agafia, who seemed slightly bemused.

"You are interested in bondage?" Agafia asked coyly. She pulled the sash around her waist loose. She shrugged and the robe rippled down into a puddle of fabric around her feet. Naked, she stepped into the middle of the room.

George caught his breath. Agafia was exactly the sort of woman he could enjoy the whole night, but there was no time for that now. He had to finish the task at hand and then go meet Fen'ka and Jarnvithja.

"Yes," he answered, his rising desire making his voice a rough growl. He picked up the rope and ran his palm along the smoothly braided cord. He and Agafia smiled at each other. He joined her next to the chair. He stood behind her and leaned forward, bringing his head down to brush his cheek along her throat. She leaned her head back, exposing the length of her

13

neck, sighing and relaxing against his body. He guided her into the chair and wrapped the rope snugly around her torso.

"Not too tight, is it?" he asked, as if concerned about Agafia's welfare, standing behind her and pulling the cord gently up beneath her breasts. He leaned down again, running his tongue up her throat and tickling her ear.

"No, it is not too tight," she answered. She sounded delighted, in fact, enjoying herself, no doubt relieved that her guest did not seem to be dangerous. The ropes were snug but not so tight that she could not wriggle her way out of them easily, if needed.

George's cheek rested against her neck. Desire rumbled in his throat. He closed his eyes. Agafia's scent filled his head and momentarily distracted him. She murmured something he did not understand. He nuzzled her earlobe again and slowly stood upright behind the chair. She leaned her head back against him and he heard the sounds of desire rising in her throat too.

He rested his palms on her shoulders, gently stroking her upper back with his thumbs.

"So beautiful," he whispered. "So very beautiful." He gazed down over her shoulder. He slipped loops of rope loosely around her wrists and the back legs of the chair. Then he pulled the whole rope tight. So tight that it cut into the tender flesh beneath Agafia's breasts. She gasped.

"Rough, heh? You like it rough?" she snarled, as if changing character from smooth seductress to wild tigress. "You like a girl who fights, heh?" She bucked in the chair, nearly knocking George over.

"Yes, I like it rough," he agreed, pulling the cord even more tightly around her and tying her hands firmly against the chair legs. "I like a woman who fights but ultimately knows her place."

THE CHARIOT

Agafia struggled against the rope but George could tell that it was not heartfelt. It was only an act to please her client. She seemed to feel that she was in no real danger. He came around and knelt before her, pulling the ends of the rope forward and binding her ankles against the front legs of the chair. She continued her muted protests.

Still kneeling before her, he buried his face in her lap. His energetic attention there quickly had her writhing and bucking in the chair again, though he was unsure if it was simply a pretense she thought would please him. Raising his head, he looked up at her and winked.

"You sly man," Agafia gasped out. "How dare you come into my flat and take advantage of me in such a manner?" He was sure this was a script she had followed many times before. He stood and came around behind the captive woman again.

"How dare I?" He mocked her question. "How dare you invite me here and drive me mad with such shameless, brazen temptation?"

"Tempt you?" Agafia retorted. But before she could continue the pretend argument, George had plucked her sash from the floor and pulled it tight between her teeth, knotting it behind her head. The gag now throttled the words she struggled to enunciate.

"I must make one more slight adjustment," George announced. He took the small object from his pocket and bent over again, tracing a small triangle on the rug that was just large enough to contain Agafia on the chair. She watched, winking at him when she caught his eye as he stood. She seemed to think this was still a part of the game they had been playing. Then he returned to his place behind her, where she could not see that he was careful to keep his feet outside the boundary of the triangle he had drawn around her. He closed his eyes and leaned forward slightly.

George ran his fingertips lightly along the tendons of her throat and then along the underside of her breasts. "Temptation? That is something we are both well acquainted with, I think," he muttered. "But for now, we must forgo temptation and get to the real purpose of my visit this evening."

He lifted his face to the north. "I conjure, O Gadriel, the lord of warfare and knowledge and beauty and seduction! I command you, who revealed the secrets of occult power to mankind! I adjure you, who taught Eve the pleasures of the flesh and became the father of her son Cain! By your delight in woman's flesh and by the blood of this whore that I offer to your honor and might and by the power of Solomon who bound you, by the authority of Lucifer and Apollyon to torment you, and by your own power: I command you to come without delay and follow the instructions that I give!"

He pulled the object from his pocket again. This time he flicked it open: it was a switchblade knife and its finely honed blade, which he noted Agafia could see out of the corner of one eye, glittered in the dim and flickering candlelight.

A muffled scream was caught by the gag in her mouth. She attempted to throw her weight back against George, fighting against him now in earnest. But he was too quick. With a deft flick, he made a long but quick gash below her left nipple.

Agafia bucked and writhed and threw herself from side to side, back to front. Blood spurted from the cut and then dribbled down her body. Behind her, George kept his hands on her shoulders and leaned his weight into her. Suddenly, she stopped fighting and she slumped against the chair she was sitting in, her body still, her head tipped to one side.

He undid the gag. Air escaped from Agafia's mouth in a

quiet whistle. Seemingly unconscious, her eyes closed, she drew another gentle breath.

"Gadriel: come with your wrath and fury and indignation, your troop of destructive angels!" he barked from behind the unconscious woman.

The flame of the candle soared high, a pillar of flame in the circle he had traced. It crackled and sizzled, the glare of the candlelight making it difficult to see anything else in the room. George held up his hand, still holding the bloody knife, to shield his eyes. The wick sputtered and popped, sending a shower of wax droplets cascading across the room.

"Why call me?" a deep, gruff voice demanded. "Why have you dared disturb me?" The voice dripped with malice and hatred. The woman in the chair lifted her head and twisted her neck, as if trying to see who it was that stood behind her. "What is it you want of me, mortal?" The furious male voice was coming from the mouth of the prostitute. Her eyes, now open, were bloodshot and filled with hatred.

"I am in the midst of combat, Gadriel," George answered, his voice icy and even. "I need your aid to set free the flood that has been building and waiting to descend on Prague."

The woman rocked in the chair, straining against the ropes. Even as the chair seemed about to tip over, it struck the invisible boundaries of the triangle George had traced around it and remained upright. The candle flared.

The demonic voice snarled at the Jesuit in rage.

"You cannot escape the triangle," George reminded the demon imprisoned within Agafia's body. "Just as I am protected by the circle against any devils you might have brought with you from Hell into this world. Now listen to me! Obey me!"

The sputtering candle within the circle dipped and rose as if buffeted by a winter gale. Gadriel screamed and roared, still trying to escape and still imprisoned within the unconscious prostitute. "Set me free, mortal! Give me my liberty and I will give you untold riches! I will fulfill your widest fantasy! Only set me free upon the earth!"

"Never!" George barked at the demon he had called. "I will give you liberty only to fulfill my command to set free the flood and wash away the bridge that protects Prague!"

The demon paused in his raving and twisted the prostitute's head to look over her shoulder again, attempting to see the man who stood behind the chair. Venomous laughter erupted from Gadriel's throat.

"Wash away the bridge that protects Prague? You are mad, mortal! The power of that bridge is infamous! Its magic is unequalled and invincible! No flood can wash it away or destroy the protection it affords Prague! You are mad!"

"I am not mad, Gadriel!" George retorted. "You are bound to obey me by the conjuration worked with the prostitute's blood and the proper invocations! I, and I alone, have found a way to poison the magic of the bridge and render it vulnerable and weak. So vulnerable and so weak that it and its protective shield around Prague can be washed away by a flood of sufficient strength. That flood, which I have also prepared, needs only to be set loose by you."

Gadriel stopped trying to look over Agafia's shoulder and faced the sputtering candle, the high flame having nearly consumed the entirety of the wax candle. The demon was silent and then nodded.

"Very well, mortal man. I will let loose this flood you say can wash away the bridge and its power," the ancient demon finally agreed. "But when your project fails and the bridge stands and your enemies destroy you, I will be waiting for you in Hell. I will be waiting and I will take special delight in tormenting you! You will be bound to me forever, as I am bound here to your command for these brief moments on Earth."

"My project fail?" snorted George. "I think not! No one before me has discovered the secret to poisoning the power of the bridge and now—once the sword of Bruncvik is removed from its foundation and delivered to me—I will also wield the power of the rabbi's staff, the sword, and the Astronomical Clock. All the most important mystical defenses of Prague will have fallen into my hands when Jarnvithja and Fen'ka deliver the sword to me! My power will become a legend among the occult practitioners of the Earth. The bridge's magic will fail and the city it protects will be washed away. Svetovit will trample it under his horse's hooves and then I will give him leave to trample the modern world beneath his horse's hooves as well. It is I, not the bridge, that will be invincible!"

Gadriel listened. Then he laughed quietly. The laughter grew in strength until it sounded like thunder to George.

"I will be invincible!" the Jesuit repeated. "Now, go! Do as I command!"

The demon continued to cackle but the sound subsided, and slowly Agafia's head dropped again to one side. The candle's flame gradually descended until it was little more than a spark wrapped around the fragment of wick that remained in the pool of wax in the candlestick. Gadriel was gone to do as George had bid.

"Fail? Never!" George repeated to himself, kneeling to wipe the switchblade clean on Agafia's robe. The quiet of her gentle breathing filled the room. He slipped the knife back into his pocket after slicing through a loop of the ropes around

19

Agafia's body so she could struggle her way out of them when she woke, though the knife caught on her skin and left a bright red line beneath the rope. She wouldn't be in good shape afterward, and she'd have an ugly scar which might impinge on her ability to attract clients in the future, but she wouldn't die. That could cause complications.

George looked around the room one last time. He had touched nothing but the rope and he knew that fingerprints were notoriously difficult to lift from textures such as the cords binding the prostitute. There was no physical evidence that could link him to this incident and he knew from previous experience that she would recall little or nothing of his visit when she awoke. He took a handful of Czech coins from his pocket and contemptuously tossed them at Agafia's feet.

"Gadriel will rue the day he thought to mock me!" the Jesuit promised as he closed the door of Agafia's apartment behind him and set out to meet Jarnvithja and Fen'ka under the Charles Bridge.

Father Dmitri and his four companions fled from the Astronomical Clock, where the Dearg-due had miraculously disappeared into the darkness with a final echoing shriek, but only after murderously feeding on Wilcox. After navigating the empty nighttime streets, they stood catching their breath in the comparative safety of the arcade beneath the Powder Tower. Fr. Dmitri, the Eastern Orthodox chaplain from Tennessee, looked at the others: his wife, Sophia, Magdalena's friend Victoria, and the other two academics, Sean from Dublin and Theo from Oxford, who like Fr. Dmitri, were visiting Prague to attend the twin conferences on Evil and on Monsters.

Theo gasped. "What just happened there?"

"Evidently, my nephews in Ireland have vanquished the

20

evil Dearg-due," Sean answered. "Either they or my graduate student. We won this round!"

"But at the loss of Wilcox, Peter, and Alessandro!" Sophia burst out.

"But many more will be lost if we fail now," Fr. Dmitri interjected. "We have only one hope of stopping the Dearg-due's ally, George. We must reactivate the power of Prague's Royal Road before he can destroy the magic protecting the Charles Bridge."

"All right, this was your idea," Theo told Fr. Dmitri. "What do you think is the best way to begin?"

George stepped out of Agafia's building and hailed a taxi that took him back toward his hotel. Alighting from the taxi near the Little Town Square, he strolled down Bridge Street past the nearly empty restaurants and taverns. He followed the road underneath the bridge to the pool where he met Fen'ka's ghost and the troll Jarnvithja the night before. The water, normally so tranquil in the pool, rushed and eddied as it poured into the alcove under the bridge and then rushed out again, leaving trails of foam on the surface that circled repeatedly as if caught in a whirlpool. The water level was much higher than it had been even the night before, let alone its usual early to mid-August level.

"There is almost no room for that boat to slide into the pool from under the bridge," George observed. "Certainly not room for Jarnvithja to stand as she steers the boat with her pole. Will she even get through? Should we have selected an alternate meeting place?" he wondered. He stepped as close the water as he dared lest he be caught in the relentless grasp of the furious river and pulled into it. He looked about and allowed a quiet smile to bloom on his face. His plan was working with more efficiency and skill than he had dared hope.

Lights from a hotel behind him played across the surface of the water. The rush of the water made it impossible to hear the approach of Jarnvithja's barge. George wondered how long he should wait before attempting to meet the troll at some other point along the river.

"I didn't bring any of the tarot cards or dandelion with me," he realized. How would he call Jarnvithja to a new meeting place? He had no choice but to wait for her there. At least it was nearly midnight on a Sunday evening and the streets seemed deserted. No one was coming or going from the hotel behind him. There were no sounds of footsteps on the bridge. There would be no witnesses to his reception of the great sword from Jarnvithja if she brought it to him as he had instructed.

He finally decided he had waited long enough and was turning to go when something caught his attention out of the corner of one eye. He paused and looked more closely across the water towards the massive stone pillars that supported the bridge.

There it was! The boat was sliding under the bridge into the stone-lined inlet. The cloaked and hooded figure of Jarnvithja sat alone in the back of the boat, where Fen'ka had sat before. There was no sign of Fen'ka anywhere in the boat. The troll's gnarled and taloned hands grasped the bargepole and attempted to guide the boat through the surging current. George saw the boat sway and wobble in the river, buffeted by the conflicting currents. Jarnvithja finally brought the boat to rest at the edge of the swollen river, near where George was standing. The wooden bottom of the boat scraped against the stone paving where Magdalena must have stood when she first met the burned woman and her spectral escort.

Under the hood, Jarnvithja's face was lost in shadow,

though George could see her eyes glinting in the darkness. A handful of tangled hair tumbled out of the hood and down one shoulder, wet and glistening in the damp mist thrown up by the churning river.

"So. You've come." It was a statement more than a question that George directed to Jarnvithja. The hood inclined as the troll slowly nodded.

"I was not sure you would come this evening," George continued. "Or, I was not sure that you would be able to bring the boat to land here." He gestured to the swollen river at his feet. The hood turned and bent as Jarnvithja seemed to inspect the water level. The hood's movement eventually ceased and the troll seemed to fix her gaze on George once again.

"The athame of Prague," George announced. "The sword of Bruncvik. You extracted it from the foundations of the bridge, yes? My breaking of the enchantment of the mortar was successful, was it not?" He could not keep the note of pride out of his voice. He had done what no one had been able to accomplish in the six hundred and fifty years since the construction of the bridge.

Jarnvithja nodded again. She pulled the bargepole out of the water and laid it down the length of the boat. A considerable portion of the pole extended out over the water from the prow. She then reached toward her feet, bringing her face nearly level with her knees. The swollen hunchback rose above her, wrapped in shadow and her dark cloak. Her talons scrabbled against the boards of the rowboat floor and then her shoulders stiffened and George thought he heard a grunt of effort. The hunchback shuddered and the giant troll woman sat upright again, raising her hands, in which she now grasped the great broadsword in its scabbard, extracted from the foundations of the bridge.

23

She held the sword upright, its great hilt resting against the knuckles of her hands. George caught his breath. The sword of Bruncvik, one of the four magical tools of Prague and one of the most powerful magic talismans of medieval Europe, was his to take. What power would be his to command once he held the sword? Had Fen'ka and Jarnvithja considered that? By taking possession of the sword, which together with his destabilizing of the magic of the bridge— which the presence of the sword, taken from its foundations, amply proved—he would be acclaimed one of the greatest Grand Masters of the ages. With the magic of the sword, he might even be able to hold death at bay and win immortality. That was more than he had dared to think when Gadriel had taunted him in Agafia's apartment.

Jarnvithja was using both hands to hold the sword and it wobbled slightly. This ancient artifact was a material reality and no mere spectral or disembodied vision. It was clearly much heavier than anything she had been accustomed to holding aloft for a great many years. "How many years?" George wondered. "Probably for as many years as the river itself has flowed through this valley," he decided.

He stepped toward the boat, the chill water rushing into his shoes and up his legs. He reached to take the sword from Jarnvithja, but in a single, swift motion, she laid the sword across her lap, causing him to nearly lose his balance and topple into the water as his hands closed on empty air. George glared at her and, cursing under his breath, closed his right hand around the scabbard, reaching for the hilt with his left. But Jarnvithja kept one hand on the hilt and another on the scabbard and refused to let the sword go.

"Do not toy with me, troll," George warned her furiously. "I can walk away from this effort to revitalize Fen'ka's curse

24

as easily as not. If I leave you and that witch, who will come to her rescue again? No one knows as much about the magic of the bridge as I. That should be self-evident; when have you or the dead in the river whom you command ever before been able to extract the sword from the foundations? That proves that the magic of the bridge is crumbling, does it not? That means, for the first time since it was built, the bridge is vulnerable. So when the bridge is washed away in the coming flood, the full power and wrath of Svetovit will be unleashed against the city. Both he and Fen'ka will be forever in my debt. But if I walk away and refuse to set them and their power free, and you are to blame for having angered me, do you not think that they have ways to make your existence beneath the river more miserable than ever in the days to come?"

Jarnvithja's hood remained steady, as if she were staring him in the eye and daring him to make good his threat. He stood there as well, the cold water crawling up his trousers, daring the troll to release the sword or see him turn away.

Then his patience snapped. "Very well. You think to wield the sword yourself? You think to be the one to set Fen'ka and her curse free with it? Hardly! You have no idea of how to wield the blade or harness its power. You can explain to both Fen'ka and Svetovit why you did not deliver the sword to me." He hissed and turned, splashing water onto the cobblestones as he stepped out of the swollen river towards the hotel and the road above.

A clatter and a splash behind him caused George to look back over his shoulder despite his intention to walk away. Jarnvithja had taken the barge pole and plunged it into the water beside her boat. It stood, quivering, as if it were a great tree caught in a windstorm. She spread her arms, raising her hands from the sword as if to invite him to take the blade from her knees.

George paused. "I should send her back to face Fen'ka and Svetovit," he thought, "and let them punish her for keeping them trapped and fettered, powerless to vent their wrath against the city." But he wanted to be acclaimed as one of the greatest Grand Masters of magic even more than he wanted revenge. He wanted to be known as the one who had overcome the magic of the Charles Bridge. He needed the sword in his hands to do that.

Did he trust Jarnvithja? Would she clasp her hands back onto the sword and refuse again to let him take it? Did she seriously think that she could be the great heroine to liberate Svetovit's power from the constraints the bridge and the other magical tools of Prague had placed on his power? George plunged back through the water and reached for the sword on her lap.

More swiftly than he could have imagined, Jarnvithja reached over with one hand and seized the barge pole from where she had wedged it between the underwater cobblestones and swung it in a wide arc. The pole crashed onto the back of his head as the troll-woman's other claw-like hand wrapped itself around his throat. The pain and surprise nearly blinded the Jesuit as the claw tightened. His feet slipped on the cobblestones and his arms flailed, momentarily useless as his mind struggled to understand what was happening.

The boat rocked and glided back over deeper water. The barge pole cracked against George's skull again while Jarnvithja struggled to keep her grasp on his windpipe. The sword slipped off one of her knees and the point of the scabbard thudded against the bottom of the boat. George kicked against the sideboards and tried to push himself away from Jarnvithja, but her stranglehold was too tight.

She dropped the pole into the boat beside her and clutched

the top of the sideboards to steady herself. George could no longer feel cobblestones beneath his feet and his lungs burned from lack of air. He stretched his hand toward the boat, hoping to reach something to use as a weapon to free himself. He kicked against the sideboards, causing the boat to rock wildly.

Even as his body fought to free himself, his mind fought to find a reason for Jarnvithja's murderous attack. The lack of oxygen, the pain, the physical effort made it difficult to think, but suddenly he realized why.

"Troll! You are known to lure swimmers and others into the river and then kill them, adding to the armies of the dead that you command beneath the waves!" George gasped at her with what little breath he could manage. "You think… killing me… I will have no choice but to do your will—and that of Fen'ka and Svetovit!" His fingers scratched at the sideboards, but Jarnvithja's reach was too long and kept him from getting hold of either the barge pole or the sword.

Jarnvithja continued to hold tightly onto the sideboards with one hand and George's throat with the other. Although she held his head at nearly the same level as hers, they were both drenched with water kicked up from the river by their struggle. He tried to swing his legs into the boat and she swept her hand along the top of the sideboards, knocking his legs back into the water with a tremendous splash that surged over the sideboards and into the bottom of the barge.

A dark miasma hovered at the edge of his mind and it was an unavoidable temptation to consider simply slipping into the dizziness and letting the darkness consume him. With a last effort of thought and strength however, George reached for the sideboards and grabbed them with both hands. Pulling up his feet and bracing them against the boat, he flung himself backwards into the river, pulling the boat over on top of himself.

The move caught Jarnvithja by surprise. Unable to shift her weight quickly enough, the boat capsized and plunged the Jesuit and the troll into the cold water.

Jarnvithja now clutched at George's neck with both hands. He heard the water roar in his ears. Clouds of frothy bubbles swirled about, engulfing them as the last remnants of air were forced from the folds of their clothes. George kicked at Jarnvithja, tangling his legs in her long, flowing cloak. He swept his arms through the water as he saw the contents of the boat—the barge pole and the sword—sinking through the waves beside him. He lunged toward the descending sword, dragging Jarnvithja along with him. His lungs were bursting with pain and—unable to stop himself—he gasped for breath underwater, swallowing the river instead of air. He knew he was dying.

But then he felt something falling past his hand and he curled his fingers around whatever it was, hoping to use it to strike back in some last futile gesture of defiance. If it was the barge pole, he would plunge it into Jarnvithja's torso; if her body was as solid as her hands around his throat, then perhaps that would drive her off.

But it was not the barge pole. It was one of the leather straps hanging from the scabbard of the sword. He couldn't so much see as feel the embossed decorative work on the leather. He pulled it, hugging the scabbard as it slowly came through the dark water towards him. He clutched the hilt of the sword and wrenched it free of the leatherwork containing it as he took one last, desperate gasp of river water into his lungs.

A shimmer of light reflected off the edge of the sword's blade, even in the turbulent water. The sword slid out of its scabbard, exposing the length of the great blade. George pushed the leather straps of the scabbard up along one arm, looping it around his elbow and grasping the hilt with both hands. Then he swung the blade in a long arc directed at the troll's midriff.

Jarnvithja's hands sprang loose from George's throat as she fell back into the water, away from the sword slicing its way towards her through the water. At the same moment, George coughed and sputtered and realized that he was breathing air and not inhaling more water. There was also a surge of something not unlike electricity in the water around him, a hum and thrill of power that heightened his senses and raised the hair on his arms and neck. The barge pole rested on the bottom of the river beside him. Jarnvithja's cloak swirled and coagulated in the river, concealing her face and hands and any semblance of a person that might be hidden in the roiling cloth, which continued its retreat from him, back towards the main body of the river.

George's head burst through the river's surface, his body propelled upward by a thrust from below. He stumbled onto the cobblestones and stood there, gasping and coughing, leaning on the sword as its point dug into the mortar between the cobblestones. He turned to look back over the river, water running down his face and clothes, streaming back to the river it had come from. There was no sign of the overturned boat, no indication of the struggle that had just taken place beneath the waves. The current surged in from the river and back out again, just as it had while he had been waiting for Jarnvithja's arrival.

George bent his neck and shook his head, scattering drops of river water from his brow like rain. The sword, whose magic was crafted to protect and defend, had done just that for him: protected and defended him from Jarnvithja's terrible assault. As long as the sword had rested in the bridge's foundations, it had lent its power to the bridge and supported its magical defense of Prague. But now the sword was in his hands. Now he would wield that magic to protect and defend himself. He had intended to use it to protect and defend Fen'ka and Svetovit, but now, whether they had conspired with Jarnvithja to drag him into the river and slay him or not, he would use it to demonstrate the superiority of his power over theirs. Even Svetovit would learn to obey George now, after the fulfillment of the curse that was an unavoidable aspect of Svetovit's liberation.

"But it will be the last time Svetovit will act on his own behalf. They will all pay for the troll's betrayal," George snarled his promise to the night sky. "Svetovit. Gadriel. Fen'ka. Jarnvithja. They will all learn to serve, rather than expect to be served."

Fr. Dmitri and his companions stood in the arcade beneath the Powder Tower at the end of the street running alongside Our Lady of Tyn.

"All right, this was your idea," Theo told Fr. Dmitri. "What do you think is the best way to begin?"

Dmitri had clearly been thinking about this very question. "I think that we should begin with a circle of salt here, in the portico beneath the tower itself, but a circle that opens out onto the Royal Road," he explained, stroking his salt-and-pepper beard. "Not a circle closed in on itself, but one that leads out through the gate onto the Royal Road through the Old Town, yes? We should also release the energy of the first tarot card here by lighting it in the circle after it is drawn. Then we can trace the route of the Royal Road, pouring a single line of salt out of the chalice and lighting the next few tarot cards as we go. At turns or intersections of the Royal Road would probably be best." He paused and looked around the group.

More murmurs of assent and nodding heads met him.

"What chalice?" Theo reminded them. "Magdalena has the chalice again. I threw it at the Dearg-due, remember? Magdalena took it, with the rabbi's staff."

"Then we shall simply have to pour the salt directly on the road," Fr. Dmitri's wife, Sophia, answered, running her fingers through her hair.

Victoria pulled the tarot deck and box of matches from between the canisters of salt and handed them to Fr. Dmitri, asking, "Which one do you think we should use first?"

He thumbed through the deck and set several cards nearly at right angles to the others. "These will be good to start with," he announced, extracting the cards he had selected and returning the others to Victoria, who wedged them back into the bag.

"We should use them in numerical order," he went on. "The 'royal road' of the cards begins with the Magician, so he should come at the beginning of the Royal Road of Prague as well." He sorted the cards in his hand according to the Roman numerals printed on them and then put them into his pocket, keeping out only the card bearing the image and title of Magician.

"Theo, open a canister of salt, please," he instructed as he creased the card and wedged it into the paving stones at his feet. "Victoria, shake the salt out and draw a circle around us. And draw the beginning of a line that leads from the circle out onto the street, along the Royal Road."

Theo wedged his thumb into the small metallic spout of the first canister and gave it to Victoria. She began to walk around the five people at the base of the Powder Tower. She tipped the cardboard canister slightly, so that the salt fell in shimmering cascades to the ground. As she made the circle, the others held their breaths. The salt sparkled against the paving stones. Victoria approached her starting point and hesitated, looking back to the priest.

Fr. Dmitri, however, was busy with the card and matches. He had squatted down and pulled out a match, striking it against the side of the box. The tip flared as the flame burst into life. As he brought the match close to the card, the flame wavered and stretched toward the card, as if yearning to leap across to the image. Sophia held her breath, afraid the card would not burn. The fire hovered at the priest's fingertips, and then it did seem to jump to the card. The flames flickered along the creased ridge of the card and then flowed out along the image, illuminating the anxious faces of the five watching it.

The face of the Magician on the card smiled at those watching, the four magical tools on the table before him— staff, chalice, sword, pentacle—seeming to grow larger as the flames spread and the card's edges blackened and curled. For an instant, the card burned, shining like a star fallen to earth, and then the fire blinked out. A delicate, twisted snowflake of ash fluttered away.

Dmitri squatted a moment longer before attempting to rise to his feet. Sean reached out to help him when Sophia gasped and pointed to the air just above them, where the last wisps of smoke from the burning card still hovered. They all looked to where she pointed.

Incandescent colors slid through the air. "Just like the Northern Lights," Theo muttered. "I gave a guest lecture once in Alaska," he explained sheepishly. Colors danced and sprang around them, gradually coming together to make a three-dimensional translucent replica of the image on the card they had just burned. The figure of the Magician stood there, his hand raised in command or blessing. The four tools hovered there as well, faint but present. The flowers that had been depicted on the card bloomed in the air. The robes of the Magician stirred in the slight breeze and he seemed to be speaking, his lips moving slightly but no sound reaching the ears of those witnessing the vision. Then the colors brightened. The intensity of the lights flickered and the image slid back into a chaotic, undulating rainbow, which then dispersed into the night.

They took a collective breath again, awkwardly looking at each other even as a reverent silence descended on them. Sean finally pulled Dmitri to his feet. The priest shook himself and cleared his throat.

"We should take turns, yes?—pouring the salt," he said gruffly, trying to hide the emotion in his voice. His wife gave him a sympathetic look.

Sean took a canister from the bag. "In Celtic practice, the chalice—or whatever is used to hold the salt—should be wielded by a woman." He scratched his chin beneath his auburn beard, apparently debating which woman he should offer the canister of salt. He held it out and Victoria grasped it.

"You take it," Victoria said, offering the canister to Sophia. Sophia took the cardboard container and held it as her husband would hold the Eucharistic chalice on Sunday. Theo and Sean took up the bags of additional salt canisters. Dmitri pulled the next tarot card from his pocket and the little procession set out down the Royal Road toward the heart of Prague.

Sophia tipped the container in her hands, scattering a thin but steady stream of salt onto the cobblestones. Some of the salt drifted to one side or the other, and none if it fell thickly enough to make a clear and discernable line down the road, but Dmitri knew they all felt the thrum, the gentle vibration of power and life that gently reverberated beneath their feet. They made their way slowly, so as not to scatter the salt in too dispersed a pattern. Sophia gave the salt container back to Victoria to carry as they passed the large windows of the crystal shops displaying delicate wineglasses and other sparkling Bohemian crystal. Sean and Theo took turns as well, alternating who carried the bags as the procession continued its quiet march.

They approached the first intersection of the Royal Road with a side street and paused. Fr. Dmitri found a crack in the mortar between the cobblestones and inserted the card, the High Priestess, so that it stood upright. He bent low and struck a match, holding it near the card. The scent of the striking match hung especially pungent in the air. Again the flame flickered and stretched from the match towards the card until it leapt onto the edge of the image. It glowed and then swept across the face of the card. Shadows shifted and danced on the walls around them. They looked up in expectation, caught between hoping for and fearing another vision.

The card withered in the flames. They held their breaths. No vision appeared. The fire of the burning card spurted up into an instant of intense life and then extinguished itself, the ash of the card falling down between the cobblestones.

Magdalena had come straight to George's room, breathlessly knocking on the door and struggling to stop herself from pounding it down and causing a scene. She stood in the hallway clutching the staff and chalice, panting, knowing her brown hair was in disarray, until finally she heard the lock click and the door opened slightly. George peered into the hallway and then stood aside to admit her. He was wearing pajamas and holding a glass of wine.

"I met Elizabeth, just as you told me," she told him, still

clutching the staff and chalice as she sat on a formal chair next to the desk and he headed for an easy chair.

George nodded. "She showed you how to interrupt the magic of the Astronomical Clock and disrupt its balance, correct?" he asked.

"Yes, she did," Magdalena hastened to agree. Unable to stop herself, the whole story of the events on the Old Town Square tumbled out of her mouth as George sat and calmly sipped his wine. She hardly paused in her urgent recounting until she reached the point at which Elizabeth had ordered her to bring the staff and chalice back to safety, sending her back to the bridge and her decision to come directly to George and tell him what had happened.

"What do you think happened next, George?" Magdalena asked at last. "Was Elizabeth safe there? Or did the professors from the conference find a way to send her back to Ireland? Is that why she insisted I leave her there? Because she knew she would not be coming back with me?"

He closed his eyes and tapped his glass against the arm of the chair, thinking as she sat, catching her breath after finishing her report. "I think I must agree with you," he concluded at last, opening his eyes and sipping his wine again. "Elizabeth has been forcibly returned to Ireland, kidnapped by magic as it were, even if you did not witness her departure. Everything points to that. Fen'ka's enemies have driven Elizabeth back into her grave and won this round of the struggle." He looked intently at Magdalena. "Do you see how these men and their unwitting accomplices will stop at nothing to prevent us from clearing Fen'ka's name? It is all the more important, therefore, that we redouble our efforts to clear her even as we take appropriate measures to protect and defend ourselves. Do you understand?"

Magdalena hastened to agree. "Yes, of course I do. We must. That much is obvious. It's just…" She looked at George, pleading, feeling her eyes fill with tears. "You said we each had a role to play. Can we manage without… without Elizabeth to fulfill her role?" She let go of the chalice and it fell into her lap as she fumbled for a tissue from a pocket. "I miss her already, George. I miss Elizabeth." She wiped her eyes and looked at him, biting her lower lip.

"Yes, I shall miss her as well," the Jesuit master of black magic conceded. "As for her role, however… If you and she did as instructed tonight and the disruption of the clockworks was successful, her role will have been completed and her mission accomplished. That achieved, we are that much closer to the accomplishment of our final goal and Elizabeth would want—more than anything else, don't you think?—that we hasten to complete the vindication of Fen'ka."

Magdalena realized the truth of his words. "Yes. Yes, I see that. We cannot let her effort be in vain. We can clear Fen'ka, just the two of us, if we must. We shall!" A new resolve formed in her mind to continue and achieve the task she had been set, as well as having set herself.

George finished his wine and set aside the glass, leaning forward and resting his elbows on his knees. "Now, it is important that you recall this as carefully as you can," he instructed. "Who was in the group that met you in the Old Town Square? Who was involved in the plot to send Elizabeth back into her grave in Ireland?"

Magdalena thought carefully, picturing in her mind those who had interrupted her and Elizabeth's magical work with the clock. "We were interrupted by… let me think… it was Theo. He threw the salt canisters at Elizabeth. Sean was also there. My friend, Victoria. Former friend," she corrected. "Also

that Orthodox priest, Father… Dmitri. And his wife, Sophia."
George looked up abruptly at the mention of Sophia.

"Hmm… troubling, that," he muttered. "But Alessandro
was not among them?"

"No," Magdalena answered. She understood the difficulty.
"We knew there were two people working to stop us—Sophia
and Alessandro, who had been to the synagogue, asking to get
into the attic—but only one was on the square tonight. Sophia.
So where was Alessandro?"

"I know Elizabeth went to speak with him," was all
George said. "Perhaps she dissuaded him from joining their
efforts to stop us."

"Perhaps he provoked her," Magdalena surmised. "She
may have been driven to protect herself against Alessandro."
She shuddered, picturing the probable carnage if Elizabeth, the
Dearg-due, had been forced to kill him. "But if so, he deserved
the punishment."

"Quite so. But I thought she also planned to speak with
Sophia. I wonder, was she unable to keep the appointment?"
George asked.

"Either dealing with Alessandro took longer than she
expected, or she was unable to dissuade Sophia," Magdalena
decided. "But it seems Sophia has drawn others into her
effort to keep Fen'ka's name darkened by false accusations of
witchcraft. She must think that Svetovit and the other spirits
Fen'ka invoked during her life were the demons and devils the
Christians claim. How naïve!" She congratulated herself on
her own sophistication.

"Our enemies are becoming desperate, Magdalena,"
George warned her. "Perhaps that is why Sophia has gotten
others involved in this struggle. Or, more likely, she has
become a pawn in the hand of her husband, Dmitri. He must

realize that he cannot stop us in the short time that remains. The noose around the throats of Fen'ka's enemies grows tighter and he knows he needs help. Their time grows short."

"How short? How is the noose growing tighter?" Magdalena pressed him. "Because we are gathering the four magical tools?"

"In part," George agreed. "We have the rabbi's staff and Bruncvik's sword, and we have disabled the Astronomical Clock. But recall the invocation of justice and judgment we performed together? How we spilled the dregs of the spiced wine and the burning charcoal onto the streets of the city?"

"Yes." That had been an amazing experience that Magdalena would never forget.

"You told me you warned the doorkeepers at the synagogue that a tremendous flood was coming to Prague and that the cultural artifacts in the attic needed to be preserved, correct?" he went on.

"Yes. I did. How are those connected?" Magdalena wondered.

"Justice is coming inexorably, Magdalena. Fen'ka's enemies, our enemies, know this. They know that justice is coming. They will stop at nothing to prevent that. There is a flood coming, Magdalena, a flood that they have summoned. The coming flood is part of their efforts to keep Fen'ka imprisoned by the past," George explained. "The magic of the Charles Bridge, built by those who murdered Fen'ka to protect themselves from her wrath, has been shaken and is crumbling. But they have taken advantage of this and created a flood, a flood that is coming to wash away not only the bridge but much of the city as well."

"They created this flood?" exclaimed Magdalena. Fear and anger bubbled up within her.

THE CHARIOT

"They created the situation that makes the flood possible," George told her. "Their invocations against Fen'ka—and those, like us, who support her—must have been extremely powerful, invoking powers and magic rarely invoked. It takes time for judgment such as you and I invoked to come to fruition, but it will. In order to prevent that, our opponents made their own invocations, and for those counter-invocations to be successful, the weather conditions had to shift. Their counter-invocation must therefore have reached backwards, as well as forward, to accomplish its work. Their magic reached the atmosphere and back into the early summer to make this flood possible." He paused, regarding Magdalena speculatively.

"Apparently, Dmitri and the others will do anything they can to stop us," George warned her. "So it seems we must fight fire with fire," he said at last. "Now that we know who is working to hinder us, we can more directly protect ourselves and further our efforts to vindicate Fen'ka."

"What should we do? How do we prevent them from flooding the city?" fretted Magdalena. "How can we stop so many people who oppose us?"

"It will take thought. Much thought," George agreed. "Their strategy is devious, cunning. Let me consider the possibilities overnight. Meet me downstairs in the morning and we can discuss possible responses as we walk to the conference."

She stood, understanding that she was being dismissed by the master. "Shall I leave the staff with you, then?"

George reflected on this before answering. "For the time being, I think that would be best. Leave the staff here. Take your chalice home, though. I doubt our enemies will dare try to enter your apartment again. But you should protect yourself,

Magdalena." He went to his luggage and rummaged about in it, pulling something out and returning to Magdalena at the door.

"Take this," he told her. "Hang it in your apartment, near the door or windows. It will keep unwelcome intruders out." He leaned toward her and she offered her cheek for a kiss. Then she was in the hallway, George closing the door behind her.

She looked at the object in her hand. It was a medal of the Infant of Prague.

"What is wrong?" asked Victoria. "Where is the High Priestess?" She searched for the vision she had hoped to see.

"I'm not sure." Dmitri stood. "Perhaps because we are further along the Royal Road and not at the beginning? Could that be the difference?"

"Does the missing vision mean the power of the card was not released?" asked Sophia.

"Hard to say," Sean replied, though Victoria knew she had been asking the group and not any one person.

"Or perhaps because the other was burned in the circle of salt at the Powder Tower," suggested Theo. "Let's try the next card here as well, but first make a circle of salt around it."

"I am sorry to have wasted the High Priestess card and lost its power, but I think you are correct, Theo," Dmitri told him. "We should burn the next card here as well, within the circle of salt." He took the next card, the Empress, from his pocket and placed it upright between the cobblestones, as he had the previous card. He looked to Victoria and gestured around them.

Victoria turned to Sophia, saying, "I made the last circle. You should make this one." With a nod of gratitude, Sophia drizzled out the salt as she walked in a small circle around the others, huddled around the card. As she completed the circle, her husband struck another match and lit the card of the Empress.

More quickly than either of the previous cards, the fire rushed to embrace the card and consume it. The cardboard image blackened and disappeared beneath the growing puddle of soot across its face. The fragments of ash burst into the air as if shot by a cannon. Along with the others', Victoria's head jerked up and back, following the flight of the ash with their eyes.

Two great writhing, rippling serpentine ribbons of rainbow light materialized above them. The colors flared and faded, pooling together and then pulling back from each other like waves retreating from the shore, only to rush back in again. Embracing like lovers, the ribbons of light rose in a column and then burst into a fountain of tumbling stars that showered down toward the earth but then, as if caught in some powerful updraft, the stars swung up toward the sky again.

In the midst of the fireworks, two images appeared, facing each other. Both were women, of regal bearing and immense authority, who sat on a throne. One was arrayed in a great, flowing robe and veil and held a scroll on her lap. A strange, horned cap rested on her brow. Her expression was serene, her eyes solemn. A crescent moon was caught in the folds of her cloak around her feet.

Facing her, the other woman was resting on the pillows of an ornate divan. Wreaths of stars and ivy crowned her brow and she held a scepter in one hand. Free-flowing locks cascaded down her shoulders. Sheaves of golden wheat rustled around her feet and a multitude of flowers adorned her gown. She seemed about to laugh.

The two women hovered above them a moment, gazing at each other. They nodded to each other, as if recognizing each other after a long absence, and then turned their attention to the people on the ground. The woman with the scepter extended her free hand toward the earth. The woman with the scroll lifted a finger toward the five gathered around the burnt cards as she arched an eyebrow. Then both images blurred and faded into the night.

No one spoke. No one dared to breathe. Quiet and confidence suffused them. Finally Victoria spoke the words that articulated what they must have all realized. "That was the High Priestess facing the Empress, was it not? They were both here."

"Which was which?" asked Sophia.

"The woman with the scroll was the High Priestess." Victoria was happy to have an opportunity to contribute what she could to the skills and knowledge of these academics who had spent their professional lives studying, if at arm's length, the magic they were all engaged in now. "She with the crown of stars was the Empress." They continued to stare in the air where the women had sat on their thrones.

Dmitri shook himself. "We shall continue, yes?" he asked at last. "We do have a task at hand to complete," he reminded them. The others nodded. As they set out down the Royal Road, Sophia sprinkled the precious white crystals onto the roadway.

The street curved gently as it led them back toward the Old Town Square but there were no intersections to cross or sharp turns in the road. Sophia and Victoria took turns pouring salt onto the road, the men taking turns carrying the bags.

"Wait a moment!" exclaimed Sean. "This building. This building here!" He pointed to a building on their right with a broad, gently arched doorway. A small plaque identified it with two numbers, one red and one blue. "When Hron led us on the tour of the Old Town our first evening here, he pointed this out as the residence of a Queen Eliška, related somehow to the Queen Judith who built the first bridge over the river. The Charles Bridge was built to replace the Judith Bridge, didn't Hron say? If George's intent is to wash away the Charles Bridge with a flood, wouldn't this be a good place to release the power of the next tarot card?"

Dmitri looked at the building and then up and down the length of the road they had come. "It has been quite a distance since we burned the cards of the High Priestess and the Empress. It seems we should burn another one along this portion of the road and yes, this does seem an appropriate place to do so, given its association with the construction of the bridges."

He took several cards out of his pocket and selected the card numbered 'IV,' putting the others back into his pocket. He bent over and found a crack in a cobblestone to insert the card of the Emperor. Victoria, who was holding the salt at that point, traced the circle of salt around them as Dmitri struck the match and held it to the card.

This time it was the card that seemed to yearn for the flame, as it fell toward the match in Dmitri's fingers. The fire struck the image and quickly ate a hole where the face of the emperor had been. The soot-edged hole grew and consumed the card from the center outward, the fragmentary frame of ash collapsing into the void that had been the image.

The quivering rainbow appeared once again as the power of the card was released to join the regenerated power of the Royal Road. The image of the Emperor shimmered into sight above them, a stern-faced man garbed in the folds of a thick cloak who sat on a massive throne of carved stone. A jeweled crown glittered on his brow, sparkling in the light of the rainbow that circled him in imitation of the salt encircling the people on the ground.

The Emperor reached out a hand toward the residence of the queen and then gestured up and down the street. The rainbow whirled about him in its dizzying dance, bursting into shards of multicolored light, which skipped along the length of the street as stones might skip along the surface of a lake. The image hung above them a moment longer and then also shattered into explosions of fireworks, the sparks fluttering towards the street but fading from sight before touching the earth.

Sean was the first to break the awe-filled silence that followed. He sighed loudly and coughed to clear his throat.

The procession began its progress along the Royal Road again, the salt gently falling toward the cobblestones. The vibration of power beneath Victoria's feet had become unmistakable when the street widened and melted into the expanse of the Old Town Square. Now it burst out of its constrained channel of the street and flooded into the cobblestones of the Old Town Square. Tiny stars and rivulets of light coursed through the air above the street and out into the square. A distant rumble filled the air. Was it the power of the Road she heard or the roar of the near-flood stage river not far away?

The path of the Royal Road led across the Old Town Square. The group stepped into the center of the Old Town, everyone reluctantly moving toward the body of their friend Wilcox and the Astronomical Clock opposite that marked the continuation of the Royal Road out of the square as it made its way toward the castle. From where they stood, Victoria could even see the illuminated prison tower at the corner of the castle, said to be haunted by the ghost of the knight named Dalibor.

The Chariot

Magdalena had to do something. She did not know what had brought the academics to the base of the Astronomical Clock in the Old Town Square, but they had hurt Elizabeth, the Dearg-due, there. George thought they had even discovered a way to send Elizabeth back to her grave in Ireland.

They were still in the Old Town somewhere, doing something to thwart Magdalena's effort to undo the miscarriage of justice that had led to Fen'ka's execution. They were trying to stop Magdalena from stripping away the lies that had killed Fen'ka and still maintained the corrupt power structures of the modern world. She couldn't be as calm about the academics tonight as George seemed to be. She had to do something. She had to avenge her friend Elizabeth. She had to do something to stop them and avert the flood they were bringing towards Prague.

First, she rushed out into her small back garden and gathered a few handfuls of the stalks and blossoms that grew there in haphazard fashion. Not sure what she was picking in the dark, she knew from her months of study before the conferences that all of these would have some magical effect. Then, in too much of a hurry to turn on the kitchen light, she dropped them onto the kitchen table and rummaged through her kitchen drawers in the half-light coming from the living room. She found a green candle stub, not as large as the one she had been looking for, but it would do. She lit it at the stove and fixed it to the charred wooden tabletop with a drop of hot wax. Then she took her ritual dagger—her athame—and first traced a triangle pointing north around the candle and then a circle around the triangle, much like she had done that night last spring, so long ago, when she had conjured the two spirits in her garden.

Then she lay the athame aside and sat down at the table, also facing north. She placed her palms down on the tabletop, on each side of the circle she had traced in the surface of the table. She closed her eyes and concentrated.

"Breathe slowly and deeply," she instructed herself quietly. "Like the meditation books instruct. Slowly and deeply." She felt her pulse slow a bit and the quiet of her steady breathing spread throughout her body. When she felt the quiet tickle the periphery of her consciousness, she opened her eyes.

Nothing in the semi-darkness of the kitchen seemed to have changed. The flame atop the candle burned like a small star and cast dancing shadows around Magdalena whenever an occasional breeze wafted through the side window. She stared at the candle, though, her eyes unable to see anything clearly in the flickering shadows and darkness of the room. Her pupils grew large and round as she focused only on the candle's flame and the rest of the room fell away from her consciousness. She was much more aware of herself there in the shadows than she had ever been in the light. She felt the tabletop beneath her palms, felt each of the tiny pricks on her hands from the rough, burnt splinters, but was aware of little else. She heard the sound of her own steady breathing and noticed it had become even slower.

She stared into the candlelight, seeing the dirty smudge of the wick at the heart of the flame. The flame dipped and wavered, then grew steady and elongated as its tip reached upward, ever upward, and the flame itself stretched and narrowed. There was a breath of a breeze and the flame severed into a pitchfork of flame, its three tines struggling to remain erect, before it melted back together into one steady point of fire.

Deep within the flame was a shimmer as colors shifted and rearranged themselves to become a vision. Magdalena saw the Old Town Square. Or at least a previous version of the Old Town Square. There were the churches and the Old Town Hall with its squat square tower and façades of buildings that looked much as they did today but were different in some fashion Magdalena could not easily identify. There was a woman tied to a stake in the Old Town Square in the heart of a fire. The woman seemed angry and defiant, proud and furious. But then she seemed to cough and choke, and her face fell forward and the fire rushed up to consume her. Magdalena wanted to look away in horror and disgust but could not tear her eyes from the fiery vision.

"Fen'ka!" Magdalena whispered in amazement, recognizing the woman at the stake.

The colors in the candle's flame shimmered and shifted again, resolving again into the Old Town Square, but this time a small group of people was emerging from beside the Tyn church into the square. She could see the Astronomical Clock as well, and the Hus memorial built over the place where Fen'ka had been tied to the stake in the first vision. Magdalena leaned forward and peered as close as she could into the flame. She saw the academics approach the Astronomical Clock. One of them seemed to be sprinkling something onto the cobblestones.

Without taking her eyes from the fire, she reached with one hand for the pile of stalks and petals on the table. Clutching one, she pulled it from the pile and held it out. The bent and crumpled leaves of the stalk shriveled as it sucked darkness into itself from the candle's wick. A thin line of smoke curled into the air. Then Magdalena dropped what she realized was a dandelion across the candle wick, where the fire ballooned out around the stalk only to then rush in and consume the plant offering. Ash coalesced where the stalk had been consumed, wrapped around the candle's wick, and then either fluttered away or dropped onto the table. Magdalena wasn't sure. She only knew that the dandelion was gone.

Continuing to peer into the fire and seeing the small figures slowly making their way toward the Astronomical Clock, Magdalena reached again toward the botanicals plucked from the garden. She found a few sprigs of woodruff between her fingertips and set them carefully in the soft wax atop the candle. Immediately, they caught fire and shriveled in the flame. A sweet fragrance hovered momentarily in the air to tickle Magdalena's nose and then faded away.

George sat at the desk in his hotel room, congratulating himself again on how easily he had beguiled Magdalena and calmed her fears. But the news she had brought him was disturbing. Sophia had survived Elizabeth's attack. Additional academics had gathered to thwart him and his plans. He left his drink unfinished on the dresser and went down to the front desk to ask the clerk for a small candle or votive light.

"I am sorry, sir," the young, pimple-faced clerk on duty answered. "No candles are allowed in the rooms due to the threat of fire. The streets here in the Little Town are narrow and fire trucks would have a difficult time reaching us if a fire were to break out. Perhaps you heard of the fire in Lisbon that destroyed the Chiado, the medieval quarter of the city, in 1988? The entire area burned because no fire trucks could navigate the narrow, twisting streets. Surely you can appreciate our difficulty."

George shook his head at the clerk, who was hardly more than an adolescent. "I can appreciate the difficulty, but surely you can appreciate my difficulty as well. I am a Jesuit, after all, as you may recall from seeing me in my collar earlier. I still must read my evening prayers and I find a candle burning in front of my crucifix a necessary aid to my concentration. Surely you could find one small candle?"

"Well, yes, Father… I can appreciate the aid of a candle in your prayers," the clerk stammered. "But I am not sure where I would find one… We do not keep such items at the front desk." The young man bit his lip. His eyes darted around the lobby behind George.

The clerk snapped his fingers. "I know, Father!" he exclaimed. "I know just where to find a candle for you!" He bolted from the front desk into the darkened breakfast room across the lobby. He returned a moment later with a tea light, which he placed in George's outstretched palm.

"The kitchen staff always set them out beneath the aluminum trays in the evening when they prepare the dining room for breakfast," the clerk explained, winking. "That way they only need to put the eggs and sausage in the trays and light the tea lights to keep the food warm. They will never miss one!"

Back in his room, the tea light burned on the desktop. He traced a small circle around the candle and set out the prescription vials filled with herbs associated with malevolent magic that Elizabeth had seen him use the night before during their preparations to poison the magic of the Charles Bridge.

George sat quietly, breathing slowly and deeply, staring into the candle flame. He saw images and colors shift and dip, curl and twist, resolving into figures and then unraveling again. He saw Magdalena staring into the candle in her kitchen and he saw the people in the Old Town Square that she saw in her own candle's flame. He saw her take the botanicals she had gathered from her garden and burn them in the flame.

"Ah, she cannot hope to accomplish this on her own," he muttered. "Good that she wants to strike back, to defend her city—she thinks!—and avenge Elizabeth. But she does not have the skill needed to do this." As he shaped the words with his lips, he reached for one of the bottles of herbs without taking his eyes from the vision in the candlelight. He dipped his tiny spoon into the vial of pennyroyal oil and then dripped the oil into the tea light, next to the burning wick. In a moment, the oil, associated with fire by the medieval alchemists, had been consumed by the fire and its magic added to that Magdalena was attempting in her kitchen.

The path of the Royal Road led across the Old Town Square. In the center of the Old Town, Victoria and the academics moved toward the Astronomical Clock opposite them, which marked the continuation of the Royal Road out of the square as it made its way toward the castle on the opposite side of the river. The clock also marked their recent encounter with Magdalena and the Dearg-due. Magdalena had been sent away with the chalice and the rabbi's staff by the Dearg-due, but the Irish undead had seemingly been returned to her grave in Ireland just as she had been about to kill them all. Even so, she had killed one of their small group, and Wilcox's mangled corpse still lay in the shadows of the alleyway across from the Clock.

Sophia, pouring the salt from the canister, paused and looked around the dark square that had once served as the most important market of Central Europe.

"Something is wrong," she announced to the others. "Something is very wrong. I can feel it. Do you feel it?"

Victoria, Sean, Theo, and Fr. Dmitri all stopped as well and examined the dark square.

"Something does seem amiss," Theo agreed. "Everything seems calm and still, but…"

"You mean, everything except for poor Wilcox over there?" Sean nodded toward the body of their friend. "We should do this part quickly before someone else comes along and discovers the body. If an alarm is raised and we are anywhere in the vicinity, the authorities will want to know why we did not raise the alarm ourselves."

"Sean is right," Fr. Dmitri agreed. "At the very least, the authorities could ask difficult questions about why we are all here in the middle of the night and did nothing. Or they may suspect us of… harming Wilcox ourselves. We must hurry."

"Wilcox would have wanted us to do so," Theo agreed. "We should burn the next card here and move along." He pointed to a spot on the cobblestones a few steps ahead of them.

"Wait," Victoria objected. "What is that smell?" A pungent, sweet smell suddenly engulfed them. "Is this something more about the Dearg-due?" she wanted to know. "Is there more mischief she can still cause us?"

Magdalena, eager to see what would happen now to the figures in the fire, saw that they had paused midway across the square. She pursed her lips and slowly exhaled, causing the candle flame to dance wildly.

The smell hung in the air around them in the Old Town Square.

"Is this something more about the Dearg-due?" Sean repeated Victoria's question. "I don't know. I don't think so. If the cairn was erected atop her grave in Waterford, I don't see how she could manage to harm us here again. But…"

"Look!" Sophia pointed toward the Hus memorial across the square. "The memorial! Do you see it?"

Victoria turned with the others.

"See what?" Theo asked. "I don't see…"

Before he could finish his sentence, a blue spectral fire burst from the base of the Jan Hus memorial. It roared and rose around the memorial as if to consume the statuary in the conflagration. Shades of blue and white rippled through the ghostly fire. The flames swirled and danced, rising higher and roaring louder. Heat radiated across the square and they all stumbled back as the heat collided with them.

"What caused that? Where did it come from?" Victoria cried. "What can we do now?"

No one answered her as they stared in fascination at the roaring bonfire.

Without warning, the fire swept out in a line across the square, much as earthly fire might ignite a trail of gunpowder. It rushed toward the three academics, who all scattered away from its reach. The sheet of flames divided into several rivulets of fire, each taller than a man and snaking after them, as if each were a living thing hunting each of the professors.

Sophia threw the canister of salt in her hand at the fire, but the fire only licked it up and continued undaunted. Victoria grabbed Sophia by the hand and pulled the priest's wife away from the racing flames. The women screamed as they ran, not watching where they were going. They only knew they wanted to get away from the pursuit of the fire. They could feel the unendurable heat of the fire bearing down on them.

Magdalena, in her kitchen, saw the blue ghost-fire erupt across the square and chase down the scattered academics. She stared in fascination at what she must have caused.

Fr. Dmitri did not know which way to run. The fire whipped across the square so quickly it was nearly upon him before he had a chance to move. Where had the others gone? Were they safe? Was his wife safe? He could hear the women screaming but did not know what that meant.

Magdalena exhaled another long, slow breath as she sat at her table, examining her thoughts and wishes. The candle flame dipped and swayed.

"I caused the ghost-fire?" she asked herself. "Do I want them hurt by the fire? Or did I only want them stopped?" she wondered. "But they hurt Elizabeth. They killed her again, just as her husband beat her to death three hundred years ago! Is hurting them the only way to stop them? Is that what I want?"

Theo found himself running toward the Astronomical Clock. The sheet of flame pursuing him swept around as if to encircle him and he veered toward the body of Wilcox, managing to dart through a gap in the blue-white flames before the circle closed him in entirely.

He glanced at the torn and bloody body of his friend as he ran, gasping for breath.

"Now is the time, old friend," he whispered to the corpse. "If there is anything you can do from the other side, do it now!"

In his hotel room, George saw the ghostly fire as well and knew he had caused it, not Magdalena. A sly grin crept across his face. "It is not enough for them to be frightened." He chuckled. The chuckle became a quiet snarl. "They must be stopped!"

He reached for another prescription bottle and extracted a few tendrils that he added to his tea light, careful to hold his breath as the fire reduced the slivers of poisonous mushroom to ash.

Theo tripped on a cobblestone and fell, knocking his chin against a manhole cover. The salt canisters in the shopping bag he carried spilled across the alleyway. His lungs felt as if they were on fire. He rolled onto his back, ready to kick at the approaching flames, as if that might stop them. The fire paused and wavered, as if searching for him, and then, seemingly picking up his scent, it raced toward him again.

The fire touched Wilcox's body and suddenly Wilcox was there, standing beside his own corpse. The standing Wilcox seemed to be wounded in the same way the corpse had been wounded, but he was standing nevertheless.

"Wilcox?" croaked Theo. "Is that you?"

Wilcox looked at Theo still sprawled on his back and nodded.

Then he was gone.

Sean found himself trapped in the arcades along the façade of Our Lady of Tyn. The flames swept along the length of the façade and around each end of the series of vaulted arches, enclosing the Dublin professor in a tunnel of stone and fire.

Sweat drenched his clothes. The heat was suffocating. He looked from one end of the arcade to the other. "Dare I try to run through?" he asked himself. "Might it part around me if I clutch the Infant of Prague medal in my fist?" He had seen Sophia throw the salt at it to no effect, so the shopping bag of salt canisters he grasped in one hand would be of no use. He searched his pockets with his other hand, trying to find the religious medal that had shown them the real Dearg-due beneath the mask of Elizabeth's face.

The heat became more intense. It was difficult to breathe. He had to get out.

"Is it waiting for me?" He looked all along the wall of fire, crackling and roaring. "It seems so… conscious, somehow. Should I chance it even without the medal and try to run through?" He bit his lip to steel himself for his attempt at escape.

"Five, four, three," he counted down under his breath, rocking from foot to foot like an Olympic runner. "Two…"

The fire rushed towards him and Sean cried out, dropping the shopping bag and throwing up his hands as he fell back against the centuries' old stone wall behind him. Then Wilcox was in front of him, facing the fire with his own arms spread wide.

The fire fell upon Wilcox, and Sean wasn't sure if the roar in his ears was the fire or Wilcox crying out. The heat was unbearable. Sean gasped for breath and his lungs felt as if they were being seared by the hot air he was gulping. Wilcox kept standing with his arms open, as though he could embrace all the flames as they bore down on Sean. Even though the fire produced no smoke, it was hard for Sean to see. His eyes filled with tears.

"The heat, the heat…" he whimpered. "Wilcox, you've been killed! What are you doing here?"

Wilcox either didn't hear him or was ignoring him. Leaning forward, he did seem to be struggling to contain the flames and hug them to himself. The fire kept pouring in through the arcade at Sean and Wilcox. It kept coming and Wilcox kept struggling to embrace it, absorb it, contain it within his arms.

Sean felt his knees buckle. He was dizzy with the heat and lack of air to breathe.

Wilcox was still there, fighting to crush the fire into his chest. Then his arms collapsed around his torso and the fire winked out.

Sean fell to his side, gasping and choking, gulping in the cool, fresh air of the night.

As quickly as Wilcox had vanished, he was again standing over Theo as the fire lunged at the Englishman down on his back. The fire howled and crackled, sparks popping and flying as the lash of fire hurtled into Wilcox's open palms. He held the fire as if it were a large swirling beach ball, the flaming sphere growing larger and hotter and brighter as the mass of flames threw themselves at the dead professor. Theo saw Wilcox fighting to press his palms together as if to crush the fire between them. He could hear Wilcox grunt and gasp and struggle to keep the fire from exploding from between his fingers.

Then with one last, great effort, Wilcox pressed his palms together and both he and the fire were gone.

George couldn't believe what he was seeing in the flame-vision of his candle. Something—he couldn't see what—was extinguishing each arm of the ghostly fire as it bore down on each of the academics.

"I have to stop whatever assistance they have called," he realized. "What can best reinforce the power of the fire?" He glanced at his yellow vials on the desktop. Picking one, he extracted a few crumbs of oleander leaves and petals, which he fed to the candle flame.

Fr. Dmitri ran as quickly as he could, certain the fire would catch him before he could find refuge near the Saint Nicholas' Church across the square. Looking down, he realized he was treading on the mosaic crosses that marked the execution site of the Protestant nobility along one side of the Old Town Hall. The fire swept up behind and around him and he was caught against the wall of the Old Town Hall, the fire pausing in a ring around the outermost of the mosaic crosses.

"*Bogoroditsa, spasi nas!*" the priest gasped, crossing himself. "Mother of God, save us!"

Then a man stood there, his back to Fr. Dmitri as he faced the fire with outstretched arms.

"Wilcox?" The priest was not sure he could trust his eyes. He raised his hands to shield his face from the blistering heat.

There was a roar and crackle as the fire leaped higher, the heat rippling across the priest's body. It felt unbearable. He crossed himself again and sank to his knees, burying his face in his hands.

The flames popped and crackled. He could hear a man grunting and wheezing, gasping for breath as if in the midst of a great physical struggle. He did not dare take his hands away from his face and thought his knuckles must be blistering in the inferno. His lungs felt seared.

"Get down!" a distant voice cried in some corner of the priest's mind. He had dim memories of a fire drill in his grade school, when the students had been instructed to keep their faces near the floor if trapped in a fire because that was where the cooler air could be found.

Fr. Dmitri fell forward and held his breath, pressing his face against the mosaic crosses and cobblestones. Tarot cards tumbled from his pockets and scattered around him. The rough stones scraped his cheek and knuckles. He wanted to weep but bit his lip, afraid to take the deep breath that was inevitable if he started to cry. Was the air really any cooler or safer to breathe here next to the cobblestones?

Unable to hold his breath any longer, he gasped and feared for the worst. The nightmarish heat surged into his lungs but even as it did so, it also surged over and across his back and up the wall behind him and was gone.

Did he dare lift his head? He tilted his face just a bit and peered through his fingers.

The wild conflagration and the man who might have been the dead Wilcox had both vanished.

Sophia and Victoria, hand in hand, were running as quickly as they could away from the flames. Their screams gave way to labored breathing and panting. Afraid to pause and look around, Sophia was unsure if they were running back down the Royal Road they had just come from or down some other lane leading away from the Old Town Square. The heat on her back was intolerable. Blue and white flickered on the edges of her vision, ghostly firelight reflected in the store windows as they passed.

Unable to breathe and unable to keep running, Sophia pulled her hand from Victoria's and bent double, clutching her knees and gasping for breath. Pain knifed through her ribs. Victoria stumbled to a halt and reached for the Sophia's shoulders.

"Sophia!" cried the younger woman, trying to pull Sophia forward. "Do not stop! Come with me!" She glance fearfully behind them and Sophia too sensed the wall of blue-white fire rising high behind them and sweeping around them. Unimaginable heat engulfed them. White-hot sparks snapped at them.

"Is this how we die also?" whimpered Victoria, bending over and burying her face against Sophia's shoulder.

A dark figure, the blurry silhouette of a man, seemed to materialize against the bright flames.

Clutching each other, Sophia struggled with Victoria to stand erect. Sophia nodded toward the figure, dark against the flames. Victoria peered in that direction. The figure seemed to be leaning forward, pressing both palms against the wall of fire as if to push it back. It was impossible to tell for sure, from where they stood, but the shadow-man seemed to be holding the fire at bay. Maybe he was even pushing it back a little. But the fire encircled them and burned all the hotter and more brightly around them for being held back.

Sweat stung Sophia's eyes, making it more difficult to see. She felt the rage of the fire on her back. Victoria turned her head back toward her, eyes squeezed closed, and pressed her forehead against Sophia's shoulder again.

Sophia glanced up at the heavens, squinting against the brilliance of the flames, hoping for help or inspiration. "How do we help him hold back the fire? How do we drive back the flames?" she asked the night sky. The walls of flame high above them seemed to lean towards each other, fingers of flame reaching out as if to crush the women and the shadow-man in the grasp of the bonfire.

Victoria, her eyes still pressed tightly shut, screamed again.

Fr. Dmitri slowly gathered the tarot cards from the cobblestones around him and stood. Breathing deeply of the fresh air that now surrounded him instead of flames, he stumbled forward and realized Theo and Sean, bringing their bags of salt canisters, were also converging on the center of the square.

"Where is Sophia? Did you see which way they went?" the priest asked the other men.

"No," Sean answered. "It was all too fast." Theo shook his head.

Dmitri turned anxiously, searching the square for some sign or hint of where his wife and Victoria had run. "Wilcox...?" he began.

"Yes," Sean agreed. "Wilcox stopped the flames."

"Do you think he has stopped the flames for Sophia and Victoria as well?" Fr. Dmitri was frantic. "But how could he? The flames were growing stronger... we must do something to help him!"

"How can we, if we don't even know where they are?" Sean asked, his own fear for the women coloring his voice.

"There." Theo pointed at the base of the Hus memorial. "The fire came from there. If we could do something to extinguish it at its source..."

A woman's cry rang out from a lane near the Tyn church.

"Sophia!" cried Fr. Dmitri.

Dropping the shopping bags of salt canisters, Theo and Sean ran off toward the Tyn church.

But the priest knew he would never get to the women as quickly as the younger, fitter men. He had to do something to stop the fire. Now.

He hurried to the Hus memorial, where a thin line of the spectral fire continued to burn around the base, and dropped the tarot cards onto a bench. He quickly rummaged through them, chose one, and picked it up. Stepping over the low chain that served as token security around the memorial, he laid the Star card at the base of the statuary.

Sophia bit her lip. The fire was blisteringly hot. The roar of the inferno and Victoria's screaming made it impossible to hear anything else. She wiped her eyes with one hand and for a moment the shadow-man flickered as if about to vanish.

Theo turned down the lane he thought the scream had come from. Sean was following right behind and nearly stumbled down onto the cobblestones when Theo suddenly stopped. The fire was raging before them, its roar filling the alleyway and its shimmering blue and white flames reflecting off all the windows of the stores on either side. Heat rolled off the immense bonfire in great waves and Theo instinctively raised a hand in front of his face for protection.

Within the depths of the translucent, brilliant flames they could see two blurry, indistinct forms huddled together.

"Victoria! Sophia!" Sean called out.

Closer to Theo and Sean, but still within the circle of fire, was a third figure that could only be Wilcox. Against the brilliant light of the fire, it was hard to make out anything more than the dark outline of the dead professor, whose throat had been torn out by the Dearg-due. He was leaning forward and pressing his palms against the wall of fire as if to push it back. He was struggling, his feet slipping on the cobblestones. He twisted slightly, pressing one shoulder against the flames.

"Wilcox… how can we help?" Theo called to their friend.

Wilcox, his feet slipping and sliding, turned his face toward Theo. But then the fire crackled and burned even more hotly, more brilliantly, and the silhouette that was Wilcox withered like a dry leaf in a campfire. Twisting up like a feather of ash, the shadow-man Wilcox shriveled and vanished.

The flames roared in triumph and swept in to consume the women at the heart of the blaze.

"NO!" screamed Theo and Sean together.

"YES!" chortled George, delighted at the scene playing out in the tea light's flickering flame. "Yes!"

At the Hus memorial, Fr. Dmitri's hands hovered near the card he had placed at the statuary's base. He hoped desperately that he had chosen the correct card, as it depicted a kneeling figure pouring two pitchers of water onto the ground and was generally interpreted as a message of hope and renewal. The blue-white ghost fire flickered around the base of the memorial and then flared out around the card, which blazed for an instant before the entire ring of fire went out as if doused by a bucket of water. Steam hissed, rising from the soggy ashes of what had been the tarot card.

Roaring more thunderously than a waterfall, the flames rose and twisted into a knot high above Sophia, Victoria, Sean, and Theo. But without warning, the flames then plummeted to the ground and vanished.

"No!" cried George, shocked to see the great ring of fire suddenly vanish. He slapped both hands against the desktop and it trembled with the double impact, causing the tea light to tremble as well and extinguish itself when the hot wax spattered the desktop.

Sophia and Victoria nearly collapsed as the cool night air rushed in where the fire had been an instant before. Theo and Sean ran to catch them before they could fall and guided them, shaking and trembling, back to the Old Town Square.

Sophia's husband was waiting for them, still at the Hus memorial. He hurried to wrap her in his arms.

"We must hurry," he urged. "We cannot be sure that the fire is truly extinguished or if it might not be rekindled at any moment."

Before he had even finished speaking, Sophia heard the wail of police sirens approaching the square from behind the Tyn church.

"Someone must have heard the screams and called the police," Sean offered, looking nervously around the square.

Collecting the shopping bags of salt, they hastily agreed that burning the remaining tarot cards on the continuation of the Royal Road would have to wait until the next day.

Theo moved as if to leave the Old Town Square along the same alley that would lead them past Wilcox's body, but Victoria pointed to another way that would lead them down a street behind the Astronomical Clock, which she said led more directly to the bridge and away from the approaching police.

"Thank you, my friend," Sophia heard Theo whisper as they nevertheless paused for a moment before exiting the square, the police sirens growing louder as the patrol cars neared the square. Then they all hurried as quickly as they could back across the bridge toward their hotels before either the police arrived or the fire could reappear.

"Curse their wives and children!"

(Fall–Winter 1356)

Petr burst through the door into the house with a burning stick in his hand.

"Petr!" cried Nadezda, seeing her brother brandishing the stick. "What are you doing?"

He dashed across the room and tossed the large stick across the hearth, into the fireplace under a bubbling kettle. The stick vanished in the flames, its fire swallowed by the larger, controlled fire cooking their dinner. Petr stood panting before the hearth, his tongue hanging out, a broad smiled plastered across his ten-year-old, soot-streaked face.

"I did it, Nadezda! I helped burn the witch," Petr exclaimed proudly.

Nadezda felt her face blanch. "Petr! How could you do such a thing?" she demanded. "How could you be so cruel?" She paused. "What witch?"

"Fen'ka," her brother answered. "The old woman from the edge of the forest. We burned her in the Old Town Square. First, we dunked her in the river to see if she was a witch, and then, when she wouldn't sink, we burned her."

Fen'ka? Burned in the Old Town Square? Their grandmother had known her, grown up with her, told them about her. Nadezda even remembered being taken by her grandmother once to visit her old friend, but that had been years ago. When Nadezda had been even younger than Petr was now. Nadezda had heard the rumors and the stories for a long time, about how their grandmother's childhood friend was a witch, but had never thought the suspicions and bad feelings would ever come to something like this. Well, this certainly explained where her younger brother had been all day, but how had this happened without her knowing about it?

Nadezda squatted down in front of her brother, taking both his shoulders in her hands and looking squarely into his face. "Petr. Tell me everything. Exactly what happened. From the beginning."

Petr cleared his throat and swallowed. Nadezda knew she sometimes made him nervous. He complained about her always telling him what to do, even before their mother died. When she had gotten married and moved into her own house with her husband, Vavrinec, she had left him alone with their father. But then their father had died, and he had had to come live with Nadezda and Vavrinec. As if that wasn't enough, the baby had been born shortly thereafter and although Petr loved his baby nephew Milos, she could tell he was jealous. Jealous of the way Nadezda hovered over the cradle, jealous of Milos having both his parents alive and well, jealous of Milos's being young and having no responsibilities, since now that he was ten, Petr was expected to go out and work every day with Vavrinec at the bakery.

Petr looked into Nadezda's eyes. "I was helping Vavrinec at the bakery this morning, just like I'm supposed to do," he began. "We went to get the flour from the mill. Over in the Little Town. I was standing with Vavrinec while the miller's apprentices loaded the sacks of flour on our wagon when all of a sudden, a big crowd was all around us. They were shouting and pushing. It was exciting. I went to see what was going on.

"The crowd went down to the place on the river, by where the gypsies always camp, you know?" he asked to make sure she understood.

Nadezda nodded. She knew the place.

"That's when I saw Fen'ka," he continued. "Everyone was saying that she was a witch, like they always do. But this time they were so mad at her, not scared at all. They were shouting and screaming at her and then the men tied her up, put her in the boat, and took her out to throw her into the river. They were all screaming but she never said anything. When they threw her in the water, she stayed down a long time and they were just about to pull her up by the ropes tied around her—you know?—when the river tossed her back up to the surface. Proved she was a witch, the river did. Then Fr. Conrad, from Tyn church—remember him, with the scrawny neck?—he pulled her skirts up to show everyone the devil's brand on her butt! Final proof that she was a witch, you know? He was so glad to finally get everyone to believe him. Remember how he's been saying for so long that no one should allow a witch to live? Well, then someone shouted, 'Burn her!' and then everyone started shouting, 'Burn her! Burn the witch!' So we took her back to the Old Town Square to burn her!"

Nadezda saw the excitement burning in her brother's eyes. Yes, she knew Fr. Conrad at the Tyn church and had heard him preach many times his shrill, angry sermons. She knew that her brother was young and angry at their parents for dying and leaving him alone, forcing him to live with her and her husband. He had a hard time keeping his mind on his chores at the bakery and had to be constantly reminded to sweep the floor, tend the fire, or watch the store. He was always running off to play with a stray dog in the street or get into a fight with another boy, or play a game with other apprentices who had a few free minutes at odd times during the day. She knew Petr was a good boy at heart and could grow into being a good man. But he was a handful now.

She had been the firstborn and was ten years older than

Petr. Even though her parents had several other children after she was born and before Petr, they were the only two who had survived. Their mother had always been a hard worker alongside their father, selling vegetables in the market, and her mother—the children's grandmother—had lived with them and taken care of them during the day. Grandmother had gotten sick first and died, just as old grandparents are wont to do, but then their mother had gotten sick and died too, leaving Nadezda in charge of the house. She had been almost seventeen then and her father had postponed finding her a husband as long as he could. He loved his family and could not bear parting with his daughter so soon after his wife and mother-in-law had died. But finally, he had relented, giving in both to the expectations of his neighbors and his own good, common sense. He knew that he could not keep hold of Nadezda forever and that she needed to marry and continue her own life. She had always been friends with Vavrinec, whose family lived nearby, and as the children grew older, he had seen the love blossom between them. Even though Vavrinec and Nadezda had both tried to hide it from the families—"such a shy, modest girl," her father always remarked—the look in their eyes when they glanced at each other and the nonchalant way they tried to say the other's name of course gave them away. Nadezda's father had been delighted to finally agree to Vavrinec's request to marry Nadezda. Vavrinec had served as the neighborhood baker's apprentice and so her father knew that Nadezda and his grandchildren-to-be would always be cared for and have enough to live on.

Her father had kept Petr with him at home, although she knew it was hard. The boy was left by himself during the day while her father was at his stall in the vegetable market.

Some days, Petr went to help him and was popular with the other vegetable sellers and their customers. Other days, Petr played with his friends, went fishing, or tried to help keep the house clean. Even though it was hard for her father to care for a boy Peter's age alone, he wanted to keep Petr at home as long as possible. Other boys his age were often sent to live as apprentices with various craftsmen, but he spoiled Peter, and he knew it.

The accident at the vegetable market had killed him instantly. Nadezda had been able to bid her grandmother and mother farewell before each had died, as they had been ill and death, though never happy, had not been unexpected. But the mad horse in the streets, the careening wagon crashing into the market stalls, their father trampled by the horse and then crushed by the wagon wheels as he tried to save others—that had been unexpected. She had not seen him for a few days before his death and now would never see him again. At least, not on this earth. She had not been able to say goodbye to him or tell him that he was going to be a grandfather, as she had just discovered this herself. She had been planning to see him that evening when he returned from the market and tell him the good news when people had come running to her house to tell her of the terrible accident. So she had been happy to take in Petr and give him a home. Vavrinec had been just as happy to take the boy in, doubling the size of his quickly growing family. He was also happy to take Petr in as an apprentice at the bakery, teaching the boy a way to support himself when he reached adulthood.

In his heart of hearts, Petr must have known it wasn't true, but in his darker moments—of which there were many—she knew he wondered if they hadn't taken him in simply to get free help around the house and at the bakery. He was angry, very angry, that Mother and Father had left him. He must be terrified that his sister would leave him in the same way.

Nadezda knew all this and understood the excitement in her brother's eyes. A chance to be part of a crowd, to see something up close he had only heard about in stories from towns further north along the river. But such a terrible crowd, such a horrible story had come to life in front of his eyes.

"And then what happened, Petr? Then what?" She stopped herself from shaking him roughly to get the rest of the story out of him.

He looked away. "That's when it got scary," he muttered.

That could mean anything. "Scary? How? What do you mean?"

He paused, keeping his eyes averted. Finally he looked back at his sister's face. "We took Fen'ka into the square, where a stake had been set up for burning her. Everyone kept pushing and shoving me, it was hard to see what was going on and what was happening. But then she started to scream at us. She called Svetovit to make us afraid, to teach us his power and make us afraid. She wanted Svetovit to curse us. That's when the sky got dark and the lightning started. Then we tied her to the stake," he told Nadezda, the excitement flushing his face again for an instant. "We tied her to the stake and lit the fire. She kept screaming. She wanted Svetovit to take away what we want and make our tables into traps. She wanted the earth to become iron. That's when the other apprentices ran up to the fire. It wasn't burning very well and so they brought oil. But no one would give me any to pour on the wood. So I grabbed the stick from the fire and got away when the soldiers came and tried to put the fire out, but they couldn't, and she screamed one more time that we should all receive no vindication. What's that, Nadezda? What's 'vindication'?"

Nadezda felt ill. That her grandmother's friend had been murdered in the square by the crowd that had always gone to her, looking for help, was sickening. But this news of Petr's that Fen'ka had cursed the crowd as she was dying… That worried her.

Squatting in front of her brother, with her hands on his shoulders, her legs pricked her like pins and needles. She slowly got up and sat on the bench along one side of the table. She pulled her brother onto her lap and held him, stroking his hair and trying to control herself. She finally found the words. "Tell me, Petr. Tell me exactly what she said."

"I told you already." Petr squirmed in her arms.

"Tell me again," she said softly, closing her eyes and trying to shut out the image of the old woman consumed by the fire and screaming at the crowd. "Tell me exactly what she said and what happened when she said it."

Petr cocked his head and looked at his sister strangely. "Why is that so important?" he demanded.

"Trust me. It just is." Nadezda sighed.

Petr thought hard for a moment. "She said…" He took a breath. "She said that Svetovit should teach us to fear him and pay attention to him. That's when the lightning started and it got dark and the wind started blowing. Then she said that we should all be cursed, in the town and in the castle and in the square. That's when we poured the oil on the fire and I grabbed the stick. 'Lay to their charge guilt upon guilt,' she said, 'and let them receive no vindication.' That's when the lightning hit. A bolt of lightning hit the square right in front of the fire and the soldiers came running from around the Town Hall!" His eyes lit up at the memory of all the commotion. "Everyone started running and screaming and the soldiers tried to save Fen'ka but she was a witch and they couldn't.

I watched them for a few minutes and then ran home before they tried to get me in trouble for burning the witch like she deserved."

Nadezda took a deep breath. She shook her head. That was about as much information as she would be able to get out of her brother. She held him for another moment and then let him slide off her lap. "All right, Petr." She sighed. "I'm sorry Fen'ka was burned and I'm sorry that you were part of it. But it's over now. Let's hope nothing worse happens and no one else gets burned."

Petr looked at his sister. "Should I go back to the bakery now?" he asked.

"Yes, go back to the bakery and help Vavrinec clean up before dinner," she instructed him. He ran out the door. Nadezda stepped across the room to close the door behind him but she paused on the step and looked at the sky.

It was dark, much darker than it should have been, even at this late afternoon hour. There was a distant rumble of thunder and a droplet or two of rain fell, but the wind was also blowing and it was chilly for the time of year. How had she missed what was going on in the square? That they lived on a byway in the Újezd district of the Old Town, near the New Town, far from both the bridge and the square, did not excuse her ignorance of that afternoon's events. Unsure of how her presence might have made a difference to the outcome, she was nevertheless certain that events would have played out differently had she been there. She had heard the thunder cracking throughout the skies earlier and had seen the lightning but had thought it no more than a late September afternoon storm. What had Fen'ka unleashed?

Vavrinec made his way home later, escorted by Petr, who had returned to the bakery and now sported a fine dusting of flour in his hair. Sending him off to wash in the bucket behind the house, Nadezda asked Vavrinec if he knew what had transpired that afternoon.

"Yes, I was there," he admitted sheepishly. He confirmed Petr's recollection of the day: he and the boy had been across the river in the Little Town at the mill loading bags of flour when they had become separated in the crowd that swept down to the river to test Fen'ka in the swiftly flowing water for witchcraft. All work had ceased as the miller and his apprentices were also caught up in the excitement. "It would have been impossible to get the cart back across the bridge," Vavrinec pointed out. "There were too many people, all shouting and pushing and demanding that she be burned." He had followed the mob across the bridge to the Old Town Square, where a stake had been erected before the church of Our Lady of Tyn, where the priest Conrad, who was leading the horde, served the Mass and preached.

"She called out curses on everyone in the square," Vavrinec recounted. "Everyone in the towns and in the castle, all the wives and children of the city as well. She invoked old Svetovit and demanded that he make the heavens brass and the earth iron, that he make feast days into traps, and take away what people want as well as what they have. There was lightning but no rain, thunder but no outburst. I even thought I saw a tremendous bank of storm clouds over the bluff behind the Jewish Quarter that looked like four-faced Svetovit." He shuddered. "The lightning hit the square and it became a nightmare of confusion."

Nadezda collapsed onto a bench along the table for the second time that day and shook her head. "It frightens me, Vavrinec. She was my grandmother's friend, you know. They grew up together. I met Fen'ka, Vavrinec, and she knew the old ways better than anyone. Better than my grandmother, even, and my *babička* knew more of the old ways than anyone in the four towns of Prague." She looked into her husband's eyes. "If she invoked Svetovit to avenge her death, it could mean the end of everything in the valley."

Vavrinec sat beside his wife and took her hands in his. "Do not worry, Nadezda," he soothed her. "Fen'ka may have known more of plants and herbs and their properties than everyone else in the valley all together, but everyone knows that Svetovit is only an old and powerless devil. He can't even stop the building of the new cathedral on his own hill! How dangerous can he be to the four towns in the valley? Who can tell if he even still loiters about Hradčany to listen to the complaints of anyone who cares to address him?" He chuckled.

Nadezda studied his face and finally nodded in agreement, holding his hands tightly and drawing comfort from his calm strength. "You may be right, Vavrinec. I hope so, for all our sakes."

That night, as she banked the fire, Nadezda wondered if she could trust her husband's estimation of Svetovit's inability to avenge Fen'ka's death.

"There seems to have been no immediate strike against the four towns," she comforted herself. The red coals glimmered and blinked beneath the dusting of ash that would retain the heat and allow the fire to be rekindled the next morning. Banking the fire was always the last activity of each household before retiring for bed and rekindling the flames was always the first activity on arising each morning. Fen'ka would have been doing this same activity last night at about this same time, Nadezda realized. Now Fen'ka's hearth was cold and dark. Nadezda thought of her grandmother as well, banking the fire each evening. The continuity of the fire was an image of the continuity of the family and the household; the skill of each woman to conserve the fire of her kitchen was a point of proud competition throughout each neighborhood of the four towns that together made up the metropolis that was Prague. It was a mark of shame to ask a neighbor woman— even if a good friend—for coals in the morning, as it was a badge of honor to maintain the family hearth from day to day, week to week, month to month, year after year after year. Some hearths were rumored to have not needed a neighbor's coal to be rekindled in the morning for a generation or more.

When she and Vavrinec had wed, they had brought fire—in the form of coals on a shovel—from her father's house to the hearth of the house where they would make their new family together. She could not remember the last time that either her grandmother or mother had gone to get coals to rekindle the fire she had grown up with, and she had not needed to fetch coals from a neighbor since establishing her own hearth here with Vavrinec. They had taught her well. She smiled at the memory of her grandmother first showing her how it was done when she was a small child, and then the more formal lessons she had received as an older girl. It was during those times together with her grandmother, raking through the coals and placing them just so ("here, not there, child," her grandmother would gently point out), that her grandmother had told her the traditional Bohemian tales and of the old ways that she and Fen'ka had learned from their grandmothers at the hearths of their childhood homes.

Nadezda rose and brushed the soot from her palms. Vavrinec was already in bed in the other room, waiting for her. Milos, little more than a year old, lay in his crib next to their bed. In the principal room of the house, the only light still burning—apart from the coals in the hearth—was the oil lamp that always burned before the image of the Mother of God hanging in the corner of the room. The wick of the lamp required trimming from time to time and the oil required replenishing, but it was a cost and an effort Nadezda was happy to expend. The burning oil lamp was a constant reminder to bless herself as she went about her daily tasks at home and to say her simple morning and evening prayers. The image, which depicted the Holy Mother and her Divine Child cheek to cheek as they kissed or whispered secrets to each other and was similar to those in the Slavonic monastery of Emauzy in the New Town, was something she had inherited from her mother and grandmother, who had inherited it from another, earlier grandmother. It, like the fire burning on the hearth, spoke of the continuity of Nadezda's family and the lore passed from mother to daughter over more generations than Nadezda ever hoped to count.

Petr stirred, asleep on his cot along one wall. Vavrinec had promised to make a room for Petr in the attic when Petr was older, but for now he slept here, near the fire, where Nadezda could hear him if he called out in the night and comfort him. His nightmares and frights and weeping came less and less often, but there were still occasions when she needed to stroke his forehead and sing him a lullaby, much as their mother had sung to them both when she was alive.

Kissing her brother on the forehead, Nadezda went in to her husband and son. Svetovit had done nothing to disturb her family thus far. "I hope he never does," she addressed the Mother of God as she passed the image.

Over the course of the next few weeks, Nadezda's fears came to seem groundless or even foolish. Life proceeded as usual, the day-to-day round of working and cleaning, cooking and washing. The sun rose and the sun set. Nothing dangerously inexplicable seemed to happen anywhere in the towns that lined the river. Svetovit was quiet as ever.

But then Conrad, the German priest who had instigated the burning of Fen'ka, slapped the Italian prostitute Lucrezia in the Tyn church, causing her to strike her head against one of the columns in the nave. She had died within moments, and word of her death at the hand of the priest spread almost as quickly. His pre-dawn vigil beneath Lucrezia's window near the church, now closed as a result of Lucrezia's death within the sacred precincts, became known, and when his murdered body was found beneath her window, it was considered by many an act he had brought upon himself. It was only when Conrad was seen after his funeral, still stalking the lane below Lucrezia's window, that Nadezda became suspicious. The next morning, Nadezda met her childhood friend Alena, who was also Milos's godmother. Alena was expecting her first baby and had asked Nadezda to serve as her baby's godmother as well.

"It seems like divine justice." Alena offered her opinion to Nadezda as they mingled in the crowd that filled the vegetable market of the New Town. "He had Fen'ka burned. He killed Lucrezia with his own hand. Now he cannot rest in his grave and wanders beneath her window. Is that not the justice of God, Nadezda, that condemns him to such restless remorse?"

Nadezda was examining vegetables, some of which she placed in her market basket, ready to pay the merchant when she had finished her selection. Milos slept, wrapped tightly in his swaddling bands, on her back between her shoulders. "Yes, it does seem like a suitable heavenly retribution," Nadezda agreed. "But I can't help thinking that Fen'ka's curse might have played some role in closing Heaven and Hell to him. Vavrinec told me that she demanded Svetovit make the heavens brass and the earth iron. Is it impossible that Fen'ka and Svetovit were able to entrap Father Conrad in a hell of their own devising? Do you not see that as well, Alena?"

"Perhaps," Alena was willing to concede as she added to the vegetables in her own basket, moving along the rows of a particularly large stall. "But is Svetovit able to contravene the judgment of God? How could Fen'ka's words prove more formidable than those of God in heaven?"

Nadezda shook her head,, smelling some fruit before adding it to the collection in her basket. "It does sound outlandish. Vavrinec insists that I am nervous over nothing. Perhaps God allowed Fen'ka's curse to come true because it accorded with His judgment. Who can tell?" Nadezda turned to Alena and shrugged.

Alena seemed to be mulling the possibilities as they continued shopping. "That curse—was it one curse, Nadezda, or a series of curses?—her curse was the last thing Fen'ka spoke. Everyone knows the power of the last words of the dying. Even those criminals executed for their crimes. The last words of a man on Earth can even sway the judgment of God. If God can be persuaded to show mercy, could He not also be persuaded to be strict, to show no mercy, to let the whim of the condemned stand firm?" Alena handed her basket to the merchant to tally what she owed. "After all, Nadezda, do we not collect the remains of the executed—and even splinters of the gallows that the condemned die on—like the relics of the saints precisely because they can win God's favor and persuade Him to enforce the dying wish of the condemned?"

Nadezda could not resist adding to her basket as she waited for Alena to pay the merchant. She then gave her basket to the merchant's wife, who also worked at the stall.

"Now Vavrinec would say that your words could be mine, arguing for the power of Fen'ka's curse!" She laughed. Alena laughed with her, taking back her basket from the merchant as she paid the sum he asked. "In the end, who can say?" Nadezda was constrained to admit, parting ways with Alena to continue their workaday errands.

"Truly, Nadezda. Who can say?" Alena kissed her friend on the cheek and, waving gaily, turned down the street that led to the fishmongers.

That evening, in bed as the boys Petr and Milos slept, Nadezda recounted her conversation with Alena to Vavrinec. He laughed and shook his head.

"What do you think, Vavrinec?" Nadezda wanted to know. "Yes, I know you think Svetovit is powerless and Fen'ka's words meaningless, but is not this the kind of thing she would be pleased with?"

"She would be pleased, yes, with Father Conrad's fate." Vavrinec nodded, rubbing his brow.

"So, Vavrinec, could not the rest of her curse come true as well? If she had a hand in shaping the priest's fate, making the heavens brass and the earth iron as you told me she cried out, who can say that her words could not also shape the fate of everyone in the Old Town Square that day." She paused as she realized the implication of her own words. "Even the fate of men such as you."

"It is all too hard for the likes of a baker such as me to puzzle out, Nadezda!" Vavrinec burst out, chuckling. He tussled her hair and hugged her shoulders against his own. She leaned into him, happy to have a reason to pursue her thoughts no further.

"CURSE THEIR WIVES AND CHILDREN!"

Little more than a fortnight later, Nadezda's suspicions were raised again. Vavrinec reported over their supper that word had come through customers at the bakery that one of the Tuscan masons who lived on the far side of the Little Town and had labored in the reconstruction of the castle or the construction of the cathedral—the informant had been unsure—had died and his wife gone mad. But the dead man had approached drunks and whores who roamed the dark streets of the Little Town by night and begged them to pull a nail from his skull. "It would give him rest, he said, it would." The gossip in the bakery had gone on and on, repeating the tale as another customer entered, each time adding another detail or flourish to the account. "The dead man always begs, 'Pull the nail and let me rest in peace.' He cries and wails for mercy, that he be allowed to rest, if only the nail be wrenched from his head. But, of course, none will touch him or the nail," the story always ended. Vavrinec finished his recounting of the events and silently sipped the fish stew Nadezda had prepared.

Petr looked across the table at his sister. "What do you think, Nadezda? Do you think a dead mason really walks the Little Town or are the drunks just drunk?" He was slurping happily through his bowl of stew, nearly ready for more. "I heard the story in the bakery today, Nadezda, and you should have seen how excited and frightened the old gossips were when they heard that news!"

Nadezda swallowed her last spoonful and set her bowl down. "It is odd," she announced at last.

Vavrinec looked at her. "I tell you this tale only because I am certain that you would hear it from others, whether I will it or no," he offered, glancing towards Petr, who was scraping the sides of his bowl before helping himself to more. "I wanted you to hear it from me before you heard it from others and became concerned. Before you thought that I was hiding anything from you."

"Thank you." Nadezda's voice was even more quiet.

Petr looked up and turned from his sister's face to her husband's and then back again. "Why so solemn, Nadezda?" He took his bowl to the pot hanging at the edge of the fireplace and ladled more stew into his bowl. He sat down, waiting for an answer. He looked at Nadezda and Vavrinec again, appearing perplexed.

"It is only…" Nadezda began hesitantly. "It is unusual for such an apparition to be seen in the Little Town, Petr, especially so swift on the heels of the apparition of Father Conrad under Lucrezia's window. Two apparitions, so swift on the heels of each other, is unusual indeed." Nadezda, whose downcast eyes had been focused on her hands folded in her lap, looked up and into her husband's eyes.

"Do you still think the curse is of no consequence, Vavrinec? Someone must take steps to protect the city, both Prague altogether and the four towns individually. It may soon be too dangerous to stay anywhere near here, Vavrinec. Does not thought of all this frighten you?"

Vavrinec shook his head. "The only thought that frightens me is that you take all this talk of curses and *maleficia* and the walking dead and lay it all at the feet of Svetovit and Fen'ka, holding them responsible for every tale of something strange or unusual that you hear." He reached out and opened his palm, waiting for her to rest her hand in his. He held her hand on the tabletop and continued.

"It is talk, Nadezda. It is only talk and gossip and tales for scaring children who will not sleep at night."

"It was only talk and rumor that lit the fire that burned Fen'ka; might you say as well, Vavrinec? Do you think that words and tales have no power?"

Her husband squeezed her hand. "Yes, words and tales can kill. But not because the words of a dying woman calls on Svetovit to avenge her!"

"I wish I could be as certain, Vavrinec. Too many of the walking dead make me wonder…"

"Did you hear, Nadezda?" Alena grasped her friend's arm as they exited their Újezd neighborhood parish church of St. Martin after the midmorning Mass on Christmas Day. Alena, her womb growing ever larger, was expected to deliver her child in less than a month.

"What did I hear?" Nadezda laughed, wrapped in her warm winter cloak. Had the betrothal of one of their friends been announced? Was a newlywed expecting a child? Or was a longer-married woman expecting to add to an already large family? Another possibility occurred to her. "Did Sorina give birth?" That baby's arrival had already been delayed nearly three weeks.

"No, silly goose! We would certainly have heard about that! Do you think I would have waited until the end of the Mass to tell you if Sorina had given birth last night? On Christmas Eve?" Alena hung on her friend's arm as everyone around them exchanged greetings of "Happy Christmas! *Vánoční stromeček!*" Alena guided Nadezda to one side of the crowd, away from the bulk of the congregation who still struggled to make their way through the doors of the church onto the small square.

"No, Nadezda." Alena's tone was suddenly serious. "Did you hear about the old beggar woman Božena and Anežka, the wife of the Old Town council member? They had that tremendous argument in the Old Town Square on St. Nicholas'

81

Day. Do you recall?'"

"Yes." Nadezda giggled. "I wish I had been there to see it.
They were ready to strike each other like serpents almost on the
doorsteps of the church of St. Nicholas—and on his feast day,
yet! They certainly never seem to have listened to the injunction
to love their neighbors, did they?" Both women laughed.

"No, they certainly did not. But remember—they both
died last week, just before the last Sunday of Advent. Since
then, they've both been seen circling each other exactly where
they had their fight, and look ready to kill each other again
if they could!" Alena eagerly continued, "Not only them,
but also the two gentlemen, Aleksandr and Jiri, who died so
sudden-like in November. The two gentlemen have been seen
in the Old Town Square with Božena and Anežka on moonless
nights. Or so I've been told."

Nadezda felt the blood drain from her face and grasped
more heartily at Alena's arm for support.

Alena leaned close to her friend's face. "It is too many
now, is it not, Nadezda? Too much death and too many of the
dead walking abroad. It is all Fen'ka's doing, is it not?"

Nadezda was certain of it now. Unexpected deaths were
not uncommon. But there was no way Vavrinec could explain
away so many otherwise inexplicable and twisted turns in the
fates of these folk who had been unable to rest in their graves
after Fen'ka's ashes had been deposited in the river Vltava,
swirling and lost in the water rather than resting quietly and
still in a grave somewhere.

She nodded.

"What can we do, Nadezda? We need to protect the four
towns somehow. You would know better than anyone. You
remember the old ways that your grandmother taught you."
Alena's eyes grew larger. "You are the only one who can know

how to set Fen'ka's words aside. How can we stop the curse before it consumes us all?" Nadezda could see the fear in Alena's eyes.

"I do not know. Why do you say that only I can set Fen'ka's curse aside?" Surely Alena was wrong to place so much trust in her. "There must be someone who knows the old ways better than I. Or surely one of the priests knows how to stop such a thing, or one of the theologians at the new university. They would know how to prevent a curse."

Alena shook her head. "No, they would not, Nadezda, and you know that. Only someone who knows how Fen'ka would use the old ways could know how to set them aside."

"No," Nadezda countered quietly. "That makes no sense, Alena. You are frightened and fear feeds on itself. Go home and forget all this. Go home and celebrate Christmas. Let me speak with Vavrinec and discover what he thinks now about all these things. I will share his thoughts with you before the New Year comes."

Alena looked at Nadezda and Nadezda could see that Alena's fears were not calmed.

"I promise, Alena."

"Such things are not uncommon among the dead plagued by jealousy and the desire for vengeance. You know that, Nadezda," Vavrinec pointed out to her on the night after Christmas, in the pause between their first and second sleep, when she brought up her discussion after the Mass with Alena. "Need I remind you of these things?"

"No, Vavrinec. If it were simply that Božena and Anežka were seen in the Old Town Square, refusing to lay down their feud, I would agree. If it were only Božena and Anežka with Aleksandr and Jiri, I would be willing to say that the two men were somehow caught up in the women's feud and leave it at that. But I have heard in the market that the moneylender František, the miser who lived near the Little Square, burnt to death trying to escape his burning house, and he has also been seen at night running through the streets of the Old Town, still aflame and clutching his coins. Do you remember the Tuscan bricklayer who has been seen wandering near the castle and in the Little Town, asking people to pull the nail from his head so that he can rest among the dead? So very many will not rest in their graves since Fen'ka's curse, and there were few, so very few before that. This is not natural," Nadezda insisted. "Fen'ka's curse and Svetovit must have had a hand in shaping the demise and torment of all these people. If I only knew enough about what exactly Fen'ka uttered as she burned and could see how her words were played out in the lives of these folk—the priest Conrad, the miser František, that bricklayer from Tuscany and his mad wife, now Božena, Anežka, Jiri, and Aleksandr—then I could determine if it is really her curse that is driving these events or if it is simply an unusual confluence of jealousy, anger, and divine judgment. Do you not see that, Vavrinec?"

Vavrinec sat in bed, his arms crossed across his chest, and pouted in the dark.

Nadezda groaned with frustration. "You would rather insist these events were all driven by anything else rather than admit that Fen'ka's curse is slowly working itself out here in the midst of Prague. Why, Vavrinec, why? Why could Fen'ka's curse not lie behind all these events?"

Vavrinec turned to his wife. "Why, you ask? Because if I agree with you, that Fen'ka and her curse are responsible, then you will take it upon yourself to chase her down—even though she is dead. You will force her hand in some way to remove the curse—or will die yourself in the attempt!" His eyes glistened as he spoke. "You would drive yourself to your death in the attempt to save Prague, and that I could never bear, Nadezda." One tear streaked down his cheek and he swallowed hard to stop any further tears from coursing down his face.

She realized the truth of his words even as they spilled from his lips. While she was sure that Vavrinec would bear up under his grief and eventually find some measure of happiness, it would not be fair to either Petr or Milos. Her brother Petr had already lost their parents and now relied only on her to see him safely to adulthood, and she knew from experience and from watching Petr how cruel it would be to knowingly deprive her son Milos of his mother at such a young age.

She took Vavrinec in her arms and stroked his hair gently, as he had so often done for her. "That will never happen, Vavrinec," she promised in a whisper. "Never."

It was almost New Year's Eve when Nadezda was able to find time to speak with Alena. They were in the marketplace of the Old Town Square examining some of the beautiful wares still available as gifts for Epiphany, coming in exactly one week. Although most of their gift-giving had taken place on either St. Nicholas' Day or Christmas Day among their families or their husbands' places of work, it was still the custom to give gifts throughout the Twelve Days of Christmas, which would culminate on Epiphany.

Alena was still not convinced to set aside her fears for Prague. "Surely you would have enough sense to find some way to undo the curse without it costing your own life," she argued with Nadezda. "I think Vavrinec is being unreasonable to think that saving Prague necessarily comes at the cost of dying."

"He does make the point, though, Alena," Nadezda defended her husband's view, "that jealousy and anger can drive the dead to walk, as can unrequited love—if Father Conrad was in love with that girl he killed in the church—or some other, unrelated hex." She thought of the Tuscan mason and his wife, the one who asked passers-by to pluck the nail from his head that he might rest in his grave. "All these events may simply be coincidence and... and... Why, Alena, you might even see the hand of Fen'ka in the disappearance of that novice from St. George's Convent that Petr heard disappeared on Christmas Day. Do you think that Fen'ka's curse drives everything that happens in Prague?"

Alena finally had to agree that she was too willing to see the hand of Fen'ka everywhere. "It does seem extreme," she said sheepishly, and blushed. "I would have thought the curse responsible for the disappearance of that novice if I had heard it first, from someone else. But if you put it like that..." She hugged Nadezda.

"So, on New Year's Day, what will my godson be wearing when you come to eat at our house?" Alena asked, her former bubbling, happy self. Nadezda happily lapsed into her own previous, pre-curse self as well, and described the new garments Milos had received on Christmas.

For several days after Epiphany, it was nearly impossible to find anyone willing to discuss anything other than the transformation of the banquet guests into animals that had occurred at Jan Capek's inn in the Little Town. Mad dogs, squirrels, geese, serpents, donkeys, even peacocks—the guests had been transformed as they had begun to eat the stew the innkeeper's cook was famous for. Even one of the serving girls had been transformed as she had begun to taste the stew herself afterwards. This was unmistakably a work of magic, and all Nadezda's suspicions of Svetovit and Fen'ka raged again. She knew better than to raise them with Vavrinec, though. She resolved to keep her eyes and ears open for the least suggestion of anything gone amiss that any of her neighbors or the people in the markets might be willing to talk about. Even the missing novice from the convent near the new cathedral. The missing novice had probably simply run home to her family, but Nadezda had heard a whisper that perhaps the girl had been seized by an imp conjured by one of the other novices.

"An imp that she had conjured because of Fen'ka's curse!" Nadezda suspected when she heard the tale. There was nothing Nadezda was not willing to hold Svetovit and Fen'ka responsible for.

Alena saw the change in Nadezda and joined her in collecting news of the goings-on in Prague that could possibly be construed as the result of Fen'ka and her curse. What surprised them both was the eagerness of some to also lay these events at the feet of Fen'ka and the disbelief of others who refused to consider the possibility that her dying words might have the power to work her will even from beyond her watery grave.

"It seems that Vavrinec was hiding the talk of all the taverns from me for months!" Nadezda declared to Alena. "I was at the bakery for bread yesterday and asking some of the apprentices what the latest news might be in the taverns, and they said everyone was talking of Fen'ka again, just as they had after Fr. Conrad's death and that Tuscan mason— Bartolomeo. They all said that Fen'ka's curse must be responsible and must also be behind the transformations at the inn. One of them even reminded everyone else that she had cried out, 'Curse them eating and drinking!' If that doesn't describe what happened at the inn, what does?"

Alena agreed. Her husband had finally told her a similar tale. "He said that he hadn't told me before because he knew that I would tell you, and that Vavrinec did not want to encourage you to see Fen'ka's curse as the power responsible for all these things. But he also says that many of the men laugh at the suggestion that Fen'ka might have truly been a witch. Even the men who were there and had a hand in burning her at the stake. Now they all say such things are nonsense, the delusions of old women and children, and that there are no such things as witches." She paused. "But they never say what Fen'ka was burned for if she was not the witch they all claimed she was."

Not long after Epiphany, more news reached Nadezda's ears. A German youth was found in the butcher's parish of St. Jakub on the morning of their patronal feast day, his hand grasped firmly in the fist of the statue of the Mother of God.

"It seems he had broken into the church and unlocked the alms chest in some manner, even though he had no tools for picking locks on him when they went through his pockets later," Vavrinec admitted to Nadezda when she asked him what the news in the tavern had been that night. "The hand of the thief was held so tightly by the statue that he hung there, his feet unable to reach the floor, dislocating his shoulder. Finally, the only way to get him down was to cut his arm off at the shoulder and leave it in the grip of the statue."

Nadezda was banking the fire for the night, listening to her husband, and she nodded as she tidied the coals and arranged them as she always did. He sipped at a final mug of ale as he sat at the table and watched her. Realizing that she would discover what she wanted to know from other sources, such as Petr or the other apprentices at the bakery, or even strangers she might happen to speak to in the markets, he saw no point in concealing the happenings in the town or the conjectures of the men in the taverns.

"Another act of justice, many say. The statue of the Mother of God apprehended a thief about to steal the alms given for the relief of the poor," Vavrinec reported. "Justice such as one might hope for or expect from God and His saints to protect the poor and the needy. But others say…"

"Yes? What do others say?" Nadezda prodded.

"Others say that something must have gone wrong, terribly wrong, with the young thief's plan or he would never have dared enter the church in the first place. Whatever went wrong, whatever drove him into the church and made him so overconfident as to dare open the alms chest, right there at the feet of the Mother of God, was the result of…" He hesitated to say the final words but finally coughed out the witch's name. "…Fen'ka's curse."

Nadezda sat back and surveyed her work in the fireplace. "That sounds like a witch's curse to me. Drive a young man to desperation, promise him success, and then withdraw whatever assured him that he could succeed with his plans." She searched her memory. What had Vavrinec told her that afternoon in September when Fen'ka had died in the fire? She quoted her husband's words back to him. "She invoked old Svetovit and demanded that he… take away what people want as well as what they have." Yes, that was it! "Take away both what they want and what they have. The thief found in St. Jakub's Church has certainly lost everything he wanted as well as what he already had—his arm," she pointed out.

She continued to gaze into the fireplace and think. Streaks

of red laced through the ashes, twisting and glimmering like snakes, connecting still-smoldering bits of wood or chips of coals that would not last the night. It was not always evident how the heat connected each straggling coal to another but the glowing trail was there, hidden under ash or soot. "Just as Fen'ka's curse underlies and connects all these events since her burning, even if the trail is not always evident or visible." She considered Vavrinec's concern that her pursuit of the truth about Fen'ka's dealings with Svetovit and the probable consequences for Prague would prove her undoing.

She glanced over her shoulder and smiled at him. "Behold, Vavrinec. I have simply begun to put the pieces of the puzzle together. I have not destroyed myself yet." He smiled at her in return, looked into his ale, and continued smiling.

"Every curse has a key," she continued, staring into the fireplace, "a clause that is central to it and which must be fulfilled before the full weight of the curse is unleashed and the victim bears the brunt of it. Like the tale of *Sipkova Ruzenkaye*, the beautiful princess who slept for one hundred years." Nadezda was thinking aloud as she arranged the puzzle pieces of Fen'ka's curse in her mind. "The key, the necessary clause of the curse, was that the princess prick her finger on the spindle. The last of the godmothers could then rewrite, though not eradicate, the curse. Though the princess had then to still prick her finger, the prick resulted in a century-long sleep rather than death as the original curse had insisted."

Vavrinec nodded to show he understood the logic of Nadezda's thought. "If I can sort out the puzzle pieces and discover the central key, we can rewrite it, Vavrinec, and save us all before anything worse comes to pass. All we have to do," Nadezda murmured, "is put the pieces of the puzzle together and find the key that unlocks Fen'ka's curse."

Wheel of Fortune

(Sunday night, August 11, 2002–Monday, August 12, 2002)

THE TENTH OF THE MAJOR TRUMPS, THE WHEEL CONSTANTLY TURNS
AS IT LIFTS UP ONE AND DASHES DOWN ANOTHER.

S unday night. The hydroelectric dam was several miles upriver from Prague but was designed to deliver much of the power that the city and its environs depended on. It was always a delicate balance, a dance in fact, to keep the water flowing through the dam at the force needed to generate the needed electricity. That was how the engineer on duty late Sunday night had always described his work to student tour groups.

"There is a very fine line between what is enough water to keep the turbines turning and humming with life and too much water," he always explained. "If there is not enough water, it will not turn the turbines with enough force and will fail to generate enough electricity," he told the younger students. "Prague and all the towns around it will go dark very quickly if there is not enough electricity. There would be no lights, no television, no video games! But if there is too much water, the dam will overflow. So we need to monitor the water level all the time and release any water that we don't need in small amounts so it does not cause any damage."

Older students were always more interested in knowing what disasters might result if something went wrong. "What if there is not enough water?" they demanded to know. "How long would the lights be out? What if the dam overflows?"

"The lights could be out for quite a long time," he confessed. "If the water level goes too low, it can take a long time to build up again. We need to keep a huge amount of water in reserve, just in case there is a lull in rainfall or snowmelt in the mountains where the Vltava has its source."

"But the floods!" The older boys were always more interested in the possibility of floods. "How bad would the flooding be?"

"I'm sorry to disappoint you," the engineer chuckled. "The water levels are watched very closely. Engineers on duty would release any excess water in such trivial, but constant, amounts that it would hardly be noticed. In the past, there have been terrible floods along the Vltava. Terrible! Prague was nearly destroyed, more than once, by such floods. But now, with the dam, the likelihood of such a flood ever again is nearly impossible. We can control the river so well now that its power can never destroy us again."

The boys' faces were always disappointed and glum after he explained that.

But now, he was alone in the dam's control center in the middle of a Sunday night in mid-August. He checked all the gauges and dials and monitors again. He was responsible only for the water level behind the dam. Elsewhere in the dam complex were guards who were monitoring similar screens and detectors for security purposes.

An odd fragrance tickled his nose. He wrinkled his nose to dispel the irritation.

The water levels had been building behind the dam for several days now, fed by the heavy rainfall upriver. As chief engineer on several of the recent shifts, he had been tempted to release some of the excess water. Several times he had reached

92

for the controls that would open the sluice gates of the dam. But something always stopped him just as his fingers grasped the controls. Was it the fact that the reserves had fallen low recently and they needed the excess water to restore the reserves? But there had been more than that. There had been a sense of foreboding, an irrational intuition that the right time to open the sluices and release the water would come soon but that time was not yet. So he had always held the controls for a moment and then let go of them.

That slight irritation—"Am I developing allergies?" he wondered—was back and he rubbed his nose in an effort to drive it away.

The indicators he examined all showed him that nearly impossible pressure was building up along the base of the dam under the hundreds of thousands of tons of water stored behind it. Cameras set along the top ridge of the dam revealed rivulet after rivulet of water escaping over the top. Some water escaping over the top was inevitable, given the waves and force of the river current. But these rivulets were growing in frequency and breadth, soon to become not many tiny rivulets but several broad streams and then one nearly uninterrupted surge of water coursing over the top of the dam.

Mesmerized, he watched the water cascade over the dam. Delicate, frothy clouds of feather-like droplets rose from the foot of the cascading water as it joined the free river below the dam. Although he could not hear the roar of the water from within the insulated control room under normal circumstances, the sound of it tonight filled his ears.

That unavoidable, strange smell tickled the back of his throat as well. A slightly metallic fragrance, not unlike the smell of fresh blood that he knew from bending down to kiss his five-year-old daughter's skinned knee, hovered about him.

He sensed a presence in the control room.

Thundering water. Warning lights flashing because of the increasing pressure on the dam. He reached out, but the controls moved even before he could touch them. Finally the sluice gates were opening and the flood—that he had always promised was impossible—began.

Monday morning, Dmitri was making his way from his hotel to the bridge. The five of them—himself, Sophia, Theo, Victoria, and Sean—had gotten back to their hotels safely the night before. Tossing and turning, Dmitri's fragile dreams kept replaying the attack of the Dearg-due and the death of Wilcox, the attack of crows, the screams of the Dearg-due, the roar of the blue-white fire. Each time the dream reached the point where Elizabeth's screaming reached its crescendo and was cut short, Dmitri woke, bolting up in his bed, sweating and gasping. He finally stopped attempting to sleep and simply waited for the dawn. He struggled with what his companions might be able to do to protect the city from the coming flood but was too tired to think coherently. He had finally dressed and made his way to the hotel breakfast room and was now walking to the bridge to think quietly before rousing his wife and attending the final day of the conferences.

"We need to talk, to plan what to do next," he muttered. "Sean and Victoria will be meeting to go to Alessandro's room. We all need to make changes in our flights back home. Maybe we should ask Theo's friend Professor Hron for help. Maybe the time has come to admit what we've been doing and ask for his suggestions." He ran his hand through his hair and shook his head. "We won last night, yes? It worked. Sean got someone in Ireland to build a cairn on the Dearg-due's grave and pin her back under the earth. One of our three enemies is gone! And we escaped from that fire that hunted us across the Old Town Square! So why don't I feel more triumphant, more like a winner?" He adjusted the small chain suspending his pectoral cross around his shoulders and stepped onto the cobblestones of the bridge.

The day was humid but overcast. The bridge was beginning to fill. Tourists mingled in groups, examining the statues standing guard along the balustrades. Vendors were setting up stalls to sell souvenirs to the tourists. A pipe player was blowing a few shrill practice notes in anticipation of tourists filling his cup with coins.

Dmitri pulled his shoulders up around his ears and pressed on across the bridge. He wanted to shut out the distracting sights and sounds so as to better marshal his thoughts. He glanced at the people wandering on the bridge so as to not walk into any of them and couldn't help but notice the statues he was passing.

The stone figures of the saints had stood vigilant guard along the bridge for centuries. Dmitri passed Cosmas and Damien standing together, the physician-martyrs looking ready to distribute medicine the way a priest might distribute Communion. He saw Saint Vitus, whose cathedral atop the castle hill had displaced the worship of the devil Svetovit.

"Well, Saint Vitus," Dmitri muttered, "If there was ever a time to finish your displacement of Svetovit, now is it! And you," he addressed another statue that he passed. "You, Saint Jude, you are the patron of impossible causes, yes? Well, if this is not an impossible cause, I don't know what would be! Can't any of you get down off your stone pedestals and help us? Or give us a good idea? Something?" He sighed.

The usual large crowd was already forming around the base of the next statue, a green copper priest crowned with five gold stars and holding a gold palm frond in one hand. The brass plaques on the stone base of the statue could hardly be seen through the forest of people growing at the statue's base, but Dmitri knew them to be ancient and dark scenes from the story of the priest's life, except for the three gleaming bright spots where the fingertips of the crowd had polished the metal to the highest sheen imaginable.

"If they touch the plaques, it will bring them good luck," a short and dowdy tour guide was explaining to her charges, pointing to the plaques with her tightly furled umbrella's crooked nose. "Touching the plaques also brings the saint's promise that you will return to Prague!" she concluded with a flourish, her group bursting into appreciative laughter. They all surged for a closer look at the statue of the priest and to touch the plaques.

"Ah, Saint John Nepomuk," Dmitri addressed the statue under his breath. "Tour guides always oversimplify everything!" He could never escape his academic and theological training. "They don't realize that venerating those plaques was originally done to curry your favor and win your intercession." He charged ahead again and then stopped short.

"If they can touch the plaques to win a bit of good luck and a promise that they will return to Prague, why shouldn't I venerate the plaques as they were intended and win the protection of the saint?" Dmitri asked himself. "Saint John is one of the most popular protectors of the city, after all. Why not enlist his support?" He joined the happy throng bustling around the statue.

"Plenty of time, no need to rush," the dowdy tour guide was cooing. "Mustn't knock each other down to see Saint John, now," she warned. Dmitri wormed his way into the mesh of her charges and found himself moving closer to the statue as those in front had their photos taken while touching the plaques and then moved away for the next wave of tourists.

Dmitri hadn't venerated a statue in years, not since his first visit to western Europe so long ago. He had passed the statue of the martyr-priest each time he had crossed the bridge but had not felt the need to greet the statue before. But now they needed whatever assistance the saint could provide. His veneration of the plaques might get the saint's attention and persuade him to join their efforts.

The laughing teens immediately in front of him finished touching the plaques and climbed to perch on the statue's base, followed by a whole series of photos taken to immortalize the event, then peeled away from the stonework. The tour guide, not recognizing Dmitri as one of her responsibilities, moved up the bridge, followed by the crowd. Dmitri was alone with the statue.

He looked at the saint's face, the gold stars of apocalyptic glory around his halo shining even in the half-light of the overcast morning. He was not a Roman Catholic. How had he come be standing at the feet of Saint John Nepomuk, a priest martyred here in 1393 for refusing to betray the queen's confession to her husband? The gestures and even the attitude of veneration felt foreign, out of place apart from the two-dimensional religious art found in Orthodox churches. Yet...

"Saint John," Dmitri began, still looking up into the saint's eyes. "You know what we need. Better than I do. Do what you can to help us." He closed his eyes and slowly crossed himself, kissed his fingertips and reached out to touch the plaques that showed St. John hearing the confession of the queen, his killers dropping his body over the bridge into the river, and the king's faithful hound remaining true and honest, even when the king had not. Dmitri felt the cold metal of the

97

image of the hound. He crossed himself again and kissed his fingertips, reaching out to the silhouette of the priest hearing the queen's confession. He closed his eyes, feeling a hum of energy in the air. He crossed himself a third time and kissed his fingertips again, and reached for the scene of the killers disposing of the body. Energy like static electricity tickled his fingertips.

His hand was wrenched away from the statue, his arm twisted behind his back. Dmitri dropped to one knee in pain and surprise, his eyes popping open. He cried out and turned his head to look over one shoulder, expecting to see either George interrupting his act of veneration or a young man attempting to rob him.

No one was there.

His hand was twisted more tightly, pulled further up between his shoulders. Dmitri winced, gasping in pain.

"What—? Who?" tumbled from his lips.

"I cannot allow you to get the attention of the saint!" a man's voice hissed in his ear, the breath of his attacker tickling the hair on the back of Dmitri's neck. "If you try to venerate the statue again, I will be forced to pitch you over the bridge, just as the saint was!"

Dmitri peered behind and around him as best he could. There seemed to be no one there and none of the people wandering the bridge seemed to notice his predicament. Perhaps they all thought he was kneeling in prayer?

"Who are you?" The words were odd guttural strings of syllables that Dmitri pushed out between his teeth. "What is your interest in keeping me from the saint?"

"Who am I?" the voice sneered. "It is enough for you to know that I am one of the men charged by the king with the disposal of this wretched priest. My interest has always been to keep the priest from those who would foolishly ally themselves with him."

"But why now? Why me?" Dmitri demanded. "People seek the priest's intercession all the time. They have for centuries. That tour group did only moments ago!"

"Few of those who come to the statue actually seek the priest's intercession. They touch the plaques because they are simple-minded fools, fools who follow whatever instructions they are given," the specter snarled. "Those of us who threw the saint into the river were ourselves drowned in the river at different times. Some of us drowned ourselves in foolish remorse for our role in the priest's death. Some of us were thrown from the bridge by order of the king to keep his secret. I was killed and thrown from the bridge by the mob when they discovered that I had led the king's loyal servants to kill the priest for him. I was the last living member of our small company."

"But why now?" Dmitri repeated.

"I have waited in the river for centuries, trapped by the troll Jarnvithja, who keeps all who either die in the river or whose bodies are consigned its waters. Only the priest escaped the troll, when his body was retrieved from the river." He heard what sounded like the invisible attacker spitting on the cobblestones in contempt.

"But someone has caused the power of the bridge to wither now. It is dying and nearly dead," the voice went on. "Soon it will tumble into the river as well. So Jarnvithja was able to charge me to wait here and prevent any who would truly seek the priest's assistance." There was a pause. "So I can escort you from the bridge or throw you over its side. Which do you prefer?" A snide chuckle followed and Dmitri's arm was twisted even more tightly in a direction it had never been meant to rotate.

Dmitri cringed, nearly weeping with pain. "Escort me from the bridge," he whimpered.

His attacker spat on the cobblestones again. "I thought as much. You are an old man and a coward. A fool. Stand up!" Dmitri was wrenched up from his knees and the grip on his arm relaxed slightly, enough to allow him to stand upright. His assailant roughly twisted his shoulders so that he faced the Little Town, then pushed him. Dmitri stumbled forward, nearly tripping on the hem of his cassock.

"Now go!" the guttural voice ordered. "Get off the bridge! Do not think that I am not watching your every step. Dare to come back to the statue and I will throw you over the bridge, pull you into the river to join us in Jarnvithja's watery domain, without stopping to ask you why you would disregard my warning. Go!" Dmitri felt the assassin drop his arm and, at the same time, push him forward again. Glancing repeatedly over his shoulder, Dmitri began walking as quickly as he could back to the Little Town.

As he neared the bridge's landing, he noticed police officers gathering near the towers standing guard over the entrance to the Little Town from the bridge. More than a dozen seemed to be conferring, pointing to the bridge as they spoke in hushed tones.

"What's going on here?" Dmitri whispered, stopping and glancing back toward the statues on the bridge.

As if in reply, his hand was twisted sharply into his lower back. He stumbled from the cobblestones of the bridge and onto the plaza sloping down to the right. The pressure on his hand and shoulder vanished. He turned around sharply, hoping to see some trace of his assailant.

He saw none, but did see half the police move from

the towers to the bridge and wave at those on the bridge.
Other police officers approached from the Old Town side
of the bridge, speaking to the vendors and also gesturing to
those walking along the bridge. Vendors began to pack up
their stalls, loudly complaining and pointing at the potential
customers walking by. Tourists started coming back to the
Little Town, clearly confused by directions in a language most
of them did not understand. The police who had come from
the Little Town pulled rolls of yellow police tape from their
pockets and began to string it across the end of the bridge.
Metal gates clattered against each other somewhere nearby
and rang as they hit stone.

Fr. Dmitri turned to see the police at the base of the
towers pulling metal barricades from a storeroom inside the
towers, which they proceeded to assemble into an interlocking
barrier.

"They're closing the bridge," Dmitri realized.

"We have to get to the conferences!" exclaimed
Magdalena. "This is the last morning and Professor Hron
will be angry as it is that I am getting there so late!" She had
come back to meet George as he had instructed and waited for
nearly an hour.

"Yes. We must maintain regular appearances as much as
possible," George agreed. He had risen and dressed, then had
a leisurely breakfast with some of the conference attendees
staying in the same hotel. When he had finally emerged into
the lobby, Magdalena was standing near the door, looking
frantic. He smiled and she… relaxed.

Leaving the hotel, Magdalena wanted to ask George how
he thought they should respond to the academics' attack on the
city. But the streets seemed unnaturally full of people, none

of whom were moving as quickly as they would normally. A crowd seemed to be gathering in the street ahead and Magdalena stood as tall as she could, peering forward to see what the difficulty might be.

They made their way into the knots of people at the back of the crowd and slowly inched toward the bridge. George took the lead, shouldering his way through the confused and shouting crowd. Magdalena clutched his hand, afraid of being torn from his side by the pressing throngs and being unable to make her way forward alone. Forced to walk behind him, Magdalena tightened her grip on George's fingers.

"Excuse me… coming through… excuse me, let us pass," came George's insistent and commanding voice as he made a path through the mob. Then they burst through the front line of the mob and nearly tripped over yellow police tape extending across the entrance to the bridge.

The strands of tape stretched between the statues that guarded either side of the balustrades of the bridge. A handful of policemen stood on the other side of the tape, milling about. Some peered over the stone balustrades at the rushing water. One officer still held a roll of tape in his hands, which he had apparently just finished using to close off the bridge. Metal barricades blocked the plaza leading down to the river. Was that Fr. Dmitri in the crowd near the barricade? She couldn't be sure, and the face she glimpsed was swallowed by the ever-growing crowd of the angry, the frustrated, and the fascinated.

Magdalena turned to George.

"The bridge! It's closed!" she exclaimed. "The flood…?"

George glanced around them.

"Yes," he finally answered. "It seems the authorities think the bridge is in danger of being swept away."

Dmitri continued to stand to one side, where the assassin's spirit had left him. The crowd quickly grew around him as people intending to cross the bridge arrived and were prevented from moving forward by the police and their yellow tape. From where he was standing, near the barricades the police had brought from the tower, he could tell the river had overflowed its banks and had formed a large, roiling pool where tourists had been able to rent rowboats only yesterday.

"No one can cross from here to the Old Town. The conferences will be closed down," Dmitri realized. He had to find the others and tell them of this newest treachery, the assassin who had prevented his attempt to contact the saint.

"Father Dmitri! Where are you going? What is happening?" voices called out to him as he attempted to circle around the swarming crowd with difficulty, headed back to the hotel. He looked up to find his wife standing nearby with Theo.

"I woke and found you had gone out already. So I thought to see you at the conference sessions this morning," Sophia told him. "I met Theo here on the street, as he was headed to the conferences as well. But there seems to be something going on, blocking everything. Why is this crowd here? What is blocking the road ahead? Why are you walking back toward the hotels?"

"Is this another magic trick of George's?" Theo asked.

Fr. Dmitri nodded. "I'm afraid it is, yes. The authorities have just closed the bridge to pedestrians. The Old Town and Little Town are sealed off from each other. But that is not the worst of it." He described his encounter with the assassin.

"Mother of God!" his wife exclaimed. "The leader of the king's assassins! Who is this Jarnvithja he spoke of? It seems the wicked are lurking around every corner, in league to stop us!"

"But the bridge is closed?" Theo exclaimed. "That can only mean one thing: the bridge is in danger of collapsing!"

Sophia turned to Theo. "Yesterday. When we saw the water rising. I was afraid of such a thing!"

"Yes, and now—thanks to what Elizabeth told us last night and what the assassin confirmed for your husband—we know it is part of their plan," Theo acknowledged.

"If the bridge collapses, the city will be completely at their mercy," Sophia said to her husband.

"But surely we cannot let his threat stop us!" the priest responded. "We must continue our efforts, strike back!"

"I agree with you wholeheartedly," Theo said.

"So how do we proceed?" Sophia wanted to know.

"What do you think of continuing to wake the power of the Royal Road on this side of the river?" Dmitri asked him. "I know we all scurried back to our hotels last night after Elizabeth's demise at the Astronomical Clock and the strange fire that attacked us. We apparently cannot use the salt and tarot cards to waken the portions of the Royal Road coming from the Old Town Square that cross the bridge, but we can begin again, yes? Here, in the Little Town, and follow the Royal Road up to the castle?"

"Do you think it wise to do that in the daytime? Even if people are distracted?" Theo pointed to the crowd gathered at the police tape.

"Yes, it is probably best to wait for night to resume our procession," Dmitri said. "But there must be something we can do in the meantime, yes?"

"Such as obtain another chalice for pouring the salt?" his wife interrupted. "Maybe Victoria has one. Otherwise we must continue to pour the salt from the box, but we agreed earlier that a chalice would add power."

"We should try to contact Victoria, yes," Theo responded. "An excellent idea, Sophia."

"Where did Victoria say she would meet us this morning?" asked Sophia. "When we parted last night, she turned down that street." She pointed at a lane that branched off the main street.

"She said she would meet Sean in his hotel lobby," Theo recalled. "She is probably there now."

Early that morning, unable to sleep, Sean checked his e-mail account on the computer outside the hotel's breakfast room.

His eyes skimmed the list of people who had sent him e-mail since he had written to his nephews and his graduate student about erecting cairns on the possible graves of the Dearg-due. There was nothing from his nephews. There was no message from Seamus. No message had any indication that it might have a digital photo or two attached as evidence of the cairns.

But there was a message from the Garda Síochána, the national police force of Ireland. The subject line read: "Missing Nephew Report."

Sean froze. He felt as if his stomach had fallen through the floor beneath him. Unable to move for a few seconds in the predawn darkness of the hotel, he finally dared to click on the message indicator. The screen wavered and a message from a Detective Brendon Quinn came up:

"Professor: I am sorry to report that there has been an incident involving your nephews Donal and Colm late last night in the vicinity of the French Church in the city of Waterford. We are told that the young men were there at your behest and we are in possession of an e-mail from you requesting that they construct a cairn of stones atop the possible grave of a creature known in local folklore as the Dearg-due…"

105

The message went on to describe his nephew Colm's version of events at Christchurch cathedral and the French Church that led to the disappearance of Donal and two friends. It was corroborated by two young women who had accompanied them. Sean could hardly breathe. His heart was pounding. Then the tears came cascading down his cheeks.

It was difficult enough to believe the magic and the danger he had found himself in at an academic conference in Prague. It had never occurred to him that his request to build a cairn on gravesites in Waterford might put his family in danger as well.

"I have to help!" he vowed. "I have to save them somehow! They were trying to help me and they've been… what? Hurt? Killed? Only God knows!"

He swiped the tears away with the back of his hand and read the message again, struggling to comprehend the report of the ghost of a witch stealing his nephew and friends into the Netherworld and the detective's disdain for the tale. He sensed the detective's creeping suspicion of Sean in his request to meet with the professor when he returned to Ireland.

"I have to tell Theo and Fr. Dmitri and Sophia and Victoria… they have to know what it cost those boys who were only trying to do me a favor. And they may have saved us here in Prague." He pressed his fingertips to his eyelids and tried to wipe away the still-flowing tears again so he could read the message a third time.

"No, I can't tell Theo and the others. Not yet," he argued with himself. "I have to find out more details before I tell them, and this news would only distract everyone from the work that still needs to be done here, in Prague, to stop Svetovit!" He bit his lower lip, hoping the pain would distract him from his anguish.

"When I get back home, I have to do something. Not simply talking to the police, either! I will," he whispered to the computer screen. "I promise."

Victoria was setting out from her apartment to meet Sean in the lobby of his hotel. It was a strangely overcast sky, the damp air heavy. She had slept fitfully after witnessing Elizabeth's murder of Wilcox and the magically enforced return of the Dearg-due to her grave in Ireland. In her dreams, her memories of the screams of Elizabeth and the huge flock of crows circling around her woke her repeatedly, as did memories of the searing heat of the ghostly flame that had wrapped around her and Sophia afterward. "Were any of the others able to sleep after what happened last night?" she wondered. When she had finally drifted off to a brief, dreamless sleep, it was difficult to wake up and get out of bed. But she had promised to be in the hotel lobby and go with Sean to Alessandro's room.

The streets she hurried down toward the hotel were full of the usual people making their way toward their offices and jobs. But as she came closer to the main street leading to the bridge, she was engulfed in a mob that she had not seen since the days of the Velvet Revolution and the overthrow of the Communist government.

"Why this many people? Why here and now?" she asked herself, struggling to navigate her way through the teeming crowds. She strained to hear snatches of conversation as she made her way forward.

"I don't know... The road is closed ahead... Something about the bridge... No danger of floods but a safety precaution... But we had planned to see the St. Agnes Cloister today!" The cacophony of conversations and languages assaulted her ears. People seemed confused and angry or excited, but not frightened.

Victoria shook her head. But they should be frightened, she thought. "Floods? Yes, they want to wash away the Charles Bridge!" she muttered. "Why else do you think we want to stop them?" she demanded under her breath of no one in particular. With difficulty she finally made it to the entrance of Sean's hotel and darted through the door into the lobby.

Sean was waiting for her.

"Let's go," he announced curtly. "If we have to discover something terrible, I'd rather get this over with." Without waiting for an answer, he charged onto the street. Victoria hurried after him.

The crowd blocked Sean's efforts to get to Alessandro's hotel quickly. Victoria took advantage of the opportunity to explain that the bridge had been closed.

"But I could hardly sleep after… what happened last night," she told him after explaining the bridge closure. "I am so glad that you were able to convince someone to build those stones on her grave back in Ireland. Who knows what might have happened to us otherwise? We would all be dead on the Old Town Square!"

"I would rather not think about that," Sean answered, keeping his gaze fixed ahead and over the heads of the crowd. "As it was, it cost my nephews dearly." Despite his earlier resolution to keep the police message to himself, he told her about the e-mail he had received from the Garda Síochána and the report that one of his nephews was traumatized and the other, along with two of their friends, was now missing and that an hysterical witness claimed that they were being held hostage by the ghost of an Irish witch in the Otherworld.

"No! Sean, that's terrible!" Victoria exclaimed. "We must

do something to help them! They did that for us… We cannot leave them there, abandoned! We must rescue them!"

"We will," Sean agreed. "Or, at least, I will! But we can do nothing for them now. We must finish this business and then I can turn my attention to them once this business is done and I am back home in Dublin. In the meantime, we have to find out what happened to Alessandro and meet the others."

Victoria bit her lip and nodded. It had never occurred to her that Sean's nephews might be in any danger from building the cairn at his request.

With difficulty, they made their way to Alessandro's hotel and rode the tiny elevator upstairs.

They stood in the hallway before his door. Sean tried pushing gently on the door to see if it might be unlocked, but it refused to move. They knocked. There was no answer. Victoria held her breath, hoping to hear someone stirring inside.

Nothing.

They knocked again. Victoria pressed her ear to the door before shaking her head.

"Do you think the front desk would open the door for us?" Victoria whispered.

"Not without a very good reason as to why we think he might be in danger," Sean whispered back. "Do you really think that telling them an Irish vampire attacked him last night will make them want to help us? I think anything we say will raise more questions about us than Alessandro's whereabouts, I'm afraid." He stared at the door a moment longer.

"There is really nothing we can do here then, is there?" Victoria finally put their fears into words.

"No. I think not," Sean agreed. "And we do not want to be implicated in any police investigation whenever the body is discovered by the housekeeping department. Someone may remember we were here and tell the police as it is. We really should not be seen loitering in front of his room."

Victoria nodded her understanding. "Alessandro and Wilcox would both rather we keep working to stop George than spend time tangled up with the police, implicated in their deaths, wouldn't they?"

They turned and made their way out of the hotel as quickly but inconspicuously as they could.

George and Magdalena made their way back towards the castle, away from the crowd being kept off the Charles Bridge.

"I must call Professor Hron," Magdalena fretted. "I need to tell him what has happened, keep him informed. He should know that the conference delegates staying in hotels on this side of the river will be unable to attend!"

George nodded absentmindedly. He stopped and looked in the window of a small shop.

"There." He pointed. "Those figures of dough." He pointed at several items on display. Magdalena paused in her nervous rambling and looked at the figures he was pointing at.

"Those?" she asked. "Those are traditional holiday figures, ornaments to hang on a Christmas tree." Each figure, resembling a king or a shepherd or angel, was individually wrapped in a plastic packet.

"We should get a handful," George instructed her. "Five of them."

"Five? Why?" Magdalena did not understand what George was hinting at.

"One for each of our adversaries," George told her. He stepped into the shop.

Dmitri, Sophia, and Theo searched Sean's hotel lobby and breakfast room.

"They are not here," Theo announced finally. "We must have just missed them."

"Then we should find them at Alessandro's hotel," Dmitri suggested.

Sophia shook her head. "Someone might notice. The more of us at Alessandro's hotel, the more likely that someone will see or remember one of us and implicate us in Alessandro's… in Alessandro's death." The two men reluctantly agreed.

"So do we wait here for them?" Theo asked.

"We don't know that they will be coming back," Dmitri answered, "at least, not directly. I don't think we have much time to spare. We need to awaken the power of the Royal Road on this side of the bridge as quickly as we can, yes? Even without a chalice. Even without waiting for the cover of darkness."

His wife and Theo agreed, looking at each other and nodding in concert.

"I'll go get the salt from my room," Theo said. "Do you have the tarot cards in your room, Dmitri? Why don't we meet at the foot of the hill in an hour?"

George and Magdalena shouldered their way through the still-growing crowd back to Magdalena's apartment.

"Fetch the chalice you brought back here last night," he instructed her. "Fill it with clean water and set it here." He sat in a chair and pulled himself up to the table. Taking the small bag of their dough-figure Christmas decorations, he unwrapped each delicate figure. Magdalena took the chalice from the shelf where she had placed it the night before and filled it with water from the kitchen sink. She placed it on the

111

table in front of George and the five unwrapped dough figures.

He handed her the discarded wrappings to throw out. "Now get your other tools," he told her. She retrieved her tray inscribed with a five-pointed star, the Rabbi's short staff that they had taken, and the small ritual knife and set them near the chalice.

George took the tray and placed it directly before him. He then arranged the five dough figures on the tray, one at each point of the star. He set the knife next to the chalice and handed the staff to Magdalena. He closed his eyes, sat up straight as a school boy preparing for an exam, and gently set his palms down on either side of the tray.

"Inscribe the magic circle around us," he said quietly.

Magdalena bent over so that the mushroom-headed tip of the staff she was holding touched the floor. She walked backwards around the table, tracing a circle on the floor behind her as she moved. The energy of the circle crackled in the air around her. The hair on her arms and the back of her neck stood upright. She reached the point where she had begun to trace the circle and stood upright, looking at George for his next instruction. Rainbow hues faintly rippled like Northern Lights in the air around the circle.

George continued to sit quietly, his eyes closed and palms resting on the table. He drew in a deep breath and slowly exhaled.

"Take a seat," he told her at last. "Opposite me." Magdalena sat across from George, trying not to jar the table and spill any of the water in the chalice as she pulled her chair closer to what had become an altar. She dared to set the staff on the tabletop next to the chalice, parallel to the knife.

"I hope that's correct," she whispered.

George continued to sit quietly, meditatively, slowly and deeply breathing in and out. Magdalena found herself beginning to breathe in rhythm with him. She set her palms on the tabletop, mimicking him. The lights continued to flicker and dance around the circle.

George opened his eyes and reached for one of the dough figures on the tray, the one furthest from him at the apex of the star. The unexpected movement startled Magdalena, causing her to catch her breath.

George glanced at her, then turned his attention back to the dough figure that he held gently with his fingertips. He brought the figure to his lips and exhaled a long, slow breath onto it. Then he swiftly dipped it into the water of the chalice.

"I baptize you Theo," he announced. Lifting the figure from the water, he shook a few drops from it and set it down on the tray again.

Taking the dough figure from one of the two low points of the star, he repeated his exhalation onto that figure and plunged it into the water of the chalice as well.

"I baptize you Dmitri," he proclaimed. Shaking the few loose drops of water back into the chalice, he set the figure down where he had taken it from. He looked across to Magdalena and smiled, gesturing for her to take a figure next.

Magdalena's body tingled. "This is like when I called up Flauros and Halphas in my back yard last spring," she thought. "Or when George and I conjured the judgment of Prague last week. Real ritual. Real magic." She shivered with nervous excitement. Taking the dough figure from one of the star's side points, she took a deep breath and held it momentarily before exhaling slowly onto the face of the dough figure. Then, following George's example, she inserted the figure into the water of the chalice before her.

"I bap... baptize you... Sophia!" she stuttered. She held it in the water a moment before she remembered to lift it out, shake it somewhat dry, and replace it on the tray. George smiled at her. She shivered again and blushed.

He took the figure from the other of the star's low points closest to him, exhaled onto it and dipped it into the chalice.

"I baptize you Sean," he asserted and then returned the figure to its place. He looked at Magdalena again and nodded.

She reached for the last figure, at the point of the star's remaining arm. Bringing it close to her, she exhaled onto it for as long as she could and then dipped it into the water.

"I baptize you…" She paused, mentally sorting through the names of their adversaries to determine which one remained.

"Victoria." The name caught in her throat. "I baptize you Victoria."

George picked up the figure he had named "Theo." He turned it over and around in his hands, and over again as if examining its features and limbs. Then he lifted it to his mouth and slowly, languidly slid his tongue up one leg of the figure and down the other.

Theo had collected the few boxes of salt that remained from their efforts of the previous night in his hotel room. The torn shopping bag in which he carried them seemed sturdy enough to continue using, for at least a little while. He headed to the lobby to meet Dmitri and Sophia.

Crossing the lobby, he nodded to the clerks at the front desk, who smiled and waved back. He reached the door to the street and cried out in sudden pain as he collapsed, his legs twisting into knots and giving way beneath him.

George returned the "Theo" figure to the pentacle tray and selected one of the figures from the lower points of the star, the one he had baptized "Sean." Again he examined it, considering its details, the folds and whorls of the dough that had been baked until it was rock hard. He finally extended his tongue again and drew it slowly across the figure's face.

Sean and Victoria stood in the street outside Alessandro's hotel, looking at the knots of people continuing to flow down the streets toward the blockade at the bridge.

"So, now what should we do?" Victoria asked.

"Well, we cannot get to the conference," Sean began, thinking aloud. "We can hope that Theo, Dmitri, and Sophia did not get across the bridge this morning before it was closed." He considered the best strategy. "Finding them is probably what we should do next. Discuss our options for our next move."

"So, back to Theo's hotel?" Victoria asked.

"Yes. Back to Theo's hotel," Sean agreed. Frustrated, he reached up to rub his forehead but then shouted in agony, blinded by indescribable pain that suddenly pierced his eyes.

George replaced the "Sean" figure on the tray and gestured to Magdalena to select a figure. She hesitated a moment, and then picked up the figure she had declared "Sophia." Following George's example, she considered its various appendages and extremities before selecting one. Looking across the table into George's eyes, she slid her tongue across the rough dough of the figure's torso.

Sophia and Dmitri sifted through the discarded garments in their luggage, looking for the tarot cards they had dropped into one of the suitcases after returning to their room the previous night.

"I know they are here somewhere," muttered the priest.

"Maybe we left them over there," Sophia suggested, pointing to a small table on the other side of the bed.

As she moved to investigate the nightstand, a spasm of pain and nausea tore through her digestive tract. She stumbled to the bathroom, clutching her stomach, retching vomit again and again onto the rug.

George took up the "Dmitri" figure as Magdalena set down "Sophia." Without any hesitation this time, George inserted the figure's cranium into his mouth and slid his tongue over and around and across the entire surface of the doughman's head.

Dmitri hurried to his wife's side as she collapsed onto her knees in the bathroom, wrapping his arms around her shoulders.

"Sophia!" he exclaimed, his voice full of surprise and concern. "What's wrong? Was there something bad at breakfast?"

Sophia gasped for breath as the contractions of her stomach paused. "I... am not sure..." She tried to remember what she had eaten that morning. "What did I have?"

Dmitri tried to think back to the breakfast they had shared. It seemed so long ago. "Well, there was coffee... And yogurt, yes?"

In the next instant, Dmitri too gasped in pain and shock, dropping to the floor beside his wife. He clutched his temples with his hands, wanting to both tear his hair out and stop the sharp pains that writhed and twisted through his head, the most sudden and incapacitating headache he had ever experienced.

Sophia heard the wordless moaning of her husband. Her eyes pressed shut, trying with all her might to keep the growing nausea from rising up throughout her again. She felt him on the floor beside her, his full weight leaning against her. She grasped the toilet bowl before her, struggling to both orient herself in space and support herself and her stricken husband.

Magdalena struggled to suppress a giggle. "What kind of game are we playing?" she wanted to ask aloud, but dared not disturb the quiet of the flickering magic circle in her kitchen. "What does this licking of the baptized figures accomplish?" she wondered.

George set down "Dmitri," a snarl of contempt wrinkling his mouth. He pointed to the last figure, looking directly at Magdalena. She reached for "Victoria."

Victoria helped Sean stumble back into the hotel lobby, his hands clutching at his face, weeping and gasping between ongoing screams of pain. Clerks and other staff rushed from behind the front desk and the nooks and crannies of the lobby. A flood of words offering assistance in a confusing mix of Czech and English and German and French and Russian assaulted her ears. She and the hotel staff eased Sean toward an overstuffed chair against a wall as he continued to wail. She knelt before him and tried to ease his hands away from his face to see what had caused such pain.

"Sean. Sean, let go," she urged, wrapping her fingers around his. "Let me see. I need to see what is wrong…"

Magdalena turned the "Victoria" figure over and over in her hands. Whatever she and George were causing to the academics, Magdalena had only thought of them as enemies and adversaries to be thwarted, people intent on the destruction of her beloved home city and the continued slander of Fen'ka under the bridge. But Victoria was her friend. Or at least, had been her friend. Until last night. Until the confrontation with Elizabeth. Victoria had been duped, perhaps, but had joined those determined to destroy their home, the beautiful city they had both held most dear. They had to be stopped, including Victoria and whatever assistance she was lending their efforts.

Closing her eyes, feeling the dough in her hands and with her tongue, she licked every surface of the figure that her tongue could reach.

"Sean! Let me see!" Victoria urged him again, his palms pressed firmly against his eyes as he rocked back and forth in the chair, his cries reduced to steady sobs and whimpers.

"The pain… like my eyes are being cut out… I cannot see," he moaned. Hotel staff scurried to call a doctor.

"Do you think you got something in your eyes? Or do you think George…?" she began. She did not want to finish the thought. If George was capable of inflicting this kind of suffering, was Magdalena involved too? How could they wield such power? Or be so cruel?

"This is not the Magdalena I know," flashed through her mind. "He has changed her. He is making her into a monster." She felt sick at the thought.

But then she felt truly sick, losing control over herself. She felt her bowels relax and release whatever waste they held as spasms tore through her body, throwing her to the ground, where she rocked and ground her teeth in the few seconds she was conscious before darkness descended.

George lifted the dagger, the athame, from the table and held it over the doughmen on the pentacle tray.

Magdalena held her breath. Though she was unsure what would result from licking the figures, she was certain that plunging the knife's point into one would cause extreme pain, if not death. Was George about to pierce the figures with the knife?

George held the athame over each of the dough figures in turn, tracing the lines of the star-pentacle as he moved the knife's point from figure to figure. The flickering light hovering along the lines of the circle around them shifted and rippled, similar lines of light appearing to connect the figures along the outline of the star. Then George stood and used the knife to slice through the light shimmering behind him. The lights winked out, both along the circumference of the circle and the outline of the star.

He turned back to Magdalena. "These should be buried now," he told her. "Is there a place nearby to do that?"

"I have a garden in the back," Magdalena offered.

"The place should have a ritual significance," George said. "A churchyard would be best."

Magdalena thought a moment. "It is not a churchyard," she said, "but there is a place to bury them near a church."

"That will do," George conceded. "Is it near here?"

"Not far. At the very top of the hill, past the castle," she told him. "At the Loreto chapel."

Sophia leaned against the toilet, dazed and confused. Waves of nausea rippled through her from time to time, forcing her to lean over the toilet bowl even though she seemed to have nothing left in her stomach to eject. Gradually

119

the waves of nausea came less frequently and she thought that retreating to the bed might be an option. She had continued to support her moaning husband, whose only words had been "unbelievable migraine" and "Bozha moi!"

"Can you move at all, Dmitri?" she asked at last.

"The pain becomes a bit more tolerable if I do not move," he whispered, "but I could manage, yes. Do you have an idea?"

"I am thinking that I might be ready to lie on the bed," she answered.

Dmitri was silent for several seconds and then nodded. Together, they slowly crawled out of the bathroom and across the room to the bed. Both trying to assist the other, they made their way onto the bed and collapsed.

It was midmorning and the Loreto cloister was closed, as it always was on Mondays. The streets around it were empty, all the tourists gathered at the police barricade closing off the bridge. George had brought the five figures with them in a small bag and set them carefully on the ground beside them. The bushes and trees that surrounded the Loreto complex rustled quietly as he used the athame to trace an "X" in the dirt under one of the bushes.

Magdalena then knelt down and dug a small hole in the earth where George had marked, using the garden trowel she had brought as if she were preparing to plant a new flower there. George took each figure from the bag and laid it carefully in the soil, pressing it gently into the ground. Then Magdalena used the trowel to refill the hole and pat the earth flat. They stood and brushed the soil from their hands and knees. The disturbed ground was hidden under the sweeping branches of the evergreen bushes.

"Excellent work!" George congratulated Magdalena. He smiled at her and she felt herself blush.

George looked around the small plaza. Numerous trees and bushes covered the ground across the plaza, in addition to those that surrounded the cloister complex. One tree in particular seemed to catch his attention. He walked over to it and peered at its leaves, stroking one.

"Yew," he announced. "How useful." He half-turned back to Magdalena. "Bring me that bag," he instructed. "The one we brought the doughmen in." Magdalena was quick to stand beside him, the open bag in her hands along with the trowel.

George reached up and firmly grasped a small cluster of the leaves and used the athame to cut it free from the larger limb of the yew. He dropped the bundle into the bag and reached up several more times, using the knife to cut other bunches of leaves free.

"Yew leaves are such useful things to have around," George said, apparently satisfied with their harvest. "Never pass by the opportunity to collect them," he told Magdalena. He extended the crook of his arm and together they set out back down the hill toward both his hotel and Magdalena's small apartment; she wasn't sure to which they were returning.

The doctor arrived at the hotel lobby to find Sean clasping his palms across his eyes and rocking in an overstuffed chair, weeping quietly. Victoria lay on the floor, her torso twitching occasionally in the aftermath of an apparent seizure.

"Get me a glass of water, please," he asked the hotel staff after his preliminary examination. "Help him take these," the doctor instructed the bellhop who appeared with the glass of water, handing him two tablets. The young man leaned over and helped Sean sip from the glass, easing the sedative into his mouth between sips.

The doctor turned to examine Victoria and decided she seemed to be resting peacefully, despite the slight tremors from time to time.

"Make them both comfortable," he told the clerk at the front desk. "Move them a bit to one side if you like, but not too far. They should both rest for several hours, but under someone's observation—just in case."

"What about a hospital?" the clerk asked. "I do not believe that they are guests of this hotel, doctor. Would they not be more carefully observed in a hospital?"

"They shouldn't be moved far right now," the doctor answered. "And there is no way an ambulance could come easily through the crowds in the streets today. Nor are any ambulances free for cases such as theirs. Many hospitals have begun evacuations because of the anticipated flooding. The rest are full to capacity. Beyond capacity. Even if I could get an ambulance to fetch them, where would it take them? Only to a makeshift ward in a school gymnasium. No, they are better off left here to rest."

He gave the clerk his business card. "Phone me at this private number if there is any change in their condition."

The rushing water under the Charles Bridge continued to climb the supports of the bridge like a hungry animal, struggling to reach the delicate morsel it knew was waiting above. Crowds continued to hover at the barriers that closed off the bridge as they watched the river grow stronger, deeper, angrier. Other people were collecting along both sides of the riverbank, each watching the other side of the city.

"Look!" a young woman standing in the court of a restaurant on the Little Town side of the river tugged her boyfriend's sleeve as he attempted to take a photograph of the bridge, the statues along its balustrade silhouetted against the sky.

"Wha—!" he exclaimed, her tug causing the camera to jerk and catch a smudged photo of the cloudy sky instead. He half-turned toward where she was pointing.

The river was clearly crawling into the dark, gaping entrances to sewers and tunnels liberally sprinkled across the face of the wall across the river, a wall that must have been built to safeguard the Jewish Quarter and the Old Town from the ravages of the river. But the furious, hungry river, kept for so long from the city and reaching higher than it had in more than a century, was discovering the weaknesses in the city's defenses.

A half-dozen evangelical students from an American Bible college who had come to Prague for summer mission work stood on the platform of the Staroměstká subway station in the Old Town.

"Springs from the deep!" insisted one of the upperclassmen. "I tell you, it was more than rain for forty days and forty nights that caused Noah's flood! The springs of the deep burst forth too!"

"Springs of the deep?" asked one of the girls, a younger student. "What were the springs of the deep? My pastor only ever preached about the rain for forty days."

"The springs of the deep were the waters God had sealed away from the earth, above the heavens and under the ground," another one of the girls said smugly. "The earth was surrounded by water, sealed in a bubble of air, and the springs of the deep were the water from above and under the earth that God allowed to burst forth and flood the world. To punish the wickedness of mankind."

"Because he was sorry that He had made mankind,

123

because they had become so wicked," corrected the upperclassman.

"But is every flood a punishment for wickedness, like Noah's flood?" asked the younger girl. "What about the flood they say is headed toward Prague?"

Theo had collapsed in the hotel lobby but the staff, rushing to his assistance, had lifted him onto a sofa near the elevator and called for a doctor. The pain shimmered and crawled up and down Theo's bones and joints.

"Move, damn it!" he ordered his feet, trying to make them respond to his will. Nothing. Only pain. Followed by more pain.

"Run! *Pádit!* Get out! *Pospíchat!* Hurry!" voices cried out. Panic seized the crowd waiting on the subway platform with the American Bible students. Fingers pointed at the tracks while others gestured wildly toward the stairways leading to the open air. Older people hobbled as quickly as they could toward the escalators. Younger people took two steps at a time as they raced for the surface above.

Rats, a multitude of rats, swarmed up of the sewer grating below the tracks. Scurrying over and under and around the tracks, an intrepid few attempted to clamber onto the platform and away from whatever had chased them from the sewers and tunnels under the subway. Within seconds, water gurgled through the sewer grates, river water that had seeped in through the openings in the stone walls lining the riverbank along the Old Town.

Abruptly, fountains of water, not unlike the springs of the deep the students had just been discussing, burst from crevices in the track beds of the tunnels. Some large, some small, the fountains splashed gaily and the pools of water that already hid the sewer grates congealed between the tracks and trickled into each other. The rats still down along the tracks began to swim, paddling madly to find someplace dry, someplace slightly higher underground.

The three subway stations closest to the river were shut down moments later.

Theo jerked awake as the doctor finally began to examine his legs. He realized that he had drifted into a shallow, dreamless sleep.

"What happened, doctor?" Theo asked, wincing at the doctor's touch as he tried to roll up the academic's trousers. The doctor turned and twisted Theo's ankles and knees as gently as he could, but spasms of pain ricocheted through Theo's body.

"It is hard to tell without an x-ray," the doctor finally told him, "but there seem to be several fractures along the length of the leg bones. In both legs. Very unusual." He paused and turned his attention to Theo's face. "Were you in some kind of accident, sir?"

"No, nothing like that," Theo managed to answer. "I was walking and suddenly collapsed. There was no warning."

"No warning at all?" the doctor repeated. "Highly unusual." He rummaged in his medical bag and retrieved a small bottle of pills.

"Are you going to call an ambulance?" Theo wanted to know. "I imagine that I must go to the hospital."

The doctor gestured to a hotel clerk for a drink and a glass of water was quickly brought.

"I am afraid, sir, that going to a hospital is quite impossible at the moment," the doctor explained. "We are expecting a flood, a major flood. Most of the nearby hospitals and nursing facilities have begun to evacuate patients, straining the resources of those that remain open. I am afraid there is no space for you in any facility more conducive to your situation than the lobby where we find ourselves."

Theo winced again. The doctor shook two pills from the bottle and gave them to Theo, putting the glass of water into Theo's other hand.

"These pills are for the pain. The damage seems limited to your legs. It has not spread since the initial onset of symptoms, has it?" the doctor asked him.

Theo swallowed the pills. "No," he agreed.

"Then I am afraid we must simply let you rest here. I will leave enough medication to ease your pain until sometime late tomorrow afternoon. I hope by that time we will be able to return and fetch you," the doctor said as he stood to go. He set the bottle of pills on a small table beside the sofa where Theo sat, legs outstretched.

"Tomorrow? Stay here in the lobby until then?" Theo couldn't believe what he was hearing.

"Yes," the doctor emphasized. "Are you a guest of this hotel, sir? Perhaps the staff could manage to take you to your room if you wish. Rest, and tomorrow afternoon will come more quickly than you might expect." He shook Theo's hand and was gone.

"Now that our adversaries have been detained," George announced as he and Magdalena entered his hotel room, "we have to do what we can to repel the flood from the city."

"Detained?" Magdalena interrupted. "How were they detained?"

"Let's just say that since we licked and buried the dough figures, they have not been feeling well." George smirked.

126

"Now, as I said, we must do what we can to repel the flood."

"Yes!" Magdalena agreed vigorously. "How do we do that? What can I do to help?"

George thought briefly before speaking. "There is a fairly simple way to manage it, I think," he finally told her, "but its results will not be instantaneous. I can give you the supplies and directions, but then I must leave it in your hands to accomplish. Can you manage that? I need to call New York and explain that I will be detained here for a few more days."

Magdalena was thrilled to be trusted by George to do whatever needed to be done. "Just tell me what to do and I will do it!"

He stepped to the room's small desk and cleared it, setting everything gently to one side and then lifting his valise onto it. He brought out a plastic sandwich bag, into which he placed the yew cuttings they had brought from the plaza. After putting the bag of yew back into the valise, he brought out a small ornate silver disk like the pocketwatch Magdalena's grandfather had always kept in his pocket. He set the pocketwatch thing on the desk and then produced another sandwich bag, this one full of small vials of dark liquid, from the valise. Finally, he brought out a small ceramic mortar and pestle and set them on the desk.

"I will make a paste," George announced, "that you must smear along the curbs and gutters of the Little Town. This paste should repel the water of the flood from the city, though as I said, the results will not be quick. It will take time to turn aside this flood which our enemies have conjured, but we can reinforce the charm tomorrow, if need be." He put on two latex gloves from the valise and carefully took three of the vials from the sandwich bag, uncorked them, and poured the liquid into the mortar bowl. A powerful stench, like a concentrate of mothballs, assailed Magdalena's nostrils.

"What goes into the paste?" she asked quietly.

"A friend of mine from seminary days was assigned to northern France." George spoke but kept his face toward the items on the desk, his back to Magdalena as he next took a narrow strip of brocade from the valise, kissed it, and placed it across the back of his neck, letting the ends of the vestment reach down his chest toward his belt. "In that region of France is found a certain kind of toad, the warts on the back of which produce a venom traditionally used by the clergy of that area in combination with the Eucharist to accomplish certain purposes. My friend has a parishioner who is a chemist and who keeps my friend supplied with this venom which he extracts from the local toads and, in turn, my friend generously shares some with me."

Magdalena wrinkled her nose and peered around George's shoulders at the liquid in the small ceramic bowl but had to hastily step to one side as, without warning, he genuflected before the desk. He opened the silver pocketwatch, and Magdalena caught her breath as she recognized it from church as a pyx that contained several communion wafers.

"Is it…?" she whispered. George nodded.

He took a wafer and held it in his forefingers for a moment before placing it in the ceramic bowl with the liquid. He repeated this procedure twice more, placing a total of three of the wafers in the bowl. He genuflected again, closed the pyx, and set it aside before taking up the pestle and grinding the wafers into the extract from the French toads' warts.

Magdalena was mesmerized watching the procedure. Having made the paste of the consecrated wafers and the noxious extract, George put away the stole from his neck and dropped the gloves into the trash can below the desk. He pulled another pair from the valise and turned to Magdalena.

"Wear these and take the bowl of paste with you," he instructed. "Take cotton swabs from the bathroom and use them to smear the paste on the curbs and sidewalks of the Little Town until you've used it all. But not too close to the water level as it is currently. The water may rise too quickly, before the charm has time to act, and the flood may wash away our work before it takes effect. Mark the streets a few blocks higher than the flood and the paste will have a chance to work before the water reaches it."

"How does it work?" Magdalena wanted to know.

"The toad venom, itself a defensive tactic of the animal, will work with the healing power of the Eucharist to rebuff the flood. When you've finished, go home and rest. I will contact you in the morning to determine our next move. Do you have any other questions, Magdalena?"

Magdalena shook her head. "No, no questions, George." She leaned toward him to give him a peck on the cheek. "I will see you in the morning." She put on the latex gloves, picked up the bowl, and stopped in the bathroom to collect the cotton swabs. George opened the door for her, gave her a kiss, and shut the door behind her as she set out on her mission to drive the flood from the streets of Prague.

By midafternoon, the mayor of the city was still insisting that the river situation was under control, but no one standing along the riverbanks believed the official announcements. Local magistrates, like the hospital directors, did not agree with the mayor's estimation and blockaded the riverside of the Old Town, forcing thousands away from the view of the water.

The seventy-plus academics who had come to Prague for the conferences—and other tourists—were having an especially difficult time getting information or news and could not understand most of the answers they were given by police officers on the streets. None of the academics knew how to contact Hron, and Theo was not answering the phone in his hotel room.

"I paid my registration!" several insisted to each other. "I expect a full series of conference sessions, with all the accepted papers read! Flood or no flood, there are standards that must be maintained. Otherwise I will demand a full refund!"

In the Old Town, the rector and governing board of the Klementinum cultural center near the river decided to take matters into their own hands and directed the tourists visiting their hallways towards the exits. Once the last visitor had stepped out through the elaborate gateways, the guards closed and bolted them.

A similar scene unfolded a few blocks away at the Cloister of St. Agnes, which housed the National Gallery's collection of medieval art. Visitors and scholars were escorted at first and then hustled to the gates by museum security and the older women who served as volunteers at the entrances to the cloister. When the last visitor exited, the magnificent wrought iron gates swung shut and the staff scurried out the small back entrances before the river could trap them inside.

Trucks of sand pulled up in front of the Astronomical Clock, not far from where the mangled body of Wilcox had been found near dawn by a few late-night party-goers stumbling back to their hostel. The last of the yellow police tape was being pulled down as the trucks rumbled into position. Hundreds of large, rough cloth sacks were tucked into the sides of the truck beds along with a number of shovels and scoops. Knots of people who had been aimlessly wandering about the square, at a loss for how to react to the closing of the bridge and the apparently inexorable coming of a flood that many officials still insisted on denying, converged on the trucks and the handful of workers who jumped from the cabs of the trucks.

Shovelfuls of sand flew. Hands grabbed the cloth sacks and held them open as scoop after scoop, load after load of sand was poured down the throats of the sacks. Other hands pulled each bag tightly shut and tied it with cord or twine. A rag-tag assembly line materialized and the filled sandbags were moved to one side of the Astronomical Clock, near where the cobblestone crosses marked the execution of the twenty-seven Protestant nobility in 1621, the nobility whose ghosts according to legend returned each June to see if the clock had stopped to indicate the arrival of Judgment Day. Moving the sandbags was slow, backbreaking work, but a small mountain of sandbags continued to grow as dusk descended on the square.

"Let the shadow of death stalk them in the night!"

(January–February 1357)

adezda was unable to sleep well that night.
When her eyes did close, she had dreamed only
of Fen'ka in that fire and imagined hearing her
voice calling down Svetovit's power to destroy her neighbors
who had condemned her to such a death. The next morning,
tired and bleary-eyed, Nadezda was still sorting phrases and
clauses from the curse that Petr and Vavrinec had first told
her about, and lines that others had heard and repeated in the
squares and marketplaces of Prague. She sat cross-legged on
the floor in front of the hearth and stirred the coals to life,
uncovering the flame deep in the heart of the small mound
of coals she had built in the midst of the fireplace. She threw
a handful of straw onto the coals as kindling and waited for
them to catch fire.

She poked at the coals again and the fragile construction
of kindling and coals collapsed with a shower of sparks.
"How many lines of the curse have yet to be fulfilled?"
she asked herself, mindlessly drawing designs in the ashes
with the poker in her hand. "Why is the curse so slow in
unwinding? I would think that Fen'ka would have wanted her
vengeance carried out at once, would have wanted Svetovit
to immediately destroy her enemies." Patience was never a
virtue that Fen'ka embraced. "It makes no sense for the curse
to be taking so long to demonstrate either Svetovit's power or
Fen'ka's retribution."

Nadezda stared at the kindling without seeing it. "They say Fen'ka called down her vengeance on everyone in the towns and in the castle. She demanded Svetovit lay waste everyone in the Old Town Square. Did she mean everyone from the towns and the castle that was in the square? But surely not everyone who has suffered from the curse was there that afternoon." She reviewed in her mind the victims—at least those she was fairly certain of—and thought about the likelihood of their whereabouts on the fateful day. Conrad the priest had certainly been in the square; after all, he had begun the whole terrible incident and was certainly there to see its grisly conclusion. The mason from Tuscany—what was his name? Oh, yes. Bartolomeo. Had he been there? Or František the miser? Or Božena the old beggar woman and Anežka the wealthy matron? What about Aleksandr and Jiri? Certainly not all the guests at the Epiphany feast in the Little Town who had been transformed into animals. For all that, what about the young thief who had his arm cut off in St. Jakub's Church yesterday?

Since she had not been present in the Old Town Square, it was impossible for her to say. "Given the size of the mob, though, even someone who had been there would not know for certain who else might or might not have been in the crowd. Unlikely as it seems, maybe they were all there as Fen'ka burned." She considered that possibility. A coal winked out without her noticing. Then another.

She sighed with relief that she had not been there and was therefore perhaps safe from the predations of Svetovit. But if even only one of these others who had suffered at his hands had not been present at Fen'ka's burning—and, given her suspicions, Nadezda was as certain as she could be that some must not have been—then that meant that Svetovit's destructive power was not limited to those who had cried out for Fen'ka's death.

She reviewed what else she remembered about the curse that others had reported. "All their wives and children." Yes, that was the phrase. "All their wives and children." So Fen'ka had deliberately extended her curse beyond those present in the Old Town Square. The words caught in her throat. The wives and children of the men in the square that afternoon? Vavrinec had been there. He had told her so. That meant that she and Milos were in danger.

Fear clutched at her bowels. "It makes no matter whether I pursue Fen'ka and her curse," she realized. "Milos and I are in as much danger either way. Vavrinec is concerned that I will allow my pursuit of Fen'ka and Svetovit to destroy me, but his own actions have put us all at risk." It was even more incumbent on her now to solve the riddle of Fen'ka's curse and discover its key so as to be able to rewrite it.

A sharp pain in her wrist brought her attention back to her kitchen and the fireplace. Her grasp of the poker had grown slack as she attempted to work out the puzzle of the curse, and the poker had finally dropped, twisting her wrist as it fell to the floor. She peered into the hearth. The kindling still sat there, only the ends of it singed. No red coals shone in the ashes from the night before.

"No!" Nadezda was furious with herself. "Instead of watching the fire, I was thinking of Fen'ka and Svetovit and allowed the fire to go out!" she chided herself. "I need to do one thing or another, not both things at once!" She recognized the words, so similar to those she and Vavrinec had both chided Petr with as he had allowed his mind to wander and leave chore after chore undone at either the bakery or at home.

"Has my inattention lost a generation of continuity with my fire?" It would certainly be inconvenient and embarrassing if she had to ask a neighbor for coals to relight the fire at her hearth. Kneeling to bring her face as close to the seemingly dead coals as possible, she blew gently and poked at the mounds of gray ash with the kindling.

Delicate flakes of ash swirled about. She inserted the straw further, more deeply into the ashes. She stirred the ashes slightly and blew again. Nothing.

She sighed with irritation. A few moments of inattention had lost the fire that had burned without interruption for longer than she could remember. She blew again, more strongly this time. Ashes swirled and danced. She was about to admit defeat when she saw the tiniest hope.

A coal still glowed in the midst of the ashes that her stirring and blowing had dislodged! Burning brightly, it was the last ember of the fire that had been so carefully banked by her mother and grandmother. She touched the kindling in her hand to the ember and heaved a sigh of relief as smoke curled up from the straw and then a bright flame appeared. She added more kindling and then another handful before she began to add the larger twigs and sticks from the woodpile beside the fireplace. The flames danced brightly and grew stronger. She dared to place a log in the fire, hoping that the weight of the wood would not extinguish the delicate fire she was nursing back to life.

The log caught fire and the flames danced along one edge of the bark, which crackled and shriveled, sending sparks into the room. Nadezda sat back and wiped her hand across her sweaty face. Soot and ash streaked her face and stained her apron but she gave no thought of the scrubbing it would cost her to clean the apron or her dress. She was just glad the fire had not gone cold and there had still been an ember deep in the heart of the fireplace to revive.

She pushed herself to her feet. "Is it not enough that I have to deal with Fen'ka and Svetovit?" She shook her head. "I have to make more work for myself by letting the fire go out?" She chuckled, going to rouse her family to begin the day.

Eight days later, in the midafternoon, a boy came running down the lane with a message for Nadezda. She was called to Alena's house, he announced, as Alena had gone into labor and was soon to give birth. "Labor? Now?" No matter how prepared she was, no matter that she had been expecting this news, it still was a shock when one of Nadezda's friends went into labor after months of waiting.

Having come so close to letting the fire go out this morning, Nadezda was not about to let Vavrinec let the fire go out in her absence. She could be gone for several hours or even a day or more. This was Alena's first birth and it was anyone's guess how quickly it would go. Nevertheless, Nadezda took the time to bank the fire and prepare the coals to survive her absence from the house. Then she packed up Milos so that he could come with her and nurse when he was hungry. Ready, she stepped out of the house and closed the door behind her, locking it. She sent one of the neighbor boys to tell Vavrinec and Petr that she would be at Alena's and that a stew simmered in a pot on the edge of the hearth. A light snow was falling as she walked to join the midwife and other women who would keep Alena company during the birth.

It was shortly after midnight when Alena's daughter was born and began to cry, her lusty wails bringing a smile to Alena's face. Exhausted and drenched with sweat, Alena reached out to take her daughter, hold her close, and guide her tiny mouth to Alena's breast to nurse. Then all the women who had gathered sat around the room and took turns holding the baby, passing her from arm to arm. When Nadezda took her, she squirmed and smiled and looked straight into Nadezda's eyes. Godmother and goddaughter beamed at each other and the midwife clapped her hands. With great reluctance, Nadezda relinquished her new goddaughter and allowed the midwife to return the baby to Alena's arms.

One by one, the women found chairs or corners of the room where they could curl and nap. The time for the night's second sleep to begin had come some while before and dawn was less than two hours away.

Nadezda looked about her. Milos was restless, half-asleep and whimpering. There was no place in the house where she would be able comfortably nurse Milos or lay her own exhausted body down and rest briefly. She peered out the door. The snow had stopped hours ago and only a light dusting of snow remained on the cobblestones. The winter night was dark and cold—what thieves might be abroad? though the cold reduced the likelihood of thieves—but Nadezda resolved to face the dangers of the streets and return to her own home, where she could nurse Milos in her own chair and sleep in her own bed. Alena could spare her for a few hours.

Nadezda bundled up Milos and kissed the new mother and baby. Alena was half-asleep and murmured her own "g'night, Nadezda," without opening her eyes. The midwife let Nadezda out of the house and closed the door behind her.

Nadezda stepped quickly down the dark streets running along the wall that divided the Old and New Towns, the light snowfall crunching under her feet the only sound to be heard apart from Milos' even breathing, as the rhythm of her walking had rocked him to sleep. A gust of wind whistled between the chimneys. Very soon she was at her own door. Fumbling in the purse that hung from one wrist, she found the key and unlocked the door. She slipped inside and bolted the door shut. She turned and looked about the room.

Everything seemed in order. A dim, faint glow from the fireplace illuminated the room, casting shadows on the walls that danced with each gust of wind finding its way down the chimney or under the locked door. Petr lay on his cot, his back turned to the wall and his face nuzzled into his pillow. One arm was flung over his head. She could hear the even snoring of Vavrinec in their bed in the other room. She blessed God for giving her the family she had to care for.

Hanging her cloak on the peg near the door, Nadezda thought it best to not disturb Vavrinec, who would need a full night's sleep to work safely in the bakery later that day. She settled herself on a large pillow on the floor next to Petr's cot and, wrapped in a blanket, propped her elbow on the edge of the cot to support Milos while he nursed. Milos, who was stirring again now that the walk through the streets had ceased, whimpered but found Nadezda's breast and was soon happily sucking and half-asleep again. Nadezda, drowsy and warm, felt herself slipping into a much-needed sleep. Her head gradually slumped to one side.

Nadezda jerked up with a start. What had wakened her? Something was wrong. But what? Her eyes darted around the dark room, the shadows flickering in the faint light from the coals in the fireplace that penetrated their protective coverlet of ashes. Her eyes adjusted to the very dim and flickering light. A dark, ominous shadow loomed across the room, reaching a clawed hand toward Milos in her arms. She gasped and struggled to her feet. A scream formed in the back of her throat.

Suddenly a brighter light flared in the corner of the room near the icon, as the wick—which Nadezda had forgotten and Vavrinec had ignored—in the oil lamp, which had been burning so low as to be invisible in its votive glass, flared for an instant and then was gone. The last thread of the wick had burnt itself out. The prayer light hissed as the last ash of the wick sank into the oil.

The fleeting, momentary blaze of the oil lamp startled the shadow across the room. It turned its head toward the icon and an angry, hateful hiss escaped its lips. Evidently the shadow had not realized the icon was there. The scream at the back of Nadezda's throat burst from her lips and the shadow fled the house, slipping under the door and out onto the street.

Vavrinec stumbled out of the bed and into the principal room of their little house. Petr sat bolt upright, rubbing the sleep from his eyes, looking about frantically. Milos burst into tears. Nadezda pushed herself and Milos up from the floor and into Vavrinec's arms and the four of them huddled together on a bench at the table. Vavrinec, unsure of what had happened, attempted to calm and reassure his family. Nadezda closed her eyes tightly, trying to shut out the memory of the shadow that had been reaching for Milos. She shook her head and pressed Milos tightly to her. There were no words adequate to describe what she had seen or the terror that had pierced her in the dark. She trembled in Vavrinec's arms until dawn, fear of the shadow they had so narrowly escaped slow to subside.

It was only in the full light of day, with the fire stirred and also burning brightly, that Nadezda was able to describe to Vavrinec what she had seen coming towards Milos in her arms. "I am certain it meant to take him from me," she insisted. He listened and then sat in silence after she had finished.

"Are you certain it was not simply a nightmare that woke you?" he asked.

"No, that shadow was no nightmare," she insisted. "It was

139

a shadow with weight and substance and will. That shadow was as real as you or I."

Vavrinec sat and thought a moment.

"I brought this on us, did I not?" he said quietly. "Curse their wives and children, Fen'ka said. 'Curse their wives and children' and I was there in the Old Town Square. Because of me, you and Milos have been caught up in this wicked madness and I nearly lost you." He seemed on the verge of sobbing. He bent over, cradling his forehead in his open palms.

"Nearly, yes. But not yet." Nadezda reached over to take both his hands and he raised his head. She looked into his eyes. "We are a part of this, Vavrinec, whether we will it or no. I suspect we would be caught up in it whether you had been in the Old Town Square or not. I must discover what that shadow was and devise a way to combat it, drive it from our home and leave us in peace."

Vavrinec bit his lower lip and slowly nodded in agreement. "If doing that unlocks the curse and saves Prague as a result, so be it," he added wryly.

Nadezda made her way back to Alena's home later that morning. The midwife was still there, as were most of the other women present at the birth. Many others had begun to visit and the house was a hub of female activity. Alena's husband had gone to a neighbor's once the midwife had arrived and would be invited to see his daughter that afternoon.

Nadezda set Milos down with another of the women, who had a son about the same age. The two boys crowed with delight and sat on her lap as she leaned back against the foot of Alena's bed. Alena was dozing against the pillows with her baby nestled in her arms. Nadezda approached the midwife, who was sitting at the table in the other room. She sipped from a steaming cup of an herbal tea, sitting apart from the crowd against and atop the bed with Alena and the baby.

"Well met, Nadezda," the midwife Ryba greeted her. "I see you made it home in the dark and got the sleep you wanted." She leaned towards Nadezda's ear to whisper conspiratorially, "I warrant that you were the only one to get much sleep after the birth, except Alena herself! Would that I had been able to join you!" The two women laughed and exchanged kisses on their cheeks. Nadezda sat on the bench across from Ryba.

Ryba was an older woman, much experienced in childbirthing and the health of women and children. She was the one they turned to in this district of the Old Town when they first suspected they might be pregnant or were approaching childbirth or were having difficulty afterwards. She knew the herbs that could ease a woman's labor pains and she knew which could make birthing more difficult. She knew how to properly care for newborns and how to safely dispose of the afterbirth so it could not be used for any nefarious purposes. She knew how to read the signs in the stars that might portend the fate of a child she delivered and she could interpret the meaning of the occasional birth of monsters, such as children with multiple limbs and contorted torsos or disfigured faces.

Her face was deeply lined and careworn from worry for her charges but kind and generous. Colorful bandanas always covered her silver hair—she wore a fresh golden yellow one today that she must have brought to use after mopping her brow with the red one she had worn yesterday. She held the cup in both hands and allowed the steam to rise and caress her face.

"Would you like tea, Nadezda?" she asked, indicating the mugs on the shelf near the stove and the still-steaming kettle

141

on the wood-burning stove.

"No, thank you, Ryba." Nadezda was unsure how to begin this conversation and so she decided to simply begin. "Ryba, after I returned home last night, Milos was attacked."

Ryba's eyes shot through the door into the other room, where she could see the boy playing. "Attacked? By whom?"

"We were home and I was half-asleep. He had been nursing and was asleep, half in my arms and half on Petr's cot." Ryba nodded to indicate she understood the arrangement, her eyes never leaving Milos in the other room. Nadezda continued.

"Something woke me. I still do not know what. But something woke me and I sat up with a fright. It was dark and difficult to see, but then the oil lamp in front of my image of the Mother of God flared up as the wick gave out, and I saw it." Nadezda licked her dry lips.

Ryba turned her attention to Nadezda. "Saw what?"

"I do not know for certain, Ryba. It was a shadow. A shadow with heft and substance. It reached a clawed hand towards Milos but was startled by the flaring wick. It hissed and spat at the icon as I screamed. It fled, whether because of the icon or the sound of my screaming, I do not know. But I fear—no, I am certain—that it will return." Nadezda turned to look at Milos and the other young children in the room. She could see the top of Alena's new baby's head. She turned back to Ryba. "What could it have been, Ryba? What shadow would stalk a baby such as Milos?"

Ryba gazed into her cup. She sighed and looked up into Nadezda's eyes. "Have you seen a shadow such as this in your home before, Nadezda?" she asked quietly.

Nadezda shook her head. "Never. Not in my worst nightmare."

"Then we have time." Ryba looked back into her cup and

took another sip of tea. Nadezda waited for Ryba to continue and the midwife resumed her words even as her eyes never left the steaming contents of her mug.

"There are shadows that stalk about, hoping to scare children or seduce their fathers. Some even attempt to seduce the mothers. It might have been a succubus or an incubus wandering in the night. But it is rare that they ever assume such a shape to attack a child. Are you certain the shadow was reaching for Milos and not you, my dear?"

"I am certain, Ryba." Nadezda could see the shadow's claw reaching for little Milos even now in her mind's eye.

"Then the only other shadow it could have been was Lilith," Ryba announced. She met Nadezda's eyes. "I am certain that your grandmother must have told you of Lilith, my dear. Do you recall anything she might have said?"

Lilith! The she-demon's name was familiar, but Nadezda shook her head. She knew the name and that the creature sought to kill children, but more than that she could not recall. "Who is she, Ryba?"

"Lilith was the first wife of our father Adam." Ryba told the tale as if she had told it many times before, the words falling from her tongue in measured rhythms like poetry or song. "She was lovely, more lovely than the rising sun and more graceful than the moon and stars. She had long, flowing hair and eyes as deep as wells. She was given to our father Adam by the Lord our God as a helpmeet, to be his wife in Paradise, for it was not good for Adam to dwell alone in the Garden. This was before Eve was created. Lilith was formed from the earth, like Adam, and Eve was only formed later, from his rib."

Nadezda nodded. Ryba's tale continued.

"Lilith, made from the same soil as our father Adam,

143

thought herself the equal of her husband. She refused to walk behind him or to serve him in any way. She would not cook unless he scrubbed the pot after they ate. She even demanded that in knowing her husband she have as much an opportunity to sit astride him as he to mount her." Ryba, her hands shaking gently, lifted her mug to her lips and touched the steaming liquid to her lips before continuing.

"As much as he desired her, as much as he yearned for her, he was also furious with her. Adam fought with her and argued, refusing to scrub the pot or to walk beside her or to lie beneath her. In her rage, Lilith fled the Garden and refused to have anything more to do with him."

The noises of the children growing restless and hungry in the other room intruded and interrupted Ryba's recounting of Lilith's history. Nadezda fetched Milos, who happily sat on her lap and nursed, his gaze switching from his mother to Ryba and back again. As he settled down, Ryba resumed her tale.

"Our father Adam complained to the Lord our God that the woman he had been given for company and to be a helpmeet was a disturbance to the Garden. Her insistence on absolute equality between them was driving our father Adam mad. Adam insisted that God rebuke Lilith and provide another, more docile helpmeet for him. So the Lord God took a rib from our father Adam and fashioned Eve from it, giving her to be Adam's wife and helpmeet. Adam warned her that if she were disobedient, she could be driven away just as Lilith had been, but he lied to make Eve think Lilith had been driven out rather than that Lilith had rejected Adam."

Ryba sighed and sipped her tea again. Nadezda adjusted Milos in the crook of her elbow. Ryba took a deep breath and went on.

"The Lord God sent three angels to chastise Lilith for her

144

disobedience, but she hid from them in the wilderness outside Eden. Her hair grew longer and more tangled and matted. Her nails grew long and sharp, as did her teeth. What had been beauty became hideous and ugly, though she retained her power to assume her former beauty for a few moments, should she find it necessary. Furious at Adam and jealous of Eve, hunted by the angels and rejected by God who had formed her, she came to hate all of God's creation, but especially the children of Adam and Eve, as she considered that rightly those ought to have been her children, had Adam not been so stubborn and insisted on her subservience." Ryba shuddered.

"Lilith began to attack the children of Adam and Eve and then, in the next generation, to attack and kill their grandchildren and great-grandchildren. Having left Paradise of her own accord, rather than being driven out in punishment as Adam and our mother Eve were driven out later, Lilith retained her immortality and the marvelous powers that were common to the inhabitants of Paradise, such as the ability to come and go as she pleased. Lurking in the desert and the wilderness that became the haunts of devils and fallen angels, she also learned the dark and magical arts, which she taught, in turn, to the witches of the Earth."

Nadezda held Milos close to her. She felt a sharp chill in the air, as if Lilith or one of the fallen angels were passing by as Ryba told her tale. Milos fell asleep, and his lips fell away from his mother's breast and his head rolled back. The hint of a smile played at the corner of his mouth as some happy memory replayed itself in his dreams.

Ryba studied Milos' face and then looked into Nadezda's eyes. "It is said that Lilith hates all the children of the human race and will stop at nothing to slay those she can. But her hatred is especially strong for the children of the Jews, and it

145

is their children that she attacks and kills most often."

"Why is that?" Nadezda could see why Lilith would hate the children of Adam and Eve, but why direct her rage especially against their descendants keeping the laws of Moses?

Ryba shrugged. "Some say it is because King Solomon, the king of Israel whose wisdom knew no bounds and who was able to command demons to do his will, was the first to learn the secrets to fending off the attacks of Lilith. Some say it is because the prophets, inspired by God, railed against her as one abandoned by the Lord and given over to her own desolation. Others say it because the Jews in Babylon practiced the magic bequeathed to them by Solomon and perfected the defenses that keep her at bay and frustrate her attacks, so that she desires all the more to attack their children and prove them powerless over her."

Nadezda looked into the other room, where Alena now sat up in her bed with her new daughter. Nadezda could see the joy on Alena's face and wished, more than anything, to spare her friend and new goddaughter from the visitation of the shadow she had seen last night. She turned back to Ryba.

Ryba had seen her watching Alena and the baby and nodded her agreement. "If Lilith has come to attack both the Jewish and the Christian children of Prague, it is up to us to stop her. You are lucky, my child, that your oil lamp flared up when it did and startled her. The icons are known to protect the children committed to their care, but the presence of one was clearly not enough to keep her from entering your house or drawing near to Milos. She must have been surprised and fled before she could encounter any other defensive measures.

"But she will attack again, Nadezda. Once Lilith sets her eyes on a child, she returns again and again until she kills the babe or is driven from the cradle once and for all and knows she can never return." Ryba pointed towards the door. "You must go from here and speak to the rabbi in the Jewish Quarter. The Jews know best how to protect a child Lilith has taken aim at. It is Jewish magic that is best able to drive Lilith from your house and keep her from Milos. Furthermore, the rabbis of Prague are said to be the most expert at the Kabbalah and other hidden lore. Did you know, Nadezda, that the synagogue here is said to have been built with stones brought from the ruins of the Temple in Jerusalem, which their rabbis commanded the angels to carry?" Ryba was clearly very impressed with the supernatural abilities and talents of the Prague rabbis. "If you drive Lilith away from Milos, it may be that she will depart from Prague. If not, if you keep Lilith from Milos but are unable to drive her from Prague, you will be able to teach other women here how to protect their babes."

Nadezda understood what she had to do. The residents of the Jewish Quarter had known terrible persecution, but much less here in Bohemia than in other regions of Christian Europe. It was possible that the rabbi would willingly share with her the secret ways of driving away Lilith. If Lilith had come to Prague to attack Christian children—had Fen'ka's curse called her here?—then it would not be long before she turned her attention to her more usual victims, the children of the Jewish Quarter. "Surely the rabbi will agree that is in the best interests of us all to drive Lilith from our city before she can cause the havoc that always travel in her wake, will he not?" Nadezda anxiously asked Ryba.

"I hope so, Nadezda," the midwife agreed. "I know the midwife in the Jewish Quarter. If need be, tell him that Ryba, the friend of Batsheva the midwife, sent you. Leave Milos here with us for the moment. Some of the others can nurse him if he wakes before you return. But go. Now. Speak to the rabbi and learn the magic that he knows will protect all the children of Prague from Lilith."

Nadezda slipped her sleeping son into Ryba's waiting arms. She gathered her cloak about her and stepped into the street. It had begun to snow again. Delicate snowflakes drifted down lazily from the iron-gray skies. She made her way to the bustling marketplace of the Old Town Square and then crossed it, weaving her way between the stalls and the crowds that thronged the square. She arrived on the northern side of the square and looked about her.

Although there was no wall to block access from the Old Town to the Jewish Quarter, she had never crossed into the territory on the other side of this invisible line. She had never had any real reason to cross over to the Jewish Quarter. By law the property of the king, the Jewish Quarter was protected by royal authority and an attack on it was considered an attack on the king himself. The Jews who resided there were also protected by royal law and many Jewish merchants and bankers were active members of the Old Town market and the financial world centered on it. It was a crowded, even overcrowded place, as few of the Jews had ever accepted the king's offer of free land in the recently established New Town.

Now she had reason to enter the Jewish Quarter and speak with the rabbi himself. "Will he be willing to speak with a Christian woman like me?" she wondered as she pulled her cloak tight and stepped onto the street that led to the synagogue a few blocks away. The snow began to fall more heavily.

Walking down the street toward the synagogue, she made her way through the crowd that bustled here as well. It was slow going, not because anyone hindered her because she was a stranger, but because the people were all headed in the direction she was coming from. A few small children, noticing a woman they did not know, stopped and stared or pointed and said something to their mothers. But she felt no anger, no animosity toward her. In a few steps, she found herself standing before the synagogue.

It was a squat stone building with a pitched roof. It was surrounded by the homes of the leading members of the Jewish community, and she could see the walls that surrounded the ancient cemetery down another narrow lane. Flagstones covered the small plaza surrounding the synagogue. A few men were standing together and talking near the door of the synagogue. She walked up to them.

"Excuse me, sirs," she began. Their conversation halted immediately. She looked from one face to another. Impenetrable silence greeted her.

"Pardon me, gentlemen," she began again. Again silence. This was a very different greeting than the one she had hoped for, making her way along the crowded street from the Old Town Square. Finally, one of the men quietly asked her, "Who are you? Whom do you seek?"

"Please forgive my ignorance and my interruption." Nadezda did not want her mission to fail when it had hardly begun. "I am Nadezda, a woman of the Old Town, sent by Ryba the midwife, a friend of Batsheva the midwife here." The men murmured together at the mention of a name they recognized. "I am sent to speak with your rabbi." Glances of disapproval shot from one man to the next. "Lilith has been seen in the Old Town and we need his knowledge of the ways to protect our children from her attacks."

"Lilith? Are you sure? Where was she seen? Was it your child who was attacked?" The men instantly became a cluster of concerned fathers. Their questions buzzed in the air and the man nearest her clutched her arm wrapped in her cloak. "Tell us about the child Lilith attacked. Does the baby live?"

A passer-by overheard the question. "Lilith?" The young man, a newlywed, blanched at the she-devil's name. "Here? In Prague? When was she seen?" Faster than the wind, the news rippled through the people coming and going on the streets and lanes of the Jewish Quarter. Lilith had been sighted and a woman from the Old Town had come to ask the assistance of the rabbi to drive the ancient witch away. People pushed and shoved, some eager to spread the news as they would any gossip and others racing home to slam the shutters and the doors shut and prepare to defend their children.

"The rabbi was here at the synagogue just a short while ago," one of the men told her. "But he said he was going home for a short time. If he is still at home, I do not know. But even if he is not at home, they will know where he has gone and can send for him."

"Come with me." Another man pointed down the lane. "He lives there. Let me take you to him."

Nadezda struggled to keep up with him as the panic-stricken crowd swirled around them. Children in their mothers' arms, hearing the name of the fearful witch, began to cry. Older siblings tried to cover their ears and the ears of their younger brothers and sisters so they would not hear the dreadful name. Mothers hastened to calm their children even as they felt fear rising within their own breasts. Fathers heard the name and hurried home even though it was midday, some feeling powerless to stop their ancient enemy but all wanting to be with their families.

Finally her escort delivered her to the rabbi's door. He whispered to the maid answering the door who Nadezda was and what she had come for and the maid nodded, her face anxious. She pulled Nadezda into the small parlor right inside the door.

Inside, the door shut, Nadezda could barely hear the commotion on the street. The maid indicated that she could sit on a small stool as she waited. "I will tell Rabbi Isaac why you have come," she promised. "Wait here just a moment. This is terrible! Lilith seen in the Old Town?" The maid stepped out another door and Nadezda could hear her walking down a hall, clucking in distress as she went.

The maid returned quickly, popping her head into the parlor. "Step this way, *balibt*, and come with me. Rabbi Isaac will see you at once." She pulled the door open and held it for Nadezda to step through and then led her down the hall into Rabbi Isaac's study. Knocking on the door to the study, she opened it and pointed the way for Nadezda to enter.

Nadezda stepped into a small and cluttered wonderland of books and scrolls and parchments, inkwells and quills and straps of leather, small knives and mortars and pestles. Many things were covered with dust. Tables and bookcases overflowed and a reading desk, with a dripping candle atop it for light, stood in one corner. The rabbi was perched on a tall stool on the other side of the reading desk and peered at Nadezda as she entered.

His white beard flowed down his chest, obscuring his old and torn vest. An embroidered cap sat atop his head, held in place by ears poking through his whiskers, but he seemed bald beneath the cap. A pair of lenses set astride the end of his nose, round pieces of quartz held together by a thin metal frame such as Nadezda had seen once on the nose of one of the Italian artists who labored in the castle. His eyes were kind and the lenses, which magnified his pupils, also revealed the depth of the wrinkles that seeped into his face from the corners of his eyes. He smiled and beckoned for Nadezda to approach.

As Nadezda stepped forward, the maid stepped into the

151

cramped study and took a seat on a low stool tucked into a corner of the room, picking up the stack of parchments that had been placed there and holding them on her lap.

"You will, please, excuse the presence of my maid," the rabbi apologized to Nadezda, indicating the older woman with his open palm. "You must understand that I am forbidden by our laws to be left alone with a woman other than my wife."

Nadezda nodded. "Of course, your honor." She bobbed a small curtsey, unsure of the proper gesture of respect to such a learned elder. He climbed down from his stool and approached her.

"My name is Isaac, my dear, the Rabbi Isaac of Prague, and I understand that you have come in distress and need." He folded his hands across his ample girth, careful not to touch her.

"Yes, Rabbi Isaac. My infant son is in danger. I woke suddenly last night to see a shadow reaching out to seize him from my arms, a shadow I have come to learn was Lilith." She paused and looked around the volumes and tomes that bespoke a lifetime of study. She resumed her request. "I am told that you know the secrets to driving Lilith away and I hope to save not only my son but to drive her from Prague."

"Drive her from Prague altogether?" the rabbi repeated. "That would be quite a feat, my child. In my experience, the best one can hope for is to drive Lilith from your home so that she never comes near your son again. But to drive her from Prague? I am afraid that exceeds even my quite considerable skill." He gestured towards all the manuscripts that surrounded them. "But let us see what we can accomplish together."

He stepped around her and peered over his spectacles at a series of books and scrolls, some of which he took down from their shelves, blowing layers of dust from some before examining their contents. The dust sent the maid into a fit of coughing as she shook her head with disapproval. Nadezda guessed that the rabbi refused to ever allow her to tidy the study or dust in here when he was not occupied with his reading or prayers. Nadezda covered her mouth and coughed too. The rabbi laughed and turned towards her again.

"Please, my dear. Sit down. Forgive my lack of manners. What was I thinking?" He gestured towards another tall stool near his reading desk with the scroll he held unfurled in his hands. Nadezda carefully navigated her way through the stacks of books and papers that leaned into what narrow aisles left to walk about the study, afraid she might knock them over and introduce even more chaos. She clambered atop the stool behind the rabbi's and waited as he continued his examination of texts. Selecting one thick tome at last, its leather binding coming loose from the dry, yellow pages, and carefully balancing the open book on both palms, he made his way back to the reading desk.

He settled the book on the upper portion of the desk and perched again on his stool before pulling a small sheet of vellum from the open drawer above his lap. Taking a small knife, he sliced away a strip from one side of the vellum, leaving a ribbon of vellum that he kept after setting aside the larger remnant for some other purpose later. He placed the ribbon lengthwise before him and pointed one stubby finger at a diagram in the book. Nadezda peered over his shoulder.

"This, my child, is the amulet considered most effective in driving Lilith away from a child she has in mind to slay. Do you see this line of text that runs along the upper edge of the amulet? It is in Hebrew, our ancestral tongue and the language that our Torah was given in." Nadezda was unsure of what text he was referring to but listened attentively. He translated the text. "It is a verse from the Psalms of David the King: 'He shall give His angels charge over thee, to keep thee in all thy ways.' Below, along the lower edge of the amulet, runs another text. Do you see?" He shifted his position on the stool slightly so Nadezda could see the diagram better. She recognized that this line was also in the Hebrew letters. The rabbi traced the words with his fingers as he translated them. "These are the names of the three angels given charge by God to protect mankind from the assaults of Lilith. Here reads, 'Senoi.' This reads, 'Sansenoi.' This last reads, 'Samangeloph.' These are the angels who have pursued Lilith since she first fled Paradise and hid herself in the wilderness outside Eden."

Nadezda recognized the story of the three angels that Ryba had told her at Alena's home. "What are these three figures, Rabbi Isaac?" She reached around his shoulder and pointed to three odd caricatures that stood between the two lines of text. Small words, also in the Hebrew letters, were written next to each stick figure that resembled nothing so much as three oddly shaped birds. "What are these names written beside them?"

The rabbi looked at her over his shoulder and smiled, his eyes twinkling behind his lenses. "Your eyesight is very good, my child. Alas, better than mine these days if I did not have these lenses sent to me from my fellow countrymen in the ghetto of Modena. You are clever and inquisitive. These are good qualities to have, especially if you seek to discover a way to fend off Lilith's vengeance." He turned back to the book and pointed to each figure in turn. "This is the emblem of Adam and this is the emblem of his wife Eve. These are the names of our first parents, indicating which emblem is whose." He pointed to the third, which stood somewhat apart from the other two. "Whose might you guess is this third emblem?" He looked over his shoulder again towards Nadezda.

"Lilith?" she ventured.

154

"Correct!" the rabbi clapped his hands. "It is Lilith herself poised to attack Adam and Eve, but this line of text,"—which he indicated with his finger, and was also in Hebrew, running in three vertical rows between the sigils of Lilith and those of Adam and Eve—"is what stands between them. These are two of the ten attributes of the Almighty—blessed be He!—which we call *sephirot*. These are the *sephirot* called 'holiness' and 'deliverance.' This third row of letters spell out '*Ehyeh*,' which is the name the Lord gave to Moses at the Bush-That-Burned to report to the Children of Israel: 'I Am that I Am.' Do you understand?"

Nadezda nodded. She was fascinated by the rabbi's explanation of the diagram. She considered whether she had any further questions about the talisman as the rabbi picked up one of his quills and dipped it into the inkwell resting near the still-burning candle atop the reading desk. Wax dribbled down the side of the candle and pooled along the binding of the book they were inspecting.

"Now, my child, I must copy this amulet carefully onto this ribbon of vellum which I have prepared." He touched the tip of the quill to the yellow-brown ribbon on the desk. Nadezda heard the scratching of the pen against the translucent animal skin. Slowly, with the pen tip gracefully flowing along under the direction of the rabbi's fingertips, the diagram from the book reappeared on the vellum. He dipped the quill into the inkwell time after time, carefully shaking any excess drops back into the well to avoid smudges and blots on the amulet he was creating for Nadezda, who hardly dared to draw a breath as she watched the careful work play out before her eyes.

"Any mistake and I must begin again," the rabbi spoke as he carefully looked from the original in the book to his copy and back again. He glanced at Nadezda. "We would not want to waste either our time or our effort in making an error so close to the conclusion of our work, would we, my dear?" Nadezda swallowed carefully and nodded her agreement.

Rabbi Isaac turned his attention back to the amulet and added the final flourishes to the small Hebrew letters identifying the figures of Adam and Eve. It was a breathtakingly beautiful piece of work. He waited momentarily for the last dot of ink to dry. Then he picked it up and blew on it gently, both to dry the ink and to impart, as he explained, "the breath of life to the amulet so that it might achieve all that we hope it will."

Reaching back into the open shelf below the desk, he brought out a small spike and mallet. Placing the spike carefully towards one end of the amulet but obscuring none of the writing, he tapped it with the hammer and punched a small hole at the left end of the new amulet. Replacing the spike and mallet on the shelf below, he then produced a silver locket. He rolled up the amulet and placed it within the locket, which he then carefully placed in Nadezda's open palms.

"My child, take the locket home to your child. Remove the amulet from its case this night and tie a ribbon through the hole that I punched. Then hang the protective image around your baby's neck. The child should wear this each night as he sleeps. When Lilith returns, which she will, she will be driven off by the power of God and of the angels Senoi, Sansenoi, and Samangeloph, which is contained in the amulet I have made for you. If you are wakened by her attack, you may also call out for the angels and they will come to save you in your distress." He smiled and Nadezda felt safe. Safe for the first time since she had begun to worry about Fen'ka and the curse. She placed the locket in her small purse and withdrew a coin, hoping it was enough to offer the rabbi for his work that morning.

"No, no!" the rabbi laughed, throwing up his palms as if to fend Nadezda off. "The making of the amulet is a *mitzvah*, my child, a *brokhe* that I am happy to give to you." She stared, not understanding the words he used. He laughed again. "It is my gift to you, my dear." She replaced the coin in her purse, embarrassed to have insulted the rabbi, but he laughed again, seeing her confusion.

"Do not fret, my child. It is enough that you bring us word that Lilith has come to Prague. You give us time and opportunity to arm ourselves. There will be many mothers coming for such an amulet, I fear, but they will be hoping only to keep Lilith from their own doors and not seeking to drive her from Prague altogether." He slid from the stool and stood.

"I have given you the most powerful of the variations of this protective amulet, my dear. Use it well and never let your baby sleep without it. Bring me news of your encounter with that ancient *makhesheyfe*."

Nadezda stood as well. "Thank you, rabbi! Thank you for saving my Milos and for—I hope!—helping me to drive the she-devil from Prague forever. Thank you!" She stepped toward the door leading from the study. The maid, who had been listening to the exchange between the rabbi and his visitor with concern, stood and opened the door to lead Nadezda out.

"You are always welcome here, my dear!" Rabbi Isaac called after her. "Both in our town and in my study!"

Nadezda was careful to follow the rabbi's instructions as she prepared Milos for his night's sleep. She had explained to both Ryba and Vavrinec that she had been given an amulet by the rabbi, which he had promised would protect the baby as he slept. They were both relieved to know that her mission to the

Jewish Quarter had been a success. She took a ribbon and slid it through the small hole punched through one end of the vellum and then tied the ribbon very loosely around the baby's neck. Determined to take no unnecessary risks, she also trimmed the new wick of the oil lamp that hung before the icon and lit it from the hearth with a straw. Then she and Vavrinec retired for the night, little Milos sleeping between them.

Aside from half-waking to nurse, the night passed without incident. As did the next, and the one after that. Another week passed and there was no sighting of Lilith, not in Nadezda's house or in any of the other houses of the Old Town or even in the Jewish Quarter. Nadezda listened carefully to the gossip and news that circulated in the markets of Prague and even visited the rabbi again, but there was no word that Lilith had been seen by anyone. As the days passed without another attack from Lilith against her family, Nadezda considered what she might do when Lilith did finally reappear.

"Is she biding her time? What is she waiting for?" Nadezda asked the rabbi.

"It is hard to say." He took the spectacles from his nose and tapped them gently against his forehead. "She is a vengeful, determined *makhesheyfe* who never abandons her quest to torment and slay the children of mankind. Could she know that you possess the amulet? I think not, unless she came in the night without disturbing you. But that is unlikely. Her shock and dismay at discovering the amulet would have certainly awakened you."

"Perhaps she thinks I will forget and become slovenly in my defenses against her," offered Nadezda. She dared to discuss an idea with Rabbi Isaac. "When she does come again, I would like to speak with her."

"Speak with her?" exclaimed the rabbi in shock. "Why would you, such a good woman, want to speak with such a monster as Lilith?"

"Because I think she might know something of the curse which Fen'ka called on the town last September. I think that Lilith was brought to Prague by Fen'ka's curse and came to my house first because my husband was in the Old Town Square at the time of the burning."

"Perhaps." The rabbi tapped the spectacles against his head again, staring into space as he considered the possibility. "I remember the witch Fen'ka burning in the Old Town Square. I heard it was going on but wanted nothing to do with such business. However, I know that many of the Jews of Prague were there, attracted by the mob, the flames, the excitement. But the priest who incited the burning could just have easily turned to the Jews and incited the crowd to hurl burning faggots into the Jewish Quarter. But could the curse of Fen'ka have called Lilith to the city?"

He continued to consider the possibility. Nadezda noticed that the maid, detained from her housework to remain in the study with the rabbi and his guest, fidgeted.

"It is possible," he finally conceded. "Fen'ka's curse might well have been heard by Lilith and she saw it as an opportunity to strike back against the city from which she has long been absent. Or the curse was the key that opened the door to Lilith, seizing her here whether she willed it or no. But even if that is the case, Nadezda, why do you wish to speak with her? It is a dangerous game to play."

"Yes, I realize the danger." Nadezda agreed with the rabbi, which was why she had not discussed her idea with Vavrinec or Ryba. "But if Fen'ka's curse summoned Lilith, then perhaps Lilith understands the inner workings of the curse and can explain what the key of the curse might be. If she divulges that secret to me, then it is possible that the curse can be rewritten—and Prague be spared any further suffering, not only at the hands of Lilith but from the words of Fen'ka."

The rabbi pursed his lips. "I said you were clever and inquisitive, Nadezda, that day you first came into my study to ask for an amulet. If what you say is true and you are able to discover the secret key to Fen'ka's curse and rewrite it to save the city, then you will have done us all a great boon, and be lauded for many years to come."

Nadezda felt herself blush.

"But it is a dangerous game," the rabbi reiterated. "Be cautious, Nadezda. Lilith's treachery can never be overestimated."

Resolved to attempt to speak with Lilith, Nadezda considered what other magical weapons she might need. "What would grandmother have recommended that I use to protect myself against such a one as Lilith?" She dug through her memories of her grandmother and the things she said about herbs, images, the magical arts, all the old ways. She was surprised to discover that she could recall few of the old ways in enough detail to be of assistance. Half-forgotten phrases and snatches of herbal lore came to her. Nothing that promised success.

Then she remembered! They were no secret in Prague society even now. The feast of the presentation of Christ in the Temple when he was forty days old would be celebrated throughout Christendom tomorrow, on February the second, the fortieth day since Christmas. Tomorrow, the 'Candlemas' feast would celebrate the elder Simeon's declaration that the infant Christ had come as "a light of revelation to the Gentiles and to be the glory of his people, Israel." Candles would be blessed in all the churches of Europe with prayer and holy water and incense. Everyone knew blessed candles could banish illness, drive away darkness both physical and spiritual, light the way of the dead to find their way to their eternal rewards, and dissolve a witch's most potent spells.

"Surely a Candlemas candle will be protect me from Lilith! She will be unable to bear one if I light it after she has entered the house. She will be trapped between the amulet and the burning candle and—if I call on the angels which the rabbi promised would always hasten to protect anyone who calls on them—she will have no choice but to tell me all she knows of Fen'ka's curse and then promise to leave Prague in peace." Nadezda spoke to herself, formulating her plans as she scrubbed Milos' diapers clean in the yard behind her house. Pleased with herself, she resolved to attend the celebratory Mass at her local parish and to bring a few coins to obtain one of the more expensive, high-quality candles to be blessed.

Outside the parish church the next morning were a dozen merchants hawking their wares: numberless candles in a variety of heights and diameters and qualities of wax or tallow. Some were very refined. Some much less so. Some were so cheap as to begin melting in your hand. Some were brilliant white while others were a dirty yellow or a fair cream color. Some had thick wicks that would burn quickly or erratically while the wicks of others were designed to burn slowly and evenly. This being one of the most popular feast days of the year, the entire neighborhood was converging on the church, all looking to get the best candle they could afford to take into the church for the blessing that would render each a Candlemas candle.

Nadezda and Vavrinec, with Petr and Milos, found the

161

merchant with the best quality candle wares in the plaza outside St. Martin's Church that morning. Bargaining briefly, but not obtaining as good a price as Vavrinec had hoped for, Nadezda purchased a candle nearly as long as her forearm and of a high-quality, nearly-white wax. It was clearly a candle that would burn smoothly and lazily should it ever be lit. Vavrinec hoped it would never need to be. Nadezda hoped it would be soon.

"Hurry!" a man cried from the steps of the church. "It is beginning! Hurry, or you will miss the blessing!" Was he chiding his slow-moving wife or was he announcing to the crowd that they had best conclude the purchase of their candles and enter the sanctuary? People pushed and shoved, anxious not to miss this year's blessing. Who would want to face the year without a Candlemas candle and risk whatever wraith might come stalking in the night?

Entering the dim church, Vavrinec and Nadezda found clouds of incense already hanging in the air and the choir singing the final syllables of the opening antiphons of the Mass.

...lumen as revelationem gentium: et gloriam plebis tuae Israel.

...a light of revelation for the Gentiles and the glory of thy people Israel.

A priest, standing in the midst of several clergy at the altar, all wearing sumptuous vestments of gold and white brocade, intoned the prayers. The congregation held their candles aloft so as to catch the echoes of the priest's voice, if possible, in the wax and tallow.

"Let the Shadow of Death Stalk Them in the Night!"

Domine sancte, Pater omnipotens, aeterne Deus... ad perfectionem cerei venire fecisti... ut has candelas ad usus hominum, et sanitatem corporum et animarum... et per preces omnium sanctorum tuorum, benedicere, et sanctificare digneris...

Domine... effunde benedictionem tuam super hos cereos, et sanctifica eos lumine gratiae tuae, et cobcede propitius; ut, sicut haec luminaria igne visibili accensa nocturnas depellunt tenebras; ita corda nostra invisibili igne... omnium vitiorum caecitate careant... quatenus post hujus saeculi caliginosa discrimina, ad lucem indeficientem pervenire mereamur...

Lord... pour out thy blessing on these candles and sanctify them with the light of thy grace; mercifully grant that as these lights, enkindled with visible fire, dispel the darkness of the night, so our hearts, illuminated by invisible fire... may be free from all blindness of vice... so that after the dark dangers of this world, we may deserve to attain everlasting light...

Holy Lord, Father omnipotent, everlasting God, who... has brought the labor of bees to perfection in these candles of wax... we humbly entreat thee to bless and sanctify these candles for the use of mankind and the health of body and soul...

He lifted his hand several times, tracing the sign of the cross in the air over the hundreds of candles held aloft. As the final "amen" still thundered in the air, he took the branches of willow held by the deacon and dipped them into the silver gilt bucket of holy water. He splashed the holy water onto the candles and the upturned faces of the congregation, the children giggling with delight at this, one of their favorite aspects of the celebration. Finally, he took the heavy censer, great spoonfuls of frankincense deposited on the red-hot coals within, and censed the congregation thrice. Clouds of fragrant smoke drifted lazily about and settled in the hair, the garments, the nostrils of those assembled. What the smoke glanced across was sanctified and each candle was held out to any aromatic trail that wafted by.

The choir began the antiphons that would accompany the clergy as they processed around the church, continuing to sprinkle and cense the candles so that none of them might escape the benediction of God and prove a failure in the year to come.

Adorna thalamum tuum, Sion...

Adorn thy bridal chamber, Sion...

Smiling and laughing or alternately serious and dignified, the entire congregation held out their candles for the tangible reinforcement of the priest's prayer when the holy water came splashing or the incense billowed beside them. Candlemas, with Ash Wednesday and Palm Sunday, always brought more crowds to the churches than the buildings could contain. As the Mass of the feast itself began, people already drifted out. They had obtained the candles they had come for that would drive away the evil and wickedness from their homes for the coming year.

Recalling the events of that September afternoon when Svetovit had seemed to listen to his handmaiden's cries as she burned to death in the Old Town Square, and all the strange and inexplicable events that had played out in Prague since

164

that afternoon, more than one family hoped that this year's Candlemas candle would keep them safe from whatever terror unleashed by Fen'ka was still lurking in the shadows.

That night, Nadezda kept the Candlemas candle close beside her. Protesting that her back ached and she was more comfortable sitting up than lying in bed, she arranged Milos—with the amulet, as he had worn to bed every night—to sleep on Petr's cot while Petr took her place beside Vavrinec in the great bed in the other room. She settled on a bench near the door. The fire on the hearth was banked, the only light in the room the flickering oil lamp before the icon. In order to light the Candlemas candle quickly, should she need to, Nadezda set a handful of coals from the hearth in a ceramic bowl on the table. Covered with a dusting of silver ash, the coals were invisible in the dark room but would set the wick of the candle aflame should Nadezda touch it to them.

"Will she come tonight?" This was the eighth night since Nadezda had caught a glimpse of Lilith in the brief light of the oil lamp. Nadezda settled back against the wall and wrapped a coverlet about her. "I do not know how many nights I can play this ruse on Vavrinec without rousing his suspicions that I have more in mind than saving Milos from Lilith's claws. Is there some way to lure her to a house? Hmm… Perhaps I should have asked the rabbi that." She laughed quietly, imagining the expression that would have stricken his face. "He would have had a fit, no doubt. It was terrible enough suggesting that I wanted to speak with her. Even if he knows a way to lure her, I doubt he would have told me." Another thought occurred to her. "Setting out something known to attract Lilith might have also raised her suspicions and kept her from coming for even longer." There seemed nothing to do but wait.

Snoring soon rumbled from the bed. "That will be Vavrinec." She closed her eyes, listening to all the little sounds that made a house comfortable at night. Her husband snoring. Her little brother attempting to talk in his dreams but quickly sinking back into the depths of slumber. The creaks and occasional groans as timbers settled and a mouse scurried somewhere across the floor…

She sat up. Had she drifted into a dream? She was not sure but was certain that she had drawn close to the edge of snoring herself as she sat drowsy and warm in the dark. What had startled her awake? Had Milos whined, indicating that he still slept but was hungry and wanted to nurse? Had there been an unusual sighing of the wind in the chimney? Or had the mouse she heard earlier made its way onto the street and confronted a cat, which even now was snarling and meowing?

She sat there and gradually, hearing no other noise and perceiving no movement across the room, closed her eyes again. Were those Vavrinec's snores that she soon heard, or her own?

There! She heard something! She was certain! Her eyes blinked open, alert and watchful, on guard for whatever came next.

There was a sigh and a groan, as if the door hung open in the wind and the hinges were exhausted with the effort of holding the timbers. But the door was closed tight. Nadezda had bolted it earlier that evening.

Then she saw, nearly invisible in the dark room, a pool of shadow spill under the door from the street. It curled and twisted like a serpent hunting for prey that it knew was nearby. The shadow, which was only slightly darker than the other shadows in the room, paused when it crossed before the icon and its oil lamp and Nadezda thought she heard a faint laugh. Then the shadow was on the move again, tumbling across the room as a stream tumbles over stones. It rippled and swirled, eddies of darkness within eddies of darkness.

Nadezda caught her breath. The shadow had come to a standstill near Petr's cot where Milos slept tonight. The black pool hovered on the floor, silent and still, like a terrible tabby cat poised, waiting for just the right instant to strike its prey. Carefully, with as little motion as possible, Nadezda lifted the Candlemas candle and reached its wick over the lip of the ceramic bowl towards the live coals beneath the ash. She hesitated, then touched the wick to the coals. For a moment, nothing seemed to happen. Then the wick curled and blackened. A tiny flame danced at the tip of the Candlemas candle.

With no warning, the shadow reared up, taller than a living man, and reached for Milos on the cot.

The stench of burning flesh filled the house and the shadow screamed, burned by the amulet it must not have expected to find around Milos' little neck. The shadow screamed again and lunged for the door.

Nadezda sprang up, screaming herself. She held the Candlemas candle aloft, like a firebrand. Its light seemed brilliant in the otherwise dark room. The shadow halted abruptly, apparently unsure of how to get to the door behind the now-awake Nadezda and the barrier of the Candlemas candle. The shadow leaned towards a window that opened out into the street.

"Senoi! Sansenoi! Samangeloph!" Nadezda cried. "I have Lilith trapped! Seize her and carry her away!" Instantaneously, before she could draw her breath again, the three angels were there, fiery indistinct presences in the three corners of the room across from the icon. Nadezda thought she could make out the outline of human forms hovering within the hearts of the flames but she had no time to study them closely. "Stop!" Nadezda said, startling the angels. "Leave her be—for just a moment!" She knew they wished to seize the immortal crone they had been hunting since before the sin of Adam, but they halted.

The shadow in the midst of the room screamed again and buried what might have been its face in its talons.

"Lilith! Heed my words!" Nadezda dared to order the demoness as one would a hysterical child. "Heed my words or I will give you over to be carried off by the angels." She thrust the burning Candlemas candle in her hand at the shadow as if it were a sword in a duel to the death. The shadow shuddered and in the light of the candle thrust toward its face, it shimmered and billowed and wavered before congealing into the form of a human woman. A giantess, whose head brushed the ceiling of the room, but with a human face.

Long, tangled, matted locks cascaded around her shoulders, nearly to the floor, writhing so Nadezda thought them serpents. Her fingers were talons, gnarled claws with large, knotty joints. Her lips slavered and the teeth, what few Nadezda could glimpse, seemed razor sharp. Warts and wrinkles filled her sagging skin and the tattered remnants of what might have once been a beautiful dark blue gown hung about her arms and torso, covering her feet though allowing one pendulous breast to hang loose. Hatred burned cold in the dark eyes that confronted Nadezda. Lilith roared in fury, a sound unlike anything Nadezda had ever heard.

The image of the giantess shimmered in the candlelight and its form became blurry and indistinct, colors running and shifting, pooling and separating as the hideous figure became a lovely, gracious beauty arrayed in splendid skirts and jewels. Her hair, tumbling about her shoulders, was now clean and brushed. Her fingers, though long, were graceful and her skin taut with youth. Her breasts, hidden behind a silken shawl with fringe that swayed and danced with her every movement, were large and seemed brimming with milk. Lilith laughed and her voice was like the music of the stars at dusk or the flutter of a butterfly on a sunlit summer afternoon. Only the cold hatred in her eyes revealed that this fair maiden was the same woman who had stood before Nadezda as a hag but minutes ago.

"What want you with the likes of me?" Lilith asked Nadezda. More than a question but less than a demand, the voice sparkled in Nadezda's ears like a crystal goblet reflecting sunlight, the prism breaking the streaming light into a rainbow of one thousand sparkling colors.

"What want I?" Nadezda repeated, her own voice sounding rough and course in her ears. "I want the knowledge you possess, Lilith. And a promise that you will depart from Prague tonight, never to return."

Lilith smiled, obviously amused that a housewife like Nadezda seemed to think that she was in a position to demand such things. "Depart, never to return? Why should I make such a promise at all, much less to you?" Lilith laughed again, the lilt of her voice breaking like waves on the shore, the memory of each note lingering like traces of sea foam among the stones of the shore.

"No. To these three." Nadezda knew she sounded cold and harsh. She gestured with the Candlemas candle to the three angelic forms who each took a step closer to their demonic prey. "If you do not agree to depart from Prague when I am done with you, promising never to return, then I shall give you over to the angels to bind you in whatever shackles they see fit until the Day of Doom."

Lilith considered her situation and thought aloud. "If there were a mirror here, deluded child, then it would be a simple matter to flee through the silver-backed glass into the wild region I call home and simply wait there until these three tire of their vigil." Lilith took a step back from the Candlemas flame. "Ah, you know not as much as you think. I see from your face that no one told you mirrors serve as gateways for such as me?" She laughed again, her lilting, gracious voice like the most hauntingly beautiful music Orpheus ever played.

Lilith took another step to her left and Nadezda nervously thrust the candle in her hand in that direction, spilling drops of hot wax on the floor. Lilith looked at her with pity and resumed her musings.

"However, there are no mirrors here. Alas. But there is an amulet, an amulet of such power that I have not seen in these many long, long years. There are the angels, the three that have dogged my steps far longer than any memory other than my own can recall. There is that candle in your hand, the one you thrust about so clumsily, like an earthly sword of earthly metal while hoping to cut through ethereal spirit." Lilith walked about in a small circle, glancing and gesturing at each object in turn as she mentioned them, for Nadezda's benefit, as if the mortal woman needed such assistance.

"Any one of these angels, let alone all three of them together, would be swift enough to block my escape should I attempt to slip through a window or the door," Lilith admitted, her back to Nadezda. "I cannot touch the child who wears the amulet. You possess that candle, which you still wave and thrust and parry, but which can do more damage than even you realize, foolish wench."

Nadezda smiled within herself, glad that though she had overlooked the possibility of Lilith making her escape through a mirror ("Why did not the rabbi warn me?" she fretted), the candle she had brought from Mass that morning was more destructive in Lilith's estimation than Nadezda knew.

"So, you win, mortal woman. You have conquered me, the great Lilith… for now." Lilith turned around to face Nadezda once more. "What is this knowledge that you seek? What do you, such a pitiful and small creature, hope to learn from one so great as I that you could ever use to your benefit?"

Nadezda knew that she had to consider her words carefully, lest Lilith find a way to lie without giving an answer. Nadezda took a deep breath and swallowed. "Lilith, were you summoned here by Fen'ka's curse? Did Fen'ka's curse and Svetovit's aid bring you here?"

Lilith nodded in admiration. "Clever wench. So quickly you discerned the means of my coming? Yes, the cries of the poor woman Fen'ka reached my ears as she burned but I was frustrated in coming to her aid. The great one, Svetovit, who was once worshipped on the hill, he it was who opened the doors for me at last and welcomed me here to aid him in the fulfillment of Fen'ka's dying words."

So! She had guessed correctly! If she had been correct about that, perhaps she had also been correct in her estimation of the other strange occurrences in Prague since that autumn afternoon. Nadezda asked her next question.

"Then, Lilith, have Fen'ka's dying words—the curse she called out over the city as she was burned—caused all these deaths and hauntings and disappearances since then? Is she responsible for them or are they coincidences and accidents?"

Lilith placed a finger alongside her elegant lips as she thought. She took a small step towards a window and one of the angels—which one? Senoi, Sansenoi, or Samangeloph?—was instantly there, blocking her way. She laughed her sweet, gentle laugh and stepped back into the center of the room.

"Has Fen'ka directed all these—what did you call them?—all these deaths and hauntings and disappearances?

171

That is difficult to say." She took her finger away from her lips.

With her hand nervously shaking and spilling more wax about the room, Nadezda thrust the candle she wielded closer to Lilith. "Do not toy with me, Lilith," she warned.

"I toy not!" Lilith threw up her hands in protest, her voice filled with dismay. "Deluded simpleton, what I say is the simple truth. The web of the world's fate is far more complex than you realize, mortal girl, and what seems to you the cause of an event may or may not have anything to do with it. What I can say to you is that Fen'ka's words, though perhaps not responsible in the way that you would like to think them, have lain behind all these events and steered their course." Lilith thought carefully what else to say and then added, "They would not have come to pass without her words and without Svetovit, her champion, coming to her aid to make it so."

"Just as I thought!" exclaimed Nadezda. "She is behind it all, she and Svetovit! But the curse has taken a long time in working itself out." Nadezda wondered how much of this she needed to explain to Lilith or how much Lilith even cared to know.

"But that is all behind us, now." Nadezda turned her thoughts from Svetovit and his conniving with Fen'ka to bring ruin to Prague and relished her ability to see their wicked, monstrous hands behind the fates and actions of her fellow citizens and residents. "Now all that matters is that Prague be saved," Nadezda announced. "Lilith, what is the necessary key to the fulfillment of the curse? What must happen before Svetovit is free to wreak his vengeance on Prague? How do I take control of the curse and rewrite its ending?"

Lilith stared at her as if she were a madwoman who claimed acquaintance with the king. Then she burst into laughter, doubling over.

Nadezda stared at Lilith's hilarity with confusion. The

angels stood at attention, unwavering in their vigil. Not a sound came from Milos or Petr, though Nadezda could still make out the calm and steady snoring of Vavrinec. The presence of the angels had apparently blocked any sound from reaching the sleepers.

At last Lilith stood erect and composed herself, spreading her palms across her skirts. "Clever fool, but not nearly clever enough! What is the key to the final consummation of the curse? What must you do to seize control of Fen'ka's words and rewrite their ending?" Looking directly into Nadezda's eyes, she said, "You have possessed the key to the curse within this house and been able to rewrite its ending since the day it was pronounced."

Eight of Cups

(Tuesday, August 13, 2002)

THE EIGHT OF CUPS: A CHANGE, A JOURNEY INTO DARKNESS.

George waited for Magdalena to set out on the mission he had assigned her and then made his way down to the lobby. At the front desk, he saw that another clerk was on duty, neither the bored man he had asked to arrange the date with the prostitute nor the younger man he had asked for a candle. He asked this clerk, "Excuse me, but is it possible to buy a live chicken or rooster in Prague?"

The clerk stared at him in surprise. "Ah, live chickens or... roosters, sir? May I ask why?"

George chuckled. "Yes, of course," he told the young man. "One of the reasons I came to Prague was to consult with the Charles University faculty about both poultry farming and the role of roosters in Bohemian folktales. Since I am unable to contact the faculty across the river, given the flooding, I was hoping to speak with someone in the business."

The clerk nodded. "I see, sir." He did not seem convinced. "Perhaps in the countryside, in one of the smaller towns or villages," he suggested.

"I realize there are many other things that might require your attention," George continued, "but it is vital to my research. I really must discover if there is an establishment in Prague which sells live roosters. I am especially interested in speaking to someone who has a black rooster for sale."

"Well, sir, as you say... there is quite a situation

174

developing," the clerk responded, unable to stop his upper lip from wrinkling in disdain. "It is not really possible for us to locate such an establishment at present."

George rested one elbow on the front desk and leaned toward the clerk. "I understand," he repeated gently. Dropping his voice to a conspiratorial hush, he continued, "But it would be worth your time and effort to make a few phone calls, in any case." He slid several crisply folded bills of American currency across the desk.

Theo dropped off into a mild stupor shortly after the doctor departed, the medication helping him to rest as the doctor had promised. Late in the afternoon he stirred.

"Where am I?" he asked, rubbing his eyes. "What am I doing here?" He looked around, confused. "Why am I sleeping in the lobby?"

The full force of the pain in his legs rushed into his consciousness, knocking his head back as if punched. "No," he gasped. "George! This must be George's doing! I must get up! I must!" He struggled to swing his legs off the couch to the floor.

"No, no, sir!" Another clerk was on duty at the desk but had been informed of what had happened that morning. "Your medication, sir! You must take your medication! Doctor's orders!" The clerk got two of the pills from the bottle and into Theo's mouth as bellhops converged to hold his legs still and replace them on the sofa.

"No, you don't understand! The flood!" Theo protested.

"Yes, precisely, sir. The flood. You must stay here and rest," the clerk repeated the instructions he had been given.

Theo realized that further protest would get him nowhere. He relaxed, giving himself over to the drug-induced calm sweeping through him.

The eighty-one members of the Senate of the Parliament of the Czech Republic were meeting in their usual chambers, the Wallenstein Palace along the river in the Little Town at the bottom of the castle hill.

Orders were issued that afternoon to empty the ground floor of the palace. An impromptu emergency electrical system was set up to guarantee an ongoing source of lights within the building in case the rising water shorted out the city's power grid. The gardens were ordered closed and sandbags piled along the bottom of the gates in an attempt to keep the water at bay.

Victoria followed a long struggle towards consciousness and realized she was wrapped in a light blanket and propped in a chair in an alcove of a strange hotel lobby. Slowly, she focused her eyes and understood what she was looking at. It was Sean, wrapped in a similar blanket, sitting in a similar chair across the alcove. His head was tipped back, resting against the wall behind him. A drop of spittle hung from the corner of his mouth and he was snoring gently.

A clerk must have heard Victoria's blanket rustling and came to check on the two patients. "How long have we been here?" Victoria wanted to know as soon as the clerk had explained to her what had happened and why the two stricken guests had not been taken to the hospital.

"It has been several hours," the clerk told her. "We have been giving the sedatives to the gentleman consistently. But you have been sleeping soundly all this time, without sedatives."

176

"George!" Victoria realized. Aloud, she asked the clerk, "I must contact his family, my friend's family. I must go home to get the contact information." She tried to stand and nearly collapsed. Dizziness made her head feel as if it were rotating in complete circles and nausea gripped her stomach. She cursed quietly under her breath. The clerk helped her to sit down again before she fell.

"Excuse me, miss," the clerk warned her. "The doctor left instructions that if you tried to move again too quickly, you might become agitated and should swallow these." He gave her two tablets and a glass of water, standing guard over her until she swallowed them. The alcove rotated and grew dim, and the realization that George had probably stricken all of them in one way or another clouded over any other thought she might have had. In seconds, she was sound asleep.

In the north of Prague, the large, expansive city zoo sat in one of the city's most vulnerable positions next to the river.

"The worst flood in nearly twenty years is headed straight at us!" The news reports swept through the zoo. Veterinarians and zoologists and staff mobilized at once to implement an evacuation plan. A giant tortoise lumbered its way to safety with the assistance of the staff and in a matter of hours, hundreds of other animals were moved to safer quarters.

Responding to the requests of the director, many staff members volunteered to spend the night in the zoo. They kept vigil as the water rose, alert to see what else the impending disaster might require them to do to save the other animals.

Late that afternoon, the phone rang in George's hotel room. He answered it and heard the clerk's voice from the front desk. "It took a great deal of time and many phone calls, but I was able to obtain the information you requested, sir. There is an establishment such as the one you asked about in the area of Prague known as Ďáblice. It is, unfortunately, unreachable at present on the public transport system, because of the flooding, but you may be able to reach it by taxi, which the hotel—of course—will be happy to arrange for you. The proprietor regrets that he is not able to come into the Little Town to meet you but he will be expecting your arrival sometime tomorrow, if that is convenient."

"Wonderful!" George exclaimed. "That will be very convenient! Yes, please book the taxi for me!" He copied down the address of the establishment and the name of the proprietor, which the clerk carefully spelled out for him.

Dmitri and Sophia lay together on the hotel bed throughout the afternoon and evening. Dmitri could not bear to move, each tiny shift of his position unleashing new rounds of agony in his temples and across his forehead. The light that slipped into their room from the window burned his eyes whenever he tried to open them and the sound of Sophia rushing to the toilet, driven by the nausea that held her in as relentless a grip as the headache held him, was nearly intolerable.

In one brief moment of respite, he whispered to his wife, "This is George's doing. I know it."

"But how do we combat it?" Sophia asked him. "We are incapacitated. It is all I can do to get from the bed to the toilet and back."

"Pray," he husband urged her. "We can pray, at least."

That evening, the official acknowledgment of reality finally came. A state of emergency was issued by the Prime

Minister, and all the districts of Prague alongside the river were deemed in danger of horrific flooding. Certain neighborhoods were singled out for particular attention, including the whole of the Little Town. "Residents are advised to leave their homes," the news announcers read.

News reports later confirmed the flood's first human victim, a man who had drowned in the swiftly flowing water.

Magdalena was exhausted when she smeared the last of the toad-extract-and-Eucharist paste. She had been walking from block to block and stooping or kneeling to smear the paste on the curbs and lanes and alleys in the Little Town for hours. The cotton swabs had long since been worn to shreds and she had been dipping her gloved fingers into the bowl and wiping them against the stones she walked on. Luckily, the gloves had remained intact until the paste was gone. She slipped them off and dropped them into a garbage canister at the next corner.

Entering her apartment, she set the bowl in the kitchen sink, unsure of the proper way to cleanse it.

"I will have to ask George for instructions," she noted mentally before stripping off her street clothes and changing into her sleeping wear. She sat down to rest briefly before getting something to eat but did not stir again for several hours.

Dmitri glanced around the hotel room, careful to move his head as little as possible. Evening seemed to have fallen, as the light that crept into the room from the window had the harsh glare of artificial light. He heard Sophia's even breathing beside him on the bed.

"At least she seems to have finally gotten some rest." He sighed with relief. "But what about the rest of us? If George incapacitated Sophia and me, he must surely have done the same to Sean and Victoria and Theo… We cannot all simply lie about sick until George and Magdalena have destroyed the city and set free Svetovit." The effort of thought provoked another spasm of pain across his temples. He gasped and then tried to breathe slowly and deeply, his eyes shut tightly. A tear slipped out the corner of one eye and across his cheek.

"We must… I must… Do something," he wheezed. "But what? How?"

Which saints were patrons against illness such as they had been stricken with? The pain in his head made it difficult to think. Images of frescoes and mosaics flitted and shifted through his memory, but he could not recall the names of the saints whose faces briefly peered at him from the dark recesses of his mind. Then one image, a statue he had recently seen while walking the streets of Prague, snapped into focus. The figure was that of a man, carved from pale stone, pulling up his tunic to reveal the open sores on his leg as a faithful dog sat at his feet and clutched a loaf of bread in its mouth.

"Saint Roch, patron of plague victims, help us!" he gasped as the pain racked him. "Come yourself… Send us aid… Send us your dog, even… to stop the afflictions… that plague us."

People gathered in the plazas of the Kampa district, where the gypsies had camped in the Middle Ages. Trucks rumbled along the lanes normally filled with tourists, delivering sand and bags. As the sandbags were filled, wheelbarrows were filled with as many as could be carried and the heavy bags delivered to the buildings adjacent to the river in hopes they might staunch the flow of the water. The work went on throughout the night, floodlights illuminating the scene as if it were a movie set.

The clock in the tower over the Loreto cloister chimed eleven. The plaza in front of the cloister was empty, as everyone who might have wandered leisurely in the summer darkness had gone near the river to either watch the disaster in the making or help in filling sandbags. The chimes of the clock echoed quietly and faded in the night. A breeze rustled the branches of the trees and bushes.

A large black dog emerged from the shadows on the far side of the plaza. He stood momentarily, surveying the scene before him. Not so different from other nights. He had come to this plaza nearly every night at almost this same time for what seemed like forever. He came to protect the innocent, the lost, the aimless, the foolish. He came to protect those who were in danger. The area he was able to protect was not large, but he had always looked out for those in harm's way in the plaza and a little further beyond. The plaza was not so different tonight, but different enough. A multitude of strange, new scents assaulted his nose and he lifted his head to sniff the wind. He needed to distinguish the smells that mingled in the air, determine what they meant and how he should react. Whether he ought to ignore any or all of them. He stepped further into the plaza and sniffed again.

The dominant scent was one he recognized but had not detected for many, many long seasons. It was the mixture of putrid magic and fear, a massive supernatural assault on the city and the fear of the populace in the face of the attack. Although the attack disguised itself as a natural, earthly event and the fear it inspired was a natural, human reaction to such an event, he smelled evil and power hovering over the city. He smelled Svetovit's approach.

There was nothing he could do at this point about such an attack. It was too massive, too broad, too far-flung to respond in any meaningful way. Svetovit was both too far away and too large a power for the dog to pose any real threat, and the dog knew it. He bared his teeth and growled at the sky nevertheless. He growled and sniffed the breeze again.

Another scent was in the air, a scent both fainter and closer than Svetovit. Another kind of bad magic hovered, a bad magic close at hand and more focused than Svetovit's malice. This bad magic was aimed at a few, a handful of people, and its intent was much more specific than the general destruction Svetovit threatened. The dog sniffed the air again.

What direction was this faint scent coming from? The breeze had dispersed it, scattering it across the plaza, making it difficult to follow back to its source. The dog took a few hesitant steps and snuffled along the ground, hoping to get a deeper whiff. Any of the scent that hovered near the ground was also more likely to be heavier, more concentrated than the more volatile tendrils that slithered through the air, riding the breeze. More concentrated fragments of the scent were also more likely to make a trail that led back to the approximate area of its source.

Instead, sniffing along the ground, the dog detected a third smell that had been easy to overlook before. A murky and shadowy presence lurked under the other two scents. It was human but tainted with strong notes of Svetovit's approach and the more specific rotten magic close at hand. He sniffed again and distinguished two human sources, a man and a woman, who had been involved together in calling Svetovit and working the hex the dog was attempting to track.

He moved along the side of the plaza, sniffing and searching for the human smell beneath and tangled up with the magic. He caught a whiff and then lost it again. He continued along the edge of the plaza, picking up occasional hints of the human smell. He lifted his head briefly and glanced around to be sure no one else had stumbled out of the lanes and alleyways.

Satisfied that no one else needed him tonight, he lowered his head again and continued his slow and cautious hunt for the human scent.

It slapped across the snout. The human scent had pooled in a deep, seething puddle in this spot. They must have stood here, together, for some purpose. Why? He looked up again to determine his location on the plaza's edge. The lowest branches of the yew in front of him brushed his snout.

Yew! They had stood here to cut slips of yew for some further wickedness. Yew in the hands of such people, people who had conjured Svetovit and worked some other wicked spell in this plaza, was dangerous. It was impossible to predict how they might use it, but it was to be used for no good purpose. He was sure of that.

But he was not allowed to go beyond a certain point atop the castle hill and that the man and woman who had cut the yew were no doubt safely hidden away further down the hill. He might not be able to protect whomever they would use the yew against but he could do something to protect whomever they had hexed here.

Lowering his snout to the cobblestones again, he easily tracked the dense ropes of human scent across the plaza to another cluster of bushes not far from the corner of the Loreto cloister. The tangled aromas of wicked people and wicked magic was unmistakable. Whatever hex they had worked, they had worked it here. Exploring the area around and under the bushes, a sharp tang sliced his nostrils. They had buried something! He dug at the spot, furiously churning up the earth with his great paws.

A dough figure flew up, sailing past his floppy ear. He stopped to examine it for any damage resulting from hitting the cobblestones so roughly. He saw that it was intact, no broken limbs, so he returned to his excavation more slowly and carefully. He exhumed the other figures, gently lifting each in his sharp teeth and setting it carefully beside the one that had sailed past him. Each one, in fact, half covered the one before it. The five figures made a tidy little pyramid.

The dog snuffled in the dirt to be sure no other smells rose to indicate other figures might be buried deeper. Satisfied that he had retrieved them all, he turned to examine those he had dug up.

Careful not to disturb the pyramid of figures, he sniffed again to determine as much as he could about the hex the figures had been used to work. It was a simple, uncomplicated spell that he could undermine fairly easily.

Positioning himself over the stacked figures, he lifted his hind leg.

Theo stirred in his half-sleep on the couch in the hotel lobby. Strange figures appeared in his dreams, pudgy figures not unlike animated characters made of dough that pummeled and pinched his legs. The pain crackled and shot along his nerves, and a muffled cry was buried somewhere in his throat. But then a mysterious shower, an unexpected cloudburst opened above him and washed away his attackers and, he realized, washed away the pain with them. His legs felt soothed and refreshed by the rainfall. He was even conscious of bones knitting themselves back together, picturing this in his groggy mind as peculiar sensations rippled through his shins.

Urine, associated with the water of life and healing, soaked each figure thoroughly. Urine played in the crevices

184

and spaces between the figures and drenched the cobblestones beneath them before it ran off in the cracks and fissures of the mortar between the cobblestones.

As the last of the dog's urine washed over the figures, a small cloud of rainbow-hued lights heaved and writhed above them. Startled, the dog dropped his leg and stumbled a few steps away. The lights dimmed and flared as they twisted and swam in the air just above the dough figures, along with a small cloud of steam rising and hissing from them.

Dmitri reached up and gently placed his palms on his temples. He had thought he felt water splashing his face, but no, his face was only wet from the sweat that had accumulated there in the sweltering humidity of their room. It must have been a dream.

Sophia, kneeling before the toilet, made a strange noise that caught his attention. He had not noticed her running to the bathroom again. Had he drifted into a half-sleep?

Dream or not, he still felt water splashing his face and running over his shoulders onto the bed beneath him. He was then aware that his headache was draining away with the water.

"Sophia? Are you there?" he dared to call out, hesitant to move his facial muscles that much and provoke another reaction from the migraine. But there was no reaction. The incapacitating pain seemed a more and more distant memory.

Sophia stood in the doorway of the bathroom, leaning against the wall but not dependent on it for support.

"Yes, I am here, Dmitri," she answered weakly, but he could hear the strength returning to her even in those few words.

"Are you feeling better?" he asked, and took the risk of propping himself up on one elbow.

Sophia brushed her hair away from her face. "Better?

185

Yes. I am feeling better. But my stomach feels like it is being flushed with a firehose."

The dog barked sharply at the display, unsure of what to do.

Sparks popped from the dough. The wavering crown of lights blazed bright and then winked out. A last wisp of steam curled up from the figures, followed by a lone spark and a last crackle of energy.

The dog paused and tilted his head, waiting to see if the sodden figures produced any further display. Nothing happened. Sniffing and pawing at the dough, he determined no trace of the hex-scent remained.

Turning back to the earth under the bushes, he filled the hole he had dug and then, a few steps away, dug a fresh hole. Scooping the figures into the new hole, he buried them again to protect them and prevent any further abuse by someone finding them lying there.

Done at last, he took one final look at his evening's work under the bushes. He surveyed the plaza behind him too, remembering when there had been a chasm that opened into Hell at the far side of the plaza. But the plaza was empty.

The clock above began to chime midnight. Time to end his patrol. He trotted off into the shadows across the plaza.

Throughout his drug-induced stupor, Sean was dimly aware of Victoria, of their surroundings, of their predicament. He would occasionally struggle towards consciousness, but as he neared wakefulness, the pain in his eyes increased sharply, driving him back into the embrace of the medication.

Now, though, another sensation startled him. Drops that felt like tears caressed his forehead and fell into his eyes, pooling under his eyelids and mingling with his own tears.

Accumulating until there was no more space, the mixture of his own and the other tears slid down his cheeks.

He gasped involuntarily. The pain that had gripped him seemed to be sliding away as the tears slid down his face. He opened his eyes slightly.

Victoria was sitting up, rubbing her forehead. She saw Sean looking at her and a broad smile flashed across her face.

"The water…" she whispered. "I was swimming in it and I could feel the seizures floating away."

Sean glanced at the front desk. It was unoccupied. The clerk must have stepped away.

"I think it will be difficult to explain our sudden recovery," he said softly to Victoria. "Can you move? Let's go back to my hotel now, while we can."

Victoria bit her lip, then nodded. Quietly standing up and making their way to the entrance of the hotel, supporting each other, they stepped into the night.

Theo gestured to the bellboy on duty in the lobby.

"I am feeling much better now," he explained to the teen. "I would like to return to my room for the night. Would you help me, please? Just in case?"

"Of course, sir! Of course!" The uniformed boy responded eagerly. Assisting Theo to his feet, the boy swung Theo's left arm across his back and allowed the older man to sag into him. Theo allowed himself to rest much of his weight across the boy's shoulders, hesitant to stand on his own. Together, they made their way up to Theo's room and the boy helped Theo sit on the edge of the bed, beneath the ornately carved beams stretching across the ceiling.

"Do you need any more help to prepare for bed, sir?"

"No, thank you." Theo reached down and, grasping his

shins, swung first one leg and then the other onto the coverlet. "No, I'll just lie back against the pillows. Thank you again, young man."

"Not at all, sir. My pleasure." He turned to leave and left Theo alone in the dark. Moments later, Theo was sleeping soundly.

Dmitri and Sophia held each other in the bed, in the dark, the priest's gentle snoring reverberating through the otherwise quiet room. Theirs was the sleep known to those who are healthy but exhausted, the sleep that heals weary bodies and souls and spirits.

Sean and Victoria stumbled through the streets, dimly aware of the bright lights and rumbling trucks and frantic activity of the sandbaggers working valiantly to save their city. Reaching Sean's hotel room and throwing propriety to the winds, they collapsed together on the bed and were nearly instantaneously embraced by natural—not drug-induced—and dreamless sleep.

Dawn came. Tuesday morning. Water surged along the riverbanks in the city, pounding against the bridges, struggling to burst free of the banks and walls that confined it. Like a living thing, a hungry animal, it writhed and twisted, eating away at that which constrained it. It found a crevice, a depression in the banks of the Kampa district and stealthily crept into the low-lying district.

A tank rumbled into position on the Charles Bridge, facing the Little Town in support of the security and police officers who stood guard along the barricades against the threat of the frightened crowds.

Magdalena woke to the sound of large numbers of people trudging along the street outside her apartment. Dressing quickly so as not to miss her rendezvous with George, she listened to the radio announcer report that the flood had filled Kampa. With difficulty, she hurried through the streets to George's hotel. She found him in the lobby, sitting in an overstuffed chair and sipping coffee.

"The streets are full of people going to see the river!" she exclaimed. "Everyone wants to say, 'I saw the flood!' it seems."

George laughed quietly. "Yes, disasters will always have their fans. People love nothing better than to see a car crash or building burn. A whole town drowning is irresistible!"

"A whole town drowning?" she exclaimed. "What about the potion I smeared on the curbs all day yesterday? Won't that keep the flood away? You promised it would help protect the city!"

"I also said it would take time," George reminded her. "We may need to reinforce the charm so it has time to do its work and keep the river back."

"How?" Magdalena demanded. "We must not let those…" She struggled to find words. "We must not let Professor Theo and the others destroy the city!"

"No," George agreed with her, setting his cup down. "Indeed, we must not. The charm will, of course, be better able to constrain the water if it is applied to streets on both sides of the river, in the Old Town as well as the New Town. I will give you another charm to apply on this side of the river and I will find a taxi or some means of getting outside town and around the flooded areas to apply the toad-and-Eucharist extract in the Old Town. The subways are too unreliable at this point, are

189

they not? So it is impossible to know how long it might take to accomplish this. We will plan meet back at your apartment sometime this evening, yes? You will wait for me there?"

"Yes!" Magdalena agreed. "That makes perfect sense. What should I do to reinforce the charm on this side will you are applying it to the other?"

"Come with me." He pointed to the stairs. "I will give you the perfect thing to do it with."

In his room, she saw the slips of yew standing in a glass of water on the desk near the window. George pulled his horsehair whisk from his luggage. He brought it to the desk, gesturing for Magdalena to join him.

"How will this reinforce the potion I used yesterday?" she asked, fascinated by the process she was watching. George sat at the desk chair and wrapped two of the threads of horsetail around his fingers, then snapped them off the handle of the whisk. He nodded at the yew in the glass and she retrieved a bundle of the leaves.

"We tie the yew with the horsetail," he explained, shifting in the chair to face her with a smile. He nodded at the yew in her hand, which she dutifully extended toward him. He twisted the horsehair tightly around one end of the slips of yew and knotted the horsehair several times. He took the bouquet from Magdalena and brandished it toward the window, almost as if it were a sword. She laughed.

"Now you need to be one of those 'flood tourists' who want to get to the river," he explained, handing the bouquet of yew to her. "You can use ordinary water, but water from the river would be best. Fill your chalice with it. Use the yew to sprinkle the water from the chalice along the streets. Try as best you can to match the same places where you smeared the extract yesterday." He stood and retrieved her chalice from the closet, where it had been sitting on a shelf. She took it and set the yew in it.

"How does all this work?" she wanted to know.

"Horses and horse-goddesses are associated with the dead in the mythology of many cultures. And horsehair is often used in magic to communicate with the dead. Yew is often planted around the edges of burial grounds because the dead become caught in its branches, so it helps to keep them from wandering about to harass the living," George told her. "Using water, yew, and horsehair will focus the charm you placed yesterday to drive away the specific hazards of death and water from the city."

Magdalena examined the yew in her chalice and then smiled at George.

In the Kampa and Little Venice districts to the left and right of the stone bridge, soldiers went from door to door. Knocking, in some cases pounding, to rouse the inhabitants, they were under orders to evacuate these neighborhoods.

"Everyone must go," the residents were told.

"But where? How?"

"Make your way as best you can," came the instructions. "Family. Friends. Go up. Away from the river. Now!"

The elderly—many of whom had to be helped to safety through their windows by the soldiers and emergency aid workers because of the rising water—and others who had difficulty moving or no family, no friends, no one to take them in, were loaded into bus after bus and driven to schools away from the river, where each gymnasium and many classrooms had been turned into emergency campgrounds resembling the refugee camps most of Europe had not seen since the end of the Second World War. By the middle of the day, the fears of the city had become reality. Kampa was submerged under the roaring river and the portrait of John Lennon adorning the graffiti-laden Lennon Wall soon presided over a pond that had been a plaza.

"Sir? Ma'am?" Rough knocks pounded on the door of Dmitri and Sophia's hotel room.

More knocking rang out along the hallway. Keys rattled in locks.

"The hotel is being evacuated. We must ask all guests to leave the hotel in as quickly and orderly a fashion as possible," the clerk announced as his head protruded around the now-open door.

Dmitri realized what he was hearing and sat upright, shaking his wife's shoulder. "Sophia! Wake up! The hotel is being evacuated!" Having heard voices from within the room acknowledging the occupants understood the gravity of the situation, the clerk moved on to the next room.

Magdalena stood before the pool that had blossomed at the base of the Lennon Wall. She had come this way hoping to find a place where she could reach the river without attracting attention and had nearly stumbled into the water. She stooped with the plastic jug she had gotten at her apartment to organize herself for her new assignment.

"The chalice is much too small to hold a reasonable amount of water to sprinkle in the streets of the city," she had realized. "I'll have to get a larger supply of water and keep replenishing it." She left the chalice and yew in her kitchen and found a large plastic jug in her trash that had once held juice. She rinsed it out and set out for the banks of the river to fill it.

Now she was kneeling at the edge of the flood, holding the jug so that water could gurgle into it. When it was full, she twisted the cap back into place and stood. Glancing around, satisfied that no one had witnessed her odd souvenir collecting, she made her way back up to her apartment.

Theo was unsure of what to do next or where to go. He stood on the cobblestones outside his hotel, having hastily dressed and even more hastily repacked his luggage when the hotel staff had roused him from his deep slumber.

"Evacuation" was the one word he clearly understood in his waking stupor. Now he was downstairs, in the street, with the swelling crowd of displaced hotel guests. A multitude of languages swirled around him. "Where should we go? How far will the flood reach, do you think? Is anyplace safe left? Shouldn't the hotel have made arrangements for us? Maybe we should get the next flight out? Haven't you heard that the airport is closed and the flights have all been cancelled?"

Theo picked up his luggage, wincing as a flicker of pain danced up his shins, and trudged up the hill and away from the river.

At midmorning, announcements came that the public transportation system was available free of charge—where it was still in operation. More subway stations had succumbed to the inundation of the flood coming through the sewers and medieval, uncharted tunnels under the Old Town. Even stations that were still open often had no service, as it had been suspended at the closed stations. Yet any tram or bus that could make its way along the surface would take all passengers away from the growing disaster, free, if only they could reach the tram lines and bus routes.

Magdalena made her rounds through the crowded streets of the Little Town, sprinkling river water from her chalice with the bundle of horsehair-tied-yew onto the places she could recall smearing the toad-and-Eucharist paste the day before. People were too concerned with their own welfare to pay much attention to the young woman who was going about sprinkling water, though one or two older, more devout churchgoers clucked in approval.

"Sprinkling holy water. She must be," they agreed. "Something to protect the city. Like when the holy Infant of Prague statue was carried in procession along the walls of the city. Good of that young lady to think of something practical to aid the town!"

"Come with me," Victoria told Sean as they exited the hotel along with the other guests who had not gone out earlier to look at the flood and would return later only to find themselves unable to enter the hotel or retrieve their belongings.

"Come with me to my apartment." Victoria pulled Sean from the midst of the dumbfounded, confused tourists. "I live far enough up the hill that it should be safe, at least for a while longer."

At the zoo, the water continued to engulf the enclosures where the animals lived and to isolate the park from the rest of the city. More than a hundred people struggled to move the birds and big cats and gorillas to safety. Rifle shots rang out to put down a lion and a bear that could not be saved. Frightened gorillas attacked the would-be rescuers and jumped out of the inflatable rafts, back into the still-rising water. Elephants and hippos huddled outside their enclosures.

194

"Dmitri! Look!" whispered Sophia, setting down the suitcase she was carrying and pointing ahead of them with one hand, tugging on her husband's arm with the other to get his attention.

They had finally set out from their hotel, following the crowds that meandered through the streets of the Little Town, looking for new lodging. Each hotel they stopped at had given one of two replies: "all full" or "evacuated." Sophia was no longer sure where they were in relation to the river, the streets and lanes having twisted and turned so, but Dmitri seemed to be about to turn onto a side alley that would lead them further up the steep hillside toward hotels that might still have some accommodation available.

"Where?" he asked, startled, dropping the baggage he was carrying, looking to his wife, then n the direction she was pointing, and back again. "Look at…?"

"There! Don't you see her?" Sophia whispered excitedly. "It's Magdalena!"

Dmitri looked ahead into the crowd again and saw her. It was Magdalena, walking away from them with her silver chalice in one hand and a bundle of leaves in the other. She paused and stooped, dipping the tree cuttings into the chalice and then sprinkling water onto the curbside. A few people around her glanced and snickered at her strange behavior but no one seemed to take particular notice of it.

"What do you think she is doing?" Sophia asked her husband.

"I don't know, but it cannot be anything good," he whispered back careful to watch where Magdalena walked.

"We must stop her!" Sophia insisted. "What can we do?"

"We cannot start a fistfight in the street!" her husband

insisted in response. "The police would be sure to stop the two of us from assaulting her!"

"There must be something we can do!" Sophia retorted. "Something that won't attract the attention of the police!"

"An exorcism!" Dmitri's face lit up as he thought of it.

"Is there anyone you know who can do one now? Here? That won't attract any attention?" Sophia wanted to know.

"Yes, a very quick and simple one," he answered. "In the medieval West, the priest would always read the opening of St. John's Gospel over the congregation at the end of the Mass as a general, all-purpose blessing and exorcism." He hurried to where Magdalena had sprinkled the water, crossed himself, stooped over as if to speak to the curb, and began to recite, "In the beginning was the Word, and the Word was with God…"

George, having never had any intention of smearing the toad-and-Eucharist mixture on the streets of the Old Town, was surprised that the live-chicken smell did not overpower him as he entered a low-ceilinged but long, rectangular cinder-block building in Ďáblice. The taxi, a small white boxy station wagon, with its back storage usually used to hold luggage for tourists coming from or going to the airport, had taken a very long and complicated route of back roads and small streets to avoid the swollen river and deliver George to the address indicated on the hotel clerk's note. The driver was parked outside, waiting to bring George back to central Prague along the same slow tangle of back roads. Having been hired at a much-better-than-usual rate for the day, the driver was obviously in no rush to return. He lit a cigarette and closed his eyes to enjoy the day away from the noise and confusion of the flood in the older areas of Prague along the river.

Inside were towers of large cages stacked one atop the

other, each filled with chickens, ducks, or other fowl. A few clucked or an occasional squawk would erupt from the cages, but there was none of the cacophony George had expected. "Are they all resigned to their fate?" he wondered.

A few cages even held snow-white rabbits waiting to be killed and skinned. A counter stood opposite the large glass doors George entered through, a scale at one end of the counter. Next to the counter was an office with a window looking out into the main area of the store. In the office, George saw file drawers, a desk, and an older woman hunched over a stack of invoices. An old-fashioned black telephone with square, push-button lights of a sort George had not seen in decades sat on the desk. At the end of the building, to his left, was a window in the wall through which George could see a number of butchers moving about, bright red stains smeared across their stark white aprons.

One woman was already being waited on at the counter, holding two small children by their hands as the attendant placed the rusty-brown chicken she had chosen on the scale and wrapped a long wire around the hen's feet. A large tag with a number emblazoned on it hung from the wire. The woman paid the clerk, who then delivered the hen through the window to the back room. The woman and the children stood to one side for their selection to be returned to them, ready to become dinner. The children became engrossed with examining the rabbits lying all together in a heap. Pointing and laughing, the youngsters seemed to be telling a story in which various rabbits were the principal characters.

A man in a clean white coat and a bushy mustache came up to George and said something in Czech.

"Good morning," the Jesuit replied, in English. "I am interested in a black rooster. I was told you have such a bird available?"

The man smiled broadly and shook George's hand, calling over his shoulder to the woman in the office beside the counter. She looked up, saw George through the window, and bustled out to greet her customer.

"Good morning," she greeted him, bobbing her head and shaking his hand. "How we help you?" she asked in heavily accented English.

"I believe my hotel spoke with someone here yesterday," George explained, being sure to speak slowly so the woman had a chance to translate his words in her head. "I am looking for a black rooster and was told you had one for me."

The woman studied his face a moment and then burst out into a broad smile. "Yes, yes. One of last phone calls we get before flood... damages all phone lines. Radio only from small towns, not Prague. No television. We not know what is happening now. Your driver tell us, maybe?" She gestured towards the man outside in the car but quickly realized George was not interested in her communication difficulties. "Yes. Black rooster." She spoke in a rush of Czech to the man who had first greeted George as she stepped behind the counter. The man, who probably had never before had an English-speaking customer come into the store, made his way to a cage in a corner of the building. Pulling heavy gloves out of one pocket, he pulled them on and reached into the cage in which sat a lone coal-black rooster.

The rooster bellowed and cackled as the man grasped the bird's feet, pecking at the gloved hands that encircled its scaly talons, but the bird fell silent as the man drew it out of the cage. It hung upside down, its eyes darting about the room and looking at the world in perplexity. The man delivered the rooster to the scale on the counter.

"This rooster... you want us should dress it for you?" the woman asked George.

"No, I will take it with me as it is," George answered. "Alive."

"You want it... live?" the woman repeated, unsure of understanding him correctly.

"Yes, live," George told her again.

The woman looked at the man in the white coat and raised one eyebrow, explaining something to him in Czech. He looked back at George, snapping his thick neck back as if struck in the face. He asked the woman a few questions and she repeated her instructions. He made his way back to the corner of the building and retrieved the cage he had pulled the rooster from. He hoisted it up onto the counter next to the scale.

"The price... much more with cage," the woman warned George. She wrote several figures in a column on a pad of paper she pulled from a shelf below the counter, making rapid calculations, and showed George the total.

"I understand." He nodded. "That is not a problem." He pulled several brightly colored Czech bills from his pocket and offered them to the woman. He eyes grew wide with surprise, having obviously expected an argument. She took all but one of the bills from George's hand and gave him a few small coins in return.

"Thank you. Thank you, sir." The woman bobbed her head again.

George gestured at the door of the building. "Could you help put the bird in the car?"

The mustachioed man nodded, understanding George's request before the woman translated for him. He grunted and lifted the cage as the woman hurried to open the door to the street.

Having deposited the cage in the back of the taxi, he pulled off one of his work gloves to shake George's hand. George added another bill to the man's palm.

"Thank you." Both men nodded to each other and George slipped into the taxi's back seat. The driver and the fowl dealer looked at each other and grinned sheepishly, shaking their heads with amusement.

"… full of grace and truth." Dmitri concluded the gospel verses and crossed himself once more. He turned his attention to Sophia, who had brought their luggage to where he stood.

"Did you see where she went next?" he asked.

"That way," Sophia pointed. "I'll stay here with the suitcases and wait for you. You follow her, find where she sprinkled the curbsides, and recite the gospel passage to exorcise whatever she is doing with the water and the leaves."

The priest kissed his wife on the cheek. "I'll be back as soon as I can," he promised and hurried after Magdalena as Sophia adjusted the suitcases to sit atop one and wait for her husband to return.

Volunteers continued to fill sandbags in the Old Town Square beneath the Astronomical Clock, the hands of which crept forward unsteadily. Strange whirrings and clanking had been heard periodically from the clockworks since sometime on Monday, though most of the volunteers were too busy to notice. The complaints and moanings of the clock had become more frequent and more difficult to ignore. The rumbling of trucks, some bringing more sand while others took away the bags already filled, distracted some of the volunteers, masking the sounds of distress as the gears of the clock slipped out of position. The hands jerked ahead, paused, trembled, then moved forward again smoothly for a few minutes.

A handful of volunteers paused at midday, wiping their brows and leaning on their shovels. A loud screeching from the clock assailed their ears, metal grinding against metal. The several arms of the clock—displaying hours and minutes, planetary and star positions—shivered and finally hung still, unable to continue their struggle to mark the progression of time. The tiny star on its rod trembled violently, alone in its stalwart efforts to continue ticking, before it also succumbed to its now-inevitable death. Drivers in the square felt their truck gears slip out of position at the same time. Volunteers shouting to one another coughed and sputtered, their words caught in their throats. Silence blanketed the square for an instant and then the rumbling of the trucks began again.

The great Astronomical Clock, the pentacle of Prague, whose gears and hands were tied to the workings of Time itself, had stopped. Judgment Day had come to Prague and the clock was broken, unable to do anything to protect the city.

Basic supplies ran low and then failed altogether in the few stores that remained open. Panic insinuated itself in the city. Rumors and reports of looting circulated. People were afraid to stay in their homes and risk drowning. They were afraid to leave their homes and risk the theft of anything not ruined by the water.

The rising river breached the landing of the bridge in the Little Town, gurgling at first around the bottoms of the steel blockades and then sweeping them away as the depth and force of the water grew.

Across the river, the plaza known as Charles Square that filled the area between the first archway and guard tower of the great bridge and the Old Town was cordoned off as the rushing river consumed it. The middle of the bridge rose like an island of cobblestones and statuary out of the river, cut off from the city on both ends. News of the bridge's impending destruction, ripped from its stone moorings by the force of the quickly rising water, raced through the city on both sides of the river.

Electricity was shut off in neighborhood after neighborhood throughout the city. The Little Town and the Old Town went dark and shadows consumed them as relentlessly as the water did.

Magdalena glanced back along the street she had come down, trying to remember where she had turned and gone to next with the extract the day before. Something caught her eye and she realized that the priest Dmitri was bending over the place she had just sprinkled with river water and he was reciting or mumbling something.

"He's following me!" she muttered to herself. "Probably working some hex against the charm George gave me! How dare he? I wonder how long he has been following me?" She scowled in Dmitri's direction and looked up and down the street again.

The chalice was nearly empty. She needed to go back to her apartment and refill it with the river water in the plastic jug. "But I cannot let Dmitri see where I live!"

She quickly turned and walked as if she had not seen Dmitri and then darted down a narrow alley.

Dmitri, exhausted and sweating, made his way back to Sophia waiting with their suitcases.

"What happened?" Sophia asked excitedly. "Were you able to stop her?"

EIGHT OF CUPS

Dmitri shook his head. "I was able to follow her for a few blocks and on every block I found a wet mark where she had sprinkled water, so I recited the Last Gospel but then I lost the trail. There were no more wet splashes on the streets anymore. I tried to retrace my steps, thinking I had taken a wrong turn, but... No. I couldn't find wet marks and I could not find Magdalena. But I spent hours looking."

Sophia sighed, slumping back down onto the suitcase.

In the late afternoon, George's taxi was caught in a massive traffic jam. George recognized the streets they were driving along from the trip to the Ďáblice hen-house that morning and thought they were near the back of the castle. Cars inched along, horns blaring. Traffic crawled along in both directions. Traffic signals perched atop their poles communicated nothing to the vehicles below.

The driver fiddled with the radio station dials, changing them from the music station that had been playing. Static sizzled across the airwaves until he found one news report and listened before turning to look at George over his shoulder.

"Excuse me, sir," the driver began. "The river... the floods have risen... the Little Town near the river is being evacuated... our hotel, no longer open." He raised his eyebrows in alarm. His day away from the overanxious town did not seem to be concluding as the small vacation he had clearly hoped for.

George thought a moment. He leaned forward.

"The American Embassy," he instructed the driver. "Get me as close as you can."

Theo stood in the lobby of a hotel, waiting for the clerk to finish with a couple in front of him. He could see an ornate breakfast room or restaurant through the glass partition and a patio beyond that. He winced, the pain still dancing up his shins occasionally. He did not think he could walk to another hotel and be turned away. He had come to this one, across the flooded highway and isolated somewhat from the central area of the Little Town, hoping it was far enough from the main streets to still have at least one vacancy. He kicked one of his heavy suitcases in frustration.

"May I help you, sir?" the clerk asked as a bellhop appeared to carry away the meager luggage of the couple who had completed checking in.

"I hope that wasn't the last room," Theo answered. "Or is there still one available?"

"Yes, sir, we do have several rooms available." The clerk smiled across the counter. "We had vacancies before the... uh, situation that has developed but they are quickly filling. I can offer you one, if you would like."

"Yes! I would like!" Theo collapsed on his elbows in relief on the counter, resting his forehead on his forearms and feeling like he was about to cry.

"Excuse me, sir, but it will be on an upper floor and the elevator is no longer operational because there is no electricity," the clerk continued.

Theo shook his head. "No matter, no matter! I will take it!"

After signing the papers to register and getting his luggage deposited in the new room, he made his way down to the patio to sit, think, and have a tall drink.

As he sat struggling to think of a way to locate his friends, he sipped the beer he had been told was "the last available in our hotel, sir." Several of the other tables were also filled with the hotel's newest guests, it being more comfortable to sit outside on the patio in the afternoon light than to sit in the rooms upstairs with no electricity. The water he had skirted crossing the highway lapped the edge of the patio as if it were a predator hunting him, biding its time, patiently waiting for him to reemerge from his hiding place. A pair of geese paddled into sight, investigating the new reaches of the river, peering curiously at the people peering at them.

"Look, dear!" one woman exclaimed in a Southern accent from the United States, clutching at her husband's arm and pointing to the geese. "It's like they done gone on vacation, wondering, 'Why have we never come to this part of the river before?' They done and gone on an a'venture, just like us!"

"What should we do now, then?" Sophia asked her husband finally. "These suitcases are too heavy to carry much further without knowing where we are going." She paused. "With the evacuation, how will we find the others? They could be anywhere!"

Dmitri nodded, considering the best course of action. Wiping the sweat from his forehead, he gestured up the hill.

"Loreto," he said. "When we first met all the others, it was at the Loreto chapel because Victoria had lit a candle there. If we are going to be able to meet the others again, it would be at Loreto."

At long last, the taxi deposited George on a side street of the Little Town a few blocks from the embassy as George had requested. The driver set the rooster in its cage on the cobblestones and, having received a hefty tip from George, gave George a shiny fold-out luggage cart to wheel the cage down the street. The driver then jumped back into the car and raced off.

George wheeled the rooster along the crowded street

and easily found his way to Magdalena's building. This area of the Little Town, uphill from the river, had clearly not been evacuated and many of those ordered from their residences closer to the river were hoping to find lodging in the neighborhood. The door to Magdalena's building stood wide open, a handful of people in the lobby gawking up the staircase. They turned to George and hurled a barrage of questions at him in Czech.

He shook his head, attempting to both ignore them and answer no as emphatically as he could. He knocked on Magdalena's front door, trusting her to have followed his instructions.

She opened the door and he pushed his way in with the caged rooster on the collapsible handtruck, slamming the door closed behind him before the rush of those desperately hoping for a place to stay could push their way in.

"Let the river swallow them up!"

(early to mid-February 1357)

Nadezda caught herself on the edge of the table, grasping the Candlemas candle tightly at its base, afraid she was about to drop it in shock. "Do not toy with me, Lilith. I warn you again." She could hear the tremble in her voice. What did the she-devil mean?

Lilith looked at her calmly and took a step towards the door. Another of the angelic figures intercepted her, blocking her exit but standing beside Nadezda. "I toy with you not," Lilith insisted. "You have possessed the key to the curse since the day it was uttered."

"How can that be?" demanded Nadezda, feeling more in control and able to stand again without leaning on the table. "How can I possess the key? I was not there when the curse was spoken in the Old Town Square. No one heard all of it." Nadezda paused. "Is it here, even now?" she asked.

Lilith nodded. "No one heard the final clause of Fen'ka's dying words," she agreed, again avoiding calling Fen'ka declarations a curse. "She muttered them as the smoke filled her lungs and she collapsed. Unconscious but alive when the fire began to eat her flesh. It is also true that you were not there to hear even what she did speak loudly enough for the crowd to cower at." Lilith's mouth curled into a coy smile.

"Tell me the key! What do I possess that allows me to rewrite the curse?" Nadezda demanded, her patience wearing thin with Lilith's efforts to avoid answering her fundamental question.

Lilith stepped away from Nadezda and turned to survey the room behind her. Nadezda saw her regard Milos, with the amulet. Then the door into the other room, through which Vavrinec's snoring and Petr's occasional stirring could be heard. Then the three angelic forms keeping their ever-watchful gaze on her. Escape had to still be impossible. Lilith turned again to Nadezda.

"Svetovit will not be pleased to learn that I have divulged the secret. It is has been his only hope—lo, these several months of waiting. He has bided his time, knowing that the key would come to pass one day and then his full wrath against the city that has betrayed him and abandoned his worship could fall," Lilith informed her. "Until then, he has steered events as best he can to avenge both himself and his handmaiden Fen'ka against the people of the Vltava valley."

"Then I am sorry you, as well, must face his wrath," Nadezda said. "But I demand you tell me the key within my grasp." She felt her fingers, grasping the Candlemas candle so tightly, growing numb but she dared not shift it to her other hand and risk Lilith escaping as the candle moved.

"Very well." Lilith pointed to the fireplace. "The key to the curse burns upon your hearth."

"How can that be? There is nothing there! Only coals and ash!" Nadezda's glance shifted from Lilith to the hearth and back again, suspicious that Lilith had deposited something there that she had not seen. But, no. Only the banked ashes. Not even the flicker of a tiny flame.

Lilith strode about the room and gestured. A hazy image shimmered into focus in the air filling the fireplace above the ashes. Lilith spoke and Nadezda could see Fen'ka, tied and chained to the stake in the midst of the flames. She could see the old woman's lips moving but heard no voice. Then she saw

"Let the River Swallow Them Up!"

Fen'ka cough violently and her head loll to one side as the old woman fainted from inhaling all the smoke generated by the green wood with which the fire had been stoked.

"Let all this come to pass as surely as this fire itself will finally die." Lilith spoke Fen'ka's dying words. "When this fire dies, let all their nightmares come to life." The image above Nadezda's carefully banked ashes flickered and was gone.

"That fire has been dead for many months!" insisted Nadezda. "Its ashes, with those of Fen'ka, were put into the river the next day. There should be nothing restraining Svetovit's hand. What has that fire to do with my hearth?"

Nadezda felt the breath catch in her throat. Without moving, Lilith's face was leaning into hers, her body close enough that Nadezda could have wrapped her arms around the demon's body and singed the free-flowing hair with the candle in her hands.

"Have you truly no notion of how that fire came to be the same as that which burns upon your hearth?" Nadezda could smell Lilith's breath, the stench of long-dead bodies and rotten fruit.

Nadezda searched her memory. What had the one to do with the other?

"I cannot tell," Nadezda admitted to Lilith.

Lilith was across the room again, next to Milos on Petr's cot. From the corner of one eye, Lilith's glance slid slowly along Milos' sleeping form and the most delicate tip of her tongue slid along her lips. Nadezda feared that the monster would leap upon her son. But then Lilith turned to Nadezda once again.

"Recall that afternoon," Lilith instructed her. "How did you learn that Fen'ka had been burned?"

"Recalling that afternoon is the work of a child," Nadezda

209

replied with scorn. She would never forget, how sick she had felt in her stomach when Petr excitedly described what had gone on in the square without her knowledge. Petr, who had run into the house and wanted to know what the word "vindication" meant. Petr, who had circled the room before throwing the firebrand in his hand into the fireplace...

Nadezda caught her breath and Lilith, smiling in her beguiling way, nodded as each recognized that the other knew everything.

"Petr brought a torch that he had seized and..."

"... and ran home with it," Lilith finished the sentence. "He cast the burning stick into the fire here and joined Fen'ka's fire to this. So Fen'ka's fire still burns upon your hearth and Svetovit waits for it to die out and then..."

"... then all that stands between him and the destruction of Prague will be removed," Nadezda concluded Lilith's sentence. Lilith nodded again.

Panic gripped Nadezda's bowels and she staggered to the bench behind her. She had nearly allowed the fire in the hearth to die a week or more ago. It had seemed an irritation and an inconvenience. It would have been an embarrassment to ask a neighbor for coals to begin her fire anew. But, now... What might the consequences for Prague have been if she had not been able to rekindle the fire from that last ember in the depth of the ashes? She shuddered to realize that Prague might have been laid waste and she would never have encountered Lilith or discovered the secret of the curse.

"So, now you possess both the key to the curse and the knowledge to rewrite its ending." Lilith, now referred to Fen'ka's appeal to Svetovit as a curse. "You have all the knowledge I possess that can aid you to save your beloved Prague. But do not be so vainglorious as to think that a fool such as yourself is clever enough to stave off the wrath of Svetovit forever. However you rewrite the curse, he will find a way to serve his own ends. Rewritten it may be, but not eradicated."

Nadezda slowly nodded, considering already how she might reformulate the outcome of the fire's demise. But then Lilith was at the fireplace and Nadezda snapped her attention back to the jealous wife of Adam. She leaped from the bench and thrust the Candlemas candle towards Lilith. The flame passed through the midst of the shadow that was the ancient enemy of the human race.

Nadezda could see the flame within Lilith's frame and then the candle was beside the witch's hip, opposite to where it had entered her torso. Lilith screamed in rage and agony, contorting her mouth in fury and crying out like a wounded lioness. The air reverberated with the terrible sound. One of the angels was behind Lilith blocking her attempt to escape up the chimney.

The screams went on and on, the beautiful figure melting and resolving into that of the hag and then forming again into the seductive beauty, snarling at Nadezda and baring her teeth in rage.

"Think you that the amulet around your son is enough to protect him and your pitiful family? Know you not that I can persuade your husband to give his seed to me?" she taunted Nadezda. "In his dreams I can come to him and lie with him and bring forth children that will wreak more harm on your beloved Prague than even Svetovit could ever accomplish!" She hissed at Nadezda, a forked serpent's tongue darting out between her teeth.

"No, you cannot," Nadezda warned Lilith. "I will have your promise ere you go this night that you will depart not only from my house but will go from Prague forever and trouble the people of the city here no more for as long as the sun and moon endure!"

"So you threatened me earlier." Lilith stepped away from the fireplace. "Remind me why I would agree."

"Because if you do not," Nadezda reminded her, "I will give the angels leave to bind you hand and foot and bring you to the judgment seat of God for your insolence and murders." She gestured towards the fiery sentinels around the room with her free hand. Senoi, Sansenoi, and Samangeloph all seemed to bow their heads in acknowledgment and edge that much closer to Lilith.

Lilith looked about her again, seemingly realizing she was still trapped. She looked at Nadezda. "Depart from Prague for as long as the sun and moon endure?" she repeated, her gentle laughter mocking Nadezda. "Even you in your simplicity must realize that even I cannot make a vow of such duration. As long as the sun and moon endure? That is impossible. Who can tell what other vow might override that, just as you hope to override Fen'ka's words? I cannot make that promise."

Nadezda stepped closer. "I will plunge this candle into your bowels again and give the angels leave to seize you."

"I cannot make the promise that you ask," Lilith protested. "But I can vow that I will depart from Prague and that when I return again, I shall leave your family untouched for as long as the sun and moon endure."

Nadezda stopped. "Leave my family untouched? For as long as the sun and moon endure?" She considered the offer.

"I so vow," Lilith repeated.

"Then go. Depart from Prague for the present." Nadezda turned and rested both her hands on the table, concealing the still-burning Candlemas candle from Lilith's vision.

"Let the River Swallow Them Up!"

Another blood-curdling scream shattered the night behind Nadezda. The flaming figure near the door she faced winked out. A mighty wind blasted through the room, knocking mugs and pitchers from their places. When she turned again to look behind her, Lilith and the three angels were gone.

Exhausted, Nadezda collapsed onto a bench and licked her fingers, extinguishing the Candlemas candle with moistened fingertips, soot smudging the patterns in her skin. The wick sizzled and the flame evaporated into the darkness. She set aside the candle and allowed her face to sink into her folded arms on the tabletop. She wept, unsure that even with this knowledge she would be able to avert the wrath of Svetovit.

Nadezda made her way to the rabbi's study again the next day. She told him of her encounter with Lilith and all she had learned from the creature the rabbi referred to as "that vile *makhesheyfe*."

"Why did you not warn me of her ability to escape through a mirror?" she wanted to know.

"I had no idea," he responded. "I will make a note, however, and add that to the lore that concerns Lilith so those who hunt that vile *makhesheyfe* might know more of her tricks and deceptions and not allow her to escape through one." He picked up his quill, dipped it in the ink, and scratched a reminder to himself on the parchment before him. He shook his head in dismay when she told him she had nearly allowed the fire to die as she had pondered the puzzle of delivering Prague.

"Your attempts to save the city might have led directly to its destruction. I told you, dear one, that this is a dangerous game. A necessary one, I agree. But dangerous." He looked at her over the rim of his spectacles as he sat perched on his stool. She sat below him, on the edge of the stool he had cleared for her. The maid stood near the door, leaning against the doorframe, her eyes closed as she listened to the conversation, trembling slightly.

The rabbi cleared his throat. "Alas, my child, I fear that perhaps you have not heard the news that fills the market of the Old Town Square these past days. It is reported that the winter has grown warmer, unusually warm for these midwinter weeks. It is almost as if spring has come to the regions upriver. Heavy rain is falling there and snow banks have begun to melt, all contributing to the height of the Vltava. Floods unlike those seen for many, many years have inundated the towns along the river. Many communities of my people as well as of the Bohemians, the Germans, and others have been washed away. Have you heard no rumors of this?"

Nadezda confessed that in her concern with Lilith and Fen'ka and the curse, she had listened to little of the news that occupied most of the residents of Prague.

Rabbi Isaac went on. "The river is growing increasingly high and these floods are coming dangerously close. Word of all this first began to trickle into Prague," he paused, so that Nadezda appreciated his play on words, "just a week ago. After you nearly allowed the flames in your hearth to expire."

Nadezda gasped, her hand flying to cover her mouth.

"Yes, my dear." The rabbi shook his head sadly. "It seems that Svetovit leapt at the opportunity you inadvertently offered him. By allowing the fire to nearly die, you opened the door for Svetovit to act. In rebuilding the fire, the door was closed again— thanks be to *ha-shem*!—but Svetovit has set loose a series of storms and changes in the weather that cannot easily be stopped. Not even by Svetovit himself. The swelling river is beyond control, even if he cannot make it any worse at this point."

"LET THE RIVER SWALLOW THEM UP!"

"I should never have let my attention wander," Nadezda scolded herself. "I have brought disaster upon us all, Rabbi Isaac, all because I thought, in my arrogance and pride, that I could save us all!"

"You must not chastise yourself so," the rabbi comforted her, taking his spectacles in his hand. "You had no idea that allowing the fire to die could bring such consequences upon our heads. You were attempting to save us, and that is always a good thing. As our Talmud teaches us, child: 'He that saves a single child has saved the world.' You sought to save many worlds in saving the children of Prague and their parents. You are to be commended for that. It is not your fault that the floods bear down on us. They may yet be averted if we discover the proper way to reformulate this curse."

They sat quietly, considering what options lay before them.

"Even though you control the fire, you cannot undo the curse altogether," the rabbi reminded them. "How do you propose to rewrite the conclusion of the curse?"

Nadezda ventured to offer one idea that had come to her in the sleepless hours since Lilith's departure. "Rabbi Isaac, rather than tie the consummation of the curse to the dying of the fire, I had thought to tie its consummation to the dying of the world. If Svetovit is barred from Prague until the end of the ages, then his wrath will be irrelevant. Whatever dangers his anger poses for the city will be subsumed in the dangers of the Last Judgment. He will even face judgment, then. The Day of Doom will bring both the realization and the frustration of all his plans and hopes."

The rabbi chuckled. "How very appropriate," he agreed. "Prevented from destroying the city until it is already caught up in the conflagration that destroys and renews the world. I congratulate you, child, for your ingenuity." His eyes twinkled. "But how do you propose to phrase it?"

Nadezda shook her head. "That I have not sorted out yet. Simply telling Svetovit that he may not touch the city until the Last Day will not succeed. Fen'ka's words made the consummation of the curse dependent on the dying of the fire. To rewrite the curse, its consummation must still depend on the dying of the fire but with another condition following that. That other condition must be an event that cannot happen apart from the Last Day."

The rabbi considered that possibility. "Might it not be," he suggested after some minutes of thought, "that the additional condition, which would still be consistent with the original curse, might tie its consummation to the passage of a certain period of time?" Seeing Nadezda's shock, he hastened to add, "A very long period of time, of course, my dear."

"Such as the time it takes a fire to die?" Nadezda asked him. She had been proud of her idea to make the fruition of the curse depend on the coming of the Doomsday and was afraid that tying the unleashing of the full power of the curse to anything else might thwart her attempts to delay the curse to the point that it could do no harm. But the rabbi's idea had merit, she had to admit.

"If we tie the unleashing of the curse to an indistinct but lengthy period of time, it must involve a period of years that is important somehow to Svetovit," Nadezda built on the rabbi's idea. "It must needs involve numbers that are important to him, numbers that would seize his attention and yet be so large as to provide the delay we are looking for."

"Yes," the rabbi agreed. "It must be a number of years that cannot come to pass before the end of the world and yet the computation must involve numbers that are inherently important to Svetovit and these are fairly small, are they not?"

"They are." Nadezda was unsure which of them, she or the rabbi, might know more about Svetovit.

"What numbers are magically important to him?" the rabbi asked her, indicating his own uncertainty.

Nadezda tried to recall what her grandmother might have told her about Svetovit that would reveal his favorite numbers. "I think that four must be important to him," she concluded. "He has four faces," she offered by way of explanation.

"His horse has eight legs, does it not?" the rabbi asked her.

"It does!" The rabbi clearly knew more of Svetovit than he had indicated earlier.

"Four and eight." The rabbi scanned the rows and stacks of books about the room as if hoping the golden letters on their spines might reveal a further secret. "Four is the number of many things—such as the rivers that flow from Paradise to water the Earth or the elements that constitute the world. Our sages also tell us that 'four' indicates a door, an opening, while 'eight' is the ongoing conflict between unity and plurality. Eight is twice four, a multiple of four, so we come back to four again." His eyes rested again on Nadezda. "The number of years we choose must somehow be a multiple of four, I think."

Nadezda considered and nodded her agreement. "A multiple of four but one so large that it must not come to pass until the world comes to an end." She wrinkled her brow in thought. "But what number of years is both so large and yet so fluid as to allow for the uncertainty of when the world itself will end?"

The rabbi retrieved his feather pen and scribbled computations on the parchment before him. "Simply calculating a number of years, alas, will not be enough." He held up the parchment for Nadezda to examine but she could not make out his scrawls from her seat. He gestured for her to come closer and sit beside him, as she had when he copied out the talisman to protect Milos. Even at this close range, she did not recognize the figures Rabbi Isaac had used.

"As an example, my dear," he pointed to one set of figures. "If we multiply four years twice, we only arrive at eight years as the result. Even if we use larger multiples of four and attempt to expand the result," his pen flying across the page and more figures spilling out in a myriad of combinations, "we only arrive at longer periods of years but not so long as to encompass the Last Days."

Nadezda looked confused. He explained again.

"If we take four and multiply it by itself, we arrive at sixteen and if we then multiply that again by four, we arrive at sixty-four. But it is only sixty-four. If we multiply that by four yet again, the result is two hundred and fifty-six. To multiply that one last time by four again, making four multiplications by four, we still only have one thousand and twenty-four at the conclusion. A very large number of years. A very long time, indeed. But long enough to warrant the coming of the Messiah by that date?" He shook his head sadly. "It is difficult to say."

He considered his computations again. "Furthermore, it is a complicated computation. In the moment of declaring a new conclusion of Fen'ka's curse in addition to the extinguishing of the fire, I fear that we need an elegant but simple calculation, one that can be stated with clarity and without confusion. Svetovit will struggle with all his might against the rewriting of the curse and the delay of his triumph, so the calculation must be something that can be declared even in the midst of Svetovit's onslaught."

Nadezda understood now. "Then we need to multiply a period other than years." They both stared at the figures. Nadezda gasped as an idea occurred to her. "We could calculate generations rather than years, could we not?"

Rabbi Isaac looked at her, startled, and then at his figures again. "Genius!" he exclaimed. "Generations, not years! Truly genius! Nadezda, you prove your ability yet again!"

Nadezda blushed at the rabbi's praise, unable to think of an adequate response. She fumbled with words nervously and then gave up the attempt.

"Now," the rabbi asked her, "how shall we multiply the generations in a way that Svetovit will consider binding using numbers that already control him in some regard?"

Nadezda thought another moment. "Why not use the number of his horse's legs? Can we not multiply four generations by eight?

The rabbi's quill quickly scratched another series of computations on his page. "That brings us to thirty-two generations." His shoulders sunk and he shook his head slowly from side to side. He turned to Nadezda.

"Child, the history of my people is broken into periods both sad and glorious. The exile to Babylon, one of the most sad of all, was a period of seventy years. That is to say, a period of three—no, nearly four—generations. The years from Adam to Abraham were nineteen generations, from Abraham to Moses seven generations, and our teacher Rambam—forgive me, dear child, that is our fond name for our great teacher, Moses Maimonides—has calculated that from Moses who received the written Torah on Mount Sinai to the final compilation of the Oral Torah by the sages was forty generations. Of course, this compilation of the Oral Torah was not complete until after the destruction of the second Temple by the Romans. Shortly thereafter, the Romans drove us away and destroyed Jerusalem. They left no stone atop another."
He swallowed. He sighed. "We have wandered in exile from

219

that land promised by the Lord to our forefather Abraham for nearly seventy generations, the same number as the years we suffered in exile in Babylon after the destruction of the first Temple. Do you realize what this means, my dear one?" The rabbi's eyes glistened, wet with tears. A small smile played upon his lips.

"It is my hope, beloved Nadezda, that our exile will soon be over, that the accomplishment of the seventy generations of this exile will correspond to the seventy years of our previous exile. If that is so, then the coming of the Messiah and the End of Days will arrive shortly. If not, then the thirty-two generations of our current calculation can be added to the seventy generations of exile that we are in the midst of suffering. The resulting one hundred and two generations far exceed any of the other periods of my people's history. The Messiah must come before that time and the End of Days be accomplished prior to the fulfilling of the thirty generations we will insist Svetovit wait before he can accomplish his will." He took a deep breath. "Do you understand, my child?"

Nadezda nodded. "According to your hopes and calculations, the Doomsday of the world might be accomplished in two generations, Rabbi Isaac. But it will certainly be accomplished before the end of the thirty-two generations that result from multiplying the four faces of Svetovit by the eight legs of his great horse." She understood that much. The city would certainly be safe from Svetovit's attack if the curse were rewritten in such a way.

"That is true. Furthermore," he pointed at certain of the figures with the nib of his pen, scattering a few drops of ink clinging to the tip of the quill, "it is significant that the number thirty-two, which can be considered as a 'three' and then as a 'two,' portends what we are looking for as well. The number 'three' signifies the physical rewards and punishments of this world while the number 'two' indicates the dwelling of the Blessed One on Earth and the fulfillment of the purpose of the creation. This is confirmation that *ha-shem* will send salvation to the earth within these thirty-two generations and allot the rewards and punishments due each of us, including Svetovit."

Nadezda was very impressed, both by the rabbi's computations and his command of the esoteric meanings of the numbers.

The rabbi rocked on his stool, muttering under his breath in a language Nadezda could not make out. Then he took his page of computations and notes on Lilith's use of mirrors and slid it among his other papers on the shelf of the desk. He stood and Nadezda followed his lead.

"You must find a way to get Svetovit's attention and then inform him that the curse is now reformulated according to the terms we have discussed, Nadezda. Then you must extinguish the fire, every spark of it, leaving no ember still burning. If so much as a single coal or ember still glows red, then the curse is not rewritten and Svetovit can vent his rage to the full extent of his power when that last coal does expire." He looked at her with admiration.

"As for confronting Svetovit, I have a small thing that you may find useful." He led her to a corner of his study and found a bag of coarse sackcloth behind some books. He took it and searched through it, muttering before pulling a tangled length of red cord from the sack and handing it to Nadezda, careful that they only touched the cord and not each other. He beamed and gestured at the knotted cord in her hand. She began to untangle it.

Rabbi Isaac clapped his hands in delight. He grinned broadly. "I would be honored if you were to take this cord to use when you extinguish the fire and confront Svetovit. It will be my small contribution to both protecting you, child, and the saving of our beloved city."

Nadezda clutched the cord to her closely. "Rabbi Isaac, you have already made a much larger contribution. Thanks to you we have the information from Lilith that will allow us to hold Svetovit at bay until the world ends."

"Ah, dear child—he will struggle against this but you must remain resolute. The sages and masters of the mystical lore tell us that we must stand within the protective circle when we confront the powers of darkness, much as those who practice the old ways of the Bohemians teach. The circle may be etched or drawn with a knife or be formed by tying the ends of a cord together and arranging it as a ring to stand in. You may not have time to carefully draw a circle before Svetovit begins his onslaught. Be sure to make the circle before you attract his attention, Nadezda, and use this cord to do so. The sages teach that such a cord should be red, which signifies the energy that both creates and destroys the world. It is just such a cord that I have been saving for a purpose—I knew not what or when but I know now that I have been waiting to give it to you."

He closed his eyes before continuing. "I know that you can do this. You were given the custody of the fire by the mystery of Providence, and it is up to you to use that custody to save the city." He gestured mysteriously above her and again muttered words under his breath that she could not understand. But she knew these were the words of a prayer, another gift to aid her in her coming confrontation with the old god who was their common enemy. The rabbi opened his eyes again.

Nadezda stood before him as the maid opened the door. "I thank you for your assistance and your confidence in me, Rabbi Isaac. Together, our prayers and knowledge and resolution can accomplish the deliverance of Prague."

Now that she was aware of the floods upriver, Nadezda heard talk of them all around her. It seemed that everyone had heard of the wall of water descending on the cities along the river and threatening to wash away everything it encountered. Those that lived along the river were finding friends or family that could put them up until the water arrived and then descended or were finding inns, which some could ill-afford, far from the expected deluge. No one seemed to know how long it might take for the floodwater to arrive but all seemed convinced it was on its way.

Nevertheless, Nadezda knew her next task was discovering how best to attract Svetovit's attention so he would listen as she reformulated the curse in the way she and Rabbi Isaac had settled on.

The following Sunday afternoon, she found herself rapping at the door of Ryba the midwife for the second time in as many days. Having received no answer when she came knocking the day before, she had guessed that Ryba was assisting a woman in the neighborhood to give birth and was hoping that the midwife would be back home by midafternoon the next day. She was about to turn away from the door when it opened and Ryba was standing there in her night shift, one eye shut and her tangled hair untidily hidden under a bandana tied askew across the back of her head.

"Yes?" Ryba demanded, in the husky voice common to those who have just awakened.

"Pardon me, Ryba," Nadezda hastened to offer her apologies for disturbing the midwife's rest.

Ryba's eyes both popped open as she took in the face of the woman whose voice she recognized in her stupor.

"Nadezda! Not to worry! Come in!" Ryba pulled the door wide and gestured for Nadezda to enter. Nadezda passed from the cloudy and overcast afternoon into the dusky gloom of the house. With all its shutters drawn and the door shut, it could as easily been midnight as midafternoon. Ryba stirred the coals of the fire and added kindling and then set a kettle hanging in the midst of the fire to make tea. She turned and invited Nadezda to sit as they waited for the water to boil.

"I came yesterday afternoon," Nadezda began. "You were not here. I'm guessing that someone was giving birth and you were needed."

Ryba rubbed her forehead and squinted towards a window before looking at Ryba. She licked her gums between her missing teeth. "Yes," she answered. "It was a long and difficult labor. Verushka the cobbler's wife delivered a son, alive and healthy, thanks be to God. But it was a labor that went on for nearly two days. I was weary, too weary for words, by the time the boy was delivered. But that is why you find me so." She waved her hand about her face. "I came home this morning and was sleeping. If you had not knocked, I imagine that I should have slept until noon tomorrow!"

"Well, thank you for hearing my knocking and rousing yourself." Nadezda flattened her skirt across her knees. "I have some questions but can return another time if you are too exhausted to speak with me."

"No, no, dear child. Not at all!" Ryba rose and patted Nadezda's shoulder as she gathered mugs and dried herbs to make tea and set them on the table. "I need to drink something to restore my strength or all the sleep in the world could not revive me!" She laughed and fetched the steaming kettle from the fire, wrapping her hand in a towel to lift the kettle and bring it to the table. She and Nadezda spooned the herbs into the pot. The aromatic steam rose and caressed their nostrils as the herbs steeped.

"What have you been hoping to ask these last few days?" Ryba asked. "Is it something more to do with Lilith?"

"Not directly, Ryba. Lilith came again the night of Candlemas but I have discussed her visitation with the rabbi," Nadezda answered. "I think she will be a long time coming back to trouble any family in Prague."

Ryba poured the tea into the mugs. "That is a blessing, to be sure! Thanks be to God for that, Nadezda!" She took a sip of tea. There was a pause in the conversation, just long enough to be uncomfortable. "So. What is it that you wish to ask me, then?"

Nadezda had thought of telling Ryba the whole tale of the deciphering of the curse and her plans to rewrite it, now that she knew she had custody of the fire serving as the lynchpin of the curse. But she had deemed it unwise to let it become common knowledge. There was no telling what unwelcome attention that might bring. Even if Ryba made a vow to tell nothing of Nadezda's plans to anyone, Nadezda still considered it dangerous to say anything. If she were successful, the strange occurrences in Prague would cease and those clever enough to notice would realize something had happened to annul the curse. If she were not successful, then the city stood in even greater danger than it did now, for Svetovit's wrath would be roused to a fever pitch by her efforts.

"Lilith made a vow to depart from Prague," Nadezda ventured to tell the midwife. "But the rabbi believes that we ought to inform Svetovit of this. If the old god knows that Lilith made this vow, he can hold her to her word and will be eager to keep her far from the territory he considers his own."

Ryba mulled over Nadezda's words as she sipped her tea again. She seemed about to speak but then reconsidered and set her mouth to the lip of the mug. She drank deeply of the steaming liquid.

"I remember my grandmother telling me that Svetovit was worshipped on Hradčany," Nadezda told Ryba. "But I cannot recall if she ever said how to get his attention."

Ryba searched Nadezda's eyes, then sighed.

"Yes, Svetovit was worshipped by the cutting of the throat of a sacrificial cock on Hradčany, exactly where the new cathedral is rising on the hilltop," Ryba told her. "It was important that the cock to be sacrificed was black. Entirely black. He would always respond to whoever slit the throat of a black rooster on that hilltop, so I imagine he would still respond if someone did so today."

"A black rooster, heh?" Nadezda knew that it could be difficult to find a rooster that was entirely black, without so much as a smudge of white in any of its feathers. It might also be suspicious if she were to become known for trying to obtain such a bird. "He would never accept another?"

"Only a coal-black one," Ryba repeated. "Black as night." She sipped her tea again.

It could also be difficult to gain access to the construction area atop the hill. "Was there any other place where the rooster could be offered? That Svetovit would lurk and listen to his worshippers?" Nadezda hoped for some alternative. "Perhaps in the Old Town Square? Or on the Kampa isle, where the gypsies camp? They are no doubt fond of Svetovit and happy to offer him a black rooster on occasion."

"No doubt they are," agreed Ryba. "But, no, dear child. The only place in the river valley that a black rooster could be offered with the certainty that Svetovit would respond was atop Hradčany." She peered into Nadezda's face. "You say that you must speak to Svetovit and tell him of Lilith's oath.

226

Why not cry aloud to him from wherever you please? Fen'ka certainly did not find it necessary to stand on Hradčany with a black rooster to get Svetovit's attention."

Nadezda, about to offer another possibility—that of slitting the throat of the rooster somewhere else but sprinkling its blood atop Hradčany—halted. Ryba was clearly guessing at some connection between her efforts to speak with Svetovit and Fen'ka's death.

"But who is to say what means Fen'ka had employed to gain Svetovit's attention?" Nadezda quickly answered. "Or how frequently she might have done so? Yes, she needed only words to gain Svetovit's attention, but I have never invoked him before and have no intention to ever again. I have no desire to be intimate with him as Fen'ka might have been. I must rely on the older, more certain ways to whisper in his ear."

Ryba nodded, seemingly satisfied with Nadezda's response. "If you do succeed in rousing him and gaining an audience," the midwife asked, "how will you protect yourself?"

"The rabbi gave me a red cord, and told me that its ends must be tied together and thrown to the earth to make a magic circle." Nadezda felt it would be safe to reassure the midwife that she was taking no more risks than absolutely necessary.

Ryba nodded again. "A circle is magic, in and of itself, whether it is made of cord or inscribed with gold dust." She looked over her shoulder, as if peering into the past. "A circle attracts power and spirits the way raw, bloody meat attracts wolves in the forest." She turned to the fireplace as if to discern the future among the glowing coals and the sliver of flame that danced atop them. "Red is the color of war and power and courage. Red is an excellent choice." She turned again to Nadezda. "It will serve you well."

There seemed something else the midwife wanted to say.

227

Nadezda waited.

Finally Ryba spoke again. "The rabbi is not the only one who can give you gifts." She stood and walked to a corner of the room, where she lifted a large basket filled with cloths and rags from atop a large metal canister, such as those used to store cow milk. After placing the basket onto the floor, she removed the lid of the canister and set that aside. Rummaging about on a nearby shelf, she found another, similar canister but much, much smaller. A canister such as that milk might be carried home from the market in. She also retrieved a ladle with a long handle.

Ryba dipped the ladle into the larger canister. Nadezda heard it splash into whatever the canister held and then watched as the midwife carefully filled the small canister with water from the larger. Ryba placed the lid on the smaller of the canisters and gave it to Nadezda. "This is dead water," she explained, replacing the lid of the larger canister and then setting the basket of rags atop it again. "You know what dead water is, Nadezda?"

Nadezda nodded. "Dead water has been used to wash the corpse to prepare it for burial."

"This is the water I have used to wash the stillborn infants I have delivered over the years." Ryba confirmed Nadezda's supposition. "Do you know what might it be used for?"

Nadezda remembered her grandmother telling her once about the uses of dead water. "It can be used to inflict a curse, I think…" she answered slowly.

Ryba nodded. "Yes, Nadezda, you remember more than you think. There are ways in which dead water can be so used. But more important for you, dead water can also be used to wash away a curse."

Nadezda was unsure of what to say and Ryba must have

seen that uncertainty play across her lips. "Take the water," the midwife told her. "It may prove useful in ways that you—or even I—cannot imagine at present, either against Lilith or some other creature of the darkness. If you are thinking of confronting Svetovit, you can never have too many tools at your disposal."

Nadezda began her search for a coal-black rooster in the markets the next day. She visited each of the dealers in fowl and explained that she needed a cock, dark as pitch and black as night. When they looked askance and offered one of their many other fine, fine birds, she would always shake her head and say, "No. Only a black cock will do."

When they asked why she was so insistent, she would wink and smile at them. "It is rumored that the black roosters are the strongest, the most resilient, the swiftest and their beaks the sharpest in the cockfighting ring." The dealers would then smile and nod their approval. "It is also said that when they lose a match, they are the tastiest in the pot," she would add with a laugh, a laugh she strove to have mimic Lilith's. Light. Musical. A laugh to set her listeners at ease and lull them into trusting her.

"It may take some time," one dealer confessed. "Such a bird will not come cheaply, either, for the very reasons you say."

Nadezda pulled two coins from her purse and gave them to the dealer. "If you hear of such a bird, obtain it and hold it here. I will return each week. Or send word that you have it to the house of Vavrinec, the baker, who lives near St. Martin's in the Újezd district of the Old Town. I will gladly pay whatever price you ask," she promised. "But I must obtain such a bird or my investments will all be lost."

Making her way across town, Nadezda came to her other

destination. Opening the door to the apothecary's shop in a small plaza built around a fountain down an alleyway from the Old Town Square, she set the bell atop the doorframe jingling. The walls were lined with shelves and the shelves filled with an amazing variety of glass vials, bottles, jugs, flasks, and decanters in a wild variety of shapes and sizes. Each contained seeds or roots, leaves or stalks, granulated powders or infusions in as many colors as Nadezda could ever imagine. Some were nearly empty, with only a few, almost invisible seeds remaining at the bottom. Others were full to nearly overflowing with their dried and crumbling contents. Some infusions, she could tell simply by looking at them, were thick and oily while others were some small piece of nature still steeping in water that gently bubbled over a candle flame.

The elderly Italian gentleman who kept the shop, having come to Prague from Florence, was atop a ladder that leaned against the high wall behind the sales counter. He turned to look over his shoulder as the bell rang and, seeing Nadezda, smiled at her. His gray hair was long and clean, curling down around his jowls, which bristled with thick muttonchops. He clambered down the ladder and over to her.

"So good to see you, my dear. What can I help you with?" He was a short man. His head bobbed and his eyes twinkled. He gestured towards the thousands of medications and herbs and solutions that stocked his shelves. "What might I find for you today?"

"I am looking for four herbs," Nadezda explained. She set her baskets filled with other purchases in the markets earlier that day on the counter. The various scales and weights set out to measure the purchases were brightly polished and glistened in the dim light of the overcast day.

"Four herbs," Nadezda began again. "One for each of

the four elements. Each must be protective or effective at cleansing the air of evil miasmas. Exorcistic herbs. Only a small quantity of each," she hastened to add. "Just enough to burn in a fire to cleanse the house."

"Ah, yes, I see." The apothecary rubbed his hands together and ran his eyes along the shelves of his shop. "Step this way, my dear." He reached for a jar that held a handful of small brown and gray chunks of dried resin. He pulled out the stopper and shook a few onto his open palm. He held the chunks out for Nadezda to inspect.

"Myrrh, my dear. A resin from Arabia and Ethiopia, burned as a fragrant incense. It is obtained—like its cousin, the precious frankincense—by scratching the bark of the myrrh tree. The resin drips from the scored bark and is collected after it has dried. You can see the high quality of the myrrh I stock, my dear, though it is difficult to obtain." He gently placed the chunks of myrrh on a small brass saucer on the counter and replaced the stopper in the neck of the jar to protect the rest of his stock of the precious pellets.

"Myrrh is easy to burn, and because it is—at its heart—the sap of a tree, it is associated with the element water," he continued to explain. "It also absorbs moisture, another reason for it being associated with water. That is why it has been used as an embalming agent for centuries in the Holy Land and other places. You recall, perhaps, that the Gospel tells us that myrrh was used in the burial of Our Lord?" He winked at Nadezda.

She sniffed the yellow pellets. She could smell nothing.

"Oh, no, my dear. In that form, its fragrance is impossible to detect. But when it is placed on the coals, ah…" He kissed his fingertips. "It is then that the myrrh blooms."

He bustled about the shop, picking up one jar and setting it down in favor of another, which he then rejected as well, muttering all the while. He bent down to a shelf near the floor behind the counter to retrieve something and when he stood he held a tall, rotund ceramic pot. He nearly dropped it onto the counter, where it landed with a dull thud. He took a metal scoop from the counter and filled it with the crumbled leaves that filled the pot. He deposited the scoopful of leaves into a small bowl and replaced the pot below.

Nadezda recognized the scent of mint. It was always a fragrance that delighted her.

"This mint is the finest in all of Bohemia and I import it for only special customers. It may be burned for protection, as well as used for tea or rubbed against your temples for headache." He squinted and rubbed his own temples briefly. "Trust me, I know from most bitter experience."

Nadezda laughed. "Which element does mint go with?"

"Air," the apothecary replied, already looking for the next item to recommend. He peered into vials and pulled out jars hidden behind several others on the shelves. He sniffed some before shaking his head and returning them to their places. Satisfied with his third selection, he placed a handful of tiny seeds on the counter.

"The seeds of toadflax," he proclaimed. "It partakes of the element fire and is a potent hex breaker and eradicator of miasmas. Burning it can make your home the safest in Prague." He was clearly proud of himself for discovering this among his wares. He leaned over to whisper in Nadezda's ear, "I had even forgotten that I had it." He chuckled and shrugged. "What can I do?" he asked. "The best-stocked apothecary in Prague and with some of the most rare and high-quality herbs anywhere. But some so rare and little used I forget they are here."

Nadezda nodded. "Good sir, I have here herbs of fire, air, and water. I have need yet of one of earth. Surely you must recall one of your special items that is of earth."

The apothecary blushed. "I do, my dear, I do. It is here somewhere. Now, if only I could recall it!" He tapped his temple with one finger, he and Nadezda laughing together. He puttered around the shop again, seemingly unable to find whatever he was looking for. He became distraught. Perplexed. He tapped his foot. Then his frustration melted away and a broad grin replaced a frown. Pulling the ladder along the wall, he climbed to the tallest shelf and brought out a glass flagon filled with dried, crumbling leaves. He measured out a small quantity and placed them on another brass saucer for her inspection.

"Mugwort." He heaved a sigh of relief. "How it got itself to the top shelf, I will never know!"

"Mugwort, I take it then, is an earthen herb of protection?" Nadezda asked. She looked closely at the pale greens and browns, the delicate veins in the bits of leaves that were still intact.

"It is, my dear," the apothecary announced. "Most powerful indeed. Truth to tell, it is one of the most powerful of the protective herbs. It has been used since ancient times, when the Roman soldiers would place a sprig of it in their boots to protect them on the march. It can also be used to inspire prophetic dreams, if you so choose."

He took a breath and went on. "Of course, I am careful to stock only the mugwort that is picked during the waxing or full moon, and that only before sunrise. I take the further precaution—the only apothecary to do so in all Prague, I can assure you—that the mugwort in my shop comes only from the plants that incline to the north. The Devil's direction, you know. Even as a youthful sprig, the mugwort plant seeks to destroy the Wicked One." The apothecary pulled himself up to his full height and threw his shoulders back.

Nadezda was impressed. She had come hoping for only four protective herbs and had stumbled into what was evidently the best-stocked and most knowledgeable apothecary's shop in Prague.

"Yes, these will do nicely," she told him. "Even better than I hoped for."

"Shall I bundle these into sachets for you, my dear?"

"Yes, please do."

The apothecary hummed and sang snatches of tunes under his breath as he weighed the portions of the four things they had selected and made notes on a small chalkboard to help him calculate the prices. When all four sachets were ready, he announced the final price.

Nadezda found she had just enough coins to pay the bill, which turned out to be considerably more than she had anticipated. Nevertheless, she thanked the man for his good cheer and assistance. "Quality costs," she reminded herself, but said nothing of that to the apothecary.

"Always happy to help a young lady, my dear," he brushed aside her compliments. "Come along anytime, anytime." He bowed low and then trotted to open the door for her, her arms again laden with baskets of purchases, only now with the additional burden of the sachets of myrrh, mugwort, mint, and toadflax.

Nearly two weeks later, a boy knocked on Nadezda's door.

"We have the rooster you were looking for," he announced, "at the stall of Andrei the dealer. It is a fine and handsome bird, with great spirit." He grinned and held up the bloody knuckles of one hand. "His claws are sharp and his beak is swift. He will win many fights in the ring."

234

"Let the River Swallow Them Up!"

"Thank you so much, young man!" she exclaimed, pressing a small coin into his other hand as a reward for bringing such happy news. She hurried to finish her midmorning chores and bundled little Milos for a trip to the market in the light rain that had been falling for the fortnight since she had spoken with the rabbi and the midwife. Folk were unsure if the floods would dissipate before reaching the capital, but many had begun to pack their things into bags and wheelbarrows that could be pushed along the streets at any time if the waters approached their doorsteps. She had heard from Vavrinec the stories of more hamlets and towns upriver being washed away in the tremendous floodwaters of the Vltava. Refugees were streaming into the outlying areas of Prague, away from the riverbanks. These extra mouths to feed were an additional strain on the food markets, driving up the cost of a valuable rooster even further. By the time Nadezda reached the dealer's stall and concluded her bargaining for the black rooster in its wicker cage, she had paid nearly twice what she had hoped. Nevertheless, she thought the rooster priceless, so long as she was able to gain Svetovit's attention.

She gathered a small collection of other supplies she would need for her self-appointed task. The red cord the rabbi had given her. A lantern holding what remained of the Candlemas candle. A small but very sharp knife. The four sachets from the apothecary. The small metal canister of dead water. She placed the rooster's cage next to the hearth and her other tools in a small sackcloth drawstring bag beside that. When Petr and Vavrinec returned home from the bakery that evening, they noticed the cock beside the fireplace but had other news to report.

"The river is so high and flowing so quickly that the mill in the Little Town is having difficulty controlling the waterwheel that grinds the wheat," Vavrinec reported. "Logs and broken carts that have been swept along by the floods have become jammed in the waterwheel and nearly broken it several times. The miller is beside himself. No one remembers seeing the river this high or flowing this fast. It is even nearing the bottom of the wooden bridge that spans the river. The brothers that collect the tolls say it has been heard creaking and groaning in the current in a way none of them can recall ever hearing."

"They say it could wash away!" Petr exclaimed. "They say the river could break it up and carry it away, just as it carried away Queen Judith's bridge. Only it would be even more easily broken, since it is wooden and not stone." He knelt and peered into the wicker cage. The rooster crowed and attempted to flap its wings in its confinement.

"Get back from the rooster, Petr!" Nadezda snapped at her younger brother. "It could peck your eye or scratch your face!" Petr pulled back a bit but stayed on his knees near the bird.

"What is it for, Nadezda?" he asked. "Why such a black, black rooster?"

"It is for cockfighting." Nadezda used the same excuse with her brother that she had used in the market to explain her interest. "If he doesn't win in the ring, then we can eat him." She ran her fingers through Petr's hair and he turned toward her.

"Cockfighting? Why?" He admired the rooster again. He looked to Vavrinec. "But can I go with you to the cockfights and watch it kill the other birds?" He could hardly contain his excitement.

"Perhaps," Vavrinec replied slowly, his eyes on Nadezda, who had hers on Petr and the rooster. "In the meantime, get ready for supper!" He playfully swatted at the boy, who dashed into the back to wash his face and hands in the tub.

"LET THE RIVER SWALLOW THEM UP!"

Vavrinec knew what the rooster was for, Nadezda having explained her intentions between their first and second sleep one night a week ago. He had objected at first but not strenuously. He knew that once her mind was made up, his protests would be of little use.

"When do you plan to do this thing?" he asked.

"I am not sure," she told him. "It should be soon. But I will need access to the construction site atop Hradčany, and how simple that may be to arrange, I cannot tell."

"If the bridge fails, it could be months—perhaps years—before it is replaced," Vavrinec pointed out. "No doubt there will be ferries and other boats to carry folk across the river, but it may take weeks for the river to subside enough for even those to navigate the current. If you are certain this can only be done on Hradčany, little opportunity remains."

Nadezda bit her lip. "This may be part of Svetovit's strategy, Vavrinec. He may have started the rainfall and the flooding so that I could not cross to Hradčany and the fire would be all the more likely extinguished. The flood may even be the way he intends to destroy Prague. Who can say what he intends? I only know that our only hope is rewriting the curse, so that it comes due in four times eight generations and not when the fire is extinguished. The fire has been given to us and it is our duty to use it to save the city."

Vavrinec studied her face and finally nodded. "Then you should do it soon. While the bridge still stands. Even tomorrow may be too late."

Petr burst back into the house and Milos began crying for his supper.

"I think not tonight, Vavrinec," Nadezda said quietly. "It would look suspicious, going up to the castle in the night. But tomorrow… Tomorrow may be the best. Besides," she added, starting to laugh and picking up Milos to swing him in a circle about the room, "if I went tonight, how would all these fine men have a supper to eat?"

Petr slept on his cot. Milos lay in his cradle. Vavrinec waited for her in their bed. Nadezda sat before her hearth that night, preparing to burn her protective sachets and then bank this fire for what she knew would be the last time.

She spread the logs and embers evenly across the back of the fireplace. The carpet of red glowed warmly in the otherwise dark room. Delicate tongues of flame danced here and there above the chunks of wood and clumps of coal. She could sit and watch the fire like this for hours as a small girl. The waves of light and heat playing along the edges of the remnants of the logs, which crumbled and fell into each other with a burst of sparks, had always fascinated her. Golden hints of treasure troves lay deep within the labyrinths and coves of the coals, places where the fire fairies known as salamanders might easily hide, waiting to dart out when they thought mortals least likely to notice them.

After watching the fire for a few minutes, she pulled the four sachets toward her and set them in her lap. She had a two-fold purpose in burning these protective herbs tonight. One was to cleanse her house of any remaining vestigial presence of Lilith. The other was to purify the fire itself and, by releasing the cleansing smoke up the chimney into the city's air, to further protect the city. Though the amounts of the protective herbs were small, their power would settle wherever the smoke from her chimney drifted.

Beginning with the sachet with the elemental association most akin to her purposes, she opened the toadflax. With her fingertips, she picked up the small, dry seeds belonging to the element fire, held them aloft, and then cast them into the midst of the element that was their home.

The tiny, dull-brown seeds fell all about the fireplace and instantly began to snap and pop. The seeds burst and jumped about in the coals at the same time their faintly fish-like smell caught her attention. The dark gray smoke curled and twisted in the air, hanging above the coals. The toadflax was a long time burning, and Nadezda could see the jumping seeds turn to shiny black in the heart of the fire. The smoke and the unexpectedly fishy scent drifted into the room and then finally up the chimney and into the night air.

Next, she unwrapped the sachet of mint, the herb associated with the air. Its scent hung strongly on all the sachets, since they had been wrapped up together by the apothecary and kept in the same drawstring bag awaiting their use. Now the dark green leaves, cut and diced into tiny fragments, lay open to the air and looked as fresh and green as the day they had been harvested. Nadezda breathed deeply of the refreshing fragrance and then tossed these leaves into the fireplace.

The mint burned much more quickly than the toadflax. The light gray smoke, tinged with green along the edges of its furrows and ridges, smelled surprisingly acrid, though Nadezda could detect an occasional hint of the familiar mint smell. The shards of green quickly blackened in the fire, though Nadezda could still distinguish them in the sea of reds and oranges of the coals and embers.

The next heaviest of the four elements was earth, so she opened the sachet of mugwort. It was clumpy, and the clumps clung to one another like tufts of fur falling from a cat. The tendrils and veins of the dry leaves held the bits together both in Nadezda's palm and when she tossed them in the fire, in the depths of the flames.

239

The gray-brown smoke quickly rose and hovered above the burning herb. Nadezda recognized the smell of leaves burning in the countryside in the autumn and closed her eyes, breathing deeply of the earthy fragrance. She could see the gardeners in the countryside, where her grandmother had brought her to visit distant cousins, and they were burning the damp leaves to hasten the making of compost and mulch to protect their plots over the winter.

She opened her eyes at last. The feathery black remains of the mugwort drifted among the coals, looking denser than they had in her palm. Nadezda couldn't decide if the dried leaves had simply melted together in the heat of the fireplace or if they resembled scraps of mouse fur in the coals.

Finally, she opened the sachet of myrrh. The myrrh, associated with water and the most antithetical to the fire she intended to give it to, sat in her hands like pale yellow pebbles ranging around the size of her thumbnail. "Almost the color of bread dough," she thought.

She tipped her hands up and the myrrh cascaded into the fireplace and nestled among the embers.

The myrrh was very slow burning, the pebbles singed black along their edges and then taking on the look of toasted, even burnt bread. The gum resin seeped into the coals, causing pools of inky blackness to appear among the red embers. It was the only substance of the four that actually seemed to burn and not simply scorch in the heat. The bitter scent floated into the room as well as the chimney. It was similar to, but not as sickly sweet as, the decomposing flesh of those who had died two or three days before being taken to their graves.

The last of the myrrh's smoke rose through the chimney to join the other smoke from Nadezda's fireplace.

Teased and pulled by the night breezes, the smoke of the four substances associated with the elements drifted across the Old Town. During the course of the night, wisps of the smoke reached each of the three other towns that together made Prague, and cast a protective cloak over the city.

Even the wooden bridge, groaning and sighing under the assault of the rising river and its powerful current, seemed to draw strength from the smoke that drifted by it and curled along its handrails. Already coming loose from its moorings on the Little Town side, the bridge shivered and seemed nearly ready to careen away. Touched by the wisps of smoke, the nails stretched and grew sharper as they bored themselves more securely into the supports that anchored the bridge on the Little Town side. The planks along the length of the bridge seemed to draw together as those nails also burrowed more tightly into the joists. Even the groaning of the bridge seemed to subside, and if anyone had been standing on the bridge, it would have listed somewhat less and felt more sturdy underfoot.

The inexorable rising of the river paused as well. Swift though the current remained, the slow creep of the river onto the Kampa island halted, allowing the fraying edges of the Old and Little Towns to remain dry a few hours longer.

As Nadezda continued to sit before her fireplace, she could not stop a tear from sliding down her cheek. The fire that her mother and grandmother had tended carefully for so many years would be extinguished tomorrow.

"*Babička*, forgive me." She knew her grandmother would approve, even assist her if possible, but Nadezda nevertheless felt guilty for having to kill the fire and kindle a new one using coals from another family's hearth. "All your work, *babička*, to keep the fire alive for us. Forgive me."

That night, neither Nadězda or Vavrinec could sleep. Failing in their attempts and finally giving up the pretense of sleeping, they sat up and looked at each other in the dark. Nadezda heard Milos and Petr breathing steadily and quietly, unaware of the impending forces bearing down upon their household.

"Vavrinec, tomorrow I must extinguish the fire, all the fire, except for a small flame. This frightens me more than any other aspect of rewriting the curse. More than confronting Svetovit himself," Nadezda confessed. She leaned against her husband's shoulder and he reached around to hold her close. "This extinguishing of the bulk of the fire is the most dangerous thing I have ever done. It means that the safety of Prague rests on a small, unsteady flame. Once the bulk of the fire has died, it is only that small flame—preserved in the lantern—that stands between Svetovit and the accomplishment of his intent to destroy Prague." She shuddered.

Vavrinec squeezed her shoulders more tightly and rested his cheek atop her head.

"That small flame could die so easily, Vavrinec. A gust of wind. A drop of rain. Someone bumps my arm and I drop the lantern and the fire goes out. Anything could happen, Vavrinec, anything at all, and once it does, no other portion of Fen'ka's fire still burns to hold Svetovit at bay." She shut her eyes and tried to block the thoughts of all the small things that might go awry and cause the last remnant of Fen'ka's fire to die.

"I've come so far, Vavrinec, so far to discover the secret of the curse and now… To be so close to rewriting its end and then fail because of the wind or someone jostling me…" Her voice trailed off into silence.

Everything she said was true, and she knew Vavrinec agreed. At this point, anything could happen and all her careful planning would have been for naught. What could he say?

He said nothing and held his wife until she finally dropped off into an uneasy, restless sleep as torrential rain poured from the sky and the river continued inexorably rising.

Nine of Swords, reversed

(Tuesday, August 13, 2002)

THE NINE OF SWORDS, REVERSED:
THE "NIGHTMARE" CARD OF THE TAROT DECK.

"The sword and staff are still hidden in my hotel room," George reminded Magdalena. He had tired of listening to her telling him about how she had spent the day sprinkling river water along the streets with the bundle of horsehair-tied yew while evading Dmitri. "We will need to retrieve them."

"But what about the rooster?" she asked, pointing toward the back garden where they had placed the caged bird. "What is it for?"

Dmitri and Sophia sat down on a bench near the gateway into the Loreto cloister, breathing heavily. Sophia pulled a tattered napkin from a pocket, which they used to mop their foreheads. Their suitcases tottered on the ground beside them and then tipped over. Neither moved to set them upright again. They were too exhausted to move. Dmitri tipped his head back against the cloister wall and closed his eyes.

The haze of late afternoon and early dusk covered the sky. Finally Sophia spoke. "What if the others never come to meet us here? Should one of us try to find another hotel nearby?" she asked.

"They will come," the priest answered, his eyes remaining closed. "One of them will, at least. I am sure of it." He paused and swallowed. "But we do need some water. I will go find a store with water and you will wait here, yes?" He remained there, his eyes closed, another few minutes and then roused himself to his feet, grunting loudly as he struggled to stand. He trudged off in what he hoped was the direction toward the shops of the area.

"What about the others?" Victoria asked Sean. "Do you think there is any way we can find them now that the hotels have all been evacuated? Maybe they are still sick and have been taken to hospitals? We might be left all on our own to stop George and Magdalena."

"There must be a way to find them," he protested.

"But how? I do not have a book on magic to find lost people," she objected.

Sean considered that. "Nor am I familiar with any Celtic magic to do that," he was forced to admit. "But even without magic, there must be a way to locate them."

"We cannot simply wander the streets," Victoria answered. "Without electricity, we cannot call hotels to find them, either."

Sean thought again. "But when you were first worried about Magdalena and George, what did you do?" he asked. "You lit a candle, correct?"

Victoria nodded. "I lit a candle stub in my footprint. Near the Loreto chapel."

"And we all were carried there in our dreams," he reminded her. "We met at the chapel that morning. So that will be a place to start."

"At the Loreto chapel?" she exclaimed. "Do you think the others might be there already, waiting for us?"

"It is the best place I can think of to start looking," he

answered. "If they are not there, then we will have to think of something else."

"We need to send someone to retrieve the sword and staff from the hotel room where I hid them," George explained to Magdalena. "The police and the flood both make it too difficult to attempt to retrieve them myself. So we need a reliable emissary, someone or something that will be delighted to help avenge an injustice against the city. Are there records or stories of anyone unjustly executed in the Little Town on this side of the river?"

Magdalena struggled to remember what history of executions in the Little Town she might have ever studied. "Not that I know about," she said slowly, not wanting to disappoint George. "Not in the Little Town Square… Wait! Of course! There was an execution. Not in the square, but in the castle. In a tower on the edge of the castle hill, overlooking the Old Town and the Jewish quarter across the river. A very famous execution!" She was proud to have remembered it and embarrassed that she had not remembered it immediately.

"In the castle itself? In one of the towers? What happened? Who was it?" George wanted to know.

"There was a new prison tower built in the… When was it? In the 1490s, I think it was." Magdalena felt like a schoolgirl showing off for a favorite teacher. "Now it is called the Daliborka Tower because the first man imprisoned there was a knight called Dalibor. He was imprisoned for supporting the rebellion of another knight's serfs and so was lowered into a deep cell, a hole, called the Jug. He was kept there, alone and in the dark, until his execution."

"Excellent! Dalibor should be eager to help us. And help Fen'ka, of course." George added.

246

Magdalena barely registered George's mention of Fen'ka almost as an afterthought. "Yes, he will surely understand—and sympathize with—Fen'ka's situation. He must have felt some kindred with the poor and unfortunate even during his lifetime. Otherwise, he would not have supported the rebellion, would he?"

"No, probably not," George agreed. "Is it possible to enter that tower now? Or his prison cell? Why was his execution famous?"

"The Daliborka Tower is still there but tourists haven't been allowed into it for some years. But with my university identification, I could take you into the tower and the main rooms, though I do not think anyone can get into the Jug. Or out of it, for that matter!" She laughed at her own joke and George chuckled politely.

She covered her mouth and tried to turn her laughter into a cough.

"Why was it such a famous execution?" she repeated George's other question. "Dalibor was alone down in the Jug," Magdalena explained. "The jailor felt sorry for him and brought him a violin to play in the dark, so that he would have some way to pass the time. He played the violin in such a haunting, beautiful way that it could be heard all across Prague—the music slipped through the crevices of stonework and the narrow windows further up the tower. People all across Prague felt sorry for him and came to the base of the tower to listen to his music. They brought him food and wine, which the jailor delivered to Dalibor. The king feared a public outcry if it were known when Dalibor was to be executed, so the date was kept secret and it was only known that the execution had been carried out because the music stopped. When no one heard him play the violin, everyone knew poor

247

Dalibor was dead."

George's eyes lit up at the mention of the violin. "Violin? Really? This makes Dalibor even more suited to the task at hand!"

"What does the violin have to do with Dalibor's willingness or ability to help Fen'ka?"

George seemed a bit exasperated, and Magdalena was concerned she was missing some obvious connection between the dead knight's musical skill and Fen'ka. "The violin is thought to embody both male and female principles, since the body of the instrument is shaped to imitate a womb and the bow represents a phallus. Brought together, the womb and phallus create new music, new life. Violin music is associated with very powerful, very creative magic." He drew the shape of a violin in the air with his hands and pretended to place it under his chin and balance it on his shoulder as he drew a bow across its strings.

"I had no idea!" exclaimed Magdalena.

George continued, "The bow of a violin is also strung with horsehair, at least according to traditional violin making. Remember that I told you that horses and horse goddesses are associated with the dead in the mythology of many different cultures? And that horsehair is often used in magic to communicate with the dead? We can reuse the yew and horsehair bouquet I gave you earlier to summon Dalibor from the Jug and ask him to bring us the sword and rabbi's staff. His fondness for the violin and its magic will make him especially easy to pull from the Jug. But can we enter the prison? This evening?"

Magdalena thought a moment. "The gates of the castle complex will be locked by the time we could reach it. If they are able to follow their usual schedule, though, the gates will reopen very early tomorrow morning. We could go right after sunrise."

"Then tomorrow at sunrise it will be!" George exclaimed. "How perfect! The flood will no doubt crest early tomorrow morning. If we can get Dalibor to deliver the sword and staff to us in the cathedral plaza where Svetovit was worshipped before the cathedral was built, we will be able to defeat Fen'ka's enemies at the very moment they think the bridge is about to be washed away, leaving Prague defenseless. We will strike just as they think their triumph is complete!"

Dmitri found his way back to the plaza, clutching the one bottle of water he had been able to find left on the shelves of a local grocery. He lifted it to wet his lips. As he turned the corner into the plaza in front of the Loreto chapel, he saw Sophia still sitting on the bench. But there were two other figures with her.

"Sean! Victoria!" The priest could not stop himself from calling out their names. "I was sure you would come here!" He hurried across to the bench to embrace the Irish professor and the Czech office worker. Sophia beamed, watching the reunion play out.

The four friends managed to all squeeze themselves onto the bench and recount everything that had befallen them since Elizabeth had killed Wilcox and the ghost fire had attacked them Sunday night, and since the mysterious ailments had struck them all down Monday.

"What about Theo?" Sean finally asked. "Have you seen him? Do you have any idea where he might be?"

Sophia shook her head. "No, we have no idea. We haven't seen him and we've had no way to contact him. Now that all the hotels have been evacuated, how will we find him?"

249

"In the meantime," George continued, "there is a powerful ritual that will build our strength against those who might still try to stop Fen'ka… though I seriously doubt our academics are in any position to thwart us in any meaningful way."

"Ritual?" Magdalena voice trembled with her excitement. "Another powerful ritual? As when we poured the spiced wine and charcoal onto the street?"

"Even more powerful," George promised. "Have you heard of the sacred marriage rite of *hieros gamos*? Sexual intercourse, performed in a circle outlined with yew or cypress—yew, especially, is important because it is associated with water and femininity—and illuminated only with a green candle, would harness a great deal of creative power that would all be concentrated here, waiting to be used when we need it tomorrow. Of course, it would be even more powerful if performed outdoors." He winked at Magdalena.

"We already have the yew bouquet!" Magdalena exclaimed. "Though my landlady has told me that one of the shrubs in the garden out back is related to cypress. It might do as well?"

"Yes, we have the yew," agreed George, "which you have already used in association with the river water and our efforts to vindicate Fen'ka, poor woman."

George was silent, and Magdalena wondered what was left unsaid. She was happy to interpret that silence in accordance with what she was hoping for.

"You have a green candle, I think?" George went on. "Let me look at your shrub and see if it is indeed a suitable relative of the cypress. With all the electricity out of order and the city in such confusion, perhaps no one will notice a rite in your

250

garden tonight? At midnight?"

Magdalena could hardly restrain her excitement. Sex outdoors as the central component of a magic ritual? With George, who filled such an aching void that she'd willingly have sex with him again, under any circumstances, whether or not they involved a ritual? Victoria would be so jealous, she thought. If only Victoria hadn't gotten involved with the stupid academics! This was more thrilling and exhilarating than anything she had done in her life.

"Midnight? With only a green candle for illumination? I'll get it now!"

She was pitiful, really, George thought. And so gullible. He had not mentioned that yew was also associated with Saturn or remind her of its connection to death, dying, and the dead. Or that the horsehair the yew was tied with would reinforce its connection to the goddesses of the underworld who delighted in death and destruction. Or that cypress was similarly associated with Saturn, femininity, and death or dying. Neither did he say that the power that would be concentrated in Prague as a result would be at Svetovit's disposal for the destruction of the city that had turned away from him so many centuries ago. Or even that the toad concoction and the river water she had so laboriously spread over the cobblestones would attract rather than repel the flood waters.

Theo sat on the patio, staring at the rising water as night descended.

"How do I find the others?" He had no idea of how to answer his question. Had they been stricken as he had? Had they recovered? Now that all the hotels were evacuated, where might they have gone? He had no real idea of where Victoria

251

lived and all the phones were still out of order.

"I could light a candle in my footprint at the Loreto cloister," he mused, "the way Victoria did to call us all together that first time." But he had no candle and no matches.

"If I can't find them, what can I do to stop George and Magdalena?" The question roused itself in his exhausted mind. "What do I know that might stand in their way?"

He reviewed what he had in his luggage upstairs. He had brought with him the one canister of salt that remained from Sunday night along the Royal Road in the Old Town. But Dmitri and Sophia had the tarot cards. So he could not continue burning the cards along the Royal Road on this side of the river as it followed the streets up to the castle.

What other weapons might he have? He struggled to think of even one at his disposal.

Victoria led Dmitri and Sophia, with Sean, back to her apartment. As the light faded, she lit some of the candles she had in the house, candles she had used in small rituals with Magdalena. Seeing the candles flicker, she recalled those happier times and felt a rage rise within her. She was furious with George for trying to free Svetovit to run riot in the world and for using Magdalena to do it. She was furious with Magdalena for allowing herself to believe George's lies. She was terrified of what might happen to Magdalena, of what George might do to her. She was terrified of what might happen to the city if George's plans succeeded.

Sophia, perhaps responding to the tears that slipped down Victoria's cheek, drew Victoria to her. "We must not surrender," Sophia said, stroking Victoria's hair maternally. "We must not! Never!"

"Never!" agreed Victoria, sniffling. "But how to keep

fighting? How, when they seem to have all the power?"

Sophia pulled a chair from the kitchen table and guided Victoria into it. She then sat across from Victoria, holding her hands. Sean and Dmitri, who hovered nearby and couldn't have missed overhearing the women's voices, slid into the other two chairs around the table.

"What do we do? We take stock," Dmitri answered. "What do we have that can be a weapon, even a small weapon, against George?"

"What have we already used that we still have with us?" Sean asked the others around the table.

"We have the tarot cards, some of which we burned along the Royal Road," Sophia answered.

Sean nodded. "Do we have any salt?"

Dmitri and Sophia looked at each other and shook their heads. "No," Sophia said.

"We have my chalice," Victoria suggested. "It is not the primary chalice of Prague, wherever that may be. But it is a chalice that has been used in rites before."

"How could we use it?" asked Sophia.

"We could use it as we planned to use Magdalena's, to spread salt on the Royal Road," offered Victoria.

"But we have no salt!" exclaimed Dmitri.

"We could just go out and buy some more." Sean could not stop the sarcasm from sneaking into his voice.

"No, we can't," Victoria pointed out. "The stores were all sold out of everything, even before they were all locked down and boarded up. With all the police patrolling the streets, we couldn't break into a store either, even if we knew one did still have salt on the shelves."

They all sat in the growing gloom of the kitchen, avoiding each other's eyes.

"Wait!" Sean exclaimed, embarrassed at how he had snapped at Dmitri. "What about other herbs? Surely there must be some associated with defensive magic. Victoria, this is your kitchen! What herbs do you cook with?"

The others jumped to their feet, excitedly scrambling to search the kitchen. Dmitri got the candle from the living room. Drawers flew open, cabinets clattered. Jars of store-bought spices appeared on the table. Dried clusters and bundles of others Victoria had gotten from open-air markets tumbled with them onto the table.

"I found it!" Victoria raised her arm in triumph. "I never thought about it, but here it is by the stove! Not much, but enough, maybe?"

"What? What is it? I can't see in this bad light," Sophia peered across the kitchen.

Victoria brought her fist down on the table, rattling the jars of spices already there.

"Salt!" declared Victoria. "I found my salt shaker!"

Theo struggled to think of anything he might have to use as a weapon against George. "Salt." No matter how many times his mind circled around it, he kept coming back to that one word. "Salt." The only weapon he had was the canister of salt. "But how can I make that one canister of salt worth anything?" Other than finding more salt in some store, of course. But no store would be open now. Maybe not even in the morning. But certainly not now.

"How can I increase the power of that one canister of salt without increasing the amount of salt I have available?" He tried to think of what he could recall that might help him.

"We spread the salt on the Royal Road at night, on Sunday." He thought back over their plans. "But that was to avoid detection, so the streets would be empty. So the time when we spread the salt was important, but only in a practical way. Is there any way that the time of pouring the salt on the Royal Road might be important in a magical way?"

What had he ever read about the influence of time on magical activities? He tried to remember.

"How is time connected to magic? Well, Cinderella had to be home by midnight," he mused, tapping his finger on the table beside him. "But the wicked witches are always stirring their cauldron at midnight. So, if evil magic is black magic and black magic can be the 'dark arts,' that means bad magic is more powerful at night," he went on. "Midnight, being the darkest time of night, must be why the witches are always stirring their potions and making their brews then." He thought another while, trying to follow the logic of magic. "If midnight is the best time to work black magic, then noon could well be the most effective time for working good magic!" He congratulated himself for working out that conclusion.

"Waiting until noon to spread my little bit of salt might be too late, though," he worried. "George might be doing something tonight to make the flood worse. Noon will certainly be too late to stop him. And my little bit of salt would be lost in the rising tide of black magic tonight. So what can I do?" he asked himself, resuming his finger drumming.

Finally he came to what seemed the only reasonable conclusion. "I will spread the salt I have along the route of the Royal Road to the castle in the early morning. The rising sun will disperse what it can of George's black magic and the tide of good magic, rising toward noon, should swell the power inherent in the salt. If I sprinkle it very carefully and very sparingly so that I can trace as much of the route of the Royal Road as possible, perhaps I can awaken more of the power of the Road to oppose George and Magdalena."

He did not see what else he could do.

"But it's almost empty!" exclaimed Sean, examining the shaker.

Victoria felt herself blushing, and was glad the room was dark. "Some salt is still left," she insisted. "If we use that, in combination with the other herbs, then at least it is something we can fight with!"

"Yes, I agree," Sophia quickly agreed. "But what might be the way to use all these herbs to their best effect?" She gestured at the table.

"Let me get my books." Victoria darted to the living room and brought back a handful of simple magic she had attempted with Magdalena. She announced, "We can look up the best combinations of the herbs I have and mix those with the salt."

"That's one possibility," agreed Dmitri. "But perhaps we should leave the salt out of that mixture and save the little salt we have to make a circle in which to burn one last tarot card along the route. We should pick one of the cards, a card that can stand for all the others perhaps, and burn it to release its power. Maybe at the end of the Road, at the castle gates?"

"But that wasn't the end of the Royal Road, was it?" asked Sean. "Wouldn't the cathedral, where the king was crowned, be the real end? Shouldn't we burn the last tarot card in a circle of salt in front of the doors of the cathedral?"

Despite the dimness of the kitchen, Victoria couldn't miss Dmitri's emphatic nod. "An excellent plan, Sean! Excellent!"

"Let's get to work!" Victoria began to unscrew lids from jars, holding them close to the candle to see which herbs were in which jars. "We should start sprinkling this as soon as we can, right?"

"Wait! Wait!" Sean held up his hands. "If we want to be sure this plan has as much chance of success as possible, we should capitalize on every weapon at our disposal!"

"Yes, that is clear," Sophia agreed. "How is waiting going to accomplish that? George may already be doing something, something out there in the dark, to capitalize on his success!"

"No, Sean is right," Dmitri was forced to agree. "Immediate action might not be the most productive."

"How could that be?" demanded Victoria.

"In traditional Celtic lore, black magic always gains the ascendency during the night," Sean explained. "It is daylight which gives good magic the upper hand, intensifying and magnifying its effects. If we want this mixture of herbs to be as effective as possible, we should sprinkle it on the Royal Road in daylight. At sunrise. Or maybe just a little after sunrise, so that the daylight has clearly overcome the night."

Sophia and Victoria, seeking each others' eyes in the dark, slowly nodded in agreement.

"That does make sense," Victoria finally agreed.

"But we should still mix the proper herbs now, yes? So that we are ready in the morning?" Sophia interjected.

"Yes, yes indeed," agreed Sean. "We should do all we can now to prepare."

Dmitri brought a large bowl from where it sat on a shelf near the sink and set it on the table. Consulting her books by the candlelight, Victoria directed the others, advising which herbs were associated with protective magic, and the jars were either emptied into the bowl or set aside.

Just before midnight, using the yew bundle and a few cuttings from the shrub, which George deemed appropriately cypress related, Magdalena drew a circle in her garden, as she

257

had when conjuring Halphas and Flauros—it seemed so long ago now, so many things had happened since then! Her life had changed in so many ways! The green candle ("appropriate for attracting devils," she remembered, chuckling at the Church's readiness to ascribe devilhood to all the spirits it did not consider appropriate to invoke) already sat within the area to be circumscribed by the ritual circle, flickering in the dark.

"Remember to make the circle large enough." George's voice floated quietly out of the shadows next to her. He had already instructed her to draw the circle from right to left and told her that the most efficacious way to perform the circle making was if they were both already "sky clad," naked and vulnerable to the powers they were about to call upon. Their clothes had been laid aside indoors, neatly folded on Magdalena's bed.

The circle drawn, the candle burning, George touched Magdalena's shoulder and she felt excitement course through her as never before.

Stars hung in the sky over the swirling eddies of the river as it gorged itself on the Prague zoo. Animals that could scurried away from its embrace. Birds fluttered their wings and scampered through the air to higher branches as the water licked the refuges they had settled on for the night. Several of the birds were unable to get high enough to escape the rising water and drowned. The lone zookeeper listened for the cries or roars of distress that would signal one of the hippos he was monitoring had been trapped by the water, ever hunting for more victims. No one within the zoo, man or beast, truly slept that night. Every living creature might have dozed, but their occasional shallow slumber was always punctuated by nightmares of the water coming to swallow them, as it had already swallowed so much of the zoo.

Water continued to devour the zoo, finally discovering the top of the wall that surrounded the seal enclosure. At first, drips and trickles of river water kissed the top of the wall. Quickly the drips were more daring, progressing from kissing the top of the wall to licking it. Then, no longer satisfied with licking the top of the wall, the tongue of the river toppled over the wall, tasting the length of it on its journey into the pools of water below.

It was not long before the bulk of the voracious river was cascading into the seals' enclosure, mingling with the pools that had always been the seals' home. The river's gluttony was not sated until the water of the pools had completely intermingled with the water of the river, flowing into the main streams of the flood and forging a bridge over the wall for the seals within.

As relentlessly as the river consumed the zoo, it continued its exploration of the tunnels and underground alleyways of the Old Town. Just as the river had found, and filled, the subway tunnels and stations, it also made its way further into the sewer tunnels and discovered the medieval tunnels that had served as hiding places for those who had resisted the Nazi occupation of the city. The relentless river seeped through cracks in medieval mortar and chewed at medieval stone, clawing its way into the ancient underground halls that snaked below the Old Town Square and extended like the tentacles of an octopus throughout the neighborhoods around the square. Old buildings and homes, their basement and subbasement entrances to these tunnels long bricked over and forgotten, saw the tiny rivulets trickle in from the tunnels.

The streets of the Jewish quarter around the Old-New

259

Synagogue, set back from the river but lower than more modern streets in the area, were quiet except for the echoing footfalls of one man who stumbled home from the mountain of sandbags he had helped erect along the riverbank. He blundered down the steps that led to the ancient synagogue, intending to turn down a side street toward his apartment. But he heard a muffled gurgle as he passed the sewer grates and manhole covers.

He shook his head, refusing to believe his ears.

Inside the Old-New Synagogue, the old stones and wooden benches kept their silent vigil around the bema where the Torah was read each Sabbath morning, as it had been for centuries. Dust motes occasionally drifted down into the sanctuary, unseen by human eyes in the night. The echoes of prayers sung over the centuries reverberated as well, unheard by the ears of the living. This night seemed no different from any other night in the seven hundred years the synagogue had stood there.

But this night was different. The gurgles of water beneath the streets became louder, undeniable, inescapable. Then, in addition to the sound of running water came the scraping of iron against stone as the water pushed up from below and attempted to dislodge the manhole covers and escape into the streets. Here, in terrible mirror-like fashion, the magic of Magdalena's yew-and-horsehair asperges in the Little Town across the river was reflected in the streets surrounding the synagogue. Drawing the water up to the surface, pulling it further and further into the city and away from the river, the destructive power of Magdalena's sprinkling exerted itself as Magdalena was gripped in the ecstasy of the *hieros gamos* for the third time.

A clatter rang out. One of the manhole covers was thrown aside by the water. The river, freed from the constraints of the medieval tunnels and modern sewers, burst onto the cobblestones and quickly submerged them. The water tumbled down the street and passed the entrance to the synagogue, swirling as it pooled and regathered its strength, wavering in which way to go next. It hesitated, as if unsure where the tastiest, most delectable morsels of the neighborhood might be found. It looked like a snake, testing the air with its forked tongue for the presence of its prey. Then it struck.

Throwing itself against the door of the synagogue, the water tumbled down the stairs into the lobby where the synagogue ticket takers, Aviva and Milka, had attempted to keep Magdalena from the attic the Sunday before. No more able to stop the flood than the women had been to resist Magdalena in her efforts to retrieve the rabbi's staff, the table where the women had been posted was knocked aside by the river. One fork of its tongue crept into the sanctuary while another fork lapped the bottom of the stairs leading to the attic.

At the top of the stairs, the ghost of Rabbi Judah ben Loew, creator of the Golem, was awakened from his uneasy slumber by the sound of the flowing water below. Robbed of his staff, he was unable to do more than clench his fist and shake it at the water below as it invaded the synagogue.

Within the yew-drawn circle in her garden, Magdalena lay on her back, spent. George attempted to roll off her and onto his own back, but she clutched him more tightly. Her fingernails dug deeply into his shoulders, gasping for breath. Slowly her gasps subsided and her inarticulate whimpering began to sound more like words, though George could not understand the Czech she seemed to be muttering. But he was finally able to extricate himself.

Kissing her hand, he pulled her to her feet and together they stumbled into the apartment to collapse beside each other on the bed.

The sirens and alarms of the police gradually filled the air of the Old Town as the stars winked out above the now-silent Astronomical Clock. Men, women, and children who had collapsed in their beds a few hours ago, exhausted with the work of sandbagging the town but thinking they would be safe, heard the sirens in their dreams and nightmares. No one was sure if they were awake or asleep. Some thought they could hear water running in the pipes and only realized it was running in the streets when they peered out their windows.

Police using bullhorns made their way slowly up and down the streets around the square where Fen'ka had met her death, announcing, "Evacuation! Evacuation! All residents of the Old Town are hereby ordered to evacuate their premises!" Officers began ringing doorbells and pounding on doors. "Evacuation! The flood has reached the Old Town!"

Early the next morning, only a couple hours after coming in from the garden, Magdalena woke George. She made a small pot of coffee, surprised there was still gas in the pipe to the stove, as the electricity was still out. George retrieved the caged black rooster from the back garden as Magdalena put the horsehair and yew bouquet into her bag with a ball of twine and scissors as he had instructed. Then they set out, away from the river and the great stone bridge. She took George down a small lane that branched off the main road.

"If we go along the side streets," she explained to George, "and come at the castle from behind, we will have to skirt the edge of the flood but we'll be right at the Daliborka Tower." He followed her through the confusing maze of alleys and lanes, the rooster on the luggage trolley bumping along the cobblestones behind him. Magdalena finally brought them to the base of the great staircase that rose up the hill to the back of the castle, as she had done the morning that Professor Hron had sent her shopping on Golden Lane and she had encountered Madame de Thebes, the tarot-reading woman executed by the Nazis for predicting their downfall. She prepared to flash her university identification at the guards at the gate at the top of the stairs. She was ready to explain that she was bringing a distinguished American visiting professor with her, though she was unsure how she would explain the rooster. But there were no guards standing at the open gateway.

"I am afraid they have more pressing concerns this morning," George pointed out, nodding his head down the hill behind them toward the flood. Magdalena agreed, her smoldering anger at the academics for having endangered the city with the flood they had conjured now burning white-hot again, and led him into the courtyard within the castle precincts.

George glanced around the small courtyard. "Which way now?" he asked.

"It is in this direction." Magdalena pointed and led him up and down a series of short staircases and through other small courtyards, finally stopping in a small weed-infested courtyard where the stones were crumbling beneath their feet. A tall, wide archway rose before them, a length of chain stretched across it at knee height.

Magdalena glanced behind them and towards another alleyway that led further into the castle precincts.

"All the tourists begin at the front entrance of the castle," she whispered excitedly to George. "On a normal day, none of them would get this far into the castle for several hours."

"But today is not a normal day," George agreed. "There will be no tourists at all, I suspect."

Magdalena looked around nervously again. "But I feel like a spy, breaking into an embassy or something." She giggled.

"Is this it?" George asked, pointing at the chain across the archway. Magdalena nodded, pointing to a small sign posted where the archway met the wall of the courtyard: "Daliborka Tower," it read in English.

"For the tourists," Magdalena pointed at the sign. "The signs are always in English."

"Shall we, then?" George walked briskly to the archway and stepped over the chain. Magdalena, after one last nervous glance around the courtyard, hurried to the chain and followed George over it.

Victoria got up to make tea for her guests early the next morning. Even with their plan to sprinkle the herbs along the Royal Road and use the last bit of salt while burning the last tarot card in front of the cathedral, worry and anxiety had made it impossible for her to really sleep during the night, and she'd noticed the others were restless in the night. Coming into the kitchen, Victoria found Dmitri sitting on a chair, staring out the window at the dawn slowly creeping in.

George and Magdalena stood atop a broad, shallow flight of steps in what seemed to be a square vestibule, open to the weather from the courtyard but with a ceiling of crumbling stonework inside the arch. At the bottom of the steps, a short,

264

narrow wooden door was set in the wall on their left.

"The cell is through that door?" George indicated the door with the yew tied with horsehair. Magdalena bit her lip and nodded. They made their way down the steps with the rooster in its cage, and George examined the door.

The wood was old, very old. It was rough and weather-beaten, great splinters breaking off it. Two studded bands of iron held it together, and a small opening, protected by a few thin iron bars, was set near its top. A ring of iron was set midway down the right side of the door, opposite several pair of great rusty-iron hinges.

"I don't see any keyhole," George muttered, squinting at the area near the ring handle. "Does it lock from the other side? Is there another entrance?"

"No, this is the entrance," Magdalena explained. "There was probably a way to barricade the door on the other side, but this part of the castle was considered too secure to need many locks on the interior doors. We just need to pull it open." She reached for the ring handle and tugged.

Nothing.

"Let me," George offered, giving the yew to Magdalena. Taking the iron ring in both hands, he leaned away from the door and pulled. Joists grunted and wood creaked. George paused, panting with the effort, and tried again. Wood scraped against stone and the door inched open.

"When was the last time anyone came in here?" he asked, gasping for breath again.

"It has been closed to the public for some time," Magdalena repeated what she had told him the previous night. "But I would have thought other researchers, or perhaps curators, would have seen that it was maintained."

"I… guess… not," George grunted, pulling on the door

again. The hinges suddenly cooperated and it swung wide open, the rough wood scraping the stones they stood on.

Magdalena looked back toward the top of the steps they had come down. "Will the noise have alerted any guards who might still be here?" she asked.

"No, I think not," George reassured her. "They would be here by now if it had."

"I guess you are right," she admitted, surprised at how nervous and guilty and giddy and excited she felt. She turned back to the door, which George was already stepping through. She hurried after him, leaving the rooster to watch the steps behind them.

Inside the door, another flight of steps led down further into the tower but these steps were much more narrow and rough as they twisted in their descent. George and Magdalena made their way, dragging their hands along the rough walls beside them, and nearly tumbled into the room at the bottom of the stairway.

It was a shock to Magdalena's eyes to step into the half-light and shadows of the small room. The only illumination was the filtered daylight that struggled through the open door above and behind them. Shadows flanked the walls, though she recognized rough stonework walls, a low ceiling supported by stone arches, and deeper shadows hanging along the vaulting. A variety of iron implements, used in centuries past to encourage prisoners to confess, were scattered along the walls. A low cauldron or brazier faced the door on a low stone platform. Magdalena shivered, but whether it was because the stone walls kept the room several degrees cooler than the air outside or because she knew what these tools had been used for, she could not say.

George stepped to one side. A shaft of slightly brighter

light burst through the door and onto the floor in the center of the room. Magdalena gasped. There, clearly illuminated, was the hole into the Jug below.

Crumbling stones rose up and circled the small hole, just wide enough for a man's shoulders to pass through. An iron ring kept the circumference of the hole intact and an iron cross had been affixed to the ring at some point to prevent any modern intruders accidentally falling into the Jug beneath.

George knelt with caution at the hole, staring into its black depths. The shaft of light from the doorway showed no more than a few inches of the stone esophagus leading down into the Jug, which was itself impossible to see. He ran his hand along the iron, tracing the crumbling mortar with one finger. A slight smile appeared on his face, and he licked his upper lip.

"Give me the yew, Magdalena. Cut a good length of twine as well," he instructed, never taking his eyes from the hole.

Magdalena nodded, understanding her assignment. She pulled the yew from her shoulder bag and placed it in his open hand. He brushed the yew along the stone just below the iron ring in the floor. She pulled the twine and a small pair of sewing scissors from her shoulder bag and cut a length of string at least twice George's height. She knelt next to him, rather clumsily trying to put away the ball of string and scissors as she handed him the cord she had cut. He reached for it, still never taking his eyes from the black depths of the Jug. He tied one end of the string around the yew, just below the horsehair, so it remained exposed to the air. Then he deftly brushed the entire circumference of the hole several times as well as possible, given the iron cross fixed to the ring.

A cold puff of air rose into Magdalena's face. As much as she wanted to maintain a reverent silence, she could not help exclaiming, "What was that?" She shuddered. "A draft of air from below? How can that be? There is no ventilation down there… at least, that is what the stories say." Another whisper of cold air rose from the Jug to caress her cheek. A slight sound caught her attention next. "Was that a pebble falling? Or a rat down below?" she asked George.

He shook his head. "We are attracting the attention of the dead," he replied. "But we need to attract the attention of one of the dead, in particular." He brushed the yew against the stones once more and then, holding the free end of the twine securely in one hand, he slowly lowered the horsehair-tied yew into the Jug. Magdalena anxiously followed its descent and disappearance into the shadows with her eyes.

The whispers and rustling she heard in the darkness below increased, both in volume and intensity. The attention of whatever or whoever was below was clearly aroused and growing more agitated.

"They sound like birds flapping in the dark," she whispered.

"Yes," George agreed. "Birds in the dark with broken wings." He let the yew slip further into the Jug. Wordless cries, gentle sighing wafted up to George and Magdalena. A multitude of voices seemed to be joining the chorus of the roused. Magdalena thought she could distinguish a handful of women's voices from the more numerous men's voices. George peered down at the string and let the last few inches of the string go, the yew swinging freely in the air at the other end.

Magdalena closed her eyes, hoping to improve her hearing by closing one of her other senses. Could she hear the yew scraping the floor of the Jug? No, but something was definitely scrabbling at the stones and loose mortar below.

She opened her eyes. "Is something trying to climb up the

268

wall and out?" she whispered nervously, pulling away from the edge of the hole.

George paused before answering. "No, not out of the Jug. But climb out of the netherworld and into the Jug? Much more likely." He gently jerked the string with his free hand as if he were fishing. The whispering voices burst into a quiet cacophony of muffled struggling. Were they desperately trying to catch the yew, as fish struggle to swallow a baited hook?

George swung the string in a small circular motion, causing Magdalena to imagine the yew at the other end swinging in broad circles below. Cold air swirled up into her face. Mournful sighs and angry whispers assaulted her ears, as if the dead were struggling against each other, clambering over and around and under each other, each trying to catch hold of the dangling, tantalizing yew.

The string in George's hand jerked taut. "Dalibor!" his voice snapped. "We are looking for Dalibor!" The string shivered as something pulled on the other end in the dark. George seized the string with his other hand too, leaning back and away from the hole. Magdalena could hear gasps and panting from below.

"Are they fighting each other?" she asked. "Why?"

"Because they want out of the Jug!" George answered curtly, struggling to keep hold of the string, playing with it exactly as a fisherman might play with a fish. "Caught on the yew… pulled up into the light… is their one way of escape!" He pulled up on the string, straining to raise his hands as high as his shoulders, when an angry snarl from below—a sound more substantial than any Magdalena had heard before— startled her. Something seized the string and snapped it tightly down and across the Jug below. George was caught off-guard and fell forward, barely able to keep hold of the string with

269

both hands and still brace himself against the iron cross he nearly collided with.

"Help me... hold the string!" he hissed at Magdalena. She scurried to his side, grabbed hold of the string with both hands and pulled. The weight and strength of whatever was caught on the yew surprised her. Together she and George held the string taut, struggling to rein in whatever was on the other end. Feeling the string begin to slice into her palm, Magdalena managed to make a fist with one hand and wrapped the string several times around her knuckles. The snarling below grew more vicious, like a rabid dog trapped in a corner.

"I thought... you said... they wanted to escape," she managed to slip the words out of her lips. "Why...?" she could not complete the question. The pressure of the string tightly wrapped around her fist was intense, making it difficult to concentrate on anything else.

George gave the string a sudden snap and whatever was below seemed thrown off balance for an instant. "Most of the dead would be happy to escape their prison down there," he gasped. "But some prefer the dark. They prefer their miserable solitude to serving our cause." Seeing the sweat running down his face, Magdalena knew it was not the time to ask for a more detailed explanation.

"I want Dalibor!" he thundered down into the hole. "The rest of you... the yew is only for Dalibor," he repeated. The string snapped tight again and then went limp, a quiet whimpering beginning down below. George panted, wiping the sweat away from his forehead with the back of one hand, never letting go of the string. The string remained limp.

"Did they... it... give up?" whispered Magdalena, glancing back and forth between the darkness of the Jug and George's face.

The Jesuit nodded, breathing heavily. He struggled to get to his feet, and Magdalena, rapidly disentangling her fist from the string and letting it go, stood and took his arm to help him rise. The sound of shadowy footsteps came from below, as if a crowd were dispersing, shuffling away from whatever had caught their attention and drawn them together. The whimpering continued, breaking into an occasional muffled sob.

George began to pull the string up. It swung freely but there was clearly something heavier than just the yew at the other end. Magdalena reached out and helped pull the yew and whatever it had caught up into the light.

The string jerked tight. The yew seemed caught on something below. George shook the string, attempting to dislodge the yew from whatever had caught it. Magdalena looked around. Most of the length of twine lay on the floor around them.

"It must be just below the light," she pointed out to George. "Maybe caught on the rim of the stone hole?" The whimpering had subsided now, and nearly all of the shuffling footsteps had faded away.

"Maybe," George said. He peered at the shadows below, bobbing his head about, trying to see what had snagged his catch. He gave the string another large swing and whispered, "Dalibor? Let go of the stones… Come into the daylight."

Magdalena scrambled onto her knees again, reaching one hand into the shadows of the Jug. "Let me see if I can get it loose," she offered. She ran her hand along the twine as far as she could reach. She lay as flat as she could on the rough stonework around the hole, extending her reach. She could not see over the rim of the hole but could feel the stones under her fingertips, the mortar crumbling in places. She stretched her arm as far as she could, feeling the rough stone against the

271

skin of her forearm when suddenly… She gasped in shock.

A strong hand from below locked itself around her arm. She could feel the rough garments, a sleeve of some sort pressed tightly into her palm. The hand held tight, and then…

With an abrupt jerk, Magdalena was pulled forward across the rough, sharp stones of the floor. Whatever or whoever held her arm pulled sharply again. With her free hand, she tried to push herself away from the hole.

"Help! George!" she exclaimed. "It's trying to pull me in with it! It's trying…" She attempted to brace herself and deep, hearty laughter rumbled below them as her arm was wrenched a third time. "George! It feels like it's pulling my arm out of the socket!" Terror of the dark, of the shuffling of the dead, of being trapped below was the only thing she was aware of besides the pain. She pictured herself lying on the floor below, her neck broken by the impact of her fall.

Theo made his way back down to the hotel dining room early the next morning, the sun struggling to pierce the veil of clouds and humidity that wrapped the city. Fortifying himself with tea and a roll, he examined the tourist map of the Little Town he had found on the desk in his room. Spreading the map on the table, he struggled to read the tiny print.

"This is where I am now," he muttered, establishing the location of the hotel on the map and then tracing a path from the castle with his finger back toward the hotel. He pulled a pen from his pocket and marked an "X" on both the castle and the hotel and drew a line to connect the two, following the route he had traced with his finger.

"This street must be the Royal Road," he decided, determining which street emerging from the tangle of the Little Town Square led directly to the castle gates. When he looked up from the map, he noticed the flood waters outside the hotel. The water had risen during the night, but there was still an area free of water outside the hotel's patio.

"This is probably not enough salt to make much difference," he grumbled. "Against everything that George has, I can't imagine this will work at all. But I have to try!" Folding up the map and tucking it into his back pocket, he picked up the canister of salt from the floor, returned the pen to his pocket, and went to sit on the short wall surrounding the patio. Swinging his feet over the wall and onto the ground outside, he stepped off and made his way toward the Little Town Square, skirting the edge of the water.

"Dalibor!" George barked his stern command. "Come up into the light!" He wrenched the twine upward and the yew flew up through the grating, the string tangled on the iron cross that Magdalena had forgotten blocked the entrance of the hole. The yew bounced against the iron rim of the Jug's entrance and Magdalena felt her hand suddenly released. She scrambled away from the edge of the hole as quickly as she could, panting with fear and relief.

George stood between her and the hole now, his back to her. The string hung from his hand, wrapped over and under the arms of the cross, the yew at its other end sitting on the floor on the other side of the hole. Next to the yew, kneeling over it, was the figure of a man slowly materializing like dust gathering in a sunbeam.

He was tall, dressed in the rough and simple workday garments of a medieval Czech peasant. One hand held the posy of yew-and-horsehair on the floor, his fingers tangled in the knots of the horsehair. His hair and beard, dark and scruffy, added to the shadows of his emaciated face. Magdalena

273

thought, "He must have been handsome, once." Then she remembered that this—what? This entity? This ghost? This man?—had tried to kill her by pulling her down into the Jug with him. She shuddered, and any sympathy she might have felt for him died. She hurried to George, careful to stand behind him. She looked over his shoulder at the man across the room.

"Dalibor." George said the name simply, with no emotion.

The man lifted his head toward George and Magdalena, his dark eyes hard to distinguish from the shadows of his face. Except for the anger that glittered in them, Magdalena would not have been sure he had eyes at all.

"Yes." The voice was deep, warm, strong. But the man's lips had not moved. He and George seemed to understand each other, but they seemed to be speaking to each other directly with their thoughts, not their lips and tongues.

Magdalena heard George's voice but strained to make out the words. He was speaking to Dalibor, not her, and she realized that she was eavesdropping on his thoughts.

"Those that oppose me." She could make out those words in George's voice. Then he gestured behind him, toward her. "Those who oppose us," he corrected himself, the words coming through to her slightly clearer.

"You would have me do what?" Dalibor asked, his voice—unlike George's—clear and distinct.

"He must be aiming his thoughts at me, as well as George," Magdalena concluded, and Dalibor nodded in response as if he had heard her thoughts as well as George's. He studied her face, then stood. His fingers were still tangled in the yew and horsehair. He looked at his hand and a wave of anger and disgust rolled across his face. George glanced over his shoulder at Magdalena and she read his instructions in his eyes: "Do not interrupt."

"He tried to kill me!" she protested.

George looked startled, then pleased. He smiled at Magdalena. "Very well," he agreed. "You do have a point." He turned his attention back to the knight.

"Dalibor. You attempted to destroy my… apprentice." George's voice was cold and dangerous. "You had to know that you would not succeed. Why the futile gesture?"

Dalibor stood seething and silent.

"You deserve to be punished for such insubordination," George went on. "You forget yourself, knight. Provoking my anger is never a wise thing to do. I would have thought you had suffered enough punishment in the Jug, playing your violin there in the dark, before your death. Why risk something that terrible again?"

Dalibor refused to answer, his eyes defiant and proud.

"Very well. You shall be punished, for your refusal to answer as much as for your attack on my apprentice," George warned him. "But first I have a task you must complete."

"How can I complete any task, or suffer any punishment for that matter, so long as I am entangled in this yew and horsehair?" Dalibor retorted. "You forget yourself as well, coven-master."

"If I allow you to remove your hand from the yew and horsehair, I do not want you to escape back into the Jug," George instructed him.

"You know that I cannot," Dalibor answered. "Not so long as…"

"I give you leave to remove your hand," George interrupted. The knight easily cast the magical posy to the floor, rubbing his fingers against his jacket as if to restore circulation. He finally examined his fingers and then turned his

275

attention back to George and Magdalena.

"You would have me do what?" Dalibor asked again.

George's voice dropped in volume and the words slurred together. Magdalena felt like her ears were filled with cotton. Concentrate as she might, she could only make out occasional phrases of George's instructions to the dead knight.

"I have retrieved two of the magical tools of Prague… the rabbi's staff and Bruncvik's sword… hidden in my hotel room… bring them to us, in the plaza outside the cathedral, where Svetovit was worshipped…"

Dalibor stumbled back, his mouth open in shock. "Bruncvik's sword? How?" he stammered. "That was buried in the foundation of the bridge! The power of the bridge— surely it would have made the sword impossible to remove!"

Magdalena struggled to hear George's answer and her ears seemed even more densely packed with cotton, making the Jesuit's voice sound distant and nearly incomprehensible.

"… egg… bridge poisoned… power unimaginable…"

The knight slowly climbed to his feet and nodded. "I understand," he replied. "Your instructions seem clear enough."

George's response was muffled again. He pointed to the yew on the floor. Dalibor's reaction was… What? Magdalena thought she saw fear in his eyes, but that seemed out of character with the Dalibor of the old stories. Anger, maybe? Or contempt? Perhaps some duel involving all three.

"Very well," Dalibor agreed. "I will bring them to you in the cathedral plaza." He glared across the room at George and Magdalena, then clumsily bowed his head and gradually faded from sight, the stones in the wall behind him shimmering through his increasingly translucent form. Then he was gone.

Magdalena stayed behind George. He slowly turned to face her.

"You do understand, don't you?" he asked her. "It is of paramount importance to stop our foes and prevent them from destroying the city. Punishing Dalibor, important as that is, must take a back seat to our primary goal." He put a hand on her shoulder and caught her gaze.

Magdalena was torn. "He tried to kill me!" she insisted. "I am your apprentice! You said so! How could he dare to do it? He scares me, George!" She sighed. "But Dalibor will pay the consequences at some point, yes?"

George nodded. "He certainly will," he agreed, wrapping Magdalena in his arms. "I would never let anything harm you," he reassured her, his warm whisper in her ear convincing her she was now safe. She hugged him eagerly in return, and then they turned, hand in hand, to return up the twisted stairway. As they passed the luggage trolley with the black rooster, George grabbed it to pull along behind them. Disentangling her arm from his, Magdalena darted back down the steps towards the dark hole in the prison floor and snatched up the discarded yew and horsehair.

"In case we need it again," she announced, pushing it into her shoulder bag as she emerged from the narrow doorway and wrapped her arm around George's once more.

Passing out of the prison, the rooster reared its head back and shattered the air with an ear-piercing ululation that reverberated off the stone towers above them.

Victoria and the others stepped out into the early morning light. Sophia held the mixing bowl, fragrant scents wafting from the mix of protective herbs it held. Dmitri had the deck of tarot cards and matches while Victoria carried the chalice.

277

The all-important salt shaker had been entrusted to Sean. Following Victoria's lead, they set out for the Little Town Square, where they would pick up the Royal Road to the castle. Blessing themselves with the sign of the cross, Dmitri and Sophia nervously glanced at each other as Sophia took up a position beside Victoria so that Victoria could easily fill the chalice with the herbs and then sprinkle them from the chalice onto the cobblestones.

Theo stepped out from the narrow side street and entered an open plaza, which he recognized as the Little Town Square. Across the square, another slightly broader street began its steep ascent up the hill to the castle. Clutching the canister of salt, he made his way toward the last stage of the ancient processional route of Bohemian kings to their coronation in the cathedral atop the hill.

Stepping from the square onto the street, he tipped the canister and sprinkled a few crystals of the precious salt onto the Royal Road.

Although he was not sure exactly what time it was, he knew it was early. The streets had been empty once he left the hotel and he could see no one on the street ahead of him. No one to stop and ask him what he was doing, or why. No one to stop him. "No one to help, either." He grimaced. Either struck down by strange ailments or lost in the hectic evacuation, the others who knew the real cause of Prague's desperate situation were not available. He was the only one left of their small band to stand against George. He took a few steps and gently tipped the canister again. Salt splattered onto the road at his feet, some of the crystals jumping excitedly as they struck the ground while others adhered to the stones as if glued by the humidity, dissolving and vanishing as he made his way forward.

Slowly he trudged up the hill, partly because he was easily winded by the climb and partly to sprinkle the salt as he went. "Even sprinkling this little, the canister won't last long," he realized, looking up the hill ahead of him. He tried to sprinkle even fewer crystals each time he tipped the spout of the cardboard container. "Just let me make it up to that sharp turn ahead," he muttered, remembering the hairpin curve in the road from previous visits to the city. "Let me make it that far, so I can at least see the castle gates before the salt runs out."

Victoria entered the Little Town Square from the southwestern corner and led the other three across the trolley rails set into the street. The square was empty, silent in a way Victoria had never experienced it, making the roar of the river that much more ominous. With only a nod, as if by keeping silent they might evade George's notice, she indicated the direction they needed to go. Hugging the western side of the square, they hurried along the palaces there, stopping abruptly when a street opened on their left. Peering around the corner, Victoria then stepped into the middle of the road.

It was a steep hill they faced, nearly empty except for one lone man far ahead of them who seemed to be making his way slowly up the hill.

"This leads up to the castle?" whispered Sophia. Victoria nodded.

"The Royal Road?" Dmitri looked back across the plaza and then up the hill again. Victoria nodded a second time.

"Time to begin, then." Sean was businesslike, matter of fact and to the point. Victoria nodded for a third time and dipped the chalice into the fragrant mix of herbs in the bowl Sophia held. Trembling, Victoria then tipped the chalice

279

slightly and an herbal cascade tumbled to the cobblestones.

"Careful! Not so much!" warned Dmitri. "It has to last all the way up to the castle."

"To the cathedral," Sean reminded them.

They walked up the hill, Victoria spilling a much smaller cascade of herbs from the chalice every few steps. The chalice still trembled embarrassingly in Victoria's hand as she reached to refill the cup from the bowl. Turning, Victoria cast a thimbleful of the scented mixture to the ground.

"Do you think it's working?" whispered Sophia. "I don't see anything happening. Not like the other night in the Old Town."

"There was nothing to see when we were sprinkling the salt," Sean answered her. "There were only things to see when we burned the tarot cards."

"Yes, I forgot." Sophia blushed and, smiling sheepishly, momentarily turned her attention to her husband. In that moment, she tripped over a cobblestone. Crying out, nearly dropping the bowl of herbs, she knocked into Victoria and the chalice jumped from Victoria's already nervous grasp. In the empty street, the clang of the metal cup on the cobblestones seemed nearly as loud as the roar of the river behind them.

The man ahead of them, nearly at the turn in the road leading to the front gates of the castle, stopped and looked back at them.

"No! Tell me that's not George!" whispered Sophia hastily. "Now what do we do?"

Theo was nearly to the U-turn in the road that would bring him to the front gates of the castle. He lifted the canister to his ear and shook it gently, estimating there was almost nothing left inside.

"If I tear the spout away and rip open the top, I can

get the last few crystals out," he reasoned. Under any other circumstances, those last few crystals would not be worth the effort to extract. Now, every precious crystal counted. He wedged his thumb into the spout and began to rip it out.

A loud clang down the hill behind him startled him, causing him to nearly drop the box. He turned to looked back down the street. He saw a group of four people. From this distance it was hard to tell, but he guessed it was two men and two women. One of the women seemed to be clutching a bowl to her chest while the other was running to pick up something rolling back down the hill. A metal cup. A chalice.

"Sean! Victoria! Father Dmitri! Sophia!" Forgetting his previous caution, Theo called out to his friends down the hill.

"Theo!" all four voices down the hill rang in chorus. Victoria, managing to grab the chalice as it rolled into the edge of the sidewalk, stood and waved. Hastening as much as the steep incline of the road allowed, the four hurried towards Theo, who was trotting down to meet them.

There was a flurry of handshakes and embraces, all navigated around bowls and cups and nearly empty boxes of salt. For a moment, their laughter competed with the roar of the river. Then, in a burst of voices as they began speaking at once, the reunited friends learned what had befallen each other since they discovered the bridge closed on Monday morning.

George and Magdalena went up Golden Alley, the rooster and its cage bumping along on the cobblestones behind them, and turned up Jirska, one of the tangled streets running through the castle grounds. Coming into the plaza, in the center of which rose the great cathedral of Saint Vitus, George paused and stared at the wrought-iron angel perched high atop the apse. The angel faced them but was blind to their presence, intent on blowing its horn to wake the dead for judgment.

"Blow now, angel!" he taunted the figure. "Judgment has come!"

The Jesuit led Magdalena forward into the plaza. She looked around at the familiar buildings as if seeing them for the first time. "You told Dalibor to bring the sword and staff to the cathedral plaza. Is this the place where Svetovit was worshipped?"

"It is. When Dalibor delivers them, we will make the magic circle and sacrifice the rooster to summon Svetovit," George told her. "The magic of the bridge is nearly gone. It can no longer prevent his coming or stop the consummation of Fen'ka's dying wish." He smiled at her. "The hour of her triumph has come, Magdalena. Did you ever think it would actually arrive?"

"No," Magdalena admitted. "I was never quite sure it would all come to pass. But here we are!" She felt giddy with excitement.

When George didn't immediately respond, she asked impatiently, "How long will it take Dalibor to retrieve the sword and staff, do you think?"

"Not much longer, I am sure," George answered.

To fill the time, Magdalena pointed to the row of buildings opposite the northern side of the cathedral. "That tower is an old armory, although it is set up now as an exhibit about alchemy, not munitions."

"Very interesting," George said, apparently musing as he stared at the tower silently. "Those were the alchemists living along Golden Lane?" he asked, pointing in the direction they had come.

Before Magdalena could answer, a form shimmered into visibility near the armory tower. It was Dalibor, holding the great sword in its scabbard in one hand and the rabbi's staff in the other.

"Excellent!" George clapped his hands together, hurrying forward to retrieve the objects. "Come, Magdalena!" he called behind him. "You take the staff!" Magdalena scurried after him. George took the staff and handed it to her. She could feel the power within the wood, awake and waiting to be used again after its centuries of quiet rest in the attic of the synagogue.

George lifted the weapon with two hands from Dalibor's grip. Magdalena was amused to watch George running his eyes along the scabbard and hilt, how he was nearly salivating with anticipation and pleasure.

"Is that all?" Dalibor asked, eyeing the Jesuit suspiciously. "No other tasks?"

"None," George answered him, turning back to the caged rooster. "But stay and see what unfolds here, before you return to the darkness of the Jug," he added, glancing back over his shoulder at the knight. Dalibor seemed to focus on both the sword and the staff. He nodded but did not move, remaining where he stood. George walked back to the rooster, ignoring Dalibor. Magdalena followed his lead, holding the staff upright but eyeing it with care, as if it might suddenly become a viper and strike at her.

"It will be best if we sacrifice the rooster with the sword," George explained to her, "although it may be awkward, given the size of the sword. You will have to hold the rooster down so that I can strike the head off. You can do that, can't you?" He grinned. Seeing his excitement and near-triumph, Magdalena nodded.

"I can do that," she answered.

"You had a canister of salt and you've nearly emptied it on this part of the Royal Road?" Sean asked, to make sure he had understood Theo correctly.

"Yes. You were sprinkling herbs along the road to do the same thing?" Theo countered.

"Yes. We have just enough salt to burn one last tarot card before the doors of the cathedral," Victoria answered.

"Well, then, lead the way!" Theo exclaimed. He ripped the spout from the box of salt and turned the container upside down, spilling out the last few white crystals onto the cobblestones. Together, the friends formed a small circle and, following the road as it sharply doubled back for the final ascent to the castle, Victoria resumed sprinkling bits of the herbs from the chalice onto the ancient stones they walked on.

The scent of the herbs wafted into the air, mingling with the humidity and a smell Victoria guessed arose from the river water as it continued its assault on the city. Looking out over the edge of the royal route, the rooftops of the buildings and houses in the lower parts of the city appeared as if they were islands in the river. Victoria hardly recognized Prague.

"Look!" Sean pointed across the retaining wall they walked along. "The bridge!" Victoria turned her attention that way. Along with the others, she gasped.

The two ends of the bridge, where it connected the Old Town and the Little Town, were submerged. The towers at each end rose from the rushing water as massive boulders that might interrupt but not stop the great rush of water. The central portion of the bridge rose like a sea serpent from the waves, but only barely. Some of the statues that stood on the balustrade of the bridge were up to their knees in the water while others seemed to be walking on the surface of the current and a few looked down on the torrent from their precarious perches along the central length of the bridge.

"It looks ready to float away!" gasped Sophia.

"It can't!" Victoria shuddered, frozen with shock. "It has been there forever! What will happen to the city without the bridge?"

There was an uncomfortable silence. "There will be no more city," Dmitri finally spoke quietly. "Without the protection of the bridge, there will be nothing to stop George—and Svetovit—or whatever other demons he is intending to summon. They will be able to do anything they want. The people will be at their mercy."

"Then we must awaken the power of the Royal Road and burn that last card before the doors of the cathedral!" insisted Victoria. "We must!" She sprinted ahead of them, shaking herbs from the cup in her hand onto the cobblestones.

The others hurried to keep up with her, not an easy task given the steep hill and the fact that they were all several years older than Victoria. "Victoria! Wait!" Sophia called after their friend as loudly as she dared. "Victoria!"

They caught up with her where she stood before the great gates that opened into the complex series of buildings making up the great castle of Prague. She faced the open gates, clutching the empty chalice in both hands.

"Is it… always open like this?" huffed Dmitri as he came up behind her. Without thinking, they all formed a line before the open ironworks, guarded by great club-wielding stone giants at either end.

"No, it's not," answered Victoria. "At this time of the morning, it ought to be closed. And there should be guards on duty." She pointed to the two guardhouses in the shadow of the giant statues. "Is this more of George's work? Has he already done something terrible here?"

They all stared a long moment before Dmitri spoke. "No, I don't think that George has been here. There is no sign of violence or blood. I suspect the guards have all been called away to duty elsewhere in the city, because of the flood." He gestured down the hill toward the river. "It must be a stroke of luck in our favor, though, that the gates were left standing open. Otherwise, there would have been no way for us to get to the cathedral, correct? The gates would have blocked the end of the Royal Road."

Everyone else slowly nodded in agreement. "A stroke of luck. Or Providence," agreed Sophia. "Shall we?" She took a step forward and turned to look at the others.

"Cowards die many times before their deaths; the valiant never taste of death but once." Glancing sideways at his companions as if embarrassed, Theo added softly, "Shakespeare."

"A man prepared has half fought the battle," Sean retorted. "Cervantes."

They stepped through the gates into the empty courtyard beyond.

"Now where?" asked Sean. "Where is the cathedral?"

"This way," Theo and Victoria answered, both pointing to the left.

Sophia offered the bowl of herbs to Victoria. "There are just enough left for one more cupful," she announced. She turned the bowl upside down and poured what remained of the crumbled herbal remnants into the chalice Victoria held. Turning left, Victoria poured a thin but steady stream of herbs onto the ground as they walked. But when the last, fragrant motes of herb dust fluttered into the air, she glanced at the priest's wife, fighting tears.

The older woman wrapped an arm around Victoria's shoulder. "We must go on, dear. We must go on. We still have the shaker of salt and the card." Victoria nodded, keeping her eyes on the ground.

Theo took the lead now, since the others knew he had visited the castle complex on previous visits to Prague. He escorted the others through another courtyard, past a chapel that now served as book and gift shop, and turned right before passing through the arches they had been walking toward. Coming through another archway they might have passed without noticing, they found themselves standing before the great bronze doors of Saint Vitus' Cathedral.

"So this is where the Royal Road ends, eh?" Sean asked. Without waiting for a response, he knelt and sprinkled salt from the shaker onto the pavement, making the circle. Dmitri reached towards him, the tarot card and matches in his hand.

"No!" Victoria cried in consternation. "No! This is not the end of the Royal Road! Do not sprinkle the salt here! Don't!"

"I will draw the circle with the sword," George continued explaining to Magdalena. "You set the staff there and then take the rooster out of the cage." He gestured with the sword point at the cage on the luggage cart. Magdalena obediently set the staff down, leaning it upright against the handle of the cart. She dropped her shoulder bag to the ground beside it. The bouquet of yew tumbled out onto the plaza. At the same time, George pulled the scabbard from the blade and dropped it to the ground beside the staff. It clattered against the cobblestones. He lifted the blade so that its tip pointed to the sky. The blade glinted in the dull light drifting from the overcast sky.

George took several steps away from Magdalena, looking

287

around the plaza, judging how large to make the circle he was about to draw. Choosing a place a few more steps away from Magdalena and the rooster, he closed his eyes and drew a deep, slow breath. He touched the point of the sword to the cobblestones and breathed in and out, slow and deep. He began walking to his right, tracing the route as he walked in a fairly large circle with Magdalena, the rooster, and the staff near its center.

If Magdalena had known more about the drawing of magic circles, she would have realized that George was walking widdershins, opposite to the sun's course across the sky, the hallmark of circles drawn to perform black magic. She would have also realized that the circle he had instructed her to draw in her garden for the *hieros gamos* rite the night before had also been widdershins, cast for the working of destructive magic. But George knew she only noticed him wielding the great sword with both hands wrapped around the hilt, hacking at the air as he drew the circle around them.

George felt the blade twist as he used it to cut the widdershins circle in the air. The blade seemed as if it were attempting to pry itself free of the hilt in George's hand.

"Careful, George. The sword seems very heavy," Magdalena advised. George could sense her concern, and redoubled his efforts to hold the sword firmly enough to draw a steady circle.

"It was made to protect, to defend Prague," George realized. "Making this circle is bending its power to a purpose for which it was never intended." He congratulated himself on his skill at manipulating the power of the sword in opposition to its original purpose. He kept struggling to maintain his grip on the hilt, struggling against the strain in his neck muscles and his urge to walk more rapidly as he forced the sword to cut the widdershins circle. Still, the blade occasionally dropped and hit the cobblestones of the plaza, the iron striking sparks from the stones.

Finally, he completed the circle with as much dignity as he could. Magdalena gave him an adoring smile.

Immediately, he felt a change in the air as if all the static electricity from the hovering clouds had dropped into the space of that circle on the hilltop. Sparks popped and tiny fireballs sizzled along the circle he had drawn. He smiled at his handiwork, sweat dripping into his eyes. He pointed to the rooster with the sword.

Magdalena moved slowly but deliberately to avoid disturbing or frightening the bird. George approved of the approach, surmising that she was familiar with handling chickens. She released the latch on the cage door and reached in with both hands. Her hands moved cautiously until, at the last instant, she clutched one hand around the bird's neck and the other around its torso. She pulled it from the cage, accompanied by its squawking and protesting.

Sean stared at Victoria, dumbfounded. Dmitri turned to her, a wordless exclamation of confusion forming on his lips.

"What do you mean, this not the end of the Royal Road? It is the entrance to the cathedral, yes?" Sophia wanted to know. "Was it not the plan to sprinkle the salt here?"

"No, she is right," Theo hastily spoke up. "The bulk of the nave and western end of the cathedral was added to the original church, beginning in the 1870s. These doors were only completed in the 1920s."

"We came on school trips here!" explained Victoria. She could not stop the tears falling down her cheeks. "We were taught that the kings of Bohemia would enter the cathedral for their coronation from the Golden Gate! On the side of the church!" She pointed to their right. "Now we have no more salt left to burn the card in the proper location!" she wailed in despair.

"That door on the side was the main door of the church for most of the church's history," Theo agreed.

Sean stared at the salt he had sprinkled on the paving stones. Dmitri glanced at Theo. Sophia hugged Victoria's shoulders while biting her lip and gazing at the magnificent rose window above the cathedral's doors.

"We burn the card here," Dmitri finally announced. "What else can we do?"

"But will it be effective here?" Victoria demanded.

"We were never sure that burning one last card, without burning all the others, would awaken the power of the Road," Sophia reminded her.

Without saying anything more, Dmitri handed the card to Sean, who Victoria watched trying to wedge it between the stones on which he had drawn the circle of salt. But these stones were set together more closely, more tightly than the medieval cobblestones in the Old Town. He could not get the card into the pavement. He looked at Dmitri, who was kneeling beside him and striking a match.

"Hold the card down with your finger," the priest said. "Hold it against the stones as long as you can without burning yourself. We will have to hope that is enough."

Sean nodded his head and bit his lip. "I'm sorry," he said while staring at the ground.

Dmitri touched the burning match to the card, which Sean held against the stones with his index finger. The flames hovered along the edge of the card and then swept across the image, darting towards Sean's fingertip. The image hovered in the flame, dark smoke curling in the air above it.

The card suddenly curled into a feathery ash, the fire licking at Sean's finger. "Ouch!" Sean exclaimed, popping his fingertip into his mouth.

The smoke hovered within the circle of salt as the ash that had been the card kept curling smaller and tighter. It disintegrated, its tiny shreds wafting away. A black smear remained on the stone.

Dmitri looked up into the air above them, waiting.

Nothing.

"Now what do we do?" whispered Sophia.

Then the familiar rainbow of lights danced in the air above them, rippling and curling and undulating like a python encircling its prey. Colors shimmered and shifted as an image materialized in the midst of the eddying light. A nude woman, wrapped in a scarf or shawl that swirled in the wind as she danced, was holding a mushroom-headed staff in each hand. Four other figures—another person of indeterminate gender, an eagle, a bull, and a lion—shimmered around her, peripheral participants in her dance, seemingly centered within a great ribbon-wrapped wreath swinging at the end of an unseen rope. The nude woman smiled down at them, gesturing with her staves, but then returned her attention to her dancing partners. The whole scene hung in the air just above the topmost point of the cathedral doors and then faded and flickered in and out of focus before vanishing altogether.

The five on the ground stared in silence at where the image had hung.

"Is the power of the road awake now?" asked Victoria at last.

Sean pulled his burned finger from his mouth and laid his palm flat against the paving stone. Dmitri placed his hand on the ground next to it, but then the two men looked at each

291

other and shook their heads.

"No ripple of energy, no shift of power in the ground," Dmitri announced.

"No," Sean confessed. "No difference."

The others stood there.

Victoria forced herself not to burst into tears. Sophia, her free arm still wrapped around Victoria's shoulders, held her tightly, the older woman gently shaking her head and pressing her lips together.

"We can still burn one more card before the Golden Gate," Dmitri announced. He looked around the frightened, disheartened band. One by one, the others each turned and faced him and nodded in assent.

Dmitri and Sean stood. The small group moved stealthily to their right and around the corner of the cathedral. Another grand plaza opened before them. Across the plaza stood the grand doors that led into the central throne room of the castle buildings. Keeping close together, they made their way along the base of the cathedral walls. They passed an age-blackened statue of Saint George on his prancing horse, piercing the dragon on the ground beneath him with his lance. Victoria noticed that Dmitri crossed himself and asked the saint for his prayers. Sophia kissed her fingertips and brushed them gently against the base of the statue, pausing as she passed it.

"Here." Victoria spoke at the same instant as Sean, and both stopped and turned to face the Golden Gate. Sophia gasped. Sean and Dmitri stood speechless.

Three great arches soared up to Gothic points, grillwork gates barring anyone who might attempt to walk up the few steps and through the archways. Within the portico created by the arches, stout wooden doors were guarded by flanks of saints and angels who stood in rapt attention. Above the arches, a tremendous mosaic of gold and colored tesserae glittered.

The breathtaking golden mosaic showed Christ the King enthroned in majesty on a rainbow, angels gathered to support the radiant Judge coming to raise the dead and save or damn mankind. Angels hoisted the dead from their graves while the living knelt in supplication before the Judge. The Mother of God with John the Baptist and the apostles soared before the rainbow throne as they interceded for the men and women of all times and places. In the bottom-right corner of the mosaic, angels delivered the damned into the mouth of Hell.

Inside the portico, two other golden mosaics glittered. One showed Eve, her nude body hidden by her long, cascading tresses, with Adam on the other side of the Tree of Knowledge as the serpent tempted them to take the forbidden fruit. Opposite that, the other mosaic showed Mary and the evangelist John on either side of Christ on the cross, Adam's skull nestled in the rocks on which the cross had been erected.

The magnificent art stunned them all into silence, as it had stunned countless others for hundreds of years.

"Doomsday," Dmitri whispered at last, crossing himself. "It is the history of salvation."

"No wonder they call it the Golden Gate," muttered Sean.

"Burn the card, Father," Theo urged Dmitri. "Everything now hangs on this."

Magdalena pressed the rooster to the ground in front of her, kneeling and holding its throat with her right hand and its torso with her left. From its head pressed down flat against the ground, one eye stared up into Magdalena's face. Seeming to realize what was about to happen, the cock opened its beak to call out to the dawn one last time.

George lifted the sword and drew its point across the base

293

of the rooster's neck, between Magdalena's hands, silencing the black bird once and for all. Blood dribbled onto the feathers at first but then exploded in an arc that shot into the air, a few drops splattering onto George and Magdalena on either side of the fountain of gore.

"As this fire dies…"

(mid-February 1357)

Vavrinec kissed his wife as he and Petr departed for the bakery the next morning.

She set a clay bowl of coals, scooped from the fireplace, on the hearth for safekeeping. As soon as she finished, Vavrinec burst through the door, followed by a bewildered Petr.

"The river! It's flooding!" Vavrinec exclaimed. "Everyone is fleeing!"

"Then you must take Petr and Milos and go to the house of Ryba until I return." Nadezda stood and gathered the things Vavrinec would require for the baby. "You will need someone to nurse Milos."

"Where are you going?" Petr demanded.

"She must tend to important business in the Little Town," Vavrinec interjected. "It has been postponed far too long and must be settled today. Flood or no flood."

Nadezda was surprised to hear Vavrinec explain her impending task with such certainty. She had half-expected him to object at the last minute, point out the danger, demand that she think of her family and—now that Lilith had not been seen of late—give up her foolish notion of saving the city from Svetovit. But instead, he was explaining to Petr that she had to cross the river in the midst of a flood.

She wrapped Milos in a blanket and pressed the baby into his father's arms as Vavrinec handed Peter the bundle of goods

295

they would need for the day. Nadezda hugged Petr tightly and pushed the hair from his face.

"I love you, Petr," she said. "If the flood detains me, remember that. Please help Vavrinec care for Milos." Because it was, after all, his gift of the burning stick that would make it possible for her to rewrite the curse, she added, "I am grateful for all you have given me."

"I love you too, Nadezda," Petr begrudgingly admitted. "Settle your business quickly and come home soon."

She stood and kissed Vavrinec, long and deep, and hugged Milos.

"I will hurry back as soon as may be," she promised her menfolk as they stepped out of the house for the second time that morning, the noise of the crowds plainly audible up the lane. Vavrinec looked anxiously into her eyes one last time, then closed the door and was gone.

Alone, Nadezda took the bit of Candlemas candle and lit it from the hearth, then placed it in the lantern. She set the bowl of coals to one side in case she needed to relight the candle before leaving.

Taking Ryba's gift of the canister of dead water, she leaned over the hearth and stirred the flames and coals in the fireplace one last time. The familiar gesture reminded her of all the other times she had stirred these coals and embers, the times she had stoked the flames with new kindling, the evenings she had gathered her family around its warmth. Then she poured the dead water onto the glowing coals. "What better way to extinguish the curse than by extinguishing the fire with water that washes away curses?" Nadezda thought. Hissing and spitting, the coals went ashen and black, thick steam rising up the chimney. She stirred the coals again to see if any glints of flame remained. There was one, but it winked out as she prepared to smother it with the wet ashes around it.

She stood and looked around the room again. A thought struck her. "Have I given coals to anyone since Petr cast the burning stick from Fen'ka's fire into ours?" Was there another hearth that contained the flames of Fen'ka's curse that she would need to extinguish? She decided that no, no one had come asking for coals since last September.

She wrapped her cloak about her shoulders and tucked her knife and cord into an apron pocket. She had only to extinguish the bowl of coals now before setting out to confront Svetovit. She reached for the ceramic vessel and then paused.

"Dare I extinguish these?" she asked herself. "What if the lantern goes out while I climb the hill to Hradčany? Then all this will have been for naught. Maybe I should bring the bowl of coals?" But she could not carry the bowl, the rooster in its wicker cage, and the lantern. "Maybe I should leave the lantern here instead? But there is no way to adequately protect the coals from the weather and they may go out even more easily than the Candlemas candle in the lantern," she realized. She felt heartsick and nervous extinguishing the coals, but it seemed the only way to achieve her goals. The risks, no matter what she did at this point, were unavoidable.

She overturned the coals into the soggy ashes in the fireplace. A new round of hissing and spitting erupted. New clouds of steam rose. She took the fire tongs and overturned the coals many times, ensuring they were thoroughly sodden. Red lights glinted through the ashy overcoatings and then winked out, one by one. The die was cast. There was only one way forward now.

Gathering the caged rooster and the lantern under her cloak, she was ready. Nadezda surveyed the room, one foot already out the door.

The oil lamp was burning before the icon. "How could I have been so thoughtless? All my efforts would have been ruined!" she chided herself. The flickering, dying light of the oil lamp had first alerted her to Lilith's presence and she had lit the new wick with a straw from the fire on the hearth. She lifted the oil lamp down and blew out the wick. Satisfied that all was finally, truly ready, she set out towards the river.

The sky was quickly growing darker and the wind was growing stronger, the shrill whistle from between the towers and turrets of the houses growing louder as she neared the river. She was the only person going towards, not away from, the river. The streets were empty, as the impending flood had driven everyone away from their homes. Broad puddles stretched across the streets and small rivulets came bubbling out of narrow windows opening into crypts below the houses. Even the beggars who typically lurked near the wooden bridge were gone. There was no sign of the monks typically stationed there to collect the toll. "No doubt they think no one will dare to cross in this weather," Nadezda thought.

Before her, the swollen river continued its tumultuous careening downstream. Waves broke against the bridge and occasionally spilled across the causeway. Standing before the wooden bridge, she could see it shiver against the onslaught of the current, but its moorings seemed to be holding fast. The wooden joists creaked and groaned, louder even than the wind whipping past the chimneys of the nearby houses. She stepped onto the bridge.

The wood trembled beneath her, the force of the current pushing against the joists. But there seemed to be something more to this tremor. It was almost as if the bridge were alive and had sensed Nadezda's presence. The bridge seemed to be warning the river, like a dog whose fur was rising along its back and a growl rumbling in its throat as it pulled back its lips to expose its teeth when confronted by an enemy. Nadezda took another step forward, biting her lower lip. Her hands, one holding the rooster's cage and the other grasping the lantern, were unable to grasp the handrails of the bridge to steady herself. So she kept as much to the center of the walkway as she could.

The wood was slippery from both the rainfall and the waves spilling across it. She took another step, anxious to maintain her balance and not slip on the slick planks or drop either the rooster or the lantern. Step after tremulous step, Nadezda made her way across the bridge. The wind buffeted her face and whipped her cloak about her. The rooster was surprisingly quiet. The wooden bridge groaned and creaked but seemed to be holding fast as the river roared close beneath her feet.

She finally reached the Little Town landing and stepped onto the cobblestones. As she did, the bridge sighed behind her and seemed to visibly relax after having delivered her across the river. A tremendous crack assaulted Nadezda's ears as a beam below the causeway broke away and swirled about, upended in the water, before being carried away in the frothy tumult.

The streets of the Little Town were as empty as on the Old Town side of the bridge. Nadezda made her way toward the Little Town Square and then up the steep hill to the castle. Lightning occasionally streaked across the sky as she neared the top of the hill. The castle had been opened earlier that morning as a refuge for those attempting to escape the river's onslaught, so the guards at the gates into the castle complex must have assumed Nadezda to be a straggler, a latecomer who had been delayed because she had not wanted to abandon a pet rooster. One guard pointed her towards a courtyard to the left and she followed his instruction.

The courtyard was full of workmen and their families. The wealthier merchants and minor nobility who lived close by the river must have been inside one of the buildings. Aiming for an archway on the other side of the courtyard, Nadezda made her way through the crowds, careful to hold her lantern high and avoid its being jostled. Reaching the arch, she followed the wall towards her destination.

Across the large open space that opened before her, she saw the centuries' old St. George's Basilica and the women's cloister dedicated to him. She entered the construction site that stood between her and the convent. Large piles of stone littered the hilltop around her. Across the open space, she saw the jagged shards, like the crumbling teeth of giants, beginning to rise in a gigantic semi-circle around the old rotunda dedicated to the Mother of God. Heavy droplets of rain began to splatter down. Nearing the stones that were slowly becoming the apse of the cathedral, she set down her supplies and turned to face the north. She reached into her apron pocket and withdrew the length of red cord she had brought. She tied the ends together—no mean feat, given how cold and wet both her fingers and the cord were becoming—and threw the cord to the ground around her, creating a makeshift protective circle. Thunder rumbled in the distance.

Inside her circle, the lantern burned brightly, the flame strong and steady. She opened the wicker cage and reached in to grasp the black rooster by the throat from behind, deftly managing to avoid being pecked by its sharp beak in the process. It struggled briefly but could hardly move in the confined space. She slowly withdrew it, backwards, and held

300

it down against the dusty cobblestones that were quickly becoming muddy in the storm. Its wings flapped once and its feet scrabbled against the stones. With her other hand, she pulled the knife from her apron pocket. Grasping it firmly, she took a deep breath and then quickly sliced open the rooster's throat. She released her grasp of the rooster.

The bird's head slumped to one side as its body sprang up and began to run around the haphazardly arranged piles of stone waiting for the masons. Blood spurted everywhere like a palace fountain gone wild. She watched it as it ran in and around the stones, the blood forming bizarre patterns on both the cobblestones she stood on and the larger stones for construction. The bird finally collapsed near the front doors of St. George's.

The rain was falling harder now and the lightning drawing closer, flashing more frequently. But where was Svetovit? Ryba had promised that the slaughter of a black rooster on the hilltop was the surest way to call him. Why didn't he appear?

Above Nadezda, lightning ripped the sky and thunder boomed, echoing among the stones on the hill. A mighty wave crashed against the bridge below, washing across the walkway. The storm clouds congealed into a massive masculine figure with multiple faces astride a great horse with several pairs of legs. The horse's hooves pawed the sky, sending a cascading shower of sparks down the hill.

As the thunderclap rumbled out from the hilltop across the city, every dark thing in Prague—the shadows of the living and the shades of the dead—turned, as if summoned by the clarion call of a sentry warning of impending battle, and looked towards the hilltop where Svetovit was about to unleash his will on the city. Father Conrad, lurking behind

Our Lady of Tyn and looking up at Lucrezia's window, turned to look instead toward Hradčany, as did all the animals along the riverbank or in the farmyards surrounding Prague who had been human before attending the Epiphany feast at Jan's inn. Bartolomeo, the nail in his head trapping him between the realms of the living and the dead, felt his neck wrenched about so that he had no choice but to look towards his former employment site. Even his mad wife, Daniela, rocking on the stool where she sat, sensed the importance of what was happening on Hradčany and cried out. František, running from his house wrapped in a sheath of flame, looked over his shoulder toward the castle, and Bonifác, wrapped up with the black dog near Loreto, growled at the nearby castle forever denied him. Seïa, the novice missing from St. George's since Christmas, heard the thunder and peered through the icy darkness in which she found herself toward what seemed its source. Božena and Anežka, Aleksandr and Jiri in the Old Town Square paused in their suspicious circumambulations and glanced towards the old god and the young woman. The statue in St. Jakub's Church, which had seized Hans' arm, shifted ever so slightly in the direction of Hradčany as well. Hans, sitting on the doorstep of the closed and shuttered shop that had been Albrecht's and staring at the ground, felt pain surge through his phantom arm as fresh as the morning it had been severed and looked towards the castle without knowing why. Everyone who had been caught up in the web of Fen'ka's curse was being summoned to witness the power of their tormentor.

"Svetovit!" cried Nadezda. "I have the fire now. I control it! It has not been extinguished yet!" The figure, which had apparently been directing its attention toward the bridge, tuned towards her on its great horse. Even she could hear the groaning and cracking of the bridge timbers as the river crashed against it and crashed against it again.

Thunder rumbled. "Svetovit! Listen to me!" She took a deep breath to make herself heard above the storm. "The fire is all but extinguished, but not quite. You cannot destroy the city. Not yet. And since I control the fire, I can rewrite the curse." She held up her lantern, showing the steady light within to the angry deity.

The massive warhorse pawed the sky again and then, released from its standstill position by Svetovit, who dropped the reins and kicked its ribcage, bolted down towards Nadezda. Sparks burst from the air where the hooves struck and Svetovit leaned down and opened his hand as if reaching to pluck Nadezda from among the piles of stones waiting to be dressed and assembled into the cathedral's walls.

Seeing the great cloud-figure bearing down on her, Nadezda cringed, bracing for the onslaught. Wind rushed past her and thunder collided with her eardrums. Icy fear gripped her bowels. Would her little circle of cord prove strong enough to keep Svetovit from seizing her?

The cloud-horse and its rider descended from the heavens towards her, the wind ripping fragments and wisps of cloud from its great torso. Then, as it breached the radius of the magic circle, it dissolved and lost its shape, re-forming and coalescing as it reared up behind Nadezda. The horse whinnied in frustration and Svetovit roared with anger. The fragile cord had saved his prey from this first pass. Pulling tightly on the reins, Svetovit drew the horse around behind Nadezda so it faced her again. Its front hooves gouged lines of fire in the sky. Svetovit dug his heels into the horse's ribs a second time and the steed charged towards Nadezda.

Seeing the angry four-faced god galloping towards her, she again braced herself for his attack. But this time, at the last instant, he turned the horse to one side and instead reached with an open hand to seize her as the eight-legged steed fell onto its side and slid along the rising cathedral wall. Again, the cloud-hand dissolved and then reconfigured itself as it passed into and then beyond the circle of red cord around Nadezda. Svetovit cried out in fury and shook his fist towards the sky. The horse clambered upright and pawed the sky, its thunderous whinnies mingling with the storm. Svetovit pulled hard on the reins and the horse reared up, dancing about, as Svetovit considered his next move.

"Svetovit!" Nadezda could not wait for him to tire of his attacks. "I control the fire and will not allow you to destroy the city or bring all our nightmares to life as it dies. No! Your vengeance is tied not to the dying of the fire but to the passing of the generations—you must leave Prague in peace until…"

Svetovit did not wait for her to finish the sentence but drove his heels into the steed's ribs. The horse lowered its head and charged at Nadezda for a third time. Sparks burst from the gouges its hooves cut in the air. Thunder boomed from the hilltop as Svetovit brushed alongside the power of Nadezda's magic circle. This time, however, he clutched a handful of stones from the construction site and swept them towards Nadezda.

The large stones whistled toward her, unimpeded by the magic of the circle, as they were earthly, not magical, weapons. One struck Nadezda on the shoulder, nearly knocking the lantern out of her hand. Svetovit pulled his great horse around behind her and paused, laughing. She immediately understood her predicament. She was trapped in the circle—if she stepped outside the cord, Svetovit could seize her, but if she remained in the circle, she was an easy target for the stones he could hurl.

She shook the lantern at Svetovit. The pool of light from the lantern was the only illumination that pierced the strange darkness engulfing the hilltop. "Heed my words, Svetovit!" she demanded. "When this fire dies, you may not touch the city but you must wait until…"

Another stone flew past her and shattered on the ground behind her. The horse pawed the air, showing itself anxious to charge at her again. The animal snorted, steamy clouds puffing from its nostrils, and its hooves scraped sparks from the sky.

Something moved amid the stones along the edges of the construction site. She glanced in that direction. Shadows and dim, transparent figures seemed to be gathering around her.

A shadow peacock strutted between the piles of stone. A man in a cassock—a priest?—stood there, his arms crossed. A party of four—two men and two women—slunk between the piles of stone. A young girl, a novice nun if her shadow-habit was to be believed, darted behind the rising walls of the new cathedral.

There were other figures in clothing that Nadezda did recognize. A man who was looking away from her at first but then seemed to notice her. He held a great sword, needing both hands to support its weight. He slowly turned and then moved towards her, carefully watching where he stepped. A woman, about the same age as Nadezda, stood behind him and—after watching him—also moved slowly towards her. On her other side, the hazy forms of several people were intently watching the man stalking her with the sword. One pointed at her and seemed on the verge of crying out.

A large stone hit Nadezda's leg and she cried out, falling to one knee. Her attention was wrenched back to Svetovit and she saw him pluck an even larger stone from among those the stonecutters had set aside for carving.

"You must wait for four times eight generations to pass, Svetovit! Four times eight generations must follow the extinguishing of the fire before you may touch the city again!" Nadezda called out.

Svetovit paused, seemingly startled by her assertion that his final onslaught against the city could not be accomplished immediately. Then with an even greater fury and strength than displayed before, he threw a stone directly at Nadezda.

Nadezda ducked her head and the stone struck her shoulder. She crumpled onto her side, clutching the lantern as her other arm splayed out beneath her. Her left hand touched the ground outside the red circle.

Immediately there was a flash as Svetovit seized a silver javelin from the air and in a single, flowing movement sent it sailing towards Nadezda's fallen form. The lance pierced her wrist and a great spurt of blood burst from the wound. She cried out and attempted to pull her hand back into the protection of the magic circle but the lance pinned her wrist to the ground. The shadow-man who had been approaching her amid the construction site debris darted up to her and the sword in his hands sliced through the air. She screamed again in shock and pain as she fell back, her hand—still pinned to the earth by the javelin—severed from her arm. Blood splashed everywhere around her. She felt sick and dizzy.

Lightning flickered around the hilltop again. Nadezda, unable now to both hold and open the lantern, set it on the ground beside her. Had her falling back extinguished it? Melted wax had splattered about inside the lantern, and she held her breath as she unclasped the hinged pane that opened outward. In the midst of her pain and nausea she saw that the Candlemas candle stub within still burned.

Nadezda knew she would never escape the magic circle alive. The blood kept spurting unstaunched from the stump of her arm even as she plunged it into her apron pocket and tried to wrap her cloak about it. How long did she have? She wasn't sure. A wave of darkness swept across her vision and then receded. It was difficult to breathe. She bent forward and blew on the wick of the candle. The flame stirred but did not go out.

"Four times eight generations, Svetovit," she whispered and blew again. Another stone came sailing out of the air and crashed onto the lantern, splintering the glass and twisting the lead that had held it together. Wax splattered. A wisp of smoke curled up from the wick, now buried in the soft white wax. It hovered for an instant and then melted into the air. Nadezda collapsed onto the ground beside it, unable to hold herself upright any longer. She felt the muddy cobblestones beneath her cheek and, peering up through the miasma that swam before her, saw Svetovit charging towards her once again. She was dimly aware that she could feel the red cord under her shoulder. That must mean that her shoulders and head lay outside the protective circle, exposed to the full brunt of Svetovit's wrath. But she had rewritten the curse and extinguished the fire. His wrath should be stayed. He should not even be here any longer.

A shadow-face flickered into focus before her. It was the woman who had walked behind the man with the sword who had severed her arm. A strange expression was on her face. Concern. Sympathy. Confusion. Anger. Nadezda could see her lips moving but could hear nothing over the roar of the wind and the thundering approach of Svetovit's horse.

Nadezda swallowed and attempted to gather her strength. She reached out with the hand that was still hers and asked the woman, "Did we stop Svetovit? Did we save Prague?"

The Tower

(Wednesday, August 14, 2002)

THE TOWER: THE SIXTEENTH OF THE MAJOR TRUMPS,
IT PORTENDS SUDDEN AND UNEXPECTED CHANGE, DISASTER.

"**A**re you sure no salt is left?" Dmitri asked Sean.
Sean pulled the shaker from his pocket.
Maybe a few grains. Virtually nothing."

Victoria watched as Dmitri bent down and pulled another card, this one at random, from the deck. "Pour out whatever is left," he told Sean. "We've already burned the last of the Major Trumps at the other door. We can only hope that this card will stand in for all the others whose power we have not released. We can only trust in Providence."

Sean unscrewed the top of the salt shaker and turned it upside down. A few crystals fell onto the face of the card Dmitri held flat against the smooth paving stones before the central portion of the mosaic. Dmitri held out the matches to Sean, who took them, struck one, and held the fire to a corner of the card.

The edge of the card embraced the fire, which slid across its upper edge. Hesitating, as if afraid of the character in the center of the card, the fire hung back before engulfing the image. The salt sizzled and popped. Dmitri jerked his fingers back at the last instant, but not before the fire had singed his fingertips. The black ash that had been the card curled and twisted and fell away.

Sophia removed her arm from Victoria's shoulder, passed

the empty bowl from her right hand to her left, and crossed herself. Victoria held her breath.

Silent fireworks burst in the air directly before the great mosaic. Incandescent colors rained down before the Golden Gate. Bloom after bloom of multicolored light blossomed and faded. Barely visible in the center of the fireworks stood a young man in a multicolored patchwork coat, walking toward the cathedral as he gazed up at the spires and flying buttresses supporting the stone walls. He had a staff and knapsack swung over his right shoulder and held a white rose in his left hand. A little dog jumped excitedly around his feet, seeming to bark but making no sound. The man kept walking, seemingly distracted by the intricate masonry above him. Without once looking ahead of him, as if he had not a care in the world and was uninterested in where his feet might be taking him, he walked directly into the Doomsday mosaic and vanished. The fireworks continued bursting and exploding for long moments after he had vanished, but as they faded from sight, Victoria felt a tremor roll through the pavement beneath their feet and heard a rumble in the distance.

Victoria, accompanied by the others, gasped and coughed, unable to hold her breath any longer.

"Did you feel it?" Victoria was unable to conceal her excitement. "The Royal Road! It trembled beneath us. It must be awake!"

Then, seemingly at their elbows, a great cock-crowing pierced the air. It echoed and resounded all around them, bouncing off the stone walls and the paving stones. The crowing rang on and on as if it would never stop, then was cut short, silenced as abruptly as it had begun.

"What's that?" Sophia cried out.

"A rooster! Svetovit was worshipped on this hill with the

sacrifice of a black rooster!" Dmitri reminded them all with a shout. "George is summoning the old devil-god!" Rushing further along the cathedral wall, Victoria and the others tumbled into another portion of the plaza surrounding the great Gothic church. Ahead of them, in the center of the plaza, were George and Magdalena.

George, with his back to them, was standing over Magdalena, who was kneeling slightly to one side. She was hunched forward, pressing a black bundle of feathers to the ground with both hands. George was leaning on the sword, which he must have used to cut the rooster's throat. Fountains of blood spurted and shot from the wound.

George must have heard their commotion, because he turned around. Magdalena, keeping the rooster pressed to the ground, turned her head too as the blood continued to spurt, though in shorter and smaller arcs.

"Well, well," chuckled George, seeing Victoria and the academics. "How is it that you five are here?" His voice hovered between anger and incredulity. "You should still be ill, much too ill to be here… Unless the poppets we buried…?" He glanced at Magdalena.

"We were ill," Dmitri answered him. "But we have recovered and are here now. To stop you. Both of you," he announced, looking from George to Magdalena and back again.

"A bit late for that," George taunted him. "The bridge is nearly washed away, its power gone. We hold the sword and staff and have disabled the Astronomical Clock. I have sacrificed this black rooster within a circle drawn with the very sword from the bridge's foundations. There is nothing to stop Svetovit now. The city is vulnerable, defenseless. When the rooster dies, Svetovit will come. You have failed." He lifted the sword and pointed at Dmitri.

THE TOWER

"Magdalena!" called Victoria. "Don't you see? He's calling Svetovit to destroy the city! Our city! You must see that!"

Magdalena continued to hold the rooster down. "He is not calling Svetovit to destroy Prague, Victoria! You and your friends have conjured this flood! You and your friends have destroyed the power of the bridge and brought this disaster upon us!" Though Magdalena said the words forcefully, Victoria noticed that she seemed to be trying to remember something. Was she under some spell?

"Failed? Maybe we have," Dmitri shouted in concession. "But the city will protect itself! The power of the Royal Road will rise up to stop you!"

No more blood bubbled from the rooster's throat. Magdalena stood and faced Victoria and the others opposing her and George.

The moment she stood, the humid clouds above shuddered and darkened. They drew tight, seemingly sucking other clouds towards them and staining the new-arriving clouds with inky filaments. The clouds congealed and condensed, hanging low and almost scraping the spires of the cathedral.

"The Royal Road?" George mocked Dmitri. "That power has slept for centuries! Even if you were to waken it without a coronation procession, it would be a feeble swat at a spirit as powerful as Svetovit!"

A tendril of lightning flickered between the massive cloud-boulders above them.

Victoria heard Sophia whisper to her husband, "How do we summon the power of the Royal Road now that it is awake?"

Dmitri shook his head, hoping George would not notice. "I don't know," he confessed.

"Wouldn't an awakened Road respond if Prague were

in danger?" Sean turned to the priest. "If so, it should come without any further prodding from us!"

George laughed, apparently amused at their consternation. He gave an order to Magdalena. "Bring the staff and stand here with me."

Magdalena hurried to get the staff and returned to George's side, resting one end of it on the ground and holding it upright as if it were a flagpole. George rested the sword's point against the ground, between his feet, continuing to look across the plaza toward the academics and at the sky above the cathedral, where the clouds continued to gather and grow heavy in addition to darker and darker. The hilltop seemed shrouded in shadows even though it was still early morning.

Lightning flickered above them again.

"You have failed!" George shouted again. "Neither you nor the Road can prevent Svetovit's arrival now!"

Victoria turned to the others, tears running down her face. "No! We can't have failed!" she cried.

A cold breeze ruffled the feathers of the dead rooster and then Victoria's skirts.

"Svetovit is coming. I can feel it," Magdalena shouted with awe. She searched the sky above the cathedral. "He is nearly here, is he not? Fen'ka will be vindicated at last!" She smiled up at the sky and closed her eyes, the breeze playing in her hair.

"Fen'ka should be here to share in this triumph," Magdalena announced. She opened her eyes and looked at George. "I brought river water. Can we use that?"

"Possibly." George glanced over his shoulder at her. "Pour the water into your chalice and use the yew to stir it." He turned his attention back to the sky.

Victoria watched helplessly as Magdalena rushed to her

bag, setting down the staff and pulling out a small plastic bottle of water, then pouring it into a chalice.

"Fen'ka." Magdalena's low call was carried to Victoria by the wind. Magdalena jerked on something green in her hand, sending water droplets splashing around her.

The faint, translucent image of an old woman stood in front of Magdalena where the water had splashed onto the cobblestones. The woman seemed startled, unfamiliar with where she stood, and her head darted from side to side.

A flash of lightning and thunder crashed around them, nearly knocking over Magdalena and several of Victoria's companions. The image of the old woman winked out.

Wind gusted down the hilltop, and with it, a look of awe struck both George and Magdalena. George stood taller, straighter, and both prouder and more reverentially.

"Svetovit is here," muttered Sophia. "See how George and Magdalena are looking at the sky over the cathedral?" Victoria twisted her head to try and glimpse the ancient devil-god but could not see him. However, she felt an electric charge in the air, a malevolent energy crackling around the hilltop.

"Svetovit!" called George eagerly. "I have prepared your advent! Welcome to your ancient home!" Thunder crashed around them as lightning sizzled and hissed across the sky.

A neigh like thunder and a war cry of fury burst from the sky and echoed across the city. A great eight-legged horse with the ancient four-headed god astride it came galloping along the roof of the cathedral, clouds of sparks showering down from its hooves. The devil-god and his horse careened around the bell tower next to the Golden Gate. The horse, hardly pausing to make the turn, nearly slid around the baroque spire atop the bell tower and sent another great shower of sparks raining onto the plaza where Victoria and the academics stood.

Victoria screamed and the others also cried out as they ran for cover. Sophia dropped the now-empty bowl of protective herbs and huddled with Victoria and Theo, pressed against the rough stone walls of the cathedral. Dmitri and Sean darted across the plaza to take refuge on the porch of an entrance.

The cloud-horse and its rider came skidding to a stop over the western end of the cathedral, the horse again rearing up and scraping showers of sparks from the air with its hooves. Svetovit cried out again, tangling his fingers tightly in the horse's tangled mane, and the two came charging toward the apse a second time. Lightning flickered.

Without warning, a great wall of rippling and undulating rainbow light sprang up in the air over the apse. Seeing it, the horse screamed and tried to break its forward hurtle. Svetovit tugged on the horse's mane, trying to turn it aside before it crashed into the wall of light. The horse slid and tripped and stumbled but did not fall. Svetovit clutched the horse's body with his knees and its mane with his fingers, retaining his balance on the animal's back.

"Look!" cried Dmitri, pointing at the wall of light in the air. "The tarot figures!" Victoria peered up to see what Dmitri was pointing at with such excitement.

"He's right!" Victoria exclaimed, jumping up and down and darting into the open plaza to see better. "The power of the Road is awake!"

Dmitri gazed at the four figures standing in the midst of the quivering light now slithering through the sky to make a circle around Svetovit and his eight-legged horse. The figures began to walk as the light moved, and as the light pulled away from the figures to encircle Svetovit, the four entities from the tarot cards were clearly visible. The Magician held his staff upright, now with a small sword in his other hand. The figure of the Emperor stood beside him, wielding his great unsheathed sword. Next to him stood the Empress, her flowing gown tumbling behind her in the wind, the scepter she held a torch in the dark sky. The last figure was also a woman, the High Priestess, her vestments curling about her and behind her as if they were living things, the crescent moon still snarled in them. The scroll she held was now unfurled.

The horse stood, snorting and pawing the sky as the circle of light closed around it. The four tarot figures—Dmitri was not sure if they were best described as spirits or archetypes or phantoms—took up positions around the horse and Svetovit, one at each cardinal point of the compass. The horse kept snorting, furiously pawing the sky as it turned first one direction and then another as if trying to discern a weakness in its prison through which it might charge. Svetovit grumbled with it. Dmitri felt the reverberation of that grumble in the stones.

Was it the Magician who began speaking? Dmitri thought so but was unsure. It was a male voice. He was certain of that. But as the Magician spoke, George cried out to Dmitri and Sean.

"Four figures of the Major Trumps? Is that all?" he taunted the priest and the professor. "You only were able to awake four of the powers of the Royal Road?" He laughed in mockery and derision. "If you had been able to waken all twenty-two, you might have been able to accomplish something! But four? Do you honestly think four can stand against Svetovit?"

Dmitri struggled to hear what the Magician was saying to Svetovit. It seemed to be a challenge, as the figure pointed his staff first at Svetovit and then back toward the western horizon, but Svetovit's only response was to throw his head back and laugh. The old cloud-devil reached one hand into the air and pulled a lance out of nowhere, which he then tucked under his arm, the long spearhead protruding along the horse's shoulder and far past its nose, which it flared and snorted, pawing the air with its left front hoof.

The Magician seemed to repeat his demand that Svetovit depart, again gesturing with his staff toward the western horizon. Thunder rumbled.

Svetovit bent down, nearly rubbing one of his faces in the mane of the horse. The spear's tip was pointed directly at the Magician's torso as the horse leaped forward, charging at the Magician.

As rapidly as the horse charged forward, the Magician snapped his hand back with the staff and held it horizontally before him, swinging the dagger in his other hand upwards as if to eviscerate the cloud-horse. The horse reared and whinnied, Svetovit clutching its mane and the spear jerking upward, missing the Magician's chin by inches. The razor-sharp hooves came crashing down and the horse charged at the Emperor standing at one of the other compass points along the curling circle of lights. The Emperor shouted at the horse and its rider, swinging his broadsword sideways as if to cut open the horse's breast. Again the horse reared up, the front four of its eight massive legs pawing frantically at the air, Svetovit gouging its ribs with his knees to drive it forward. The horse reared again, its whinny like the shriek of a hurricane's wind. The Emperor thrust his sword forward, and as the great forelegs came tumbling down, the horse turned aside and charged back towards the Magician.

The Magician figure slashed at the air beneath his feet with his staff, as if drawing a line and daring the horse to cross it. The now-terrified horse bolted towards the Empress standing opposite the Emperor.

THE TOWER

The Empress held her scepter up as if to illuminate the darkness of the storm-cloud steed and then darted forward to thrust the scepter towards the horse's eye. Vines and thick thorny stems of roses came curling from beneath her feet, wrapping around the eight legs of the horse. The horse stumbled and whinnied and nearly threw Svetovit from its back as the thorns cut shreds of cloud from its legs. Svetovit swung his javelin over the horse's head to strike at the Empress, but she was already back wrapped in the safety of the rainbow lights. Svetovit slashed at the vines and roses tangled around the horse's legs, cutting away most of the quickly growing greenery. The horse again reared and whinnied, this time coming down on its hooves and chasing its own streaming tail. Svetovit roared in anger and drove his knees into the horse's ribs, and the animal charged at the High Priestess.

Her vestments still curling and twisting about her, she held the unfurled scroll in one hand as if it were a matador's cape taunting an infuriated bull in the ring. The horse lowered its head and galloped toward the scroll, Svetovit aiming his javelin at the High Priestess, who stepped nimbly aside at the last instant. The horse screamed as it collided with the circle of twisting, curling light. Black smoke and ruddy flames burst from the light, the thunder of the explosion ricocheting off the stone walls of the cathedral and castle below and nearly knocking over Dmitri, who was still crouching with Sean on the castle porch.

The horse stumbled back and shook its head as if to clear its thoughts. Its ribs heaved and shook as it struggled to control its breathing. Then, slowly, with Svetovit whispering words to calm the beast and nodding his head as his four faces smiled, the horse turned to face the empty space between the Magician and the Empress.

317

As Dmitri continued to watch, enthralled by the battle in the sky, the horse took a handful of backward steps, brushing its tail against both the High Priestess and the Emperor as it swung from side to side. Svetovit again took aim with his lance, pointing it at the glittering wall between the Magician and the Empress, and pulled his head down until one cheek rubbed the horse's neck. Clutching the mane with the fingers of his other hand, he slapped the horse's side with his thighs and howled a battle cry. The horse galloped toward the unprotected wall.

"Magdalena! The staff! Stand here with me!" George barked and Magdalena scurried, stuffing the chalice into her bag, bringing the staff to stand again beside George.

Sean grabbed Dmitri's shoulder and shook the priest. "Wait! What are George and Magdalena doing?" he shouted over the roar of Svetovit's war cry.

George was speaking to Magdalena and pointing at Svetovit, the Magician, and the Empress. He raised the great sword he held. Magdalena raised the rabbi's staff.

The horse bore down on the wall of light. The Magician and the Empress moved toward each other as if to close the breach in the wall, but as they moved, George slashed the air before him with Bruncvik's sword, cutting the air to his left while Magdalena swung the staff to her right. The Magician crumpled, dropping his staff and dagger as he clutched the back of his legs as if their tendons had been severed. The Empress threw up her hands and fell backward as if struck in the ribs by a heavy club. Her scepter flew from her grasp. The horse charged through the wall of light, another explosion of smoke and fire erupting as it did so, but Svetovit rode in triumph past the barrier of light and past George in his own magic circle on the ground. Coming over the basilica of St.

George, the horse turned to face the cathedral again. The horse cantered in place as if dancing, shifting its great weight from foot to foot to foot to foot. The javelin point bobbed as Svetovit eased his grip on it.

The circle of light shuddered where Svetovit and the horse had breached it. The light tore and began to unravel. Ragged wisps of light fluttered and danced and faded. The entire wall of light slithered out of the geometric figure of a circle and resembled more a snake struggling to make its way forward. Portions of the light-wall tumbled over.

The Magician lay sprawled on his back, the Empress bent nearly double and wrapping her arms around her torso. George and Magdalena lifted the sword and staff and repeated their slashing, hacking motions with the weapons. The Empress, cognizant now of George and Magdalena, turned and looked at them. Pain was evident in her face as Magdalena's blows rained down on her shoulders. She collapsed to her knees.

The light that had come unfurled in the sky shuddered once again and dissipated altogether.

The Magician, unable to turn and face his attacker, reached one hand toward George. But the Magician had no weapon with which to fight and writhed on his back as George cut and cut and cut again. With a final, exuberant slash, George uttered his own battle cry and the figures of the Magician and the Empress, their power defeated by the principal magical weapons of Prague, faded from sight.

"No! He cannot do that! He can't!" Victoria exclaimed. "No!"

Svetovit chortled and raised his javelin, shaking it in what was both a triumphant salute to George and a warrior's taunt of the Emperor and the High Priestess, who still stood in their positions along the original diameter of the now-vanished light

319

circle. The Emperor shook his sword at Svetovit in return. The scroll in the hand of the High Priestess fluttered in the wind.

George swung around to gloat, first at Dmitri and Sean on the porch, then at Victoria, Sophia, and Theo against the cathedral walls. Magdalena beamed in triumph with him.

Svetovit drove his knees into the horse with no warning and the beast screamed, lowered its head, and charged straight for the High Priestess. George raised the sword again. Magdalena lifted the staff.

"Magdalena! Stop!" Victoria shouted, urgently trying to get through to her friend. "Don't do it!"

Fireballs sizzled and sparked along the outline of the circle George had drawn with the sword. Two translucent figures appeared just outside the fiery outline of the circle to confront George and Magdalena within it. In front of George stood a nude woman wrapped in a scarf, the woman from the card Dmitri and Sean had burned in front of the modern doors of the cathedral, minus her four companions—human, eagle, bull, and lion. The other figure, which was the Fool from the card incinerated with the last few crystals of salt, stood before Magdalena. His knapsack still hung from the staff over his shoulder but he was no longer looking into the sky, ignoring what was in front of him. He glanced from Magdalena, to George, and back to Magdalena again.

"Can't we do something to help them?" Victoria asked Theo.

"How?" Theo asked her. "We have your chalice, but it's empty. What other weapon do we have?"

Lightning flared, drawing Victoria's attention back to the sky. Svetovit's spear had struck the open scroll of the High Priestess and shattered, raining splinters and shards onto the plaza below. The horse careened past the High Priestess, past the Emperor before Svetovit could rein it in and turn the horse around. The Emperor and the High Priestess turned to face Svetovit. The two tarot figures on the ground continued to face George and Magdalena, seemingly oblivious to the battle above them.

Victoria wondered if appealing again to Magdalena might help and turned to ask Sophia's opinion.

"Why didn't we save some of those protective herbs?" Sophia said, wringing her hands. "I should have thought of that!"

Dmitri and Sean were carrying on their own debate.

"We need something to draw a protective circle of our own, if we go out there," Sean told Dmitri. "Do we have anything to draw a circle with?"

The priest shook his head.

Above them, the horse reared up on its rear four legs and charged at the Emperor. Svetovit reached out an open hand, as if he planned to seize the Emperor's crown or sword with his naked palm as he rode past.

At that same instant, the tarot figures on the ground uttered a war cry. The scarf-clad woman began a sensual dance as her four companions—even more translucent and less material than she was—appeared and rushed at George. The barrier of the circle convulsed and flared up to bar their way. Three of the woman's four companions—eagle, lion, bull—vanished.

The Fool swung his staff with knapsack around his shoulder and brought it crashing into the air above the circle's outline. Fireworks exploded there.

George apparently trusted in the strength of the circle to protect him and Magdalena from these new opponents. But Magdalena retaliated, striking back as the Fool struck at her. She swung the staff at the Fool's patchwork doublet, crossing the line of the circle as she did.

"No!" George shouted at her. "Don't cross the circle!"

It was too late. The Fool had tossed aside his own staff and seized the end of the rabbi's staff that Magdalena had swung past the protective confinement of the circle. He wrenched and pulled it, attempting to break Magdalena's grip. The androgynous human figure that had accompanied the World, the card depicting the nude woman dancing, came to the Fool's assistance and also wrapped both hands around the staff.

George swung at them with Bruncvik's sword, not simply reaching over the edge of the circle but entering the unprotected space of the plaza outside the malevolent widdershins circle he had drawn.

Dmitri saw George step out of the circle as Magdalena struggled to keep the staff in her grip. He also noticed the luggage cart with the empty cage on it and Magdalena's shoulder bag on the ground beside it. Something had tumbled out of the bag. A bouquet of some sort. Or a bundle of herbs.

"Look!" Dmitri grabbed Sean's elbow and pointed toward the bouquet of leaves. "One of their own tools! We can draw a circle with that! Now, while they are distracted!" Without waiting to see if Sean was following him, Dmitri scrambled across the plaza toward the bundle of leaves.

Coming up to the circle, he didn't pause or worry that he might not be able to cross the magical barrier. But the circle had been cast to harness destructive magic and act as a barrier to magical, not physical, opposition. Dmitri stumbled over the sputtering fire of the circle's boundary, grabbed the leaves, and bounded back across before Magdalena or George could respond to the noise of his footfalls.

Sean stood waiting for him outside the circle, gesturing and attempting to get the attention of Theo, Sophia, and Victoria. But the three others, attempting to watch both

Svetovit's battle in the sky and George and Magdalena's battle
on the ground, had seen Dmitri steal the bundle of leaves
and must have guessed what he was about to use it for. Theo
rushed from the shadows of the cathedral wall with one hand
firmly grasping Victoria's arm and the other hand grasping
Sophia's. The trio scurried over to Sean and Dmitri.

Dmitri bent over and touched the bundle of yew to the
cobblestones, stumbling in a circle around the others and
tracing his route on the ground with the leaves. As he came
back to his starting point and closed the circle, there were slim
wrinkles along the ground of the same rainbow light that had
formed the now-vanquished circle in the sky. Dmitri stood,
raising his eyes but afraid of what he might see.

George and Magdalena stood a few feet away, Magdalena
now outside the widdershins circle, as was George. Magdalena
still held one end of the staff, although the Fool and the
other human figure seemed to have a firm grip on it as well.
George swung the sword as if to slice through the torso of
the androgynous figure that was closer to him than the Fool,
but the figure slipped in and out of materialization as George
attempted to harm it.

Meanwhile, the feminine World figure seemed to be
ignoring the struggle before her and remained content to lazily,
luxuriously, sensuously dance and weave her way around
the plaza. The images of the lion, the bull, and the eagle had
returned and were shimmering in and out of view around her
as they participated in her dance.

Dmitri could make no sense of the World's behavior.
There seemed no other way to assist the Fool than by
distracting George. Shaking the yew leaves in front of him,
Dmitri shouted, "George! Look! We have your leaves! And
we've cast our own circle with them!" He shook the leaves

vigorously again.

George glanced over his shoulder at the sound of Dmitri's voice. Startled, then furious, George turned and slashed the air in front of him with the sword, probably thinking to disrupt the protective power of Dmitri's circle. The lights that danced along Dmitri's circle crackled and popped but the circle held.

As George turned to face Dmitri, the Fool and his partner nearly wrenched the rabbi's staff from Magdalena's grip. She cried out and wrenched it back towards her hip, afraid of what would happen if she lost this tug-of-war with the Fool.

Meanwhile, Svetovit seemed more intent on watching George and Magdalena's struggle than in pressing his attack against the Emperor and the High Priestess. The two remaining powers of the Royal Road seemed momentarily unsure whether to come to the aid of the Fool and the World or to rush at Svetovit in his distraction.

Then Svetovit roared in defiance and tossed aside what bits of the javelin he still held. He shook his fist, slapped his thighs against the horse's ribs, and charged at the Emperor, who raised his sword as the High Priestess stepped closer and extended her open scroll as if it were a shield to prevent Svetovit's dodging past the Emperor.

Svetovit roared again, slapped the horse's rump with his open palm, and the horse leaped up and sailed over both the Emperor's sword and the High Priestess' scroll to come down in a shower of sparks directly over the Fool.

"What are you doing?" Sean cried in alarm to Dmitri. "George will be able to cross this circle as easily as you crossed into his!"

"But he will not be able to bring the sword with him," Dmitri answered. "He will have to set it down."

"Perhaps I will be able to seize the sword if George

attempts to cross your circle," a shadowy man said, appearing just within their circle. His hair was long and his beard unkempt. Victoria recognized his clothing as that of a medieval Bohemian peasant.

"Who are you?" she asked, as startled as the others by the shadow-man's sudden appearance and apparent cooperation with their efforts.

"I am known most simply as Dalibor," the man answered.

Victoria stumbled and caught hold of Dmitri's arm. "How did you come to be involved in this?" she asked.

"The man named George involved me," Dalibor answered her. "He did it using that posy of yew and horsehair, which you have now used to construct this circle. The same yew that pulled me from the Jug allows me to cross the circle you have made with it. If you allow it, I would gladly help you stop him."

"Yes! Do whatever you can!" Sophia urged Dalibor. Dmitri nodded in agreement, not taking his eyes from George, who still stood near Magdalena and had seen Dalibor materialize within Dmitri's circle.

"Dalibor! Your place is here!" George shouted in fury, striking the ground between his feet with the point of the sword. "Here… or in the Jug!"

Magdalena shrieked. George whirled around, only to witness that the Fool and the other figure, undistracted by George for an instant, had pulled the staff from Magdalena's grip. The Fool turned and looked up to the Emperor and High Priestess, shaking the staff in his fist. George screamed and ran straight for the Fool, swinging the sword before him. Svetovit, seemingly unsure if he could win a duel against the Emperor and the High Priestess without the aid of the staff and sword, hovered above.

The Emperor and High Priestess, seeing Svetovit's

hesitation and doubt, vanished from the sky, only to reappear on the ground between the Fool and George's sword. George slashed, the sword hissing through the air as he aimed at the Fool, but struck the unexpectedly appearing protectors instead and hacked a ragged cut through part of the scroll in the High Priestess' hand.

The Emperor raised his sword to deflect George's next strike, the ringing echoes of the swords' clashing together reverberating across the plaza. The swords clashed again and again. George's strokes were unrelenting and drove the Emperor stumbling backwards a few steps, knocking into the Fool he had sought to protect. The Emperor and the Fool together fell against the border of George's magic circle.

Ruddy fire and oily smoke exploded from the magical barrier of the circle where the tarot figures fell against it. The staff went tumbling from the Fool's hand. George pressed his attack, swinging the great sword of Prague at the torsos of both the Emperor and the Fool. The sword sliced cleanly though both tarot figures and struck the wall of magic they had fallen against around George's circle. Sparks exploded and hissed as the sword cut through George's circle. The Fool and the Emperor collapsed and vanished, as did the shadow of the man who had been aiding the Fool.

"No!" Sophia and Victoria wailed together from within the safety of Dmitri's circle.

George seemed like a swordsman possessed. Hardly pausing for breath, he lifted one arm in an apparent attempt to wipe the sweat from his face and whirled about, swinging the sword in a wide arc and striking the High Priestess across her back. The tarot-woman shuddered and threw her hands up. The scroll flew from her hands up into the air and vanished as she collapsed onto the plaza and vanished in turn.

In the confusion of the sword fighting, Magdalena went running for the staff as it clattered across the plaza after the Fool had lost his hold on it. She bent and closed her fingers around it again just as Dalibor appeared before her, reaching for the staff as well.

"You tried to pull me into the Jug!" cried Magdalena in fury, standing and swinging the staff at Dalibor. She hit Dalibor in the ribs and the knight crumpled from the impact. "You tried to kill me!" She swung again with the staff against his shoulder.

"I was following instructions!" gasped Dalibor, lifting his arms to protect himself from the blows of the staff.

"Whose instructions?" demanded Magdalena, gasping for breath and swinging the staff again and striking his forearm.

"The one holding the yew!" snarled Dalibor. "Are you really such a fool, woman?"

Dmitri, taking advantage of Magdalena's attention on Dalibor and sure that the yew and horsehair in his hand would be some protection, darted from his own circle as Theo and Sean cried out in surprise.

"George! Stop this while you still can!" Dmitri shouted, brandishing the yew posy as if it were another sword equal to the one George held.

Seeing Fr. Dmitri outside the protection of the yew-circle, George called back in furious amusement, "Have you gone mad, Dmitri? Why should I stop this?" He took a deep breath and strode toward Dmitri but then hesitated.

The woman that was the World had continued her dance around the plaza and Dmitri realized in the same instant George must have that she had been casting another circle as she danced, a large circle that encompassed nearly the whole of the plaza. She was nearly back to the point where

she had begun her dance and the circle was almost complete.
Would the circle of the World supersede and override the
other circles? Would it keep Svetovit from the area above the
hilltop? Apparently, George was taking no chances. Raising
the sword above his head and shouting a battle cry, he charged
at the dancing World.

George brought the sword swinging down onto the
pavement in front of the World, sparks showering her bare
feet. He raised the sword to swing at her, to cleave her in half
if he could, when Dalibor was suddenly in front of him and
shoving him in the chest and shouting his own war cry into the
Jesuit's face.

George stumbled back but kept his grip on the hilt. The
sword descended and cut through Dalibor's collarbone. George
wrenched the sword free and swung again, this time at Dalibor's
knees. Dalibor threw himself at George, but the Jesuit saw
what was coming and managed to twist to one side. Dalibor
fell forward onto the plaza and George brought the sword down
one last time across the knight's lower back. The dead man
shimmered and rippled, fading from view. George, gasping for
breath, leaned on the sword and looked around the plaza.

The circle of the World was complete. She took the
last step, closing the magical ring around the courtyard, and
looked up at Svetovit. She smiled and beckoned to him, still
seemingly oblivious of George.

With a final cry of rage, George drove the sword through
her breast. She vanished an instant before the sword touched
her, as did the shadows of the lion, eagle, and bull that had
been her dancing partners.

Dmitri still stood half-way between George and the circle
he had cast with the yew. Would the World's completed circle
have any effect on their apparently doomed efforts to stop

Svetovit? Or had the World intended to do something else with her circle before George had cut her down?

"They are all gone!" Victoria turned to Sophia in disbelief. "The tarot powers of the Royal Road have been destroyed!"

"Impossible!" shouted Theo, looking wildly about the plaza, seemingly convinced that one of the figures must be hidden somewhere on the hilltop. "They must be here! They must!"

The storm clouds above the cathedral began to rotate in a slow and lazy tide around the spire of the church's bell tower. The clouds darkened yet further, becoming an opaque hue that hovered on the cusp between black and the darkest shade of green that Victoria had ever seen. Svetovit threw his head back, clapping one hand against his knee as he shook and rocked with uproarious laughter. Thunder rang out and pealed above them, echoing across the city. The breeze stirring near the ground now followed the same widdershins flow of the storm above.

The cloud-horse pawed the air, anxious to charge again. In the gloom, Victoria could hear, rather than see, the horse snort, but then the sparks its hooves scraped from the sky illuminated the steamy clouds puffing from its nostrils. Without warning, Svetovit leaned forward as he had before and drove his heels into the horse's ribs. It charged down at the hilltop, lightning shattering the darkness, showing the clouds rotating more rapidly, and the force of the breeze growing stronger.

In the circle together, Victoria, Sophia, Sean, and Theo all cried and shouted, ducking down and clutching each other. Across from them, Dmitri cried out and dropped to his knees as well, covering his head with his arms and dropping the yew. Driven by the wind, it scuttled across the plaza in the dark.

Even Magdalena covered her head with her hands and bent over, though she kept hold of the staff.

Just as the horse seemed about to crash into the hilltop, Svetovit pulled it back up, causing it to scream and roar, rearing and prancing on its back four legs as the front four scraped shower after shower after shower of sparks from the black-green clouds.

Lightning flickered in the still-deepening darkness, throwing all the figures on the hilltop into stark relief for an instant. The lightning flickered again and this time Victoria was sure of seeing something.

It seemed to be a convocation of shadow figures assembling on the hilltop. A bird—a peacock?—was strutting along while a group of four people seemed to be slinking across one corner of the plaza. Victoria was sure a young nun darted in another direction and vanished into the cathedral before she glimpsed a man in a cassock standing near the dead rooster, his arms crossed across his chest, staring up at Svetovit.

Svetovit also seemed to see the shadows in the dark, his thunderous voice joining that of his horse, which continued its angry prance in the sky. He held onto the horse with his knees, disentangling his fingers from the animal's mane and smashing one giant fist into his other oversized hand's open palm. The hilltop shook and reverberated. Svetovit roared again and reached out, pointing down at the courtyard toward an open area where no one was standing.

Lightning oscillated between the clouds.

Victoria saw a young woman where Svetovit had pointed, a young woman who seemed to be standing inside a circle of red cord, the only detail she could make out in the all-too-brief flicker of light. The woman was holding up something that glittered in the dark as if she held a star, though Victoria could not make out what it was.

George stared at this young woman, ignoring the other shadow people on the hilltop. He lifted the sword with difficulty in both hands, perhaps exhausted by the morning's duels. He walked towards her, slowly and carefully, as if seeking new obstacles that might have appeared in the dark to impede him. Magdalena, standing upright now, took a step towards the shadow woman as well. She held the staff in front of her as if to protect herself if anyone or anything attempted to block her. She took another step. As she came closer to the woman, she was also coming closer to George and then following in his footsteps.

Victoria and the others slowly stood and watched George, followed by Magdalena, come closer to the shadow woman holding the star in one hand. Victoria held her breath, afraid to move and disturb the strange tableaux, the seeming dance between George and the two women—one a shadow, the other Magdalena—playing out before her eyes. But then Victoria, unable to stop herself, raised her arm and tried to warn the shadow woman to beware of George, but no words could escape her suddenly parched-dry throat.

The shadow woman fell to one knee.

A large stone hit Nadezda's leg and she cried out, falling to one knee. Her attention was wrenched back from the shadowy figures around her and back to Svetovit. She saw him pluck an even larger stone from among those the stonecutters had set aside for carving.

"You must wait for four times eight generations to

pass, Svetovit! Four times eight generations must follow the extinguishing of the fire before you may touch the city again!" Nadezda called out.

A shiver seemed to ripple through Svetovit and then across the rapidly circling storm clouds above. He raised his arm and, half standing from where he was mounted, he threw something toward the fallen woman. Lightning crashed around them. Everyone on the hilltop covered their eyes. Victoria cried out. The shadow woman fell onto her side, clutching the star to her with one arm as the other fell past the red cord she had been standing within.

Svetovit reached into the clouds and threw another handful of lightning across the city. The hilltop rocked in the simultaneous thunderclap that ricocheted among the stone walls of the plaza. The shadow woman on the ground seemed to struggle, trying to pull her hand back over the red cord but apparently unable to move it.

Then he launched something silver like a lance that pierced the woman's wrist, and a great spurt of blood burst from the wound. She cried out, but the lance pinned her wrist to the ground.

George was unsure who this woman was or where she had come from but realized that her presence was the reason the World had created the magic circle encompassing the entire hilltop. The circle of the World had clearly conflated times or dimensions, and this woman was somehow a threat to both Svetovit's plans for the city and George's plans to establish himself as Grand Master of all Grand Masters, the only occult practitioner ever to overcome the magical defenses of Prague, that most magical of cities in Europe. She had to be stopped.

He had to stop her. He dashed up to her before she could do anything else to actualize the threat she personified. He swept the sword through the air, but it struck the protective power of the red cord encircling her and slid to the ground. Rather than striking off her head, as he had planned, he severed her hand.

Lightning flickered around the hilltop. The woman, freed from her hand, fumbled with the star she held in her other hand and attempted to sit up.

Again Svetovit roared and raised himself from the back of the horse, clutching its ribs with his knees as it cantered about the sky above the cathedral. He shook his fist at the hilltop, with deafening thunder. George stared at the woman on the ground and knew that in whatever dimension her physical body had been struck, she was rapidly bleeding to death from the stump of her arm. She would be dead in moments. Whatever threat she had posed was no longer a menace. He turned away and strode briskly back toward the cathedral apse, raised the sword above his head, and shook it as he shouted at Svetovit in what was both a half-salute of victory and a half-challenge to the old god.

"Svetovit!" George shouted but no one could make out the words in the rolling thunder. "Can you do anything without me?" The Jesuit was giddy, the old god seemingly unable to accomplish anything without his assistance. Svetovit shook his fist back at George and blinding lightning struck again and again.

Magdalena came up to the woman, who had fallen back onto the ground, her body shifting in and out of focus, her head and shoulder outside whatever protection the circle of red cord might offer. Magdalena knelt down on one knee, steadying herself with the staff, and peered into the woman's face.

For an instant Magdalena could see the woman clearly.

Pain was etched across her face, but it held more than pain. Magdalena saw calm in the woman's face, but more than that as well. Magdalena saw a peace that far surpassed anything Magdalena had ever experienced. Who was this woman? Why did Magdalena feel so drawn to her and recognize something in her that was present and yet missing from Magdalena's own life? Was this shadow woman also tied up with Fen'ka in some mysterious way?

But this woman also made her angry. Magdalena was angry that someone apparently intimately involved in the affairs of Fen'ka and Svetovit seemed to be fighting against Svetovit, against his vindication of Fen'ka's name, as misguided as Victoria and the academics huddling together across the plaza. But then that made her wonder: was there something the shadow woman knew that Magdalena did not?

"Who are you?" Magdalena asked. "Why…? What do you know of Fen'ka… and of the truth?"

The woman stared at Magdalena and swallowed, apparently struggling to gather strength. She clutched Magdalena's hand with a strength and a ferocity the modern woman had not expected from a dying shadow. The shadow woman opened her mouth and shifted out of focus again. A thin, distant, raspy whisper tickled Magdalena's mind even as she could hear the thunder of Svetovit's horse galloping across the sky. She leaned down more closely to hear the woman.

"… stop Svetovit… save Prague..." Then she was gone and Magdalena was staring at paving stones.

"Stop Svetovit? Svetovit's coming will save Prague!" Magdalena shouted at the stones.

Wouldn't it?

Magdalena repeated the woman's words to herself and then slowly pushed herself upright with the staff like an old woman might rise from a chair with her cane. Her legs and feet tingling as the blood began coursing through her lower limbs again, she turned to where George stood beside the apse wall of the cathedral.

He was standing with his back to her, looking up at Svetovit whose horse had paused in its wild gallop across the skies, and the old god was reaching an open palm down toward George. George had the blade of the sword in his hands and was delivering the hilt to Svetovit.

George heard Svetovit's voice thunder in his head. He heard the voice but it was not words that Svetovit communicated to him. It was more like his experience of communicating with the dead, with Dalibor and Fen'ka. His mind and another mind would reach out to each other, sharing images, desires, emotions, and his mind would then manufacture words to give shape and body to the messages received.

"Give me the sword and the staff," Svetovit instructed George while Magdalena was kneeling over the dying shadow woman across the plaza. "The time has come! MY time has come, priest! The number of generations four multiplied by eight have come and gone, been born and died. You have brought them here but the magical tools of Prague are now mine!"

"I have freed the tools from their hiding places," George declared proudly. "Together, we can work our will against Prague and any who stand against us! But we must work together, Svetovit! I will not surrender the tools to you!"

"I do not ask you to surrender them," Svetovit took a more cajoling, less threatening tone. "Let me feel the heft of the sword in my hand, the wood of the staff in my grip. You have done much, more than any before you, to make ready my path to victory, and it is right that you share the fruit of that labor. You have my word that I will simply hold the sword to appreciate its workmanship and then return it to you." Svetovit reached down his open palm.

George knew that none of the old gods or devils could break an oath they had made, though they might lie or cheat in any one of a thousand other ways. But an oath, once made, was binding on all the parties involved.

"Your oath is that you will feel the heft of the sword, admire its workmanship, and then return it to me?" George asked.

"It is!" Lightning cracked across the sky.

George had triumphed! Even Svetovit had capitulated to him! Letting the devil-god savor the heft and workmanship of the sword that had been fashioned to defeat him but whose power had instead been twisted by George to overcome Svetovit's enemies seemed a small enough gesture. He had not only overcome the magical defenses of Prague—most importantly, its famous bridge!—he had outmaneuvered Svetovit! He could afford to be magnanimous with the jealous old deity.

George took the blade in his hands and lifted the hilt towards Svetovit's open palm.

Magdalena saw George lift the hilt of the sword to Svetovit.

"No!" screamed Sophia and Victoria together, cringing and turning their faces.

"Stop!" shouted Theo.

"Do not give the sword to Svetovit!" Dmitri cried. "Do not believe his promises!"

"Don't do it, George!" Sean roared.

Even as the words spilled from their lips, the men began running toward George.

THE TOWER

In that instant, Magdalena saw the truth and realized everything she had believed about George, about Elizabeth, about Fen'ka had been lies. George had told her that the academics had poisoned the bridge so that they could wash it away with the cataclysm of the flood they had unleashed. But she had heard George tell Dalibor that he himself, had poisoned the bridge's magic to retrieve the sword from its foundation. Dalibor had attempted to throw her down into the Jug, leaving her for dead if not killing her outright. But Dalibor had professed that he was simply following the instructions given by the one who had held the yew. George was the one who pulled him from the darkness of the Jug with the yew. Now George was handing the sword to Svetovit and there was only one outcome possible: Svetovit would use the sword to destroy whatever part of the city still stood after the flood.

Stop Svetovit! Save Prague! Those had been the words Magdalena had heard the shadow woman whisper. The shadow woman had been right! Svetovit had not come to vindicate Fen'ka. He was here to destroy the city for abandoning its worship of him all those centuries ago.

"No!" cried Magdalena, charging at George with the staff in her hands. "No! You lied to me!" She could think of no more damning charge to hurl at the man she had thought she loved. She swung the staff and struck George across the shoulders.

The crack of the staff across George's shoulders rivaled the crack of the thunder around the hilltop. Svetovit, reaching for the sword, closed his hand around empty air as George stumbled forward and dropped the sword, the blade somersaulting as it tumbled from his fingers. George threw himself toward it, half-falling to the ground on top of it. The staff whistled in the air and grazed his lower back as Magdalena swung a second time. He jumped up again,

337

brandishing the weapon. He swung around with fury to face
Magdalena, raising the sword over his right shoulder.

"Magdalena!" screamed Victoria.

George swung the blade in an arc but in his haste, he
swung the blade so that its flat side, not its cutting edge, would
strike his foe. Magdalena held the staff before her cheek as
she stumbled back, the sharp point missing her face by a
hairsbreadth. But she felt the shock wave of the power of the
sword despite the staff deflecting the brunt of the blow.

As she braced herself, she saw that Victoria and her allies
had no such protection. The waves of power radiating from the
flat of the sword bowled them over like dry leaves caught in
an autumn wind, and they tumbled across the plaza.

Svetovit, cheated of his chance to wield the great sword,
howled in his enmity of those below him. Fire exploded in the
clouds whipping around him.

George swung the sword again, not even bothering to
offer any words to justify his behavior. Magdalena knew now
that he had used her to obtain the power and fame he had so
lusted after, and now that those things were within his grasp,
he no longer needed her. He brought the sword down across
the staff she now held out horizontally, aiming to smash the
wood with the blade. But the wood held and the sword sprang
back up toward George's face. He swung again.

The duel began in earnest, Magdalena using the staff to
thrust and parry George's sword strokes. The staff seemed
to fight of its own volition, Magdalena simply holding it and
allowing it to swing and deflect George's feints and cuts.

But George was driving Magdalena back across the plaza
with his furious ripostes. The staff was defending Magdalena
but she had no opportunity to attack George. She twisted her
head slightly, to see where she was on the plaza, what was

around her, if there was any doorway to take refuge in from the onslaught of the sword.

She saw Victoria and the others picking themselves up unsteadily from the paving stones, apparently dazed and bruised from their tumbles across the courtyard.

She returned her attention to George just in time to notice him turning the blade in his hand ever so slightly. He struck the flat of the sword not against the staff this time but against Magdalena's knuckles. She cried in surprise and pain, dropping the staff and tripping over her feet. She fell onto her back, darting her eyes wildly about to identify anything she could seize to defend herself and realized that she had fallen in almost the exact place the shadow woman had lain when George struck off her hand.

George loomed over Magdalena. "You are a nuisance! You have always been one! Now you're a nuisance I no longer need to tolerate!" he spat at her. He raised the sword above his head.

"Liar!" screamed Magdalena, raising an arm in a feeble effort to shield herself.

"No!" shrieked Victoria.

"Magdalena!" wailed Sophia.

"Save yourself!" Theo shouted.

Magdalena saw Victoria drop to her knees and pound her fist against the plaza paving stones, crying out "Royal Road, help us one more time!" Dmitri and Sean, battered by the winds, were running, bellowing, toward George's back, but she knew they could never reach him in time to save her.

The sword swung down.

Magdalena closed her eyes and screamed.

Fire exploded in the sky around Svetovit again as he charged, his horse snorting lightning from its nostrils as it galloped down toward the hilltop.

Dmitri raced after Sean to stop George, intending to tackle him or knock the sword from his hands. Sean tripped over something and nearly fell, reaching out with one hand to steady himself. Dmitri saw his fingers close around the staff Magdalena had dropped. Sean swung it in a circle, catching George's knees and knocking the Jesuit to the ground. The sword fell, tumbling along the cobblestones of the plaza toward Dmitri, who grabbed the hilt with both hands. He raised it and swung at the prone figure of the Jesuit.

George screamed with rage and raised one hand as if to deflect the great sword while pushing himself up with the other.

"Saint Vitus!" cried Dmitri as a war cry of opposition to Svetovit and George together. He swung the magical blade, intending to strike George with the flat side, but the sword, forged to protect Prague, jumped from his grip and plunged through the Jesuit's ribs.

Next to Dmitri, Sean swung the staff again, perhaps without realizing that the sword had thrust itself into George's torso. The staff struck George's shoulders and tumbled from Sean's grasp across the plaza, even as it impaled the Jesuit more firmly on the sword's sharp blade.

The sword wrestled with the muscles and cartilage along George's ribs and in doing so, the blade tore deeper. Blood sprayed everywhere and splattered on the plaza. The Jesuit's body fell back onto the cobblestones and the sword jumped back into Dmitri's hands.

With no warning, a great lion sprang down from the cathedral buttresses onto George's body. The beast roared at the sky and shook his shaggy mane.

Dmitri dropped the bloody sword in horror.

Death

(Wednesday, August 14, 2002)

DEATH: THE THIRTEENTH OF THE MAJOR TRUMPS,
IT COMES BETWEEN THE HANGED MAN AND TEMPERANCE

The sword fell to the pavement, clattering across the plaza.

Magdalena, realizing that the sword had not struck her and that she was still alive, pulled her arm from her face and struggled to sit up and make sense of the scene beside her. She saw George's prone form, the blood splayed across her and the courtyard. She saw the lion, his paws on George's now still chest, and cowered as the animal roared again. Guessing what had happened, Magdalena began screaming and pushing herself back from the man who had betrayed her.

"Magdalena!" burst from Victoria's throat.

"The lion! Get away from the lion!" Sophia shrieked.

"Saint Vitus, pray for us," whispered Dmitri, crossing himself and trembling. "The lion, the lion... Is this the lion associated with you, Vitus?" the priest asked the saint, staring at his own blood-smeared hands.

Magdalena, still screaming in terror but rooted to the ground, watched the lion, which had stepped off George's body and now stared at her. Was he coming for her next? She registered Theo and Sean circling behind the lion, but they didn't seem to be trying to help her or divert the beast's attention. They seemed to be headed to retrieve the two magical tools of Prague.

But they were challenged by Svetovit, who was making another mad run on his horse at the plaza on the hilltop. He reached down with both hands, one to seize the hilt of the sword and the other to clutch the staff. Lightning pummeled the sky as thunder deafened the city.

Sean and Theo looked up, saw Svetovit, and began running toward the sword and staff. Their running diverted the lion's attention from Magdalena, and he turned first to them and then looked up at the sky. Lips pulled back from his sharp teeth, the lion rumbled and leaped, running back across the plaza towards Svetovit. A bull materialized beside the great cat, and both leaped into the sky towards Svetovit.

The air shivered beside the lion and bull to reveal the eagle flying beside them.

"It worked!" cried Victoria. "The Royal Road is helping us one more time! It sent the animals!" Magdalena's screams finally froze in her throat. She did not understand what Victoria had to do with them, but the three animals were charging Svetovit and the cloud-horse.

Then she realized that Svetovit was charging toward the ground not far from her, where the rooster's lifeless, blood-drained form lay. She could feel the impact of the horse's hooves in the air. Half-pushing herself up from the pavement, she propelled herself across the ground, stumbling as she reached for the staff. Her fingers just missed closing around it.

Simultaneously, Svetovit leaned down low and forward on the horse's back, stretching his fingers toward the staff and sword. Further away, Magdalena saw Theo headed toward the sword, but caught no glimpse of Sean.

As Magdalena's fingers missed the staff, another woman was suddenly standing beside the staff and picking it up one-handed. Magdalena gasped, recognizing the shadow woman whose hand George had severed. The dead woman looked at Magdalena and nodded, cradling the staff in the crook of one arm while reaching for the living woman with her one remaining hand. Magdalena grasped the offered hand and the dead woman pulled Magdalena to her feet and then handed the staff to her. Magdalena clutched the staff with both hands. She swung the staff in a wide arc up at the horse. Lightning shattered the sky. Showers of sparks rained down from the horse's hooves. Magdalena swung the staff again, nearly striking the dead woman, who ducked down but then vanished.

The horse screamed and fell onto its side, all eight legs knocked aside by the staff in Magdalena's hands. Svetovit sprawled to one side, falling from the horse's back, roaring in fury. The horse slid across the sky toward the cathedral roof, still kicking and screaming, struggling to stop itself but unable to do so. As it was about to crash into the cathedral, its cloud-body dissipated but almost immediately re-formed on the other side of the church, still sliding across the sky, showers of sparks shooting down onto the ground.

As the storm-cloud devil came crashing toward the ground, the trio of lion, bull, and eagle abruptly changed course and bounded toward Svetovit, who was now sprawling in the sky above the plaza.

The lion leaped to sink his great teeth into Svetovit's throat as the bull lowered his horns to gore the old god's chest and the shrieking eagle opened its beak and prepared to rip open the god's stomach. But the cloud-body of the old devil melted away and the animals threw themselves at empty air. Lightning blinded everyone in the plaza. Svetovit reappeared, kneeling just above the plaza and reaching for the sword. Snatching the weapon up in his gigantic fist, the sword became as proportionately large as Svetovit. Svetovit swung the blade in a circle above his head with a roar of triumphant of laughter. Thunder cracked, shaking the hilltop. The plaza shook and reverberated with the repeated impact of thunderclap after thunderclap after thunderclap, knocking everyone over.

Looking up, Magdalena saw that the black-green clouds were still rotating in the wind above the cathedral, dropping down long, thin tendrils toward the church's roof. The wind braided the tendrils together, lengthening and thickening them into a funnel cloud.

Over the residential wings of the castle, the great horse skidded to a stop, the impact knocking a shower of tiles from the roof that rained onto the pavement and shattered. The horse shook its head and then scrambled up onto its eight legs. Rearing up on its hind legs, whinnying and scraping brilliant cascades of sparks from the air with its forelegs, its head turned in a frantic search for its lost rider. Svetovit stood, sword in hand, saw the horse, and whistled. The horse crashed down onto its hooves and ambled toward Svetovit, who lumbered toward it. Coming up to its master, the cloud-horse stopped and pawed the sky, bowing and dipping its head as it whinnied again in greeting. Svetovit swung a leg up and over the horse's tail, pulling himself once more onto the stallion's back. Brandishing the sword, Svetovit shouted in defiance at Magdalena and the others strewn about the plaza and then gouged the horse's ribs with his heels. The horse reared again and bolted across the sky, turning in a wide arc over the city and beginning another descent to the river.

"The bridge!" Dmitri shouted, struggling to his feet and pointing. "He's charging the bridge!"

The lion, panting in the air over the alchemist's tower, where he had finally stopped himself after his failed attempt to rip out Svetovit's throat, raised his head and roared. With the roar still hanging in the air, the shaggy beast loped down to the plaza and seized George's corpse in his great jaws. Then, leaping back into the air, he also set out across the castle walls and down toward the bridge. The eagle and bull followed the lion with his gruesome prize.

"Quickly! We have to follow them!" Dmitri's urged. Magdalena got up on her feet again, prepared to join the others struggling to stand.

"We can't let Svetovit wipe out the bridge!" Dmitri said. "If that happens, nothing can stop him from rampaging across the face of Europe!"

The lion saw the river beneath him, the water pounding against the bridge. Svetovit was still above him, still descending from the sky over the Old Town toward the stone span; though its magic had been poisoned by George, it remained the one shackle on the devil-god's reclaimed power. The great cat dipped down and opened his jaws. George's body dropped the short distance into the midst of the floodwaters with a splash and vanished, pulled by the current beneath the surface of the waves. The lion shook his mane and, with the eagle and bull beside him, turned around to face Svetovit.

"Magdalena!" exclaimed Victoria, hugging her tightly as the others hastily followed Theo back down the Royal Road, retracing their steps to the imperiled bridge. Magdalena hugged Victoria back, dropping the staff and stammering with embarrassment, not sure what to say. Tears spilled from her eyes after she struggled to find the words to express herself and she collapsed against Victoria, sobbing.

"Oh, Victoria! I am so sorry! So sorry for everything! What have I done?" Magdalena cried, still uncomprehending of how she had been so duped. "What have I set in motion?" She burst into a fresh downpour of tears.

Victoria stroked Magdalena's hair but then grasped her firmly by the shoulders and gently shook her.

"The important thing is that you know you were lied to," Victoria told her. "Lied to and manipulated. But now you can use what you know of them to intervene in the destruction of Prague. We have to follow them, Magdalena. We have to stop Svetovit." She began to guide Magdalena out of the plaza.

"Wait," sniffled Magdalena. "We cannot leave this." She bent over to retrieve the staff she had let fall. She gestured to the yew bouquet that Fr. Dmitri had dropped.

"We should take that also," she told Victoria. Victoria picked it up and the two women made their way after Dmitri and the others.

Svetovit galloped toward the center of the bridge, swinging the sword down toward the stone path across the raging river. Lightning sliced through the sky toward the bridge. The black-green clouds tumbled from their perch in the sky above the cathedral and rolled toward the bridge. The beginnings of the funnel cloud unraveled and drifted apart. Svetovit, no longer high above the ancient center of his cult, drew the storm to the bridge.

The great lion saw Svetovit charging the bridge, the sword flashing in his fist. The fur bristled along his back, his lips pulling back in a snarl that exposed his sharp teeth. The bull lowered his great horns and pawed the ground with a front hoof. The eagle circled around the four-footed beasts, its talons extended as its shriek mingled with the roaring of the

346

bull and lion. Svetovit saw the three animals and there was a
flash of hesitation, a quiver of uncertainty in his swinging of
the sword. But then, with a battle cry, he pulled the horse up
and charged, not at the bridge but at the lion.

The streets of the Little Town were still empty as Dmitri
and his companions hurried down the hill from the castle
to the bridge, the residents and hotel guests having all been
evacuated. As they tumbled across the Little Town Square
and down the street leading directly to the bridge, lightning
flickered incessantly above. The shadows beneath the arcade
along the street danced and writhed in the half-light of the
lightning under the black-green sky. Coming to where the
street passed through the bridge's guard tower and then melted
into the plaza—where the bridge landing was hidden beneath
the flood—Dmitri pressed against the interlocking police
barricade that still blocked access to the plaza. Sean, Sophia,
and Theo pressed up next to Dmitri. Moments later, Victoria,
grasping the yew, and Magdalena, clutching the rabbi's staff,
arrived and pressed up to the barricade too.

"There! See?" Dmitri cried, pointing to the sky above the
bridge. Sophia crossed herself.

The lion and bull were darting in and around and between
the horse's eight legs, nipping and snapping, while the eagle
screamed and charged at Svetovit's four faces. The horse neighed
and whinnied as it pranced about, attempting to avoid the sharp
jaws of the lion or the horns of the bull. Svetovit struggled to
maintain his balance on the horse, swinging the great sword
wildly in arcs that might intimidate a lesser fighter but did nothing
to frighten off the fearsome animals from the tarot. Then the
sword sliced through the winged ox, and it was gone.

The remaining eagle and winged lion seemed to be

347

struggling to keep the horse and rider distracted until the academics could reach the bridge. Watching from below, gasping for breath and exhausted, Dmitri was sure that either the sharp blade in Svetovit's hand would deeply slice across the back of one of the remaining tarot beasts or one of the sharp hooves of the horse would come down heavily and crush a limb or paw. But watching from the barricade, Dmitri realized that as the beasts harried the cloud-horse and its rider, they were also attempting to lead the horse away from the river. Dmitri dared not think what might happen if Svetovit or the horse injured one of them, causing it to tumble into the river below.

Then the pair of tarot animals paused, seeming to notice Dmitri and his companions at the barricade blocking access to the bridge.

The eagle shrieked at the lion and madly flapped its great wings. The lion ran from Svetovit's horse and both tarot beasts made a large turn in the sky and seemed to come straight toward the academics.

"The animals! They're charging at us!" Sophia cringed and huddled behind the barricade.

Dmitri and the others ducked down as the tarot beasts skimmed over their heads through the guard tower passage and then rose back into the sky behind the tower to charge again at Svetovit.

Magdalena felt the rush of wind as the great eagle swooped through the air above them, felt the pummeling of the lion's paws in the air. Looking back towards the bridge, she saw Svetovit hesitate as if deciding whether to pursue the animals or attack the bridge.

She thrust the staff into Fr. Dmitri's bloodstained hands.

"Use this," she urged him. "Strike Svetovit or the horse. Knock them down if you can." Startled, he stared at her and then the staff, his mouth dropping open.

Magdalena grasped Victoria's free hand.

"Come with me. Bring that," she said, pointing to the yew bouquet Victoria still held. Magdalena led Victoria back through the passage and around the base of the guard tower to the edge of the flood that occupied what had been the small, low-lying plaza on the right side of the bridge. The inundated hotels and restaurants stood as dark and silent witnesses, debris bobbing in the swirling eddies.

Magdalena took the bedraggled yew from Victoria, the worn length of string still tied around the stems bound with fraying horsehair, and inspected it before handing the end of the string back.

"Hold this tightly," Magdalena instructed her friend. "I saw George do this earlier this morning to raise Dalibor from the Jug and it was difficult to hold the string, even then, with both of us." She made sure Victoria wrapped the string tightly around her fist and then the two women knelt at the edge of the water. Magdalena, holding a loop of the string tightly, tossed the yew as far across the water as she could toward the central body of the river. It hovered on the surface and then the current pulled it forward, towards the place where Magdalena had met Fen'ka under the bridge.

"Fen'ka!" Magdalena barked the old woman's name, surprising herself with the animosity in her voice. "Fen'ka!" she repeated. "Are you awake? Can you hear me?"

"Why did the animals charge us before charging Svetovit again?" Sophia asked Dmitri and Theo.

"Maybe to invite us to join the fray?" Theo suggested.

"They want us to do something, I think."

Dmitri stared at the staff Magdalena had thrust into his hands.

"How do I use this?" he asked the others. "It must be the rabbi's staff from the synagogue attic, but how do we harness its power?"

"It looked like Magdalena simply swung it," Theo offered.

"Swing it now!" Sophia exclaimed, pointing at the sky above the bridge, where Svetovit was raising the sword as if preparing to strike the bridge. His horse continued to prance and caper, as the eagle and lion continued to nip at its flanks. Svetovit made a sudden twist and turn, swinging the sword behind him, and cut through the lion. The lion vanished. Svetovit tossed the sword into his other hand and in a fluid swing, nearly cut through the eagle, which darted aside at the last moment. A handful of wing feathers fluttered in the air.

"Knock the sword from his hand!" Sophia shouted.

"How?" Dmitri shouted back, afraid to take his eyes off the cloud-devil, who swung again at the eagle and toward the bridge below.

"Swing the staff! Knock the sword from his hand!" Theo and Sophia both urged Dmitri.

"Swing it?" Dmitri repeated. "But what if I miss Svetovit and hit the eagle?"

"Aim high!" Sophia urged. "But swing it now!"

Dmitri, remembering images he had seen of Moses with his staff at the Red Sea, held the staff upright in both hands and brought it down in a quick stroke that slashed the air.

Walls of water burst up from the flood, struck by the magic of the staff, crashing into Svetovit and his horse, the unexpected force of the water knocking the god from his horse and sending him tumbling through the air. The horse was tossed whinnying onto its side, its eight legs flailing as it slid through the air. The tarot eagle was also knocked aside. The walls of water hung shimmering in the air momentarily before collapsing into the river amid great splashing and clouds of spray.

Shadows glimmered in the depths of the water. Was the dim light that illuminated Magdalena and her friend a reflection from the black-green sky or was it escaping from the flooded cobblestones? The shadows circulated and plunged beneath the yew, rising toward it and then veering away. The roar of the river rushing past the bridge made it impossible to hear any whispers from the water here, but Magdalena suspected she would have heard them if the river had not been so loud, as she heard them in the depths of the Jug when the yew had been dropped into its darkness.

"Magdalena!" Victoria exclaimed. "Something pulled on the yew! Or was it the current?"

"I felt it too, Victoria." Magdalena twisted her head to one side as she peered across the water at the yew hovering in the waves. "I don't know if it was the current, but hold on because…"

The yew was wrenched forward and down. Magdalena cried out in the same instant Victoria did as the string she held was pulled taut enough to cut into her hands. Magdalena could see the wake of the string as it broke through the water, the yew somewhere beneath it.

"Fen'ka! The yew is for Fen'ka alone!" ordered Magdalena, imitating George's command to the ghosts in the Jug to leave the yew for Dalibor. Who knew how many other ghosts might be in the river, as eager to escape the water as those others so eager to escape the Jug? She struggled to stand, keeping the string tight in her grasp. Victoria stumbled to her feet as well.

Come Hell or High Water, Part 3: Deluge

The water boiled and seethed around the yew. Magdalena slowly pulled the yew toward her. Victoria gathered up the length of the string that Magdalena fed her.

"Something's caught on it," she whispered. "Something that doesn't want to come out of the water. Is it…?"

Magdalena nodded, holding her breath and struggling to keep pulling the string and bringing the yew into the shallows at their feet. The boiling fury of the water followed the string, just as the thrashing of a large fish caught on a hook traced the route of the line to the fisherman's pole. Magdalena shut her eyes and turned her face to one side, leaning all her weight away from the river so as not to be pulled forward into its depths. Without warning, an explosion of spray burst from the water's surface and the twine in her hands jerked again, wrenching her off balance so that she let loose of the twine, stumbled forward, and fell into the river.

Storm clouds of boiling froth enveloped Magdalena as she plummeted into the cold water. She coughed and sputtered, her lungs nearly empty, as she had been holding her breath while pulling the twine. Unable to see in the water, she swung her arms and legs, expecting to meet the stonework of the inundated plaza.

But she found no foothold and seemed to be continuing her descent into water that should not have been this deep along the edge of the flood. Terrified and confused, she fought the urge to scream.

Something—a hand, perhaps?—wrapped around her ankle and dragged her even further into the murky depths. Then the hand was joined by another clutching at her clothing and then the hand released her ankle and… a pale light glimmered around her and the hand released her clothing but two hands wrapped themselves around her throat. George's face pulled close to hers through the illuminated froth and bubbles around them.

"This is your fault!" she heard his thoughts snarl in her mind. "Your witless friends called the Royal Road to block Svetovit's entrance into this world and stole the sword from me! The lot of you have robbed me of my victory—my triumph! My fame! And now my corpse has been thrown into the river and I am trapped here in bondage to the troll-woman!"

The voice of his thoughts became a furious screech in her head. "But I will not be trapped here alone! You will pay for your insolence and troublemaking, girl! You will die in the river with me, and be forced to remain here. Even if I cannot see Svetovit's triumph, at least I will know that I made it possible for him to destroy the bridge and that you and your friends have failed even more miserably than I!" His fingers gripped her throat more tightly. His thumbs dug into her windpipe.

"Not—my fault!" Magdalena sputtered, half-forming the words with her lips as she struggled. River water surged into her mouth and she clamped her lips shut to block it. "You—lied! You—wanted—Dalibor—kill me!" She spat her thoughts at her attacker.

Victoria stood at the edge of the flood, stunned. Magdalena had lost her balance, stumbled into the river, and vanished in an explosion of spray and foam. Now Victoria stood clutching the end of the twine wrapped around her fist, unsure of what to do.

"Magdalena!" she shouted at the river's surface. There was a momentary surging and frothing in the middle of the flooded plaza, but the river was too busy filling the courtyard for Victoria to tell if the agitation in the water was due to the river's currents or Magdalena's struggles below the surface.

"Magdalena!" Victoria shouted again. Without another thought, she waded into the river to find and help her friend.

Dmitri watched as Svetovit, still clutching the sword in his hand and drenched with river water, struggled to his feet upriver over the outskirts of the Little Town. Each of his four beards dripped madly as the river water streaked down his torso and both arms. He looked across the river, apparently searching for his horse. He whistled long and shrilly, turning his attention up and down the river.

A lonely whinny answered him and the horse came trotting from between the clouds across the river. It shook its head and whinnied again. Sighting the god, it lowered its head and crossed the sky above the river. Svetovit mounted the steed and shook the sword in his clenched fist at Dmitri on the ground. Thunder crashed through the air. The green-black clouds over the Charles Bridge began to congeal and rotate above Dmitri and the staff.

Dmitri was wielding the staff when a muffled explosion came from one side. The sound of spraying and slashing water and Victoria shouting barely registered when Sean exclaimed, "I'm going to help Magdalena and Victoria!" Sean ran in their direction before Dmitri had a chance to respond.

"Where is Svetovit?" Theo asked Dmitri, leaning over the barricade as far as he could and looking along the course of the river. Sophia stretched out over the barricade too, but apparently neither of them could make out the cloud-god in the half-light.

Sophia grasped the barricade in both hands and rattled it fiercely. "We need to get past this," she grunted. "We can't use the staff to its full extent trapped behind this fencing!"

Dmitri, the staff still pointing forward, gestured with an

elbow at a link in the barricade. "There. It can be pulled apart there," he suggested. Thunder rumbled above them.

Sean hurried to the edge of the water, where he had seen Magdalena and Victoria vanish into the river before dashing to their aid. He stood there a moment, knowing it was too dangerous to plunge into the water. They were clearly victims of a supernatural attack and attempting to rescue the women as if they were victims of a boating accident would not help them. He stared at the surface of the water, rapidly struggling with his memories.

"Water… drowning… what myths?" he demanded of himself. "Who—forced water to disgorge its victims?" He could think of no folktale that would answer his question. What could he do to pull the women from beneath the waves?

Magdalena struck out at George but her hands swung through the water and found nothing to grab hold of or pummel. She swung her feet to kick him away but the water slowed her movements and she felt only the water swirling around her, no contact with George's shins. She gasped and choked, her lungs struggling to take in air. Darker shadows clouded her vision and she was afraid she was losing consciousness. His stranglehold on her throat grew stronger and tighter. He pulled her face even closer to his. She saw his rage and hatred, felt his fury engulf her. Her lungs were nearly exploding.

Suddenly a second presence plunged through the waves beside Magdalena, adding to the turbulence of the water. This other presence flailed and floundered in the depths. Even in the glimmer of the spectral light, it was impossible to see any detail or make out who or what was there.

"Magdalena!" She heard the thoughts of the new neighbor in the water call her name.

"Victoria!" she answered. "What—why—?" George's thumbs felt as if they were about to tear through her throat. Then she heard Victoria's thoughts gurgle and choke and she saw a vast cloud of swirling cloak wrap around her friend. It was Jarnvithja and the troll's claws clutched Victoria's throat.

"Now—both of you—bitches—get what you deserve!" Magdalena heard George shriek with glee. Magdalena couldn't feel her arms or legs any more.

"I have come for you, mortal man, as I promised." A new voice, deep and cold and as full of hatred as George's face had been, pierced Magdalena's fading consciousness. She was dimly aware that Victoria's struggles and flailing beside her were quickly fading too and she could only imagine the grip Jarnvithja must have on her friend's throat.

"We'll both—die—together," Magdalena realized, unsure of where her limbs—which were growing numb—were, though she could feel the pressure of Victoria's grasp on her hand. Something rough scratched Magdalena's palm and she realized Victoria still grasped the twine tied to the yew. She forced her fingers to move and flex, pulling the twine along as quickly as she could until the yew was in her grasp.

"George!" she shrieked in her mind, remembering Dalibor's hands stuck to the yew. "The yew is for George!"

Magdalena heard George scream in desperation as his fingers were wrenched free of her throat. She struggled to stop from gasping in relief while still trapped beneath the water.

"You have failed, mortal man, as I knew you would," the new voice went on. "You have failed and now you are mine!" George choked and sputtered and Magdalena imagined such sounds resulted from someone else's hands

356

around the Jesuit's ghostly throat.

"Gadriel!" Magdalena heard one word escape George's mind and the water boiled anew with the struggle between George and the entity whom he seemed to recognize.

Then Magdalena heard Victoria gasp and sputter in the water and was aware of Jarnvithja turning her attention to this new presence.

"Gadriel!" a voice hissed and Magdalena realized it could only be Jarnvithja, whom she had never heard speak. "The man is mine! His body is in the river so he has been committed to MY care!" she insisted.

"Nay, troll," Gadriel snapped. "The man dared to conjure me and make me part of his petty schemes despite my warnings to leave me be. I promised him that when he failed, I would claim him!"

"Nay, devil," Jarnvithja turned back Gadriel's rebuke. "He is dead but the project has not failed! Svetovit will destroy the last shreds of the bridge's magic… and then he will be free!" A slow and hideous chuckle rumbled from the depths of Jarnvithja's mind through the water.

"Whether Svetovit can free himself of the shackles of the bridge is of no concern to me," Gadriel answered her. Magdalena was aware that George was still struggling, evidently still in Gadriel's clutches, but Gadriel seemed to be thinking as calmly and clearly as if he were simply standing and having a barbed conversation with the troll. "The man is still mine!"

Jarnvithja threw herself at Gadriel, apparently to reclaim George as her prize.

Magdalena felt the yew being torn from her grasp as George was being fought over by the devil and the troll. She could not afford to lose it or the answers she needed.

"Fen'ka!" she repeated her earlier command, gasping the words in her head. "I release—George," she added, remembering his dismissal of Dalibor. "I release you into—the hands of Jarnvithja and—Gadriel. The yew is for Fen'ka!"

Two names came to him! Sean recalled two royal women who were drowned in mystical wells and had become goddesses of the rivers Shannon and Boyne in Ireland. He thrust his hands into his pockets and rummaged around until he found the Infant of Prague medal, which had worked its way into the bottom seam of one pocket. Dropping to his knees, he leaned over the water, holding the medal in the fingertips of one hand while careful to support himself with his other hand on the paving stones.

"Sinann! Bóinn!" he called across the water. "If you have any power here… You, together with the Infant of Prague— save them from the clutches of the flood! Bring Magdalena and Victoria back to land!" Afraid to breathe, he gently tossed the protective medal as far into the stream as he could and heard its plunk.

There was a violent wrenching as some new power grasped Magdalena by the shoulders. The yew was torn from her cold, numb fingers. With a force she had never experienced, she was shot up through the water in an explosive fountain of spray. She gasped and gagged, able to breathe at last! Dropping back into the water, her feet hit the cobblestones and she fell onto her knees, but the water was barely deep enough to cover her heels.

Victoria was beside her, pulling Magdalena to her feet, even as she also struggled to breathe. Together, Magdalena and Victoria blundered forward and nearly tripped over Sean, who scrambled onto his feet and out of their way.

Victoria wrapped her arms around Magdalena, pulling the twine up sharply as she did so. Sheets of water exploded from the water's surface again, drenching Sean as the angry fountain tossed the yew into the air. It splashed back onto the water's surface, and out of the shallows, clutching the yew bouquet, trudged the old woman Magdalena knew.

"How dare you?" The hunchbacked old witch grimaced and tried to throw the yew away but could not. It seemed stuck to her skin as if some resin from the leaves had permeated her spectral flesh.

"How did you know how to call me?" she demanded. "This is beyond your skill, girl!" She craned her neck forward, struggling to see around them. "Where is the coven master? Did he teach you?" She paused and peered at Magdalena as if recognizing her for the first time. "Wait! It was you who tried to call me earlier today…" She turned her twisted torso so that she could look in the direction of the castle and then back at Magdalena.

"The coven master is not here, is he? You have come on your own. You foolish, foolish girl! You should be with him, calling Svetovit to clear my name!" Fen'ka spat at Magdalena's feet.

"We did call Svetovit!" Magdalena startled herself with her brave retort to the ghost. "But the coven master is dead now and in the river with Jarnvithja and you lied to me! You did not want Svetovit to clear your name. You wanted him to destroy the city!"

Fen'ka stumbled back as if Magdalena had slapped her across the face. "I would never have lied to you, child!" she snapped. "I do want Svetovit—I need Svetovit—to clear my name and my reputation. But only you could summon him, set him free from his prison, so that he could do so!"

"Then why did I need the assistance of George and Elizabeth? Why did you tell me to seek Flauros and Halphas and bring George and Elizabeth to Prague?" Magdalena demanded.

"What prison was Svetovit in?" Victoria wanted to know, and Fen'ka looked ready to gouge her eyes out.

"Yes, what prison was he in?" Magdalena prompted.

Fen'ka turned her attention back to Magdalena. "Prison is such a harsh word. Svetovit was not in prison so much as…"

"Liar!" Sean shouted. "This is Fen'ka, right?" he asked Magdalena.

"Yes," Magdalena answered. "This is Fen'ka."

"I thought as much." He looked around the ground. "Ghosts are notorious liars. But Magdalena already knows that because she has seen through your lies. The real question is, how do we get you to tell the truth?"

He saw what he must have been looking for and darted to retrieve it from the gutter along a curb behind them, barely above the water mark. He stepped back beside Victoria and held his prize up proudly. It was the jagged, broken fragment of a cobblestone, washed up by the flood from the depths of the inundated plaza.

He knelt down and used the fragment to scratch a figure on the stones that looked like a three-legged swastika. "This is the symbol of Manannán mac Lir, an Irish god whose goblet could distinguish between a lie and the truth," he explained. "Put the yew there, on the sigil," he instructed the women. "She will have to speak the truth then."

Victoria's face lit up. "The truth—at last!"

Fen'ka shrieked and tried to dart back into the flood, but

Victoria seized the soggy yew in Fen'ka's hands and wrenched it toward the dry cobblestones. Magdalena grabbed hold of the yew too, Fen'ka still shrieking and spitting and struggling. But together, Magdalena and Victoria dragged the yew onto the character Sean had drawn and Fen'ka tumbled atop it. Sean jumped toward her and scratched a circle on the cobblestones around her with his sharp fragment of stone.

Sobbing and wailing, Fen'ka struggled to her feet. "Free an old woman!" she implored Magdalena. "Do not listen to your lying, so-called friends! They want to keep my name besmirched with the charge of witchcraft! Set me free, Magdalena, as I begged you to do when you first came to the bridge to answer the call of a frightened, maligned old woman!"

"Quiet!" barked Sean. "You will answer her questions and you will speak only the truth! None of your lies this time!" Lightning erupted from the darkness above them.

Theo and Sophia wrestled with the links that joined the sections of the barricade until they wrenched them apart. Together with Dmitri, they spilled into the plaza, searching the sky for Svetovit. Dmitri could hear Fen'ka shrieking.

Bolts of lightning flashed in the darkness, revealing Svetovit charging toward the bridge, accompanied by the thundering scream of his cloud-horse in the sky. He was swinging the sword above his head.

"Get the sword away from him!" Sophia shouted again. "Knock it from his hand!"

Dmitri swung the staff. His stroke was immediately answered by the wild cries of the horse, bucking and kicking its back legs against the painful goading of the staff and nearly throwing Svetovit from its back. Dmitri, hoping to make Svetovit drop the sword, swung again and knocked the horse's legs out from under it. It skidded down the river, past the bridge, cascades of sparks showering toward the earth from its hooves. Svetovit, his leg trapped beneath the horse, was dragged along. The sword slashed a flaming gouge in the clouds, ruddy flames sputtering along the wound in the sky. The tarot eagle swooped from behind a cloud to peck at the eyes of one of the god's four faces.

"Yes. Tell us the truth, Fen'ka," Magdalena instructed the ghost, composing herself even as she nervously twisted the tangled string, the end of which Victoria still held, that was tied to the yew in Fen'ka's hands. Magdalena and Victoria stepped closer to the shuddering witch, who cringed and forced her shoulder up as a shield between herself and them, as if she feared they would strike her.

"Why now?" Magdalena asked.

Fen'ka cringed and doubled over, screaming and hopping from foot to foot as if the rune beneath her were burning them. "Because he could not come before now!" she sobbed at last, the pain in her feet appearing to subside. She stood and glared at Magdalena.

"Why not?" Magdalena wanted to know.

"Because... because that girl, Nadezda her name was, rewrote the last words of my call to him," Fen'ka answered with a grimace, her voice halting and stumbling as if the words were being pulled from her throat against her will. "She rewrote it so that rather than coming to vindicate my name as the last of the flames I was burned in died, he could only come when sixty-four generations had passed."

"Yours was a curse to revenge yourself against Prague, not to vindicate your name!" Sean accused Fen'ka.

"Call... curse... Call it what you will," Fen'ka retorted.

"Did you—or anyone else—try to call Svetovit before?" Victoria asked.

Fen'ka spat on the cobblestones in fury. "Whenever Jarnvithja and I attempted to call Svetovit to Prague—and we have tried several times!—his coming was always prevented because the sixty-four generations had not yet passed. But this is the sixty-fifth generation since I was burned and finally it was only the magic of the bridge prevented Svetovit's answering my call! But the coven master found a way to poison the power of the bridge!"

Fen'ka paused, as if trying to decide if she should continue. "Not only was Svetovit able to come," she sneered as she finally continued, "but the sword of Bruncvik was extracted from the bridge and given to the coven master."

"That sword is the sword of Bruncvik?" exclaimed Sean, gesturing wildly at Svetovit in the sky behind them. "The sword that Svetovit is using to attack the bridge?"

"But it was made to protect Prague, not destroy it!" Victoria was aghast.

Fen'ka laughed. "But the coven master must have turned the sword against Prague, because Svetovit wields it now. It will protect him, as it must protect the one who holds it. But to protect Svetovit, it must destroy what feeble shreds remain of the power of the bridge."

"Then how can Svetovit be defeated?" Magdalena wanted to know. "The truth, Fen'ka."

Fen'ka laughed again and looked towards Svetovit. "Defeat him now? I think not!"

Dmitri swung the staff again, scraping the surface of the water with its power. Sheets of spray hurtled toward Svetovit, blinding both the horse and its rider. The horse, still skidding across the sky towards the castle, whinnied and neighed like a wild animal. Svetovit, all his eyes clenched shut against the spray, clutched the ribs of the horse more tightly with his knees as he tightly wrapped the fingers of his free hand in the horse's mane and swung the sword in wild, blind circles over his head.

Lightning stippled across the sky, giving the whole scene the appearance of a stop-action movie. Sparks rained onto the river from the horse's hooves scraping the storm clouds. Deafening thunder burst in the air.

"Sophia! Theo!" Dmitri shouted. "Do you still have the medals of the Infant of Prague? Throw them onto the bridge! They might help strengthen its power!"

Theo immediately plunged his hands into his pockets and rummaged around.

"I swung mine over Elizabeth's head!" Sophia replied. "Remember? That's how I escaped her. My medal is gone, Dmitri!"

"I have mine!" Theo exclaimed in triumph, pulling his out of his pocket. He took a deep breath. "May it help to strengthen the bridge!" he mouthed as he threw the small medallion. Dmitri watched it sail toward the bridge before hearing the small clatter as it fell onto the cobblestones of the bridge's central span.

Ripples fluttered through and across the cobblestones of the bridge, the usual solid stonework appearing as insubstantial as gossamer for a fraction of a second. Dmitri glanced at Theo and Sophia, seeing hope darting across their faces.

Svetovit and the horse righted themselves in the sky near the castle and turned to face the bridge. With one hand, the cloud-god swatted aside the eagle, which had again begun to peck at one of his eyes. Svetovit kicked the horse in its ribs,

364

and as the animal charged the bridge, he reached toward the bridge with the sword and roared in seeming triumph. Dmitri swung the staff once more with a furious snap, smacking the cloud-devil firmly on the knuckles.

Svetovit cried out in pain and shock, dropping the sword in his surprise.

"The sword! Catch it!" screamed Sophia.

The sword tumbled through the air, falling toward the plaza where Magdalena stood with Sean, Victoria, and Fen'ka. Falling away from Svetovit, the sword tumbled blade-over-hilt in the air, reverting from gigantic to human scale. Fen'ka shrieked and cowered as the clang of it striking the cobblestones reverberated through the air. Svetovit leaned over the side of his still-galloping horse, reaching for the sword.

Magdalena dropped the twine she had been clutching and darted toward the enchanted weapon. She seized its hilt, shocked by how heavy it was. Using both hands, she struggled to hold it aloft.

"Bruncvik's sword!" she shouted defiantly at Svetovit. "I have it now, Svetovit! It will protect me and I will use it to protect the city!"

Svetovit roared in fury as his cloud-horse veered up and away and then began another charge down toward Magdalena. He swept his empty sword hand through the green-black clouds and gathered a handful of sizzling lightning, which he threw at Magdalena. She cowered, but managed to keep the sword aloft. It swung and darted in her grip, deflecting the lightning. Sean and Victoria were struck nearly blind and deaf by the brilliance of the lightning ricocheting off the sword and the thunder that accompanied it.

Svetovit continued to cast bolt after bolt of lightning and

the sword continued to dip and weave, keeping Magdalena safe from Svetovit's assault. But the sword was heavy, too heavy to keep holding upright much longer, and she knew that once she dropped the sword, she would be all but handing it back to Svetovit. There was only one thing to do, though in the moment that she realized what must be done, she also realized what the cost would be.

She splashed through the shallows of the flood toward the nearest pier supporting the bridge. She raised the sword above her head to drive it into the stonework.

Svetovit roared in fury, rose to half-standing as his knees gripped the horse's ribs, and hurled another fistful of lightning toward Magdalena.

The stonework of the bridge rippled and shimmered as it absorbed the sword back into the foundations of the bridge. Magdalena's hands were empty.

"NO!" screamed Victoria. "Magdalena!"

Horrified, Victoria watched the lightning strike both the bridge and Magdalena, hurling her across the plaza against a wall. The stuccowork cracked from the force of the impact.

Multicolored rainbow ribbons of lightning exploded from the point of contact between lightning, bridge, and sword, ricocheting back to Svetovit and slicing him and his horse to shreds. The base of the bridge above the plaza rumbled and shook violently, knocking Dmitri, Sophia, and Theo to the ground. A wild gale screeched across the city, shattering windows and blasting grit and sand from the ground into the façades of buildings as if to scour them clean.

Spray whipped by the wind drenched Victoria and Sean as they cowered and tried to shield their eyes. The ground on which they stood rumbled, causing them to stagger into the walls of the buildings behind them. Victoria lost her balance, snapping the string taut in her hand, and the yew shot away from the rune and out of the circle Sean had etched. In the instant the yew was pulled from the magic circle, Fen'ka vanished. Victoria snatched up the yew before it could tumble away in the wind.

Storm clouds collapsed from the sky around Svetovit. Thunderclap after thunderclap rolled over the city, shaking the hills of the Little Town and the spires of the Old Town. Another roar—Svetovit? the collapsing of the bridge under the weight of the onslaught against it? the rushing of the river to consume whatever remained of the city? Victoria could not say—deeper, more solid even than the thunder, staggered into the sky.

The wall of sound assaulted the city. For Victoria, the world was nothing but spray in her face, stone walls at her back, and the roar in her ears.

Victoria gradually realized the wind had died away, the spray was no longer washing over her, and the half-light of a sky that was only overcast and no longer green-black had returned. The roar in the air was gone. Nothing was pressing her into the stonework.

She took a deep breath and dared to half-open the eye that was not pressed into the wall against which she had been driven. In the sky, she saw no sign of Svetovit, his horse, or the winged animals from the Royal Road. Turning her head, she saw Sean half-fall from the same wall and stumble a few paces into the water near their feet, rubbing his eyes. He looked around them, squinting, then pointed to the landing of the bridge. She saw Theo standing with difficulty and helping Sophia to her feet. Then she turned her attention to the pier of the bridge where the lightning had struck and remembered what had happened. Her glance darted around the edge of the plaza frantically until she saw Magdalena's crumpled body on the ground against the cracked wall.

"Magdalena!" she cried, running to her friend, dropping to her knees, and clutching Magdalena's shoulders. She dropped the yew bouquet and pulled Magdalena's face towards hers.

"He's gone! Svetovit is gone!" Victoria shook her friend and tried to pry open one of Magdalena's eyes. "Magdalena! Wake up! Are you all right? He's gone!"

Sean joined her, pocketing the sodden yew as he knelt beside the women.

"Sean! Why isn't she waking up?" Victoria demanded. She pressed her cheek to Magdalena's and began to rock.

Sean reached for Magdalena's wrist to search for her pulse.

One eye fluttered open. Magdalena's voice was little more than a dry whisper. "Svetovit is gone, isn't he?"

"Yes, yes he is!" Victoria said.

"We stopped Svetovit," Magdalena murmured, closing her eye again. "We saved Prague." She smiled weakly as her head tipped gently to one side. She shuddered as she drew her next breath and Sean set her hand down to touch Victoria's shoulder. "No!" Victoria choked out and burst into sobs.

Magdalena shuddered again and took another breath.

Victoria was still sobbing and cradling the unconscious Magdalena as Dmitri, Sophia, and Theo came down from the bridge. Sean explained what Fen'ka had said.

"You made him drop the sword," Sophia said, facing Dmitri, picking up where Sean left off. "Then Magdalena took it and…?"

"It protected her from Svetovit's lightning as long as she

held it, but then she drove the sword back into the foundations of the bridge," Sean resumed his report. "Then Svetovit threw another handful of lightning, but she was no longer holding the sword and the lightning threw her against the wall."

"Isn't there something we can do?" Sophia demanded.

Sean shook his head. "It's hard to say. I'm not sure if anything is broken or how badly she struck her head. "

Magdalena stirred.

"Magdalena! Are you all right?" Victoria exclaimed. "Can you walk?"

"I think so," she said after flexing her fingers and feet. "But I'll need help."

Eventually, they made their way back to Victoria's apartment as they all took turns supporting Magdalena. Although there was no electricity, the gas was still in service and she was able to light the stove. As the tea was brewing, the kitchen was filled with the quiet, excited chatter of the triumphant friends. Only Magdalena was resting on the sofa, quiet and apart from the others. Sophia pulled up a chair beside her.

"How could I have been so misled?" Magdalena wanted to know, asking the question with no preamble. "How can I make up for all the destruction I've caused?" A tear slipped down her cheek and she stared at her folded hands.

Sophia reached out and wrapped both hands around Magdalena's. Dmitri came and stood beside the women, wrapping an arm around Magdalena's shoulders. The apartment grew quiet.

"Fen'ka no doubt told you what you wanted to hear," Sophia answered softly. "She made it easy to believe her words, twisting the truth to gain your sympathy and pity. She

369

was an expert at lying and deceiving. Any one of us could have believed her if she had approached us."

"But the flood. All the destruction. How could I have helped to nearly destroy the city?" Magdalena's shoulders collapsed as she burst into great sobs of regret and despair.

Victoria stood with the others, letting the grief pour from Magdalena. Sophia kept her hands wrapped around Magdalena's. Gradually Magdalena's sobs subsided and she raised her tear-stained face to them.

"Why do you think you listened to them?" Victoria asked.

Magdalena thought a long moment; Victoria wondered if she was afraid of what she might discover within herself.

"I think… I think I listened because I wanted to do something important." She considered again. "No, I wanted to be someone important," she said at last. "I wanted to escape being lonely and afraid."

"Loneliness and fear can haunt you only if you allow them to do so," Sophia said gently. She clutched Magdalena's hands tightly and looked into Magdalena's eyes.

"You have Victoria. You have us now, as well," Sean told her. "If that doesn't make you important, what will?" They all laughed and Magdalena slowly smiled.

Sean went on. "You need to make changes in your life, Magdalena. We all need to make changes sometimes. But those changes never come quickly or easily. But now that you know what you are looking for, that alone is a tremendous step forward!" Magdalena blushed and bobbed her head in agreement.

"In the meanwhile, what can you do? You can help drive the flood from the city," Dmitri told her. "Go to each of the places you sprinkled water with the yew and recite the opening verses of the Gospel of Saint John," the priest instructed. "That will counteract the charm's attraction to the river and force the water back into its normal course."

He paused and then asked, "Can you tell us anything else that you or George or Elizabeth did to conjure the flood or endanger the city?"

"Elizabeth and I—we used the staff to jam the gears of the Astronomical Clock and break its magic. George—he said that he had poisoned the power of the bridge," she whispered.

"The clock? Its magic was in its timekeeping gears and I think the best way to repair its magic is to repair its gears," Dmitri said. "I am certain that the city will see to it that repairs are made to the clock as soon as possible. Even if the authorities are only concerned that tourists see it in operation again, yes? But the bridge? Even with the sword in its foundations again, I do not know how best to heal the damage—the poison, you say—George has done."

"I recall a 'Great Antidote' against all known poisons," Theo told them. "Something from the Greeks and Romans. We could look it up and give the bridge a dose of it."

"Then that should be our immediate concern," Dmitri said. "Victoria, give us all the books you have that might have something to say about the Great Antidote. Let's get to work, yes?"

"Wait—I still have this," Sean announced, pulling the drooping and bedraggled yew from his pocket. "What should we do with this? Is Fen'ka still tangled in it?" He scowled at it as if it might bite him.

"I think she might still be," Magdalena told them. "I had the impression that the ghosts whose bodies were in the river could not escape the water or go far from the river. But George had to give Dalibor permission to be free of the yew. I released George from the yew when I used it in the river to get his hands off my throat so it would catch Fen'ka instead. Did we ever give Fen'ka permission to be free?" She looked

371

at Victoria and Sean, who looked at each other and then shook their heads.

"But she is too dangerous a ghost to let go free," Sophia insisted. "We cannot simply let her return to the river and snare someone else to destroy the city."

"What can we do with it, then?" Theo asked.

"We should do what should always be done with the dead," Dmitri answered the group. "It should be buried. But we need a safe place, yes?" He looked at Victoria and Magdalena, who looked at each other.

"Loreto!" Victoria exclaimed in the same instant Magdalena did. She continued, "We should bury it on the Loreto grounds where I lit the candle in the footprint."

"Where George buried… where George and I buried the dough figures," Magdalena whispered. "Whatever hex that placed on each of you…" She looked around at all of them. "I am so sorry!" She wept again.

Dmitri took her hands and lifted her chin to look into her eyes. "Regret is meaningless without action," he told her softly. "It is by acting to undo all that you have done that you will be able to set this all behind you, yes? Each time you recall something to regret, find a way to correct it. Do you understand?"

Magdalena nodded but continued to quietly sniffle. Victoria took her friend's hands from Dmitri and sat beside her on the sofa as the others milled awkwardly around the room.

"The antidote!" Sophia exclaimed. Victoria pointed to her shelf with the magical handbooks that might contain a reference to the antidote against all poisons and Sophia took the books down. Then Sophia, Theo, Sean, and Dmitri each took one or two of the volumes, found chair, and looked for the antidote's recipe. The apartment was quiet except for the rustle of pages turning and Magdalena sniffling as Victoria continued to sit with her.

"Here it is!" Sean exclaimed at last. "The 'Great Antidote of Mithridates,' it says!"

"What does it say?" Sophia, Theo, and Dmitri put aside the books they had been examining.

"Well, it is not a specific recipe," Sean apologized. "But it says the antidote included walnuts, rue, figs, and salt." He looked further down the page, turned the page, and examined the text there. "No, that is all it says," he announced. He looked up at Victoria and Magdalena.

"Do you have any of those things?" Sean wanted to know.

"I have walnuts," Victoria told them. "I imagine I also have figs—one or two dried ones. I did have salt," she added. "We used it all this morning."

"I think I have salt at home," Magdalena told them.

"What about rue?" Sean asked. "It's not something people cook with anymore."

Victoria thought a moment. "Wait! That I might have!" She jumped from the sofa and darted into the bathroom, returning holding a small sachet aloft in triumph.

"From the flower market!" she announced. She sat down on the couch again and pulled the string to open the sachet, spilling the thimbleful of dried gray-green sprigs and yellow buds into her palm.

"I got this in the flower market months ago for use in bathwater," she explained. "But I never used it."

"Excellent!" Sean congratulated her.

"But how do we administer the antidote?" Victoria asked, looking from Sean to Magdalena and back to Sean.

"The bridge has to ingest it. We have to insert the mix of ingredients into the bridge. But how to do that? I have no idea," Sean admitted.

373

Magdalena spoke hesitantly. "I remember George explaining how the bridge was a masterpiece of occult workmanship. One of the ways its inherent power as a bridge was bolstered was the inclusion of eggs in the mortar. He said eggs were emblematic of the four elements—earth, air, fire, and water—and that including them in the mortar strengthened the bridge immeasurably, both its chemical and its alchemical structure. He also mentioned something about an egg when he told Dalibor that he had poisoned the magic of the bridge, so maybe he used an egg for that."

"An egg then!" Sean concluded. "We add the ingredients of the Great Antidote to an egg and then insert the egg into the bridge!"

"I have an egg!" Victoria went into the kitchen area and retrieved an egg from her refrigerator.

"Do you have a needle? A sheet of paper?" Sean asked. Victoria nodded and retrieved those as well, the needle from a sewing kit and a torn page from a tablet near the telephone.

"Prick open a small hole in the top of the egg," Sean instructed as they all sat around the kitchen table. Magdalena hobbled from the sofa into the kitchen to join them. He curled the paper into a funnel, and Magdalena watched closely as Victoria carefully pierced the top of the egg several times and then pulled away the small triangle of shell she had outlined. Sean inserted the tip of the paper funnel into the opening and Victoria slid the dried rue from her hand into the funnel. It rasped down the paper and into the egg.

"Now we only need to add the other ingredients and insert it into the bridge," Victoria declared, rummaging through the kitchen and placing the walnuts and figs on the table.

"Someone should get the salt from my apartment. Or come with me to get it," Magdalena announced. She struggled to push herself up from the table.

"We'll go," Sophia told her.

Dmitri agreed and, taking Magdalena's keys and directions, set out to fetch the salt from Magdalena's apartment.

Victoria chopped a walnut into tiny chips. Theo sliced one of the dried figs. Sean added each ingredient of the Great Antidote in turn to the egg. Then he returned the egg to the darkened refrigerator for safekeeping. When Dmitri returned a little later, he added the salt.

"What shape is the city in now?" Theo asked.

"People are out on the streets," Dmitri said.

"They say the flood has crested and begun to recede," Sophia elaborated. "But there is still no electricity."

"But if people are on the streets, we cannot get past the barricade and onto the bridge," Dmitri warned them.

"We can if we go very early in the morning," Sophia offered.

Given the small size of Victoria's apartment, she was glad when Magdalena suggested that Dmitri, Sophia and Theo spend the night at her flat. They all agreed to meet back at Victoria's early the next morning.

That night, as Theo was preparing to sleep on the sofa in Magdalena's apartment, Dmitri and Sophia retired to the bedroom and sat on the edge of the bed, holding hands in the pool of flickering light from the candle on the bedside table. Shadows twisted and furled around them.

"I never meant to kill him," Dmitri confessed to his wife. "George. I wanted to stop him. Wound him, even, if I had to in order to stop him. But I never meant to kill him, Sophia." He stared into the darkness across the room. Sophia stroked the back of his head.

"I know," she whispered. "I know."

"But the sword… It seemed to have a life of its own," Dmitri went on. "I picked it up and it… felt alive, Sophia. I swung at George, to stop him, and… the sword jumped out of my hand as if it were a snake attacking a rat. It was uncanny. It killed George of its own free choice and then jumped back into my hands. My hands were stained with George's blood."

Sophia shuddered involuntarily.

The two sat quietly.

"I might have to surrender the priesthood, Sophia," Dmitri said at last.

She looked at her husband.

"But serving as a priest is all you have ever wanted, Dmitri!" Sophia objected.

"If a priest kills, even accidentally, he can longer serve at the altar," he reminded her. "You know the rules of the Church."

"But you also know that the rules are not always strictly applied," she reminded him. "If we explain to the bishop…"

"Explain what? That a magic sword jumped from my hand to kill a Jesuit practicing black magic and then a lion from a tarot deck jumped from the sky and carried the body to the river?" Dmitri chuckled. "If we explained that to the bishop, he might want to remove me for a great many more reasons!"

"No one else was there," his wife protested. "No one will ever know that you were the one wielding the sword when it killed George."

"I will know, Sophia," Dmitri answered quietly. "And I will be unable to stand at the altar knowing my hands were stained with blood."

Sophia thought a moment. "Well, if you must surrender the priesthood, it was a sacrifice that saved… well, nearly everyone! Yes?"

Dmitri wiped away a tear that had slipped down his cheek. "If Svetovit had been set free, who knows what damage he would have wrought. Yes, that vision at Loreto did imply that modern civilization would fall." He wiped away another tear with the back of his hand.

"Do you remember the tarot readings we each had after the Ghost Tour on the first night of the conferences?" Sophia asked him. "Your reading ended with the Ace of Cups and mine with the Hanged Man. The reader said we would be leaving Prague with a new spiritual life, with clear knowledge of what is truly most important.

"Do you see? This must be the new spirituality the cards promised. But we are safe, the world—that we know—is safe, and we have each other," she gently reminded her husband. "But you will miss the priesthood. I know." Sophia pulled her husband's head down onto her shoulder and he sobbed like a small child who had lost his mother.

Over the next few days, they made their plans. They were able to move Magdalena back into her own apartment. She was badly bruised, tired easily, and was occasionally confused or nauseated, making Dmitri think she'd suffered a small concussion. But she was growing stronger each day. Victoria and Sophia stayed with her in her flat while Theo, Sean, and Dmitri remained in Victoria's apartment. Magdalena promised that she would see to the safe return of the rabbi's staff to the synagogue attic when the flood had receded enough to cross the bridge to the Old Town and the Jewish Quarter. She and Victoria both promised to go to Loreto when Magdalena was able and would bury the bedraggled yew bouquet under the shrubs at the cloister. By Saturday morning, the streets of the

Old Town had been reopened, allowing residents to return to their homes and survey the damage done by the flood. Chaos had erupted as the displaced rushed back to see what was left of their homes. The residents of the New Town were also being allowed home by the police. The residents of Kampa could only stand on the bridge and look down on the upper-floor roofs of their homes, sprouting like mushrooms from the deluge still covering the area.

The airport finally reopened, and there were reports of untold numbers of tourists standing in lines, hoping to board planes to take them home.

"I have to get back to Ireland—now," Sean announced when Victoria related the reports on the airport. "I need to find out what happened the night Elizabeth was put back in her grave." He told them about the e-mail he had received from the Irish police and his fears for his missing nephew Donal and Donal's friends in Waterford. "I have to find the truth—and find a way to help the boys, if at all possible."

"Yes, you must go," Sophia urged him. Dmitri and Theo promised to come to Ireland and help, once Sean knew what had gone on and had an idea of how to proceed.

"I'll come with you to the airport," Victoria said. "To help with translations, or anything."

"No! Please don't," Sean answered. "I may be in lines for days to book a flight back to Dublin. I wouldn't want you wasting precious time loitering around the airport with me. But I do appreciate your help. I will let you know what I discover as soon as I can." Less than half an hour later, he had set out for the airport and was gone.

Victoria and Magdalena housed their remaining new friends until they heard that the airport lines had become

378

somewhat manageable. Victoria went to the airport with Theo, Dmitri, and Sophia to help with any issues that might arise.

But no difficulties arose, beyond standing in long lines. They saw no sign of Sean and decided he must have already boarded a flight to Ireland. Finally, all the visitors stood at the security checkpoint, ready to board their flights. Victoria promised to keep them informed by e-mail about the recovery of the city.

"We can all meet again at next year's conference!" Theo announced. "Before we heard the airport was open, Sean and I spoke about Dublin being the perfect place to hold the next conference on Evil—or the conference on Monsters. Or both."

"And if Sean needs help sorting out the trouble with his nephew, he will e-mail us and we will meet him in Ireland long before that, yes?" Dmitri spoke up. "After all, his nephews and their friends did save us from the Dearg-due, so we must go to help them if we are needed."

"Well, when the announcement is posted online," Theo resumed, "I will expect all of you to submit abstracts to attend! You too, Victoria—you and Magdalena! We'll find some way to get you both there and be part of the conference team!"

They all hugged and kissed and shook hands and clapped backs, shedding a few tears. Then the academics were gone and Victoria stood as the crowd of other travelers surged around them, eager to return to their lives that had been interrupted by the flood.

Magdalena, accompanied by Victoria, retraced her steps as best she could recall and recited the verses of the Gospel as Fr. Dmitri had instructed at each of the places she had anointed with the toad venom or sprinkled with river water.

That evening in Magdalena's apartment, the two women

were sitting at the kitchen table, leaning forward on their elbows. A steaming cup of tea awaited each of them. In the center of the table sat a tarot deck.

"Oh, Victoria," Magdalena objected. "I don't know if I can do this. Not again. Dabbling with magic… with tarot… that's how this whole nightmare began. That tarot reading back in New York. If only I hadn't…"

"I know, Magdalena," Victoria soothed her friend. "But now that we know how real magic is, how can we ignore it?" She paused. "And how better to be sure the whole thing is over with than by having another reading, like the one in New York that started it all?"

Magdalena thought about that while she sipped her tea.

"All right," she announced at last. "I'll do it."

Victoria picked up the cards and shuffled.

"How else can I help to repair the damage I have caused?" Magdalena asked the deck. Victoria drew a card and set it face down on the table. It was the depiction of Death.

The card of Death in the Major Trumps of the tarot deck was rendered as it most often was, a skeletal knight wearing armor and riding a great white stallion, with a white rose emblazoned on the banner hanging from his lance and flapping in the breeze. The horse was walking over the corpse of a king and the broken crozier of a bishop. A woman and child were about to be crushed under its hooves. The bishop, whose fallen staff lay broken under the horse, stretched out his hands to plead with the knight for a reprieve. A river flowed past in the background and the sun was peeking over the battlements of a castle on the other side of the river.

"That could have been Svetovit on his horse," Magdalena whispered. "Trampling us all up at the castle or down alongside the river."

380

"But it wasn't!" Victoria reminded her. "He didn't! The card does not mean defeat, Magdalena! It can't!"

"What does it mean, then?" Magdalena closed her eyes and waited, biting her lip.

"Grow. Change. Life goes on and is transformed," Victoria interpreted the card, checking her words against the text in the guidebook she had set out to consult.

Victoria looked at Magdalena. A tear slipped down Magdalena's cheek.

"I hope I can," she whispered.

"I know you will!" Victoria promised.